The Ph[...]

By
Eleanor Swift-Hook

Copyright © Eleanor Swift-Hook 2022.

The right of Eleanor Swift-Hook to be identified as the author of this work has been asserted by her in accordance with the Copyright, Designs and Patents Act, 1988.

First published in 2022 by Sharpe Books.

THE PHYSICIAN'S FATE

Paris, Saturday 29 November 1642 (Gregorian Calendar)

In a splendid chamber of the Palais du Cardinal, which was one of the most splendid mansions in all of Paris, a man sat lost in deep reverie. His head resting on his hands, he leaned over a gilt and inlaid table, covered with documents. Behind him, a vast fireplace was alive with leaping flames. Thick logs blazed and crackled on brass-ended firedogs. Their flickering brilliance combined with that of the wax lights set in the twin grand candelabra which illuminated the room. All set and lit by the precise habit of the Palais' household servants.

It occurred to him that if anyone had been there to see, and he thanked God they were not, they might have mistaken his cape with its rich colour for a gorgeous red simar, robes of office due to a cardinal. They might have thought that against all possible hope and expectation the owner of the Palais had risen once more from his sickbed to sit at this table and work.

But he had no time to dwell on such fancies. He creased his brow in anxious reflection, grateful for the solitude of the suite of rooms he was in, relieved by the continued silence from the chamber beyond and aware, very aware of the measured tread of the guards outside on the landing. They were there to ensure the safety of the master of the house. That thought made him shake his head. They could no longer keep safe a man who lingered on the threshold of death, reluctant to release the agony of life for the promise of eternal bliss because he felt his work was not yet done.

And neither was his own work, the man in the red cloak knew. He had come to this room as it was the one place in the entire Palais where he could be certain to remain undisturbed, the private cabinet of L'Éminence Rouge. A place where he could sit and think as the pounding of his heart grew less, and somehow come up with a plan that would save his life. In his hand was a list of names that he had just written. He had known them already but seeing them written out seemed to give him some sense of control.

It was as if he held the fate of each of those men in his grip. And in a very real way he did. It was a matter of choosing a name—choosing the right name.

It was a very short list but from it he had to choose the name of a man with few connections in Paris, a man who had no friends in powerful places who might step in to defend him. He needed it to be one of the men on the list in his hand, because they were the only ones who had the right access, who could have been there—apart from himself, of course.

A couple were men he would very much enjoy seeing accused, humiliated, convicted, broken by torture, and removed from life on the gallows. But he also knew they would have friends, family, and possible patronage. It was not a risk he could afford to take.

But there was one name on the list which did not belong to a Frenchman. Someone of no significance—someone who no one would stand up for, and no one would miss. And someone, he realised with a growing delight, who was perfectly placed to serve the role required.

Smiling to himself, the man in the red cape screwed up the list and dropped it into the hearth. Then waiting for the tread of the guards to be distant, he left the room before his presence there could be marked.

THE PHYSICIAN'S FATE

Chapter One

Oxford, Tuesday 29 November 1642 (Julian Calendar)

It was a bitterly cold day at the end of what had been a bitterly cold November, although for once the sun put in an appearance.

Looking out over the quadrangle of Christ Church in Oxford from his seat at a writing table by the window, Gideon admired the elegant architecture. It looked lovely, despite the mud of the churned ground below where too many boots had walked. Today King Charles and his close household had arrived from Reading, his sons now recovered from a dose of the measles that had delayed them there.

The last of the king's entourage crossed from the gated entrance to pass within the main buildings, allowing Gideon a glimpse of the young princes, Charles and James, with their retinue. It seemed strange to find himself an inside observer in the seat of royal power. But then much about his life had been strange since he had left London and his work as Gideon Lennox, lawyer in chancery, in the summer.

Even without the added benefit of being able to see the great come and go, he liked this room. It was one of a suite of three which had been granted to his employer, Colonel Sir Philip Lord, a notorious mercenary commander also known as the Schiavono. Presently the rooms were occupied by Lord's wife Lady Catherine and their immediate household of which Gideon was now a part. Only those who had great favour with the king were offered such accommodation. Places to stay were at a premium in a city heaving to the point of bursting upon news the royal court was going to winter there. Civil war kept them from the capital which was held by Parliament.

This room, the largest of the three, was both a bed chamber for the Lords and a day chamber for the household. With Lady Catherine—Kate—bedridden as an effect of a presently untreatable bullet wound, and her husband away with the army, the arrangement worked well.

Lord had been absent for the last three weeks. As one of the more senior and most capable commanders available to the king's nephew, Prince Rupert, he was much in demand. The prince was energetic in prosecuting his uncle's war and expected no less of those who served under him. News of the progress of the war reached them daily. Abingdon, Aylesbury, and Reading were taken, although Windsor Castle had first refused and then resisted the prince's summons. All this time there were ongoing attempts at peace negotiations. The horrific battle beside Edgehill in late October had been enough. No one wanted another. Gideon had even begun to hope that the war would indeed be over by Christmas.

Then word came that Brentford had been set ablaze by Prince Rupert and rumours flew about that there had been murder and rape. More sober accounts agreed there had been looting and some houses caught fire, but no egregious attacks on civilians. Gideon, haunted by memories of what the Lord Digby's horse had done to Parliament's baggage train after the battle, wondered which account he should believe.

Then, the day after whatever happened in Brentford and three weeks to the day after the battle of Edgehill, the Royalist advance faltered. At Turnham Green, a name Gideon thought most apt, the king's army was confronted by the superior numbers and grim determination of the trained bands of London and surrounding counties. Commanded by the Earl of Essex and leavened by his now veteran troops from Edgehill, they halted the Royalist advance. A Londoner himself, Gideon heard the news with relief. Even though he knew it would be regarded here in Oxford as treasonous, he nurtured a silent pride that his fellow citizens had taken arms to defend themselves.

Having been lost in thought and gazing through the window for quite a while, Gideon brought his attention back to the work he was supposed to be doing. Kate, whilst restricted to her bed, was far from ailing in her mind. He and Kate were kept busy reading and sifting intelligence reports from Kate's network of spies—

most of whom were women as far as Gideon could tell—and such as came to Oxford from other sources. Some in complex ciphers that needed decrypting. In addition, there were letters from Sir Philip Lord's network of correspondents, from across England, Scotland, Ireland, Europe and beyond.

New such letters had arrived that morning and he had just finished ploughing through a very gossipy one from a correspondent in Rome who wrote in Latin with a florid style. Gideon turned his attention to the next, which was written in a neat French hand that he translated without effort.

It seems unbelievable that his eminence is dead. They say he had more illness than most men could bear and that until the end he was more concerned about the work he wished still to do than making sure of the state of his soul.

Gideon had to read the letter twice before he understood what it was saying.

Cardinal Richelieu, the man that had ruled France for King Louis for the last twenty years had just died.

It needed little political awareness to realise this would have an incalculable impact across Europe. Richelieu had been involved in the wars and peace-making, alliances and betrayals that had characterised the states of Europe for as long as Gideon had been alive.

Gideon was very sure Sir Philip Lord would want to know as soon as possible. He checked the date. The fourth of December, which was... he ran through the usual necessary rapid calculation turning the new calendar date used by most of Europe into the old-style system England still held to which was ten days behind. It was only five days ago. The letter had been sent at speed and Gideon knew he should get it into the hands of the man it was addressed to as fast as humanly possible.

He was about to tell Kate, to confirm the urgency, but as he turned to do so another letter, as yet unopened, nearly fell from the desk. He caught it and was about to put it down when he saw the direction upon it was written in a familiar scrawl. Gideon's heart picked up a beat. This should contain something more important to Lord than even the changing pattern of power caused by Richelieu's death would be.

Opening it, Gideon saw the letter contained a dense cipher in neat rows. But at the bottom was a hasty postscript jotted in plain English.

At last. This was the news they had been waiting for.

A was heading to France. He said he had an open invitation from someone he knew in Paris - D.

"What is it? You look shaken." Kate was frowning at him.

Instead of answering, Gideon crossed to her bed and offered her both letters. Her eyes scanned the pages then looked up to meet his gaze.

"The news about Richelieu is not unexpected, but Philip will need to know, he has certain interests in France that he may need to protect. This other is from Danny, so A is for Anders? Anders Jensen?"

Gideon nodded and saw a flicker of emotion brush Kate's features.

If anyone could remove the bullet lodged deep in Kate's body with safety so she might walk again, it would be Anders Jensen. He was a skilled Danish physician-surgeon who had spent a few weeks with Lord's mercenary company, becoming good friends with Gideon, before finding the harsh reality of that life little to his taste. When Anders left, it had been with Danny Bristow, one of Lord's most trusted officers, who had been charged to escort Anders wherever he might wish to go, before attending to the work with which he himself had been tasked. So, the first thing Lord had done upon their arrival in Oxford at the beginning of November was to send a message to Danny asking what he knew of where Anders might now be.

"Paris," Kate said, her tone thoughtful. "It will need a week to get there and as long back again—assuming the sea crossing is easy, which it seldom is this time of year. Although that would not be including such time as it might take to find Dr Jensen in all Paris. And who knows how France might react to the Cardinal's demise? That too could delay matters."

"At least we know where to look now," Gideon said.

THE PHYSICIAN'S FATE

"Paris is a large city. Even bigger than London," Kate shook her head. "My real concern is that the prince will not be happy to have one of his best commanders away for so long."

"I can speak French well and have been to France before," Gideon assured her. "A couple of years ago I was paid to find some old property deeds in Calais for a client who had the improbable name of Sir Paston Appletree. They had been left there by his grandfather—of the same name—when the French captured the city from us."

Kate was still looking at the pages she held. "It seems odd to think that Calais and the land around it was as English as Oxford not so long ago. Then she looked up. "You are most kind to make such an offer."

"I'll find Shiraz so as to get word to Sir Philip as soon as possible," Gideon sketched a bow towards Kate. "With your permission."

"Yes. Of course." Kate's attention was back on the sheet in her hands, and she was frowning now at the ciphered letter. "But please ask Zahara to come and help me work out what else Danny has to say."

Zahara, just the mention of her name made Gideon's heart beat faster. His thoughts were filled with her as he crossed the room. Gideon loved her beyond reason, even though he knew he might never make her his own. Because, the daughter of an enslaved English woman and a merchant of Aleppo, Zahara was a Muslim. It added to his anguish that she returned his feelings but could never fully reciprocate them. Even had the barrier of religion not been there, the wall of her past suffering at the hands of a brutal Barbary Pirate rose ever between them.

Sir Philip Lord had redeemed her from that captivity and now she served Kate, as much her companion and friend as she was at the moment both Kate's nurse and personal maid. Never far from Zahara was Shiraz. A man, Gideon had learned, who once held high status in his homeland before falling foul of the changing political tides from which he escaped with his life but not his tongue. He was as protective of Zahara as a brother or father might be, having rescued her from the floods that left her an orphan, and he was just as loyal to Sir Philip Lord. It was Shiraz who looked to their security, commanding the handful of Lord's men who were left both for their care and to ride at need bearing messages to and from Sir Philip. It was Shiraz whose approval Gideon knew would be the final bastion he had to conquer if he were ever to win Zahara as his bride.

Pushing such depressing thoughts aside, he found Zahara sitting by the window of her room to get the best light on the sewing she was doing, repairing one of Kate's fine lawn shifts. As soon as Gideon entered the room, she set it aside and rose, smiling. Gideon felt her smile like a physical warmth, as if the sun shone upon him.

"Does Lady Catherine need me for something?"

"There is news from Danny," Gideon said, knowing she would guess what that news would be. "I need Shiraz to see a message gets to the Schiavono—and yes, Kate would appreciate your help with the cypher for the rest of Danny's letter."

Her green eyes widened.

"Shiraz is in the stables. I can send Martha for him if you wish."

But Gideon was already opening the door. "I will go myself, that will be quicker. Martha has enough to do I'm sure"

Gideon made his way down through the college building. The arrival of the king had meant the place was now packed. Men and women wearing gorgeous clothes were swept along, cheek by jowl with those much less well-attired. He was glad he had not sent the serving girl Martha. She was slightly built only in her teens and would have made little headway in the packed throng. It took Gideon about three times as long as it would have the previous day to reach the door and head to the stables.

"Fox."

The call stopped him in his tracks before he was ten paces from the door. Fox. The nom-de-guerre, given by Lord's men in appreciation for what they saw as his lawyer's cunning. It had become so familiar to him that he responded to it now as to his own name. Turning back, he saw Sir Philip Lord, with two men behind him who were wearing the grey and blue that Lord had been using to equip his regiment.

Lord himself was dressed in peacock and silver, with gemstones in the points and from beneath a black hat, trimmed with a real peacock feather, his white hair lay over his shoulders and down his back.

"I thought I saw you being pressed like a felon by the crowd here," Lord said, clapping a hand on Gideon's shoulder once he had regained the door. "You looked like you were in a hurry. Did you need help getting something?" But there was a different, silent question in the turquoise eyes.

"Lady Catherine is fine," Gideon said, answering the unspoken question first. "I was indeed in a hurry. I was seeking Shiraz to get an urgent message to you."

Lord tilted his head in enquiry. "Then it is as well I am here. You have received a letter from Danny?"

Gideon supposed it was not that hard to deduce.

"Yes, and he says Anders is—"

The hand tightened on his shoulder.

"Not here. Let's go upstairs. There will be time enough when I have greeted Kate."

So, preparing himself like a salmon about to endure rough waters returning uphill to its spawning, Gideon followed up the stairs in Lord's wake. But far from having to push through, people parted before them and a respectful murmur of the name 'Sir Philip...' preceded and followed them. Lord responded to some of the greetings with a nod, a look, or a brief bow. As if, Gideon thought, he accepted it as his due.

But then Philip Lord had been brought up to believe far more than that to be his due. He had been raised to believe he was the legitimate descendant of Queen Mary Tudor and Philip of Spain. And somewhere in England, Lord believed lay proof of that fact. Gideon himself had seen evidence enough to believe it was possibly true. One reason Lord employed him was that if the documents ever came to light Gideon could verify their authenticity.

When they reached the entrance to their suite of rooms, Lord told the two men with him to keep anyone except the prince or the king himself from entering, then opened the door and went within.

"Philip, God is kind and brings you back to me." Unalloyed joy lit Kate's face.

In response the mask of indifference that Lord usually maintained, fell away. Beneath it, the raw yearning was almost too painful to witness and in the moment it took before Lord was able to regain his composure, Gideon had to look away.

Lord crossed the room in three swift strides to drop to one knee at Kate's bedside, his hand cupped over hers, head bowed as if asking for her blessing. Then he looked up and Gideon could see in his face something close to awe, as if he were rediscovering his wife and his love for her anew. Then kissing the fingers he held cupped, he spoke in verse. His voice was gentle with wonder.

"Do but look on her eyes, they do light
All that Love's world compriseth!
Do but look on her hair, it is bright
As Love's star when it riseth!"

Before the lines were halfway spoken, Zahara had moved to touch Gideon's arm and taking the hint he withdrew with her to the room he shared with Shiraz, closing the door on the final words.

Zahara smiled at him.

"You will go to France," she said, with no hint of a question in her voice.

Gideon nodded. "Either with the Schiavono if he is permitted leave to travel, or alone if he is not."

"I will miss you and pray for you," she said. Then she hesitated as if unwilling to ask. "Do you think Dr Jensen will come back with you?"

It was something he hadn't even considered. But Zahara was right to question it. After all, Anders had left Lord because he had been filled with a profound repugnance for the mercenary company. Things he had witnessed that didn't sit with his straightforward nature. Things he had been forced to do which had required him to condone and engage in duplicity and deceit.

"I hope he will," Gideon said and Zahara reached out to brush a stray hair aside from his face. From her it was the most intimate gesture.

"When you find him, tell him I still have his copy of Ambroise Paré's book and I should like the opportunity to return it to him."

Gideon shook his head. The more he thought about it the less reason he could see for Anders to choose to come back to England at all, let alone back to the very heart of Lord's world.

"You think he will come back for a book?"

"Not at all," she said. "But if he needs a reason that will allow him to set aside his pride and his promise, then that gives him a reason."

"His promise?" Gideon was confused. "What promise?"

"The promise he will have made to himself that even though he has much liking for you, for me, for Daniel, for the Schiavono, that he will keep himself apart from us and our affairs. He left because he did not wish to become what he thought we were turning in to—bad people like the Graf von Elsterkrallen—and he did not believe he could resist doing so if he stayed."

The more Gideon thought about that the more sense it made. Anders had tried to persuade him to leave as well. The Dane might refuse not from lack of care for his friends but from fearing he might care too much. He would see it as a man sworn from drinking would view a tavern. It meant that there was another layer to the task beyond that of just a journey and a search.

"He has to come," Gideon said at last. "So I will find a way to persuade him."

Zahara nodded and her look of trust lifted his heart and made him feel he could meet any challenge.

"I believe that if anyone can, you can," she said.

An impulse made him slip the gold swivel ring he always wore from his finger. It was the one token he had from his mother's side of the family and the one thing he had to remind himself of her. He knew nothing of it or of her family except she had told him it had been her grandfather's ring. But the heraldry on its hidden seal was too worn to be discernible anymore. Lifting Zahara's hand he placed it in the palm.

"I want you to have something of mine when I am away," he said, uncertain he was being wise. "Something so you know... to show... to..."

Words failed him and he found he was staring at the ring in Zahara's hand unable to bring himself to meet her gaze for fear of what he might see. Then her fingers closed about the gold, and he found the courage to look at her face.

The glow of her smile was like radiant heat.

"I love you very much, Gideon Lennox," she said. "I will keep your ring so you must come back to me."

"And then?" he found the question asked itself without any conscious intent or permission.

"And then," she said, "we will see. *Allah hu hassan.*"

There was a tap on the door and Lord's voice.

"Pack what you need to travel, Gideon, we will be leaving for France as soon as I have obtained permission from the prince."

THE PHYSICIAN'S FATE

Chapter Two

"How long do you think it'll take?" Nick asked, his gaze fixed on the bridge spanning the river Tees.

Danny Bristow sucked in his freckled cheeks, studying the makeshift fortifications with an expert eye.

"They have five or six hundred men and those barricades," he said after some thought. "Could take a couple of hours and they'll make us pay a high toll to cross that bridge. I'm glad we are not with the lucky souls chosen for the privilege of trying the first forcing. I feel sorry for Howard's dragoons."

The royalist dragoons had quickly occupied the village of Piercebridge, but the enemy had never intended to hold it. Instead, they left a handful of men to delay the advance. Once those were flushed from the houses and gardens, they had retreated behind a barricade which blocked the bridge a short way onto its length. The bridge had been damaged in the middle making the passage difficult for feet and impossible for hooves or wheels. Another barricade guarded the far side of the damaged span and some more substantial defences had been thrown up on the south side of the bridge.

The Earl of Newcastle, Nick's commander, had placed all ten of the guns they had with them on a small hill to the northeast of the bridge from where they could threaten those defences. The boom of the firing cannons made Nick's mount dance in anxiety. He tried to calm it and realised it didn't help that his own nerves were frayed and not just by the present circumstances.

The last weeks had been a frustrating time for Nick as he was sent from one garrison to the next, used by the Earl as a means of strengthening the morale and defences of each small town or stronghold. Something the earl had said he seemed to be very good at. Too often he had been required to leave some of his men to reinforce the troops already there.

In truth though, Nick was painfully aware that it wasn't Captain Sir Nicholas Tempest who had the magical effect that Newcastle noticed. It was his lieutenant, Daniel Bristow, who amongst his repertoire of talents included swordsmanship, card playing, cipher breaking and military engineering. But if Danny was doing the bulk of the work, Nick was getting the bulk of the credit for it.

If this war had been the only issue Nick needed to contend with then he would have been pleased with how things were going. But, although his commander in the war was the Earl of Newcastle, his real masters were the men who controlled the cabal he knew as the Covenant.

For three generations Nick's family and their close relations, the Couplands, had been bound to that secretive and powerful organisation. It had been established nearly a century before with the noblest of ideals—universal peace and religious unity. The men who created it sought to provide a ruler bred from royal bloodlines, who could rule with a new philosophy that could transcend, and so heal, the religious schism that plagued Europe and thus end the unceasing wars between Protestants and Catholics.

But whatever its founders might have intended, Nick was sure that today the group's motives were far less praiseworthy. They seemed to him more concerned with grasping power than any grand and worthy enterprise. They had forced him to marry a woman he disliked and who loathed him. One supposedly of the bloodline they nurtured, albeit not legitimately so, Christobel, who was half-sister to the man they really wanted to control. Sir Philip Lord. In his veins they believed ran the pure and legitimate royal blood of Tudor and Hapsburg.

Nick had been given another task by the Covenant men. That was to win to their cause the mercenary commander who was once Graf von Elsterkrallen. He was Francis Child, an illegitimate cousin to Nick and known to most as 'Mags'. But Nick's own intention was to see Mags dead and his mercenaries under the command of himself. He believed he could achieve this through the auspices of Danny Bristow, who had worked for both Lord and Mags before declaring himself to be Nick's man.

They could do with the men. So far in terms of the number of troops he commanded things had gone contrariwise. By the time the Earl began marching south at the end of November Nick was reduced to a pitiful twenty-six cavalrymen and had been attached to the vanguard of the army to serve as scouts.

Now a rider approached them where they waited a safe distance from the village. He wore a sash to mark him as one bearing commands from the earl to his officers at need.

"A message from the earl to Sir Nicholas Tempest," he said. "He requires you to move in support of Sir Thomas' troops." Nick acknowledged the command, and the messenger rode away.

"I spoke too soon," Danny said in a low tone only Nick would hear. "This is what comes of being with the vanguard. They have a couple of cannons on their side of the bridge as well. Those will make a mess when we get in range."

Nick heard the echo of Danny's earlier comment and felt his guts tighten and wondered if that meant he was a coward.

"Ah well, we'd best get to it, sir," Danny said, his voice suddenly loud and cheerful. "Sooner started, sooner done as my grandmother used to say when my granddad knocked on her bedroom door."

That raised a laugh from the men behind them. Nick looked over to where a handful of Sir Thomas Howard's men were holding their company's horses and realised they were going to have to go in on foot themselves.

Dismounted Nick felt more vulnerable. He led his men through the village at speed and found Sir Thomas positioned behind a low wall at the far side. The dismounted dragoons were keeping the rebels behind the barricade on the bridge from being able to rain fire onto the infantry which were forming up to storm them. Sir Thomas pounced on the new arrivals as soon as Nick was beside him.

"Spread your men along the wall and in that hedge, the more we can keep those on the bridge occupied the better. Lamberton will charge and clear them from their position."

From beside him, Nick heard Danny draw a sharp breath.

"Lieutenant?" he asked, giving him permission to speak.

"I don't see any bridging with the infantry, sir. Without it they will be held up there once the enemy retreats to their second barricade"

Sir Thomas made a dismissive sound.

"There will be materials in the first barricade we can use, I can see some from here."

"But—"

"Get your men spread out, Sir Nicholas. Sir William is waiting."

A short time later Nick found himself crouched beside Danny who was reloading his carbine. Nick himself was armed with pistol and sword, and both lacked the needed range for this task.

"You're not happy to use things from the barricade to cross the bridge?"

"I'm sure they will work well enough." Danny pulled the scouring stick from below the barrel and rammed the wadding hard over the bullet and the charge.

"But you think it a mistake?"

"I *know* it's a mistake," Danny corrected, sliding the stick back into its rest and reaching for his powder flask. "While they are standing there choosing planks, they will be fully exposed to the men at the second barricade," he said, closing the pan as he did so then blowing at the excess powder. "If either commander had an ounce of sense, they would have already prepared a solid bridging piece and have men behind the infantry with it so they could rush the second barricade without pause." He sighted down the barrel of the carbine. "If I had command of the men on the other side of that bridge, I would have set this up with that as my first intended killing ground, because they know they can't stop us. Damaged bridge or no, they can only ever delay us and hurt us as much as possible." The pan flashed a moment before the gun barked.

"Missed," Danny said, peering past the smoke of his own firing. "Make him keep his head down a bit though, he must have felt that by his ear."

As Danny reloaded, Nick heard the tramp of feet from behind over the hollow boom of the cannons in the hills.

THE PHYSICIAN'S FATE

"One more volley and they'll send in the infantry," Danny predicted. "The defenders won't wait for them. They'll be off like rabbits after we've fired. Job done."

"Don't you find it at all annoying when you can see these mistakes being made and yet you can do nothing to stop them?" Nick asked.

"I'm too used to it," Danny told him, repriming his carbine. "I used to mind how many got killed and maimed because of it, but nowadays, unless I'm in command, I don't let it get to me." He aimed his carbine and Nick could see he was not aiming it at the barricade but at a place beyond where there was a part of the bridge exposed behind it. "It's like the weather. No point cursing what you can't control. Just dress as best you can for it."

"Give fire!"

Sir Thomas bellowed and all along the scattered line of hedge and wall Nick could see flashes and then blooms of smoke. But Danny hadn't fired. As he had predicted, the men on the barricade had started running for the gap after the volley and Danny fired as they did so. One of the running men screamed and collapsed.

"Got him that time," Danny said with apparent satisfaction.

Then they were being given orders to form up and Nick saw what Danny had predicted playing out. Under the merciless fire from the second barricade which had perhaps four times as many men as the first and was at the advantage of having their targets massed and at effective range.

"We don't seem to be downing many of them," Nick observed.

"And we won't. Soon as Sir Thomas and Sir William storm their barricade, they'll be off back to form up for the real battle—us coming off the bridge into their welcoming arms in defensive positions that they've had a couple of days to prepare."

Looking at the far side of the river and what awaited them there, Nick's blood ran cold.

"Sir Nicholas," the bark came from away to the side. "Reform your men with my horse at the rear."

"Horse?" Danny echoed. "He has horse, and yet we are here playing at being dragoons and they are not?"

"Enough, lieutenant," Nick snapped, afraid such words could be reported back to Howard by his men. "Tempest company, withdraw."

It felt good to be mounted again and no sooner had Nick taken his small company to join the fifty or so men which formed Sir Thomas' cavalry contingent, then there were cheers from the direction of the river. The enemy had been pushed back.

As Danny had predicted there was no further attempt to try and stop the earl's army crossing to the far bank. Instead, as they came off it, they were subjected to withering fire from the well-prepared defences of the enemy. But at least now, Nick realised with relief, he and his men were at the rear of the advance not in its van.

Even Nick could see this was no fight for cavalry. He was sure that until the foot had pushed the Parliamentarians from their defences, Howard would keep them back. Getting horses over the damaged portion of the bridge would be a challenge, but once the enemy were in the open and in retreat, then the cavalry would come into their own harassing the withdrawal and hoping to turn that to a rout.

But it didn't play out quite like that.

By the time the Parliamentarian forces withdrew, Sir Thomas was dead, shot in the assault he had insisted upon leading. That left Nick commanding the cavalry. But the enemy cavalry, screening the retreat, was in greater numbers than Howards' horse even combined with Nick's.

The afternoon was spent trying to avoid the enemy as much as engage with their stragglers and more than once it was only Danny's skill that kept them on the right side of that fine line. When darkness came, Nick was relieved to abandon all pretence of pursuit and withdraw to the bridge. Nick had his men make camp in the enemy's old defences. He gave Danny permission to go and see if he could help with repairing the bridge to an adequate strength to allow the rapid passage of the army in the morning. Left alone with his thoughts, Nick reflected on the day and the chance of war that could take life in a moment from a man so energetic and vibrant as Sir Thomas had been.

THE PHYSICIAN'S FATE

When he woke at dawn, Nick found a sturdy construction now spanned the damaged section of the bridge, strong enough to bear the weight of even the artillery. He crossed it to answer a summons from the earl, grateful that no comment was made about his appearance. Instead, the earl praised Nick for his part in the fight and gave him a commendation for his men's help with repairing the bridge. Then before Nick could respond to that, he was given orders to continue scouting towards York and dismissed.

Riding back to his company, he found Danny sitting with a group of civilians playing cards. His uniform was filthy, and his hands boasted a new selection of cuts and grazes. When Danny saw him approach, he stood up and pulled off his hat to make a short bow.

"Sir Nicholas, we—that is myself, these gentlemen here and a few others—managed to achieve what you asked, and the bridge should withstand the weather and the passage of traffic, until better repairs in stone can be made."

"So I noticed," Nick said, deciding not to mention that he had made no such request. "So has the earl. I was commended by him for your work."

Danny made another bow. "Thank you for telling me so, sir. I take it we are moving out?"

"We are scouting again, so it is time to pocket your winnings and find your horse."

There was little activity between Piercebridge and York. They saw a handful of small patrols of enemy horse, who withdrew when sighting them, but the road was clear. No doubt news of the earl's advance was enough to persuade the enemy to keep away.

The army arrived outside York two days after the battle on the bridge. Then, to Nick's incredulity and despite the pressing nature of the times, ceremony and etiquette took over.

It made for an impressive display.

The entirety of the Earl of Newcastle's army, all six thousand men stood on parade in a field to the north of the city of York. Looking over the flat ground, Nick could see the round walls of the rebuilt keep of the castle high on its mound, known as Clifford's Tower. Beyond that the immense mass of the cathedral rose above the city like a guardian angel. The lesser buildings, spired churches, towers and houses, spread about the two as skirts around a seated woman, encircled by walls that provided an uneven frill.

Nick sat at the head of his company alongside the rest of his father's regiment. For some reason Nick wasn't privy to, his younger brother Henry was not there. He had been left with a command in the garrison of Newcastle. The rest were lined up with the cavalry of Sir William Wriddington, Sir Marmaduke Langdale, Colonel George Heron and of course the Earl's own. The king's appointed commander-in-chief of his armies for the county of Yorkshire, Henry Clifford, Earl of Cumberland, rode out of the city. With him was Sir Thomas Glemham, who was Governor of the City of York and a large group of eminent citizens vying to outdo each other in their apparel.

Removing his hat in a grand salute with the rest, Nick cheered as Sir Thomas presented the keys of the city to the Earl of Newcastle, and then joined the procession into the city. There the inhabitants greeted them with as much enthusiasm as they might a relieving force after a siege.

Once the pomp and ceremony were done, much of the army was found quarters and able to take their rest, exploring the taverns and the women of York. But Nick and his men had no such luxury. No sooner had they been assigned quarters, than they were being sent out again. This time it was south-west towards Tadcaster, where Lord Ferdinando Fairfax, the Parliamentarian commander, was based. So too, according to Danny Bristow, was Mags.

Tadcaster was a small town that was set on either side of a river, the two parts connected by a bridge. It was clear that the Parliamentarians were expecting an attack of some kind. They had built a small breastwork fortification as a redoubt across the road from York on a rise of ground at the edge of the town, occupied by a force of musketeers. In addition, they had holed the bridge over the river Wharfe in a substantial way. Doing so protected the larger part of the town, which lay on the west bank, from any attack mounted from York. Guns were set on the west side of the bridge and there was some more artillery in a strong looking placement in the main part of the town itself. To Nick's inexperienced eye it looked like a strong defensive point.

Armed with a Dutch-made perspective glass that he claimed he had won at cards that night at Piercebridge, Danny looked over the town from a safe distance.

"There are no walls so they can't hold it," he said after a short while. "Although they can make us pay a stiff price for it if they choose to fight. If I was them, I'd not cos they'll take losses too and for no real gain. But this is a strange kind of war."

"How many men?"

Danny put the glass away and shrugged. "A thousand at most, I'd say, and they look as if they're not comfortable there." Then he grinned. If the earl plays this right, we'll have Mags and Fairfax trapped in there like rats and if that happens, I am very sure I could whistle Mags' men to our side."

The image of Danny as the Pied Piper seemed so apposite that Nick laughed aloud.

"If you could do that it would both please our Covenant friends and earn the goodwill of the earl." Then he had another thought. "And it would help replenish my ranks. How many men would there be?"

"There were about a hundred," Danny said. "Though last I heard he'd lost some."

"Killed and injured?"

"A few. Most just walked. I'd like to think we had a small part in that."

Nick recalled a game of piquet in which Danny had humiliated Mags in front of two of his men.

"Those men didn't come to us, though."

"The main thing is they left him," Danny said. Then, "If it comes to it, I may have to go in alone during the attack, to hunt for Mags. We need to be certain he's killed in the fighting, and I could make sure of that better on my own."

He glanced at Nick as he spoke and for just a moment the amiable expression Danny always wore seemed more of a mask through which his eyes looked with smouldering darkness. Nick felt a shiver of creeping flesh across his shoulders.

"If it's needful, you must do it," he said.

Danny smiled and gave a nod of satisfaction. The dark moment was gone, and Nick felt a bit foolish to have thought of it as he had.

"I think we've seen all there is to see, sir," Danny told him, putting away the perspective glass. "I'll make some drawings for you when we get back and you can show them to the earl and explain what is here."

The earl was impressed with the sketches and the explanation that Nick delivered with them. The next day he sent for Nick again to ask for some points of clarification and this time the earl was in company with Mountjoy Blount, Earl of Newport who was both Lieutenant-General to Newcastle and Master of his Ordnance, such as it was. The earl asked some questions about artillery to which Nick, a little to his own surprise and entirely thanks to the things Danny Bristow had told him, was able to muster serviceable replies.

"You are very talented with this work, Sir Nicholas," the Earl of Newcastle said when they were done. "I must consider how best we can use you with the army. It seems to me you are being wasted where you are at present. When we have taken Tadcaster, which your designs seem to suggest is well within our grasp, I will consider this further."

This Nick later related to Danny, as they sat together over a cup of wine and a friendly game of piquet. He was more than a little confused by what the earl was implying.

"It's simple, sir," Danny told him. "He's thinking of appointing you to scouting duties on a permanent basis and attaching us to his own regiment." He paused to take some cards from the talon and then flipped the two he left over so they could both see them. "Eight of hearts and king of spades. And if we get Mags' men from Tadcaster, you never know, the earl might even make you a lieutenant-colonel."

It seemed a bit farfetched, but the notion that the problem of Mags would be solved soon was enough to bolster Nick's confidence. Which was as well because his father demanded his presence the next day.

THE PHYSICIAN'S FATE

Since he was a colonel, Sir Richard Tempest enjoyed the privilege of being accommodated in the comfortable home of one of the leading citizens of York, one who had no doubt ridden out to welcome the army two days before. Nick was shown into a parlour that was private for his father to enjoy and found him sat, legs spreadeagled and arms wide on the arms of a chair set close before the hearth, as if he was cold and seeking to warm himself. He looked pale and his eyes were more hollow than Nick recalled them being even at Newhall a little over a month before.

"You may as well sit," his father said by way of greeting, sounding as weary as he looked, "there is news you should have, though I am unsure what to do with it."

Nick took the other chair that was near the hearth.

"What news?"

"Our friends have told me they are not pleased with what you did."

Nick felt his heart stand still for a moment.

"What I did?"

"Yes. Or rather what you failed to do. It seems whatever actions you took regarding Francis Child were not the ones they wanted." Nick's father held up a hand. "No. I don't want to hear the details. None of that matters anyway; what matters is that you failed. Now they are considering that his petition for legitimacy might have some value and as you have yet to be entered on the rolls as Baronet Howe, that means it could all be granted to him."

The words were like a frost on Nick's skin.

"But the petition was granted to allow me to inherit after my uncle, so we can go to the king and—"

"That would make no difference. In this nation divided what the king might honour, Parliament will not. It will make the two of you claimants and the matter settled by this war."

Nick made himself draw a breath.

"Then I do not see how. I—"

His father slammed both hands down on the arms of his chair.

"It does not matter whether *you* see or do not see. All that matters is what *they think*."

Nick said nothing, his heart hammering.

"There is still a chance," his father said heavily. "If you have the courage to take it."

His throat closing up with dread, Nick found it hard to speak and when he did the words came out hoarse and rasping.

"What should I do?"

"These men see the future of this country under a new king, not this one. They seek legitimacy for their power-grab. You can give them that."

"You mean—?"

"You know exactly what I mean. She may not be willing, but you need not be so fastidious as you are legally wed. You have every right. She is the one in the wrong to refuse you. Just do what needs to be done. Get her with child."

Nick tried to think but his brain wouldn't move beyond the appalling act his father was suggesting. How could he explain his wife had tried to take her own life rather than sleep with him? That she had to be watched night and day for her own protection? That Nick felt sick at the thought of forcing himself on her? She needed time, he knew that, time to adjust to her new life. Then he remembered.

"What if Francis Child were to die?"

His father stared at him from hollow, hooded eyes.

"Are you come to that?" There was weariness not condemnation in his voice.

"If need be," Nick said.

His father drew a breath.

"I will tell them that your wife is with child and it is due in the summer. For now that will satisfy them. If things go on, they can always be told the infant miscarried. And in the meantime, should you be able to do what you just said, it would remove a blade from our throats."

There was no time for more because a messenger arrived asking them both to attend upon the Earl of Newcastle for an urgent council of war. Nick helped his father to his feet, and they went together to the castle where the earl was sharing accommodation with the Governor of York, Sir Thomas Glemham.

THE PHYSICIAN'S FATE

It seemed the earl was determined to act immediately upon the intelligence Nick had provided and planned to move troops into better positions the next day. After some more discussion during which Nick kept silent, the earl held up his hand.

"I believe I have a design which will deliver the town to us and ensure we also crush the rebels who hold it. It would serve us little to rescue the town and have them still at large to work whatever mischief they can devise elsewhere."

Using a map based on the sketches Danny had made, the earl showed what he intended.

"What we shall do gentlemen is divide our men. I shall take the main force and attack when they are not expecting it. They have strong points here," he pointed to the breastwork on the road, "and here," indicating the position that defended the broken bridge. "But they lack numbers to hold either and I am sure we can overcome them." He made a circling motion to the west. "Meanwhile Newport will take a smaller force of horse and dragoons, cross the river at Wetherby bridge and come at them from the west, stopping the bottle so we can deal with them completely."

He stood back and looked at the men in the room with him as if expecting an argument. When none came, he gave a nod of satisfaction.

"This is the plan as it stands, but that still means the flanking attackers have nearly thirty miles to cover to reach us. So, Sir Nicholas, you will see if you can find a suitable place to cross the river which is closer to Tadcaster. I have some local men from Sir Thomas who seem to believe it can be done."

The Earl of Newport lifted a languid hand, his gesture more courtier than military man.

"I will be taking two light guns."

It was a challenge and Nick expected Newcastle to deny him. Clearly even the lightest artillery would slow down a force of horse. Instead, the earl nodded.

"Indeed, my lord, that will put some heat under them." His tone implied it was a topic they had debated already.

Nick spent the rest of that day and into the evening riding along the River Wharf upstream from Tadcaster checking the places the local guides believed could serve as crossings. At each one, Danny sucked on his teeth and shook his head. Except the last. There the river both narrowed and had a protruding bank of mud and sand. At a warmer time of year, it would have been soft and sucky, hazardous for men or horses, but in the bitter cold of December, it was almost solid. It was also the point furthest from both York and Tadcaster of those suggested but would cut eight or ten miles off the route. Danny studied it critically, tested the mud by walking on it and probed the depth of the river, then gave a reluctant nod.

"If it were just horse we could likely ford it with little problem, but with artillery… anything with wheels..." He wrinkled his nose then brightened. "If the need for secrecy was less, I'd put piles in and make a temporary bridge that way. But we need something we can install quickly. If we have time, I can make a small pontoon bridge. But if his lordship wishes to attack tomorrow—"

"The day after," Nick assured him. "The morning of the seventh. Tomorrow he will make much of getting his men in quarters in the villages towards Tadcaster."

"We'll make the bridge sections tomorrow, carry them with us and assemble them when we get here."

They got back to York at dusk and Danny gave Nick a list of the supplies he would need. The earl was not immediately willing, but Nick made it clear that to move artillery over the river there was no other choice except the Wetherby bridge itself. At that, the earl authorised the purchase or requisition of all that was on Danny's list.

The following day as troops moved out of York, Nick stayed with Danny and the team of men who were preparing the pieces of the bridge. The problem was making them small enough to be portable, yet big enough to be effective. Normally bridging would be transported on wagons with an artillery train, but these needed to be carried more swiftly. They were made in pieces designed to be transported by two men, slung on a rope harness between them. As the last of the sections were loaded onto their human bearers to be sure they could be carried, Danny announced himself pleased with what they had done.

His confidence was infectious. When Nick reported to the Earl of Newport, who was dining with his senior officers, he managed to convey enough of it that the man rewarded him with a supercilious smile.

"Well done, Templeton, good work."

"Tempest, my lord," Nick corrected him, "Sir Nicholas Tempest."

The sudden shift in the quality of the smile told him he had made a mistake.

"Quite so. What's in a name? Would not dung by any other name smell as foul?"

There was laughter and one of the men made a show of covering his nose as if there was a noisome stench about with the undeniable interpretation that it was emanating from Nick, himself. Grinding his teeth, Nick was considering calling the man out, but then remembered what was at stake and managed to offer the briefest of bows before retreating.

After getting a couple of hours of sleep, Nick was woken by Danny. He had the entire construction and the team needed to place it, together with their armed escort, ready to make the night march. The plan was to have it all in place for Newport and his men, who were due at the crossing point by dawn.

Somehow Nick wasn't surprised that with Danny commanding the operation, they made the march without any problem and had the bridge in place and assembled under cover of darkness.

Dawn broke and they waited.

Half an hour later there was still no sign at the river crossing of Mountjoy Blount and his fifteen hundred men, plus two pieces of field artillery. It was early morning on the seventh of December and downstream at Tadcaster, The Earl of Newcastle would be preparing to take the town by surprise, unaware that his flanking support had yet to stir.

Even the phlegmatic Danny was getting restless. "If we are going to get all the men across and allow time for issues with the guns, they should have been here long since, sir. Do you want me to go back and see where they've got to?"

In the end, Nick decided they both should go, leaving the majority of their men to guard the precious crossing and taking only two with them.

They came upon the Earl of Newport's men quartered in and around a village a good six miles back from the river crossing point and easily ten miles from both York and Tadcaster. These were the quarters Newport's men had been moved to the previous day. They were rousing themselves having clearly slept the night with no idea of an early start.

Newport himself was not there. They were directed another couple of miles further back towards York and found the earl in a comfortable wayside tavern, sat with the same men Nick had seen him with before, in the tavern in York. Blount seemed surprised when Nick burst into the room and strode over.

"The bridge is set, my lord," Nick said, holding the fringes of his anger as tightly as he could. "You need to bring your men right away. We may still be at Tadcaster in time to support the Earl of Newcastle as planned."

"There is no need, Tempers, we have been told to await further orders."

Nick shook his head.

"We have been given very certain orders, my lord, I—"

"Show him the message, Mountjoy," one of the others suggested. "I know the type. You won't shut him up otherwise."

Blount raised an eyebrow and sighed.

"You are probably right." He reached into his coat and pulled out a folded paper and held it out between finger and thumb to Nick who by now had Danny beside him. "It was delivered by a running footboy just as we were leaving York. I suppose I should have sent someone to tell you, but you never know, the next message might be to advance again and then we will need your little bridge after all."

Nick unfolded the sheet, his eyes scanning over the words.

My lord,

THE PHYSICIAN'S FATE

Though your commission was to come and assist me, yet you might now spare your pains and stay where you are until I send you new orders in the morning.
Will.
Newcastle.

Nick read it without really seeing or understanding what it signified. It was Danny who muttered a curse under his breath.

"This is Mags' doing," he said in an undertone. "I know his hand."

Nick felt sick. Despite all their hard work in preparing the crossing, the Earl of Newcastle was now committed to a frontal assault of Tadcaster and there would be no supporting attack from the west.

Chapter Three

What Sir Philip Lord said to Prince Rupert to gain permission to travel to France at such short notice, Gideon had no idea, but the documents were in Lord's hands that evening and they left Oxford together the following morning. Gideon's last words spoken with Zahara had been sweet and tender. Even so, parting was hard with the knowledge he might not be back for a month.

Their first destination was Southampton, a large port city on the south coast. It had been chosen because, with most of the southern coastal towns and cities being held by Parliament, Southampton had an active Royalist community and was still not garrisoned against the king. It was also a place where Kate knew of someone who she said could be trusted to arrange their passage to France, no questions asked.

Lord posed as a professional gentleman of modest standing, dressed in the kind of attire that Gideon once wore on a daily basis when he had lived in London. Gideon, more humbly clad, passing as his clerk, and the two of Lord's men with them wore the garb of household servants. To complete the impression, the horses they rode were very ordinary beasts, far less glamorous than Sir Philip Lord might normally be expected to ride. Lord had even dyed his betraying white hair a shade of brown. Indeed, the only mark of his real status and profession was in the cat's head pommel sword he wore.

But even thus disguised, getting to Southampton was far from easy. The southern counties stood strong for Parliament in general, which meant they had to rely more on the power of coin and on their wits rather than the documents Lord carried, signed by the prince. But a mixture of evasion, avoidance and at times simple deceit, took them safely south without any major incident. Gideon surprised himself with how natural it had become to him to behave in such a way.

Getting into Southampton itself was easier than expected. The port still teetered in its loyalty. It seemed a warship belonging to

THE PHYSICIAN'S FATE

Parliament had docked recently and was demanding the surrender of the city. There were arguments and negotiations going on, but until those were resolved the politics of visitors to the place were not being questioned.

Once they were through the impressive gate and in the port their luck held, and they found the man Kate had directed them to without any difficulty at all. But that was where things stopped being easy.

Although he was keen to help them, Kate's contact, a merchant of some standing, explained that it wouldn't be straightforward. Normally, he assured them, passage could have been found on a merchant vessel and they could have travelled in some comfort. But with the ironically named Parliamentarian warship *The Charles* and its belligerent Captain Swanley occupying the harbour, shipping was being restricted.

The merchant seemed keen for them to leave as soon as possible. Although he did allow them a heartening supper in his house before he took them to the outskirts of the docks and the home of a humble fisherman. Gideon saw coins change hands. The horses they had ridden were left with the merchant as further payment.

They made the crossing that night, in a tiny coastal fishing boat that slipped unnoticed from the river estuary of the Solent and out to sea. It was so tiny they were packed cheek by jowl with their possessions. The dark waters of the Narrow Sea, when the wind bellied the sails and heeled the craft, seemed to Gideon at times barely a hand's width away from the gunwale.

Luck was with them and the wind highly favourable, speeding the little vessel along. They landed safely in France the following day, with Gideon as shaky legged as a newborn foal and his stomach churning. He wasn't just physically disoriented. It would have been the fourth of December back in England but was now become the fourteenth thanks to the calendar change. That was a very strange sensation, as if they had travelled in time as well as in distance.

Lord, no more affected by their voyage than had he spent it in a comfortable cabin, hired mounts to take them to Rouen. There they had spent the night in a pleasant enough auberge, and Lord took pains to wash the brown colour from his hair. The next day he negotiated to purchase horses for their onward travel. That night they spent in a town called Gisors, where their accommodation was much less desirable, and the brooding castle on its high mound seemed to frown on the very presence of Englishmen.

"Where do we ride for today? Paris itself?" Gideon asked as they set out just after dawn.

"Saint-Léon-du-Moulin," Lord told him.

Gideon had never heard of it. "Where is that and why are we going there?"

"Saint-Léon-du-Moulin," Lord said, his tone patient, "is about ten miles outside Paris. It is a place where we can be sure of a decent meal and a comfortable bed."

Which seemed good enough reasons to Gideon, who was finding the pace of travel—the fastest they could go without over-tiring their horses—grinding. In the late afternoon they came to a cluster of houses with a sturdy stone-built church and a pleasant looking inn. Gideon was delighted to be told this was indeed their destination for the day.

The village of Saint-Léon-du-Moulin had an air of prosperity about it. The houses looked beautifully kept and there was a colour and vibrancy that Gideon hadn't noticed in some of the other communities they had passed through. He assumed the comparative affluence was due to its proximity to Paris.

Their way led through the village and on the far side, Lord took a tree-lined side turn towards a fine house built of brick and stone in the French style. Before reclining into elegance, it had clearly once been a fortified building. There was evidence of where stone walls had been pulled down and the remains of a moat had become a fishpond.

Someone had put a tremendous amount of work into the house and grounds in recent years. Gideon could see that even in the first bite of winter it looked cared for. Well-tended fields with healthy livestock surrounded them and they approached the embracing arms of the chateau through a small formal garden with clipped evergreens, statuary and even a fountain.

THE PHYSICIAN'S FATE

It was not so surprising that Sir Philip Lord should know someone who lived in such a house. Gideon sometimes forgot that Lord had a colourful history which trailed across swathes of Europe. In fact, he reflected, it would be more surprising to find that Lord knew no one of note he could repair to at need within striking distance of the French capital.

It was with real relief Gideon slipped from the saddle, secure in the knowledge that there was no hard journey to be made the next day by land or sea. Instead, a few gentle miles to Paris where Lord would discharge his diplomatic duty and they could seek Anders.

The man who took their horse had a heavy limp and some fingers missing. He greeted Lord with profuse respect, making it clear to Gideon that Lord was a frequent visitor.

They were welcomed into the house itself by a man with greying hair, and a pleasant smile. The quality of his clothing was, perhaps, a little less than Gideon would have expected from the owner of such a prosperous estate, but it had been carefully tailored to help disguise the fact that there was only one sleeve needed by its owner.

"Schiavono, sir" he said, making a deep bow. "Welcome home,"

Home?

Gideon had one of those moments when his understanding of the world seemed to tip on its axis and realign in a completely new pattern. Slightly dazed, he managed to make the polite response to the introduction that followed.

"Fox, this is Gervais Poirier who is my tenant here, and manages most of my affairs in Saint-Léon-du-Moulin."

"If I had only known you were coming, sir…" Poirier trailed off and spread his hands in a Gallic gesture of accepting the inevitable. "No matter. I will have a fine supper prepared in no time and have your room opened, aired, and made up with fresh linen. The blue room for Monsieur Fox? As you say, sir. It will all be done. Of course, some refreshment will be sent in for you whilst everything is arranged."

A very short time later, feeling dazed, Gideon found himself sitting in a wide windowed room and admiring it unstintingly. Lit by a hanging chandelier, there was an elegant modern fireplace that provided warmth to the whole room. The walls were lightly panelled in pearwood with garland motifs. The furniture was both comfortable and beautiful, with velvet upholstered fauteuils that had tapestried cushions.

One wall was dominated by a broad, geometric cabinet decorated with tortoise-shell and ivory marquetry. It had turned ebony balusters below, and above the cupboard doors were carved with mythological scenes, wreathed round in the same garlands that adorned the wall panels. There was a set of matching side tables with round tops set to serve the chairs. These were covered with embroidered cloths so only the very bottom of their single pillars and spreading supporting feet could be seen.

In one corner was a plinth on which sat a broken statue's head that looked to be of classical antiquity and above the fireplace was a magnificent painting of a man wearing burnished armour, holding a sword aloft and mounted on a fiery looking stallion. His long hair was white against the armour and his focus fixed over the head of anyone viewing the portrait, and behind him the outline of a city in flames in the distance.

"*Others at the Porches and entries of their Buildings set their Armes; I, my picture; if any colours can deliver a minde so plaine, and flat, and through-light as mine.*" Lord spoke from the door and then crossed to stand by the hearth as if to allow Gideon a comparison. "It's a little flattering, I know, but when I am in my dotage I might enjoy the reminder."

"So all this," Gideon spread his hands to imply more than just the room they were in, "this is *yours*?"

"The house, the estate, the village. Yes," Lord agreed. "Mine in return for services rendered to the crown, the cardinal, and the grateful citizens of Paris. There was something of a crisis a few years ago when the Spanish came dangerously close. They were within a dozen miles of the city at one point. I was in the fortunate position of being able to play a role in turning the tide." he lifted a hand in a self-deprecating gesture and smiled. "Whores are paid in silks and jewels, mercenaries they pay with chateaux. It is one of several such I have."

THE PHYSICIAN'S FATE

"*Several?*" Gideon heard his voice squeak. The value of just this one estate would make Lord a rich man by any standards. "You mean you own more than this house and its estate in France?"

"This is my sole French property," Lord assured him, "I have one or two elsewhere, if not as substantial. The income from them funds my needs, pays the company's wages when we lack a paymaster and enables me to be more particular about who we serve. And the property provides employment for those of my men who are too old or have been wounded and can no longer fight and have no other home to return to." He broke off and gave a slight shrug. "It is useful."

There had been a time when Gideon wondered a lot about the source of Lord's income. How it was he seemed able to fund whatever he was undertaking in England and not need to lead armies abroad. Not for a moment had he thought the answer might be something like this.

"I don't understand why you bother with England if you have such a place here. Does it come with a title?"

"It could have," Lord admitted. "I thought Monsieur le Baron de Saint-Léon-du-Moulin was a bit too much of a mouthful. Besides, accepting land is less binding than accepting nobility, which carries with it altogether too much responsibility and commitment to the bestower."

Then another thought occurred to Gideon. "But surely to hold land here you must be French by nationality? That is how things stand in England, either that or at least be accorded denizen status."

Lord favoured him with an enigmatic smile. "Such things lie in the gift of the king—and his first minister."

Which was, Gideon supposed, almost an answer.

"You have land in England too?"

"It would have been illegal for me to hold, be granted or to purchase any until very recently on account of my being held a traitor there. Kate, however, has some in her own right and some she purchased and holds for me, so I am not without resources there at need."

"I don't understand," Gideon admitted, looking around at the beauty and elegance. "Why do you trouble yourself with wars, with what has happened in the past, when you could live here in peace and plenty with Kate at your side?"

Lord laughed at that.

"*This maketh me at home to hounte and hawke and in fowle weder at my booke to sitt...* It does," he said, "have some appeal. "But alas Kate is not the kind to sit at home and practise her needlepoint and neither am I. Especially when I still have things I need to resolve such as those who would use my heritage for their own ends whilst keeping it from me. And whilst I might be pardoned, I am still held guilty of a crime I did not commit." He moved to sit in the chair opposite Gideon. "Besides, were I to make this my permanent residence I would be given little time to enjoy it. His Most Christian Majesty King Louis would find the need for my services, not just the men I provide to him already for his wars. He would doubtless expect I might fund myself in whatever task he set me."

Which made a kind of sense—if you were Sir Philip Lord and had the ability he had at warfare and the management of men in war.

"If I had all this—"

"If you had all this, I am sure it would be protected by contracts like ravelins. It may be you can help me with that sometime. But for now, this is merely the means which allows what I have to do and gives support to many who need it, as well. You should not think so much of it. Just as I do—a means to an end."

It was very difficult for Gideon to see how he could ever do that, but it was also apparent that Lord wasn't dissembling when he said that was how he viewed it himself. And thinking back, of the easy way Lord wore his wealth, often quite literally in the clothes he chose, there had been many clues that Gideon had missed that this was a much-monied man. He wondered then what a man who had such wealth and the power to conjure armies from the earth like Jason's dragon tooth warriors, would want with someone like himself? What had Gideon Lennox to offer to such a man?

Lord must have sensed something of his inner turmoil.

THE PHYSICIAN'S FATE

"This is what I have, not who I am," he said, lifting his empty hands. "I have held all this for as long as you have known me. It is to me no more than the sword at my thigh—a tool."

Gideon was mercifully spared the need to frame a reply to that because Gervais Poirier returned with a jug of wine and a plate of sweetmeats, saying that as soon as Monsieur Fox would wish, he would show the gentleman to the blue room. Monsieur Fox decided he needed to retreat and allow himself a chance to absorb and consider, so he got to his feet as soon as the offer was made. Sir Philip Lord made no attempt to detain him.

Poirier took the time to serve Lord with wine, then left the room with another bow, holding the door for Gideon to follow him. Gideon wondered if he were supposed to bow to Lord here as well, at least in front of others. Did French etiquette demand it? Hesitating, Gideon made a slight attempt, only to see Lord's expression change to disappointment.

"I will see you at supper," was all he said.

The blue room was well named. The panelled walls were the colour of bird's eggs and small ceramic plaques set on them with pictures of peacocks, tails spread wide or sweeping behind them. The bed was undoubtedly one of the most comfortable Gideon had ever had the privilege to lie on. And, having seen to his minimal ablutions where a bowl of warmed water had been set on a stand for him, lie on it he did. Staring into nothing and thinking.

Of course, nothing had changed, even though everything had. He was still here to find Anders, to persuade him to come back to England and assist Kate, that was all that really mattered. After that... Well, that could wait until the urgent task was accomplished.

When he was called down to supper soon after, he found he had arrived ahead of his host. Gervais Poirier was at the table, now dressed in a lace-edged black and grey twill with silver points. He introduced the woman with him as his wife, Jeanne. Her round face was wreathed in smiles as she bobbed several curtsies.

Gervais Poirier bade him be seated. "The Schiavono," he explained, "instructed that we were not to hold back on his account. He said you would be hungry Monsieur Fox."

The door to the elegant dining room opened and a small parade of servants trooped in bearing a main dish of baked bass, half wrapped in leaves and seasoned with fennel, and several side plates of vegetables, bread and a tureen of some white sauce floating with herbs.

"I am sorry it is such plain fare, but you have come to us unexpectedly," Madame Poirier told him. From her girth he suspected that plain fare was not very common in the house, unless on days when the church demanded it.

Gideon assured her that he was more than content with the food on offer and after a prayer had been said, set out to prove his point. The conversation was limited to polite small talk, and they had almost eaten the first course when Lord opened the door and strode in. He held up a hand as he did so to show he had no wish to disturb anyone's meal.

In the time since Gideon had last seen him, Lord had changed and adopted the extravagances of French court fashion in a confection of dark red silk.

"My apologies for the delay, some of the men wished to speak with me." Lord swept his cape aside with one hand, so it did not get trapped beneath him, and sat at the table. "And what is this? Baked bass? Oh, and a velouté sauce. Madame, you have outdone yourself, I hope you will forgive me for not being here to eat when it was at its best." His smile had Jeanne Poirier blushing.

After Lord had been served, the conversation shifted key at his prompting. "What news from Paris? Is there any disturbance following the death of the Cardinal?"

Poirier shook his head and wiped over his plate with a piece of bread.

"They lit bonfires in the streets for joy, but they didn't riot. His last words were said to be that he wished God to condemn him if he had done anything in his life except serve the Church and France."

Lord picked a bone from the fish and nodded.

"I think that is true, by his own lights at least. How did the king take it?"

"With no mark of grief. He said, 'a great politician has departed,' and that was all."

"He may not grieve now, but he will find things much harder without Richelieu as his mentor and his foil," Lord predicted.

Gervais nodded as he spoke. "The king, they say, will keep to the same course and has taken three men to fill the shoes of Richelieu."

"Three?" Lord looked surprised. "I had heard that Jules Mazarin was to be made First Minister."

"Oh, he has been taken into the heart of affairs. The day after Richelieu's passing, the king placed Cardinal Mazarin on the royal council. But then he named two other men as well to be his close advisors—Sublet de Noyers and the Comte de Chavigny."

"As they are all Richelieu's proteges one way or another," Lord said, having swallowed a mouthful of the bass, "I can see why you think things will keep to the same course."

"Although," Poirier observed, "there are plenty who wish it were not so, who would like to see some things restored to what they were before."

"It will be interesting," Lord said, his tone thoughtful, "to see how long those three all survive on the council. I am sure there are bets being placed as to who will be the first to be removed. It must be the talk of Paris."

"But that is not what is the talk of Paris," Jeanne Poirier said. She subsided immediately as Gideon saw her husband send her the kind of look his own father had bestowed upon his mother when he felt she was speaking up in an unseemly manner in front of an important guest. Something in him rebelled.

"Then what is, madame?" he asked her. "If we are to go to the city tomorrow it would be good to be advised what we might expect."

The look she gave him made him wish all over again that he could have had more ability to stand up for his mother in such ways.

"The talk of all the gossips of every rank is of the murder of Demoiselle Geneviève Tasse. She was a lady of the Duchesse d'Aiguillont, the Cardinal's niece. Killed in the very building where the Cardinal lay dying." Madame Poirier's voice dropped to a confiding tone. "It is said that before she was killed, she was *violated*."

"*Non!*" Gervais Poirier sounded shocked. "We are at table, *madame*."

There was a frozen pause and Jeanne Poirier flushed bright red and murmured an apology.

"You are right of course, Poirier," Lord said, his tone unconcerned as if there had been no socially awkward hiatus. "But such things happen in this world, and we cannot hide from them, or pretend they do not exist. It takes courage to speak of the unspeakable." He lifted his glass in a gesture that might be seen as a toast towards their hostess. Having taken a drink, he put the glass down. "Let us hope they soon find the man who did such a terrible thing."

"Oh, but they have." Madame Poirier assured them, her confidence much restored by Lord's gentle endorsement. "He is already held in the Châtelet. They say he is a foreigner, a Danish man called Anders Jensen."

THE PHYSICIAN'S FATE

Chapter Four

Nick wasn't sure how he came to be standing outside the inn. Mountjoy Blount had brought him as close as he had ever been to drawing his sword in a blind rage. Danny must have intervened somehow, because he was standing there too, looking at Nick with the kind of expression he wore when assessing the weather.

"I apologise, Sir Nicholas," he said, with little of apology in his tone, "I didn't think it'd help matters if you forced a duel with the Earl of Newport."

"I don't think he cares if the order is genuine or not," Nick said, still appalled by the laughter that had greeted his attempt to persuade Blount that he should march anyway. "I have to wonder if he is even loyal. He opposed the king in parliament before the war."

Danny shrugged.

"Does it matter? It is like me saying that for a Master of Ordnance he knows precious little about artillery. He is a courtier, not a warrior. As I see it, sir, to be angry at someone like that for behaving in such a way is akin to being angry at the wind for blowing."

Nick shook his head.

"You spent all yesterday and most of the night working to prepare that bridge and get it in place, surely you feel *something* for having had your hard work wasted by him?"

"It is not the first time," Danny said, sounding stoic. "And if that's the last time then I will be more than surprised. 'Make this, Danny. Prepare for that, Danny. Oh, but we don't need that now.' Happens all the time, sir."

But Nick was not really paying much attention, he was already thinking ahead.

"We will go anyway. Take our men."

Danny's benign expression seemed to freeze. "There is a big difference between outflanking a defensive position with over a thousand horse and outflanking with it with twenty-five."

"But we need to get into Tadcaster if that is where Mags is," Nick insisted. "If we let him away from there, we might lose him altogether."

"I'm not saying we don't need to get to him, but we won't be able to do it that way."

"Then how?"

Danny took off his hat and rubbed his fingers into the mop of his tawny hair.

"Well, what if we fetch our men and take word to the Earl of Newcastle that he'll be unsupported?" he suggested. "Then we might still get to bring the flanking force in, if there's time—and if not, the earl will likely take the town even without Newport and we might be able to get in. Or I might, at least."

Nick's spirits rose.

"You have the right of it. The earl needs to know of this. We must tell him."

"We need to return to the bridge, with our men—"

"They can stay there. That would only slow us down. It would be adding miles to our journey to do so. We need to get this news to the earl right away."

"But sir—"

Nick ignored him and turned to the two men they had brought with them who were already on their horses.

"Go back to the bridge and tell the men to wait there. Hopefully, the Earl of Newport will march soon." Then as the two turned away he gestured to Danny as he had seen his uncle do many times. "With me," he insisted, mounting.

For a moment he thought Danny was going to refuse and disobey. But, instead, he shook his head, put his hat back on, and taking the reins of his horse, swung himself into the saddle. Satisfied, Nick turned his own horse towards the south, Danny riding behind him. He set a punishing pace that allowed no opportunity for talk, and they heard the fighting at Tadcaster soon after they saw the wreaths of smoke curling above the town.

Closer to it was broiling chaos. The outlying fort dealt death by musket fire to any who came in range. The Royalists, under cover behind walls and in hedges, were attempting to return fire but with

THE PHYSICIAN'S FATE

little impact. The big guns from both sides boomed their lethal missiles, with varying degrees of success.

Nick kept close to the river in their final approach and came to a halt just past the mill, a hundred and fifty yards or so north of the bridge. He stopped because a company of musketeers was running towards them. These were white-coated men, most with blue knitted bonnets. Newcastle's men.

"For the king and Cavendish!" he shouted. "I'm Captain Sir Nicholas Tempest."

The row of muskets wavered a little, then an officer appeared.

"Lieutenant Colonel Atkins. Leave your horses, sir, we have need of every man we can muster to seize the bridgehead."

"I need to get a message to the earl," Nick told him.

"Unless we can cut off the fort, you won't get to the earl, Sir Nicholas. Come with my men, we'll secure the bridge. Then you'll be able to deliver your message to the earl."

"But I need—"

"That is an order, captain. Leave your horses behind the mill. They'll be safe enough there from the fighting."

Having no other choice at that point Nick dismounted and Danny took their horses to the shelter of a small outbuilding behind the mill.

Atkins nodded approval. "Now, with me." He took off at a run beside his men.

"The man is a fool," Nick said as Danny thrust a carbine into his hands.

"You shouldn't be so surprised," Danny told him. "Men carrying out an order often see it as having the highest priority on the battlefield. Besides, he may even be right about getting to the earl—he's certainly right about needing to break the link between the town and that fort. But I'm not sure he's got enough men to do it"

Then they were running.

There was a cluster of houses around the end of the bridge, outliers of the town and Atkins had chosen the most substantial to put his men into. As Nick came up, he gestured to the house beside it, smaller and closer to the bridge.

"I'll give you ten men. Get them in there and hold it."

Beside him, he heard Danny draw a sharp breath.

"We'll need twice that, sir," he said. "And that would be tight, to get a sufficient rate of fire to keep an assault away from the—"

"Who do you think you are?" Atkins snapped. Then he turned away and called to one of his men and brought a group of them crouched low, who he ordered into Nick's care. Then he was gone, following his men into the back door of the bigger house.

Danny took off his hat and hurled it at the ground.

"I don't mind being ordered to die when there's some chance of it doing someone some good somewhere, but this…" he spoke in a tone low enough that only Nick would catch it. The fury was something Nick had never heard from Danny before.

Danny bent, picked up his hat, dusted it briefly on his buff coat then pushed it back on his head. He turned to face the ten men who were clutching their muskets, lit match between their fingers, and lifted his voice.

"Form up, two files." As the men moved to obey, he went on talking. "You don't know me, but I'm Danny Bristow, lieutenant to you boys, and if you listen up, we'll get this job done. When I say 'advance' I mean run. Keep your ranks in your files or you'll trip over the man in front. We'll be exposed to those bastards in the earthworks for perhaps five seconds. So keep moving and they're not going to get a good shot." Danny turned to Nick then. "This is Captain Sir Nicholas Tempest and he's the man we all follow. He's going to lead the way and I'll be right behind you all. Now, let's get into that house and ruin their day. They can't have too much more powder left in that redoubt and we're going to stop them getting any more."

He had the men now, Nick could see, with just those few words. It was ten times what Nick would have said to them, but it had made the men somehow stronger and more determined. He wondered what the magic of it was. Was it the words? Or just that Danny had taken the trouble to speak to them at all?

"Just run like hell, sir," Danny told him quietly. "You're going first so you'll be in cover before the enemy has a chance to react properly. Get the men to start finding stuff to barricade the doors—big chests, tables, anything solid and heavy will do it."

Nick nodded his understanding, wondering if the fear showed in his face as much as in those of the men he had to lead. Five seconds of exposure to enemy muskets was an eternity. Danny had been watching the earthworks and then he gave a sharp nod.

"For the king and Cavendish!" Nick shouted and shot for the door of the house. It was only as he reached it, he realised he had crossed the killing ground safely. He let the force of his charge hit the door, which burst open as he did so, nearly tumbling him into the house. The first men in behind him, he set to looking for heavy furniture. Then he counted in the men. The shots suddenly increased in intensity. Nine men were in. Seconds passed. Stretched to a minute with no sign of Danny or the last man.

Two of the men with him had found a heavy table which they were holding ready to put up against the door. Nick knew he should tell them to do so, knew Danny must be lost, knew he was now alone in this fight, knew...

Danny staggered in, all but carrying the last man with him.

"Sorry, sir," he panted, "We had to wait for them to get distracted after Clarke here stopped a bullet with his leg."

Nick's relief was greater than he would allow to show.

Offloading Clarke to one of the other soldiers, Danny took over organising what was needed, blocking the downstairs windows, barring the door they had entered by before treating the one to the main street on the other side the same. It was fortunate that the householder, who had wisely abandoned his home, had a number of heavy pieces of furniture that could be pressed into service.

Under Danny's direction, they rapidly secured the lower floor then occupied the upper, barricading the stairs, which ran up from a small entrance hall by the street door, by wedging it with broken bedsteads, bedding, and other furnishings. Then they manned the upper windows which had a good view over the bridge. The men were placed at the windows in threes so as soon as one had fired, they could step back and reload and another man, with a fully loaded musket, was ready to take his place.

"Let's give them hell, boys," Danny called. "If you see something worth a bullet, shoot it. If you don't, then hold your fire until you do."

He followed up his words by shooting dead the first of a group of men running up from the bridge. A ragged volley followed from their windows and the house next to them and the men who had been moving forward retreated sharply. Nick began reloading as fast as he could. At the window where he was there were only himself and Danny. But the injured Clarke, sat propped against the wall behind them to help reload.

For a time, Nick began to believe they were going to dissuade any further attempts to storm the houses. If anyone was foolish enough to show themselves from the town, a handful of shots from the two houses dissuaded them. It seemed almost too easy, and he wondered what had made Danny so troubled about it.

"We can do this all day," he observed.

"It may seem fine now, but they are going to feel the pinch at the fort soon," Danny told him. "They were burning through powder faster than quick match and then it'll get dangerous here. They can't afford to let us sit here for long and our own supplies won't last forever."

It might have been a prediction for less than five minutes later a larger body of men than before could be seen assembling behind the bridge barricades. Danny cursed fluently in Spanish and Italian, and another language Nick did not recognise.

"We're going to get hammered," he said, his voice pitched so only Nick could hear, "and I can't see any way to stop it."

There was something in his tone that made Nick's stomach tighten.

"We could go out the way we came?" he suggested.

"Too late for that. They have men moved to cover that door. If we go out there now, we'll be mown down. And the fort is still kicking out enough to keep our friends from coming to help."

He sent another shot in the direction of the bridge, then raised his voice. "Make ready and hold your fire."

"You have a plan?" Nick asked, hopefully.

Danny lifted the brim of his hat and met Nick's gaze.

THE PHYSICIAN'S FATE

"I have two plans," he said. "The first is to cost them dear getting in, and the second is to cost them dear when we break out. What I need you to do if you will, sir, is stay here and send a volley into their stomachs whilst I go and make them a warm welcome on the stairs. Then we might be able to leave by the window that looks over the river, if they've not thought of that—but if Mags has any say in the command of this, they will have."

"Why not just go now?" Nick demanded.

"Because, sir," Danny said, working to reload as he spoke, "that would mean leaving Clarke. We need to buy time to get him out with us."

Nick shook his head. That made no sense at all.

"One man is not worth the lives of all the rest, we go now."

For a moment he thought Danny was doing to defy him, and for that same moment he had no idea what he might do if he did. Instead, Danny rammed the scouring stick hard into the barrel of his weapon and then replaced it in its rest before he spoke.

"Of course, sir," he said, mildly, "but it is my duty to remind you we need to make some show of defiance first or you'll have a job explaining to the earl why you deserted a defendable position. That means we have to stay until they attack."

"But you just said this is *not* a defensible position," Nick protested.

"At the moment it is, sir," Danny said. "Soon as those men get inside the house it won't be. But that's a very fine line to explain to a man of honour like the earl. If we leave too late we're lost, if we leave too early we're cowards."

"Christ." The oath burst from between Nick's lips and the men in the room looked over at him. Then he glanced out the window and what he saw nearly made him blaspheme again.

It was as if he had been blighted.

He had come to warn the earl of a betrayal and been forced into this undefendable building—trapped between the earthwork packed with musketeers on one side, and a town full of the enemy on the other.

He was turning back towards Danny when a sound at the rear of the house made his blood freeze. At the same moment, there was a surge of movement from the men behind the barricades and their voices came as a roar.

"Present!" Danny's voice cut through the sound, steady and confident. He was already aiming into the mass below.

There was battering now on the door and the men in the windows could hardly miss. Except they were become easy targets themselves from below.

"Give fire!" Danny commanded.

The explosions seemed to come as one and smoke billowed through the room and Nick's ears were ringing. Danny was shouting orders to two of the men to bring Clarke, he seemed to be completely ignoring Nick and headed out of the room without a word to him. The hard pounding on the door below intensified.

A stay bullet smashed into the far wall and Nick seeing there was no safety to be had in the room, pushed past the men helping Clarke just as one collapsed suddenly, and a spray of blood splattered over Nick.

"Help me with him, please sir," the other man called, but Nick was already out of the room, hand on sword. Then he saw the matchlock musket Clarke had been reloading, now leaning against the wall by the door and scooped it up. The lit match that had been stuck in the serpent ready to fire, was pulled half-free and he managed to grab it before it fell to the ground.

Danny was on the stairs, sprinkling a trail of black powder over some parts of the blockade they had set. As he clambered back up again the pounding on the door onto the street, which was at the bottom of the stairs, turned to a heavy splintering sound. It gave way in a sudden implosion of wood, and there were men pushing over the blockading furniture to get in. Danny was still on the stairs when Nick saw one of the men below raise and aim a pistol at him.

Without thought, Nick lifted the musket, thumbed back the pan cover, and pushed the lit end of the match into the pan with his other hand. The pistol went off at the same time as the musket and in the ensuing smoke, it was hard for Nick to see what had happened. Suddenly Danny was beside him, grabbing the match from his hand and bending to push it into something that was wedged into the clutter blocking the stairs.

THE PHYSICIAN'S FATE

Then Danny ran and Nick ran with him, along the top passageway of the house to the far room which had a view onto the river behind the bridge. The eight survivors of their small detachment of men were already leaving by the window, throwing their muskets out first. Two had already gone through the window and dropped down and two more were now helping Clarke to be lowered to them. They had just done so, and the three men were running as fast as they could together, when there came a series of staccato explosions from the stairs and some yells, followed almost immediately by a larger explosion.

"Go," Danny was telling the men who remained. "Out fast and run for the mill."

There were sounds of fighting in the house next door now as well and Nick pushed through to get to the window, keen to be out and away before those in this house gathered themselves for an attack. But Danny's strong grip pulled him back.

"I know you want to see what's happening, sir," he said, tone conciliatory, "but best to keep back for now so the men can get out."

Nick glared at him and was about to snap a reply when he saw the same darkness in Danny's eyes that had been there before when Danny spoke of Mags. The ruthless brutality of it sapped strength from Nick, but then the look was gone.

"They can't get up here for a minute or two yet, sir," Danny told him, releasing his arm. "There are no stairs and a fire to deal with."

It still seemed painfully slow to Nick as each of the remaining men swung themselves over the sill and dropped down to the bank below though it must have been less than a minute. Behind them smoke was creeping through the door and Nick was increasingly convinced the fire had taken hold. When the last of the men was gone, Nick stepped forward but again, Danny's hand was holding him back.

He turned frowning. This time Danny's eyes seemed to search his face as if looking for something.

"You saved my life on the stairs," Danny said. "I won't forget that." Then he released Nick and gave him a push towards the window. "Remember, run for the mill. Don't wait for me."

ELEANOR SWIFT-HOOK

A moment later Nick was out of the window and swinging by his fingertips from the sill, the drop perhaps five feet over the grassy bank below. He let go and landed, falling forwards as he did so and catching himself on his hands, he scrambled to his feet.

The shout came as he turned to run.

"Hold!"

Glancing back, he saw the river path on the town side was now full of men. He guessed at least a dozen and more were coming up behind them from beside the bridge. With the houses being retaken there was nothing to stop them. Those in the front ranks were levelling muskets at him. He turned to run.

"Hold."

The shout came again and suddenly Nick found himself falling flat forwards, measuring his length on the muddy river path as a volley of shots sent bullets through the space his body had been occupying a moment before.

Danny lay beside him. "I think we can cry quits with that," he said.

The men who surrounded them were not gentle as they prodded Nick to his feet. Disarmed, wrists lashed with match, Nick's emotions were numb. Of all the fates he would have ever envisaged for himself, being captured as a prisoner by Parliament was perhaps the worst. He would have much rather died under a hail of bullets before enduring the humiliation of it. The thought of having to face his father and explain how such a disgrace had been wrought upon the name of Tempest, left his guts cramping.

They were not the only prisoners taken. Another fifteen men, some injured, were marched with them back over the planks placed to cover the breach in the bridge, and then through the town to one of the houses. There they were pushed into a large room and made to sit on the floor under the muskets of four men who, from their expressions, would really enjoy being given the opportunity to abuse or kill their prisoners.

There were other prisoners already there, one of whom was, by his dress, also an officer. He sat with his head almost on his knees, surely feeling the shame as acutely as Nick himself. The rest of the men seemed more anxious and weary, and he supposed their fates were less certain than his own. Danny had lost his hat and his hair was a tangled mop about a blissfully unconcerned freckled face. The look was more that of a choirboy caught supping the sacramental wine than a man who might easily be hung for fighting on the wrong side of this war.

They sat in silence, even the usually loquacious Danny.

One man tried to murmur something to his neighbour and was pulled out and beaten before being dropped back with the rest. After that, there was no sound but that of the fight at the other end of the town. If Newport had marched then this place would have been at the centre of any fighting, Nick thought wryly, and the battle would have been over and done with.

It seemed an age before the shots grew fewer and by then the narrow windows had begun to darken. Someone brought a lantern to hang from a hook. Eventually, the door opened and an officer came in. He was middle aged but wearing it very well with shoulder-length black, curly hair flecked through with grey. By his dress and bearing it was clear he was in command. He looked over the seated men, although it would have been hard for him to see more than outlines of most in the mix of shadows.

"I want the man who owned this sword," he said and held up a basket-hilted blade, gripping it in his gauntleted hand just below the quillons. Nick stared at it then shot a glance at Danny, wondering what he would do.

"That would be me, sir," Danny said and pushed himself to his feet.

There was a strong silence and Nick felt the lines of tension between the two men as solid as ropes. Then the man by the door gave a brief bark of laughter.

"Before God, I should have known. Danny bloody Bristow."

"Captain Gyfford, I presume," Danny said, his face breaking into an answering grin. "It's been a while, John."

"Major," Gyfford replied. "Though after flushing you and your fellow vermin out of those houses I've been told it is likely I'm getting a promotion off the back of it. Now let's get you out of here, we've some catching up to do. Must have been, what, five years since Breda?"

"You have a couple of other officers in here," Danny said as he began to pick his way through the seated men towards the door. Nick wished he had said nothing. Better to face whatever came as an unknown and perhaps have history record he had died in the fighting, than to be singled out and marked by such indignity.

Someone held up another lantern.

"Oh, so we have, better have them out of here too. Get up gentlemen, whoever you may be."

The other officer was little more than a boy, younger even than Nick and he looked sick as he struggled to stand, tears of humiliation were clear but unshed in his eyes. Something about his demeanour gave Nick more strength and courage. He pushed himself to his feet and met Gyfford's gaze with as much defiance as he could muster. The worst this man could do was kill him and that was nothing next to the shame of what had already happened.

The other officer identified himself as Lieutenant Richard Fane then Gyfford turned to Nick.

"And who are you, sir?" he demanded.

With Danny standing beside the man, it was pointless to prevaricate.

"Captain Sir Nicholas Tempest," he said, trying to keep the pride he once took in his name as he spoke it.

Gyfford nodded.

"My respect to you sir, you got all your men safely away having managed to hold me and mine off with a mere handful. Now gentlemen, I will take your word and you can ride with me, or you may withhold it and stay confined."

Nick wanted to say he would not give his word to a treasonous rebel cur under any circumstances. But the young officer, Fane, spoke up beside him with almost those exact words first.

Gyfford's face darkened dangerously.

"As you wish, sir." He made a curt gesture to the men with him "Strip this gentleman and confine him."

Fane was dragged out protesting and silenced by heavy blows before he was through the door. Nick looked back to Gyfford, who watched Fane's removal with a look of contempt. Beside him,

THE PHYSICIAN'S FATE

Danny was trying to catch Nick's attention with a meaningful stare.

Nick swallowed the bile that seemed suddenly thick in his throat.

"You have my word, Major Gyfford," he said and wondered why his own tongue did not rebel at such ignominy and choke him as he spoke.

Gyfford gave him a brief nod.

"Thank you, Sir Nicholas. We'll have to find you a horse as we'll be leaving this town before long." Nick allowed himself to be shepherded from the room behind Gyfford who had returned Danny's sword to him. Then, as they went, threw an arm around his shoulders and was congratulating him on killing three of Gyfford's own men with the explosive devices he had left on the stairs.

Nick knew then that he would never understand the minds and hearts of such professional soldiers.

Chapter Five

Lord had been insistent that there was nothing they could do until morning.

"If Jensen is taken, he has been for some days, and they will do nothing more with him overnight than has happened so far. I will make the necessary arrangements so we can go into Paris with the first of the wagons heading to sell their produce in the big market at *Les Halles*."

It was, of course, good sense, but that made little impact on Gideon's fear for the man he considered his friend. The Châtelet was notorious as a place of torture and abuse, a place where men could simply disappear. As a result, Gideon was up well before dawn having barely slept.

He had been provided with clothing Lord decreed suitable for Paris. It was much more expensive and stylish than anything Gideon had ever considered wearing before. He was sure he looked less lawyer and more courtier.

When he arrived downstairs, it was to find that Lord was already up and finishing a quick early meal. Lord was dressed even more superbly than he had been the day before. In his hatband as well as the inevitable white plume, was a small square of lace-edged and tasselled white silk. The kind of kerchief a lady of rank might bestow as a favour on the gentleman of her choosing. Gideon wondered at it because it was most certainly not the kind of item he would ever associate with Kate.

"We need to have strength today, so eat." Lord gestured to the table and rose as he spoke. "I want to leave in the next quarter of an hour, so as soon as you have eaten find me outside." Then he was gone.

Gideon looked at the food on offer, his stomach too tight to face the prospect of eating much. He chose some fresh bread and a round of soft cheese with a strange smell, but he found it tasted none too unpleasant. Well within the time set by Lord, he was stepping out onto the apron of ground before the house and found

THE PHYSICIAN'S FATE

one of the men they had travelled with from England holding a horse for him.

There were, Gideon counted, twenty men waiting with their horses. All were armed, clad in polished back and breast armour, new buff coats and a more extravagant version of the blue and grey uniforms he had seen Lord find for his troops in England. Lord was clearly planning an entry to impress.

When Sir Philip himself appeared, he was mounted on the kind of destrier that Gideon imagined must have carried the combatants into battle on both sides of the long wars between France and England—the wars between Plantagenets and Capetians, then Lancaster and Valois. It was a magnificent powerfully built dark bay stallion, coat gleaming like polished wood and with both mane and tail brushed out.

The horse Gideon was given, also a bay, was clearly more jennet than destrier as were the mounts of their escort.

"Who exactly are we trying to impress?" Gideon asked as they set out along the avenue that led from the house to the main Paris road. "And what is that?" he added nodding towards the banner carried by one of the men riding behind them. It showed the head of a white cat—or perhaps it was a leopard; Gideon was not too well versed with the intricacies of heraldry—facing out of the banner from a blue background.

"That," Lord told him, "is azure, a cat's head cabossed argent. I was informed by Sir John Borough, the Garter Principal King of Arms, that as a knight banneret I would be entitled to have two bare supporters. Which seemed quite an interesting notion until I realised he meant armorial bears of the furred and ferocious kind."

On any other day Gideon would have laughed, but today he managed no more than a grimace.

"And," Lord went on, unperturbed, "we are sent as an extraordinary embassy to His Majesty King Louis of France, on behalf of His Majesty King Charles, in order to offer his condolences on the death of First Minister Cardinal Richelieu. Also informally, should the opportunity arise, to ask the king, yet again, what he might do to best aid his sister, Queen Henriette Marie. I sent ahead to inform Richard Browne, the king's agent in

Paris, that we were here and late last night received his reply that we would be well advised to make ourselves presentable when turning up today as he fully expects to receive word that we will be invited to attend upon the king at some point this morning."

It all seemed a bit sudden to Gideon.

"I thought such things were only done with days of preparation and fanfare."

"You would be surprised. Often it is much lower key even at courts which stand on ceremony so hard they get piles. But in this case, when the King of England has had to smuggle his condolences out of his own country to his brother-in-law of France, in the hands of a man as disreputable as myself, you can be sure there will be many exceptions made. A major reason the prince persuaded the king to give me the job was because his majesty was assured I would be able to put on a decent display thanks to my resources here."

Gideon shook his head close to incredulity.

"So where in all that do we find time to help Anders?"

"Until we have been officially received there is very little we can do directly to help him. In person at least."

"We?" Gideon bridled at that. "Surely you mean yourself? I'm not given any position by the king. And why didn't you tell me this before?"

"I mean 'we' as you are currently part of my retinue and anything you do will reflect on me and through me on His Majesty King Charles. No matter how much you may wish to rush to the Châtelet—and you can believe I am just as keen to do so—you will have to wait until I have been formally received. And I didn't mention it before because until we were here it was not safe to let it be known to anyone what I carried. If we had been stopped in England, your ignorance might have protected you." He sighed and cast a glance at Gideon. "The problem is in agreeing to the task, as it would allow me to travel speedily to Paris, I somehow failed to anticipate that we would discover Jensen had been taken on a charge of murder."

They joined the main road and the amount of traffic heading towards Paris even that early in the morning was breathtaking.

THE PHYSICIAN'S FATE

Most seemed to be supplies and provisions of various kinds, slung on the backs of horses, mules and donkeys or piled high in carts. But there were also travellers on the road, a group of nuns trusting to God for their protection, a nobleman with a smaller retinue than Lord had who was forced to draw aside to let them pass, a couple of scholars heading to the Sorbonne perhaps, and inevitably a handful of men Gideon was sure were lawyers of some variety.

"What do you need me to do?" he asked.

"Probably nothing more than sit in Sir Richard's parlour and make polite conversation with his wife whilst he and I are at Le Louvre kissing the royal boot, or whatever the present polite practice is. With any luck, it will be done by dinnertime and then we will be in a place to help Jensen."

"May I at least try and find out if there is any news of him?"

Lord's mouth tightened.

"I would pray there is not," he said grimly. "Any news that comes now will be bad news."

Gideon shook his head. It still made no sense to him.

"There must be some mistake," he said. "Anders would never—"

"I am *sure* there is a mistake," Lord cut across him. "But until the matter I have been sent to discharge is completed, there is nothing more we can do."

And with that thin gruel of a promise for the future, Gideon had to be satisfied.

His first impression of Paris was a silhouette of spires and towers, open fields, earthworks, and the sound of distant bells. The fields were mostly empty, it being winter, and a cold white frost covered them in the early light, but they lay about the city ready to provide for its needs when spring returned them to growth. The earthworks came next, low and yet menacing, sparse with guns. A reminder that France was at war too and this was clearly a city that felt the need to keep its defences in order. The outer fortifications had been reinforced by outlying forts and ditches. As they approached closer the sound of bells grew louder as if to greet them.

There was a delay at the gate, because rank and status meant nothing to the wagon of nightsoil, hauled by two bellowing oxen, which had blocked it. Lord took his men off the road and around the growing jam of carts and wagons, but it was quickly obvious that the wagon had a broken wheel and until it could be removed there was no way to get through on horseback.

"Sir Philip!" The shout, in clear English, came from the far side of the blockage, just as Lord was turning his mount away and then a figure eased on foot past the cart where no man mounted could have fitted through and came striding over with two armed retainers behind him. The man was in his mid-thirties, well dressed, if not in quite so fine apparel as Lord and Gideon. Strangely, as well as wearing a cloak he carried one over his arm. He stopped, breathless and clearly a little flustered, making a bow in the road to Lord on his very high horse.

"Sir Philip, Richard Browne at your service, I am so glad I managed to reach you before you entered the city. The king, it seems, has had to have second thoughts about any public reception. You are still to be received at some point, but things need to be done," he paused as if uncertain what word would fit his purpose best, "done discreetly." His gaze moved from Lord to the men ranked behind him, the message in it clear.

"I see," Lord said. "I would assume I am permitted to retain some semblance of my dignity?"

Browne flushed, clearly embarrassed at the message he was being forced to deliver.

"I will explain when we are more privy, Sir Philip, but if, perhaps you were to dismiss your entourage, I took the liberty of bringing a full-length cloak of a fine but plain making so you can pass through Paris unremarked." He shook out the cloak to show it was indeed a good one. Black wool lined with what seemed to be a crimson-coloured silk.

"You believe I can pass through Paris unremarked on this horse?" Lord asked and Browne was almost squirming.

"I would ask that you come with me on foot, Sir Philip. Quite apart from the fact the gate will be blocked for some time yet, in Paris it is the fastest and best way to proceed I do assure—"

THE PHYSICIAN'S FATE

"You seem to forget that I know Paris," Lord's tone was sharp. "I have a house close by here, and this horse is to be a gift to the Most Christian King Louis from his brother King Charles."

It was not often Gideon had seen Lord in such a stubborn mood.

"Can we not send for the horse later?" he asked, frustrated that they seemed to be held up by some minor debate over the exact etiquette of a meeting. "It is not far after all."

Lord looked at Gideon, his gaze Baltic, but Browne was nodding eagerly.

"I suppose," Lord's tone was cutting, "there is little else that can be done." He swung himself down from the tall mount and turned to the men behind them, handing over the reins and issuing instructions. Gideon could only wonder why Lord was so fixed on the point when surely all that mattered was getting into Paris.

"Alone, would be best, Sir Philip," Brown said, as Gideon dismounted and handed his own reins to another of Lord's men. "I have men to escort us." He gestured to the two men with him.

Lord turned back. "Mister Fox is here on a matter unconnected to my mission on behalf of the king. He is a lawyer and needs to conduct some private business on my behalf."

Gideon was almost sure he saw relief in Richard Browne's face at Lord's words and wondered who—or what—Browne had taken him to be.

"Very well. Here," Browne said, unfastening his own long cloak and offering it to Gideon. "If you would please wear this. I am not so—" he paused as if trying to find a polite word, "*distinctively* clad as you are."

They had been speaking in English throughout and from the looks they were being given, Gideon was pretty sure that no one had understood the conversation, although when Lord had dismissed his men, he had done so in French.

"So why this change of plan?" Lord demanded as they walked towards the blocked gates, followed by Browne's two men.

Browne glanced around as if wanting to satisfy himself that they were not being overheard and even then, Gideon had to strain to hear him speak.

"The king here has received another embassy—from those who support the rebellious Parliament, sent ostensibly on the same mission as yourself, to bring their condolences. I had thought, as all the court had thought, that his Most Christian majesty was intending to dismiss them coldly. Indeed, he would have for certain, but it seems they have hinted that were he to be willing to concede some of what they asked for, it might be possible that his nephew and niece, Prince Henry and Princess Elizabeth, who are both presently held in London, might be allowed to come to France under certain stringent conditions. At which point I was sent word that you are not to be received publicly."

Lord groaned aloud.

"So how long before I can expect to be received?"

"It is likely not until this secret embassy has concluded its business. This king would not wish word to reach their ears that he has been also talking with King Charles' representative. It might mar the chance of concluding some means of freeing his sister's children."

"Of course," Lord said bitterly, "and thus why it was to be seen that King Charles' envoy has been turned away from the gates of Paris. This could take weeks and even were it settled in days, it is already the seventeenth of December. We have the Christmas season starting next week, when any diplomacy will be shut out of the room as the court dallies with festivities."

"I know it must be frustrating for you, Sir Philip," Browne said, and Gideon marvelled that he managed to sound sincere rather than emollient. "But I am sure his majesty will understand the delay and would wish to allow such negotiations to have his children set at liberty."

"I am sure he would," Lord agreed, his tone clipped. Then in a slightly less chilly tone. "And where does that leave us now? I have affairs I need to attend to that are of the most pressing urgency and yet I am not officially here so I can hardly be seen to attend to them."

"I think this matter will be resolved with more expedition than you fear," Browne said quickly, perhaps a bit too quickly as if to placate. "My own sources tell me that what these men of

THE PHYSICIAN'S FATE

Parliament ask for is unlikely to be granted by King Louis no matter the incentive and as soon as that becomes clear the negotiations will hastily flounder. I am sure whatever the matter that exercises you might be, it can wait a few days."

"No," Lord said. "It really cannot. A man's life is at stake."

"A life at stake? That sounds very serious." Browne was clearly trying hard to be conciliatory. "If you come to my house, we can talk about it, and I will see what I may do to be of assistance in the matter."

Lord made no reply as they had reached the gate and the requirements of getting into the city, passing the malodorous damaged wagon, took over from the conversation.

Once within, Gideon understood how a provincial visitor must feel on their first visit to London. London was a great city, but Paris was undoubtedly greater. It was not so obvious from without, but once within the walls, the high buildings and the crush of people made it plain. He had heard there might be half a million people living within the city, more than a fifth as large again as London. From what he could see even this early in the morning, he believed it.

Their way went through broad streets and narrow, past high-fronted houses and the occasional church. Space in the city was clearly at a premium. The river Seine wound like a broad strip of dark satin through the centre of it all, much like the Thames through London.

Walking swiftly, keeping out of the way of those riding mules and a few carriages which took the centre of the very muddy roadway, Gideon was glad of the cloak. Aside from its warmth on what was a very cold day, it served the useful function of keeping clothes beneath relatively unsplattered by the mud of the unpaved roads. Most of the local people seem to have adopted heeled boots or wore wooden pattens to lift their shoes above the mudline.

A short time later they were being shown into a surprisingly spacious and comfortable house. Browne must have caught Gideon's expression because he smiled.

"I was most fortunate to be able to rent this at a price I could afford, but we require the space as I often have stray Englishmen to stay. And then there is the chapel."

"Chapel?" Gideon was momentarily confused, then he realised the need there would be in a Catholic country. "Are there Anglican services on Sundays?"

"Yes. You are welcome to attend. We have a priest staying with us at the moment and there are a number of English residents of Paris who come every Sunday." He sounded very proud of the achievement. "We've even held a baptism here."

"You have been in Paris long?" Lord asked, looking around the parlour at the evidently settled air.

"We came last year, before things took such a terrible turn and his majesty was forced to the extreme of war."

"I am surprised he has the means here in France to pay for this."

There was a slight pause in which Gideon realised that Lord already knew that Browne was supporting the embassy largely from his own purse—and that Browne knew that he must know.

"We all do what we can," Browne said at which point Gideon decided he was indeed a diplomat of some ability. "Now," he went on as the door opened, "Sir Philip, please let me present my wife, Elizabeth and my daughter, Mary."

Elizabeth was perhaps five years younger than her husband and greeted them both with a warm smile. Mary was seven years old and already the perfect miniature of her mother, with golden ringlets, deep blue eyes and an angelic face. She made a practised curtsey, asked if they fared well and how their voyage had been. Lord spared the child at least his vexatious mood and answered her questions graciously. To Gideon's relief that lifted the chill that had been riming the atmosphere and made both her parents glow with pride and even warm a little to their waspish guest.

"Let me show you to your rooms," Elizabeth said. "Richard mentioned you may need to send for your things, but—"

"I thank you for your offer," Lord interrupted her. "There is no need. My own house is not far from Paris."

The frost returned and Elizabeth Browne looked at her husband for guidance. Browne tightened his lips.

"I had hoped you might consent to remain here as my guest for a few days, Sir Philip," he said. "Then as soon as there is any chance to carry out your commission you will be in a place to do so. Even at Saint-Léon-du-Moulin you would be too far were the king to send word he was able to receive you within the hour—and he has been known to do that."

Now it was Lord whose lips grew tight. But only for a moment, before they relaxed into a smile as he inclined his head to Elizabeth Browne.

"Then, thank you. I am delighted to accept your generous offer of hospitality."

The house was arranged over four floors. The ground floor contained the kitchen, a reception room, and the chapel. The first floor held the public rooms and above those were the family rooms and a well-appointed guest room with views over the road, which had been prepared for Lord.

There were then further stairs up to some small rooms under the roof space, of which Gideon was offered one. The others were clearly used by Sir Richard's live-in servants or for guests of lesser status.

For the dwelling of the man representing the King of England in France, Gideon thought it felt less like a projection of the monarch's power and more of a rather cramped besieged outpost. A small corner of England in the very heart of Paris, diligently preserved and defended against the surrounding Catholic culture.

He found Lord in his elegant room, leaning on the sill of the window looking out over such of the city as it revealed.

"I have sent for your things," Lord said, turning as Gideon entered. He dismissed a servant, who had been arranging the room, with a nod of his head. "I regret we have no choice but to remain here until the king will agree to see me."

"What about Anders?" Gideon asked, doggedly once the door had closed behind the departing servant.

"I have been giving the matter some thought," Lord said. "What if you were here not as a member of my own retinue but as a guest of Richard Browne and his family, at their specific invitation? Travelling with me but not one of my people. You are not named in any of the documents I carry, I was careful to ensure that for your protection. You were covered by the mention 'and servant'." Lord gestured to documents he had placed on a side table in the well-appointed room. "You should see if you have any acquaintances in common with Richard or Elizabeth Browne. I would not be at all surprised to find you have and if not, I am sure they can think of someone of sufficient prominence and obscurity who we can claim as such a party."

It dawned on Gideon that Lord's uncharacteristic short temper was born from his concern for Anders and a frustrated desire to do all that could be done to free him.

"Do you want me to begin finding out what I can about Anders?"

Lord tapped the documents with a finger.

"As long as I have these, I can do very little—in my own name."

"In your own name, no," Gideon echoed, picking up on the significance.

"I am sure," Lord said carefully, "that the Brownes will feel that their guest—come freshly from England and unused to Parisian ways—should not be allowed out without a capable servant to ensure his safety."

"And what if the king decides to send for you when I am out with my 'servant'?"

"That," Lord said grimly, "is a risk I shall have to take."

It meant taking Browne into their confidence to some degree. Without actually claiming it as a secondary royal commission, Lord managed to create the impression that the matter of Anders Jensen was of nearly an equal priority to that of the meeting with King Louis. But it still took the best part of the morning to persuade Browne that it would be safe for Lord to come and go in disguise. In the end Lord was pushed to a compromise in the face of Browne's concerns. They agreed that whenever possible and appropriate Gideon would go with Browne himself, as his putative friend, rather than risk Lord clad in servant's garb out on the streets.

It was not a compromise Lord liked, but on this occasion, Gideon thought Browne had the right of it. Although Lord had supreme confidence in his own ability, there would always be a risk of something going wrong. The embarrassment it would cause should Lord be caught out playing the part of a lackey, would not just have repercussions on Lord's diplomatic mission but perhaps even work to the detriment of whatever they might be trying to do for Anders.

Lord bowed to the inevitable.

"Let us hope, gentlemen," he said, "that this effort to avoid embarrassment is not fatal. You seem to forget what I said earlier—a man's life is at stake here."

Gideon saw Lord's tight lips and knew his true thoughts. Although Lord didn't say it, a woman's life was at stake too.

Chapter Six

When Gideon set out on his first venture into Paris that afternoon it was with Richard Browne and two of his men in attendance. They were to visit the Châtelet which, Browne had explained, as well as being a prison, included courts of law with both criminal and civil jurisdiction.

"The courts are open to the public?" Gideon asked as they walked along the banks of the Seine.

"Of course," Browne said. "Justice must be seen to be done."

"Even the prisons?"

"It is not hard to get in if you have enough money," Browne explained, then smiled ironically. "But then nothing in Paris is hard, if you have enough money."

Gideon felt the weight of the purse in his doublet. Lord had given it to him before they left the house.

"I think I have," he said. "Do people have to pay to talk to the prisoners?" It was often thus in England.

"Of course. But sometimes they pay to visit as a variety of entertainment. And if you would not draw too much attention to your interest in this Dane, that is what we must do. Speaking with him will be seen then as a morbid interest in a murderer rather than as someone seeking to succour him." He paused then added, "Also it might be best if, for now at least, you do not admit to any great knowledge of the French language, just 'bonjour' and 'merci', that way I can help you avoid any issues that might arise around your purpose there."

Gideon nodded. He was still unsure why the last words Lord had spoken to them as they left were to insist that on no account should they let it be known that Gideon was there to try and help free Anders. Gideon's own instincts as a lawyer were to state who he was, and his purpose, from the first. But Lord seemed to believe that until they knew more it was safer not to let anyone realise their true intent.

THE PHYSICIAN'S FATE

The Seine for Paris was the lifeblood of the city, even more perhaps than the Thames was for London. Gideon saw the laundry boats moored by the banks and even the peculiar sight of floating mills in the heart of the city. But as they neared the Châtelet, the smell was what struck Gideon the most—rotten offal mixed with excrement, intensifying close to their destination. It turned his stomach. Browne looked sympathetic.

"There are sewers that run out near here and the slaughterhouses which run into those are nearby. Although they should stop the worst of it by law, that seems to make little difference."

The Châtelet itself was a castle within the confines of the city, guarding the Grand-Pont, one of the main bridges which connected the Île de la Cité with the right bank of the Seine. It had rounded towers and typically French turrets. The prévôt who held it, Browne told him, acted as both investigator of crimes and judge of them.

Browne spoke quietly to one of the men at the gates and gestured to Gideon who pressed a coin into the hand that was held out and then they were taken inside.

The man who escorted them, and who expected another coin for his trouble, explained that they were in luck as there were two cases that afternoon and the first was about to start. Gideon assumed then they were going to witness some kind of legal proceedings, perhaps an arraignment or trial. Although thinking it odd that anyone would have to pay for the privilege, he had a great professional interest in how such things were done in France.

So he was not prepared when they were led onto a gallery overlooking a room in which a naked man was having his wrists bound by rope to a ring on the wall about four feet above the ground. As Gideon began to realise with appalled horror what it was he and Browne had paid to watch, they tied the ropes around the man's ankles to a ring on the other wall. Ignoring his struggles and protestations of innocence, used a device like a wooden sawhorse to press on the ties that lashed his ankles together, lifting him higher by the feet and tightening the rope at the same time. The effect was to stretch his body almost as if upon a rack.

Browne must have noticed Gideon's reaction because he hissed urgently in his ear.

"We paid to see this. You mustn't look as if you wish to vomit."

The fact he had to look at all was more than Gideon could achieve. He heard the man scream and sob breathless denials to the questions he was asked and then they increased his torment by using a higher wooden horse.

There was a pause when the men questioning had a brief discussion and for a moment Gideon thought they had decided their victim had suffered enough, but instead one of them pushed a horn, narrow at the mouth but wide at the top, into the man's mouth. Then, his head still lower than the rest of his body, proceeded to pour a full bucket of water into the horn, forcing the man to swallow or drown. When he still refused to admit his guilt, they followed that with a second bucket. At that point, the prisoner was barely conscious, his stomach distended to a horrific degree and Gideon was fighting the urgent need to vomit.

As there was another discussion about what they should do to the man next, Gideon knew he had seen enough. The notion of this being regarded as any kind of entertainment made him feel sicker in his soul than in his stomach.

"I have to go," he said to Browne, who took one look at him and then spoke quickly to their guide.

That he wasn't sick, Gideon put down to the last three months that he had spent in Sir Philip Lord's company. That had exposed him to sights as bad and taught him to deal first hand with man's inhumanity to man. Before he had been mostly shielded from the worst of it except what he might come upon in the street or have to read about in the course of his work.

He had no idea what Browne said to excuse his reaction but having spent a few minutes breathing the not so fresh air, he rejoined Browne and their guide. The latter greeted him with a jovial smile and a comment about his dinner not being well cooked. Remembering in time that he was not supposed to speak any French, Gideon returned a weak smile.

Then they were being led back inside the building, their guide explaining that the man they had seen tortured was clearly guilty

THE PHYSICIAN'S FATE

even though he had made no admission, so would undoubtedly be sent to the galleys. He would be made to row a ship of the French navy on the Mediterranean for the rest of his life. Gideon wondered what the point of the torture had been if the man was already tried, judged and condemned no matter how he replied.

Their guide had already moved on from the topic and was now regaling them with details about the crime committed by the man they were about to meet.

"He is a murderer, but worse even than that, before he killed poor Demoiselle Tasse, he *deflowered* her."

"That is terrible," Browne agreed. "What happened?

Gideon tried not to look too attentive whilst listening intently. Their guide was clearly a man who revelled in the knowledge he had and the sharing of it.

"Demoiselle Tasse was companion and attendant to the Duchesse d'Aiguillon. She was staying in the Palais de Cardinal as the duchesse was there to be with her uncle as his end approached. Duchesse Marie Madeleine was his favourite relative, you know. He, it was, had her created a duchess in her own right four years ago. She is a marvellous lady, so kind, so compassionate. Always involved in charitable works. It is such a tragedy for her to lose her companion and then her uncle so close together, I have wondered—"

"A tragedy indeed," Browne said, interrupting, clearly as unwilling as Gideon to hear a paean to the Duchesse d'Aiguillon rather than details of the murder. "But what happened to Demoiselle Tasse?"

They had gone downstairs away from the light of day and come to a dark corridor which reeked of damp and the ordure of the sewers. There were heavy metal bound doors on both sides of the passageway, but their guide stopped before they reached even the first at Browne's question.

"She was found in her own chamber, by the duchesse herself, on the evening of the twenty-ninth of November, naked on the bed, despoiled and obviously so. It seems she had been poisoned by a remedy called laudanum. Apparently, in small doses it is used for many good things, such as in the relief of pain and to promote healthful sleep. They found the stopper of a small bottle that smelt strongly of it and there was wine left in a glass which contained some. The prévôt's investigators have suggested that this man, Jensen, wished to enjoy her and as he knew she would refuse, drugged her with the laudanum, but gave her too much and so poisoned her. It is a horrible thing."

"And how do they know this Dane was the man who did this terrible thing?"

"That is easy. Laudanum is not a permitted treatment authorised by the Faculty of Medicine so none of the physicians of the Faculty would have had any access. But the physicians who work at the Bureau D'Adresses are often reproved by the Faculty for encouraging and prescribing such unlicensed chemical remedies. Of the physicians from the Bureau who had been allowed in the Palais de Cardinal this man, Jensen, had a bottle of it in his possession. A small bottle wrapped in a handkerchief which had belonged to Mademoiselle Tasse."

Gideon felt the nausea of earlier returning.

"And he has confessed?" Browne asked.

Their guide shook his head. "Not yet, but I am sure in time he will."

Those chilling words combined with the memory of the torture he had just witnessed, left Gideon close to despair as they were taken to one of the doors and it was unlocked by their guide.

"These are the rooms we keep for our special guests," he said with a wink that made Gideon shudder.

Browne looked at the blackness the door opened onto and hesitated. There was an unbearable reek of human excrement. "My friend from England here has a fascination with this matter and would ask some questions of this man."

"Then your friend is in luck, I believe the man speaks English even better than French."

"And is it permitted to speak with him privately?"

It was, of course, for a price and more of the coins Lord had provided slipped into the palm of their guide who handed them a lantern and said they would need to be locked in, but a knock on the door would see them released.

THE PHYSICIAN'S FATE

Browne, his nose wrinkling, declined and stayed outside as Gideon, armed with the lantern, stepped into the stinking darkness and the door was shut behind him.

The room was small enough that once he had taken a pace inside, the lantern, with its single candle, illuminated the whole chamber. The walls were covered in places with some kind of slime and the floor was wet. The only attempt to offer any comfort to the occupant was a hessian covered straw pallet, which was partially soaked and falling apart, and a stinking bucket that was close to overflowing.

Anders barely resembled the man Gideon remembered. He had lost weight, his hair and beard, normally so clean and well-trimmed, were filthy and matted and his only clothing was a ripped shirt. He sat on the mattress, hugging his knees and had thrown up a hand to protect his eyes from the light, so Gideon quickly shielded the lantern. As he crouched down, he wished more than anything that he had thought to bring food, drink, a blanket. The purse in his coat felt useless with its weight of cold metal.

"Anders, it's Gideon—I'm here to help you." Even as he said that he felt utterly impotent and no longer sure the words he spoke had any meaning.

The Dane lowered his hand from his eyes and blinked at Gideon for a few moments, then reached out a hand and gripped his arm, clearly not entirely convinced of Gideon's physical presence.

"Either I am finally and completely deluded, or I have died and we are meeting in some antechamber of hell, or somehow, unbelievably, you are really here. But how…?" His voice sounded hoarse and gave way to a brief rasping laugh which in turn finished in a cough.

Gideon set the lantern on the floor then took Ander's hand and held it in both his own.

"We came to find you, Lord and I," he said, suddenly uncertain how much more he could or should say.

"You heard? Even in England, you heard? And you came?" There was such a sharp and sudden hope in his tone that Gideon lacked the will to take that from a man who had nothing else.

"We heard," he lied. "We have come to help you." That was truth.

The shaded light from the lantern glistened on Anders' face as tears welled from his eyes and rolled unchecked down his cheeks. Embarrassed, Gideon released his hand and looked away.

"Have you been tortured?" Gideon was afraid to ask but had to know.

"They threaten me with it daily, but so far it is only threats. It seems the evidence against me is such that they do not need me to admit to anything."

Gideon drew a breath of relief, then wanted to choke on the foul air. "You must tell me what happened," he said quickly, "I'm not sure how long I will be allowed to speak with you."

"I do not know what happened," Anders said, the edge of desperation creeping back into his voice. "I know I am accused of the murder of a woman the Palais de Cardinal, but that is all I know. Not even who she is or how I am supposed to have killed her."

Gideon had his mouth open to explain what he knew then closed it again. For Anders' own sake he needed first to hear his account of what had happened.

"Then tell me what you do know. Why did you come to Paris and how did you wind up here?"

Anders wiped a hand over his face and drew a breath.

"I arrived in the last week of October. I came to work with Théophraste Renaudot. I met him before on a visit here. He tried to persuade me then to join him, but I was eager then to travel to London, meet with Sir William Harvey. I had a letter of introduction from my old mentor at Padua."

"So who is this man Renaudot?" Gideon said, keen to try and keep Anders more focused on what he needed to hear.

"He is a very good man, and learned, too. He holds weekly conferences where all manner of scientific and philosophical matters are debated."

"He is a philosopher?" Gideon asked.

Anders shook his head. "Not as you mean. Like myself, he studied as both a physician and a surgeon. Unlike the fools in the

Faculty of Medicine here in Paris who think of surgeons as of carpenters and that any remedy not listed over five hundred years ago is fraudulent, he is a true man of medicine." For a moment, in his remembered anger at that injustice, Anders had clearly forgotten his own plight, then he must have recalled it because he shook his head. "Not that any of it matters now."

"You were working for this man Renaudot?"

"Yes. Renaudot is Commissioner General of the Poor. Amongst other work with the poor, he offers them free medical consultation and treatments. That is what I was doing."

"You were helping the poor of Paris with free consultations?"

Gideon blinked. He had encountered few medical men willing to give their services for free.

"Yes. Why not? The poor of Paris need such help as much as their wealthy neighbours. More so, indeed."

"Then can you think of any reason someone might believe you could have been in the Palais de Cardinal on the evening of the twenty-ninth of November?"

"Because I was," Anders said simply. "I was one of the handful of physicians Théophraste recommended to Cardinal Richelieu. When the fools from the Faculty began to realise they could no longer help him, they agreed to allow us in. But, of course, by then it was much too late."

"Were you alone there?"

Anders frowned as if memory was escaping him.

"I was there for two evenings. There were times I was alone. Does it matter?"

"It might. Did you carry any remedies with you when you went to the Palais?"

"I took my bag, so yes, whatever was in there." Then, his tone suddenly became more fierce. "Is that what they are saying? That I killed someone with the wrong remedy?"

Gideon shook his head.

"No. That is not the charge."

"Then for the love of God, my friend, please tell me." The desperation in Anders' voice was hard to bear. "I have been out of my mind wondering what it is I might have done to deserve this."

Gideon could only imagine what it must be like to be locked up for so many days in the dark, threatened with torture and questioned, but never aware of what you were accused of doing.

"They say you put laudanum in a cup of wine and gave it to a woman called Geneviève Tasse. Then you raped her, and the laudanum killed her."

Anders stared at him in complete confusion and disbelief.

"How could they even think such a thing of me?"

"Because," Gideon told him, heart heavy, "they found the bottle of laudanum wrapped in a handkerchief belonging to Demoiselle Tasse in your possessions."

The Dane made a sound that Gideon did not recognise for a moment, and then he did. Anders was laughing. He seemed to find it hard to stop, and when he could it was with a gulp of despair.

"I see that not only am I supposed to be a rapist and a murderer, I am also supposed to be a fool. A bad physician who cannot design the correct dose and a half-wit who would keep the evidence to prove my own guilt. There is only one good thing in all this," Anders said. "Whoever is trying to place the blame for this on me is not a very clever man. This is the kind of thing a child might have thought up to make someone look guilty, although every fool thinks himself clever enough."

"I agree," Gideon admitted. "Unfortunately, it doesn't change that even if simple, they seem to have been very effective."

Anders shook his head.

"It is truly said that no one gets into trouble without his own help. I must have done something which made me the one chosen to bear the blame. Perhaps if I could think of that…"

"Perhaps," said Gideon. "But perhaps you were the most convenient scapegoat. We have, after all, established that whoever did this wasn't the cleverest of men. Had you ever met and spoken with Geneviève Tasse?"

Anders sighed.

"That is the problem. I met and spoke. with her, the day before."

Gideon felt his heart sink. He had assumed that one plank of his defence could be that Anders had no prior knowledge of the victim.

"You had better tell me," he said, then realised his tone was too grim and added, "If I know what is likely to be said I will be better able to counter it."

Which was when Anders looked at him as if with fresh eyes. "You will guide me in how I should conduct my defence when it comes to court?"

Until that moment Gideon had given the matter no thought. He was too concerned with looking for ways to avoid any need for the matter to go to court in the first place.

"Of course I will," he promised. "Although it would stand you in better stead to have advice from a French lawyer, but I will consult with one for you."

Anders closed his eyes for a moment then gave Gideon a small smile.

"It may not seem much to you, but you bring me so much hope, my friend."

Gideon smiled back, glad to see that the Anders he knew was still there within the shell of the man sitting in the cell.

"What did you have to do with Geneviève Tasse?" he asked, very aware that at any time Browne or the men who were in charge of things here might decide they had given Gideon enough time.

"It was an attempt to gain some interest in Théophraste's work from her mistress, the duchesse, Richelieu's niece. She is known for her care for the poor of Paris, and it seemed she might well be inclined to a joint project. Mademoiselle Tasse was to put some suggestions to her. The notion being that it would be easier for the duchesse to decline, were she of that mind, if it was all done through intermediaries without anyone needing to make it public that the projects had even been suggested to her."

"You spoke to Geneviève Tasse in private?" Gideon was appalled at the implications.

Anders nodded. "It was only on the one occasion, the day before she was—she was killed, and for a very short time, less than half an hour. She had another of the duchesse's ladies with her. I set out our ideas and was supposed to speak with her again the next day to receive some kind of reply but there was never the opportunity."

"Were you alone in the Palais at all the following evening?"

"Yes." Anders sighed. "Yes, I was. I had been given permission to access a book from the Cardinal's library to copy out a receipt—the formula for another remedy. But I had to keep it quiet as it was not one the Faculty would have approved. After, I went back to the others from the Bureau when we were brought the news of what had happened."

"What about laudanum? Have you prescribed it to anyone?"

Anders thought for a moment.

"Not that I can recall." Then he looked aghast. "Théophraste has facilities in his premises on Rue Calandre for making all kinds of remedies and as he has physicians who work for him, so he has apothecaries who do so. I did offer a new formulation I had found to one of the apothecaries together with some other remedies and the warning that I was not sure of its potency, but I never prescribed it to anyone. I can see, though, that could make me look guilty."

Privately Gideon agreed but he saw no point in saying so.

"So *anyone* who works for this man Renaudot could have got hold of some laudanum from one of these apothecaries?"

Anders frowned.

"Perhaps not anyone, but any of the physicians who work with him and the apothecaries themselves, of course."

Which gave Gideon an idea.

"Would he have records of who has asked for it—or made any?"

"I am not sure. We only needed to keep lists of any remedies we provided ourselves to patients. There was a list in the dispensary too, but many would be given a receipt and told to go to the apothecary directly."

Making a mental note to himself to check that, he tried to think what else Anders could tell him that might help provide some idea as to where he should look to find proof of the Dane's innocence.

"Do you have any enemies here in Paris? Anyone who might wish to do you harm in such a way."

Anders shook his head. "It is hardly just me they have harmed, is it? Poor Demoiselle Tasse..." His voice trailed off and then he gave Gideon a direct look. "I can think of no one here who hates me that much, or even dislikes me. And if I thought for a moment what happened to her was done purely to attack me in some way, I am not sure I could live with myself." He drew a breath still holding Gideon's gaze. "Théophraste has many powerful enemies, and his most powerful friend and protector has now died. It is possible this is some kind of conspiracy to discredit him and his work—such as his use of more novel remedies like laudanum. There are men who work for the Faculty who would kill rather than lose their privilege and most of those would think the life of a woman and a foreigner as nothing against the greater glory of the Faculty."

"Who do you—?" Gideon broke off as he heard the sound of the door being unlocked. Instead, he gripped Anders' arm. "You must stay strong and remember we are working to free you. I will find out who did this murder or at least show you did not."

There was no time for anything more because he had to be standing away from Anders when the door opened and not showing any particular care. It took all Gideon's willpower to leave the Dane alone in the darkness of that stinking chamber. Somehow his own ability to walk through the door when Anders could not, seemed an obscenity.

It was as well he wasn't supposed to speak French. If he had needed to respond in any way to the enquiries from their guide as to whether monsieur found the discussion enlightening and enjoyable, he would have likely snarled. As it was, Browne took one look at Gideon's face and gripped his elbow, walking him firmly away from the darkness and out into the thin sunlight of late afternoon.

It was only as Browne was thanking their guide and taking polite leave of him, that Gideon realised there was something he could do for Anders.

"Ask this man how much it would be to have Jensen moved to a room with a window and given a decent bed and food." He spoke quickly and seeing the expression of doubt on Browne's face, added "You may tell him I have an interest in the case and might well wish to visit again and found the accommodation too noisome." He backed up his words with a gold coin from Lord's purse.

Browne nodded his understanding and repeated Gideon's request in his flawless French. It was clear the man he spoke to was torn between venal desire with the thought of more gratuities from the odd Englishman and some other issue, lack of accommodation perhaps. Gideon found he did not care as long as Anders was moved.

In desperation, and ignoring Browne's appalled look, he dropped the entire purse into the man's hands. It was as if suddenly their guide could not do or say enough. Of course, the Dane would have a room with a window, decent food and a bed and yes, the Englishman was welcome to come and visit whenever he wished for no extra charge.

"Are you sure that was wise?" Browne asked as they walked back along the banks of the Seine.

"No, not at all," Gideon said, grimly. "But I also know I had no choice. Not if there is to be a man left to save at the end of this."

Browne looked thoughtful then nodded. "I think you are right about that," he said.

THE PHYSICIAN'S FATE

Chapter Seven

The inn's common room was too warm, too full of smoke and too packed with people. Nick's irritable mood wasn't helped by Gyfford holding forth to his personal court.

They had reached Selby that afternoon after a pre-dawn withdrawal from Tadcaster forced to do so by lack of powder to hold the town any longer. On arrival, Gyfford had taken over this inn and the surrounding houses as billets for himself, his officers and his two paroled prisoners. Evidently, he felt he had earned some entertainment after the work he had done at Tadcaster. Since their arrival, once accommodation had been arranged, he had sat in the inn drinking steadily with his cronies at a large table formed from two smaller ones thrust together in the common room of the inn. At his insistence, Danny sat beside him and Nick beside Danny.

They had just been treated to the third retelling of how Gyfford had taken the houses in Tadcaster and were now hearing about some incident that had happened two years before when he had been a major in the war with Scotland. The fact that Gyfford was now resoundingly drunk didn't help matters at all.

"He told me to my face, I can still remem—mem—berer his very words. 'Sir', he said 'you are a base, rascally, alehouse captain, a mere trooper.' Then he shook his purse at me, like I was a whore, and he said, 'If you had these ten pounds which I have in this leather purse and were in an alehouse or tavern amongst your comrades, then sure how lusty you would be then.' Gah, the scurvy, pox-ridden, jackanapes." Gyfford paused to chug down the remains of another tankard of ale, then released a ferocious burp. "Mister Too-Good-For-the-Rest-of-Us Marma-bloody-duke Someone-or-another from Dunham. He was after a duel but I took him to court and that stopped his damned lib—lub—libellous mouth."

Danny roared with laughter along with most of the rest of the men present. Nick managed to muster a polite smile.

Gyfford, for all his bluster had been one of those who managed to lose that war. The Scots had sat in the north of England for over a year after waiting to be paid off. Nick and his family who had been forced to live almost like a conquered people. It had been a small mercy Sir Bartholomew had been able to bribe the local Scottish commander to leave Howe alone. So Nick failed to find much amusement in the tale. In fact, he found he agreed rather strongly with Marmaduke Whoever's assessment of Gyfford.

"And thith—this is my good friend, Danny." Gyfford slammed a hand hard on Danny's back making him splash the ale in his tankard over Nick. "Daniel Bristow, gentlemen. He's the finest th—swordsman I ever met and he has shh...shurely forgotten more about guns and fortifications than I ever had the chance to learn. 'Sh'a privilege, privilege to fight with him and an honour to fight against him." He lifted his empty tankard in a toast. "To your health, sir." When he tried to drink from the empty cup there was more hilarity and offers were made thick and fast to refill it.

Nick sincerely wished the interminable evening would end so he could get some sleep. Any illusions he'd had that those who supported and fought for Parliament were the sober, god-fearing, puritanical sort, were dispelled by this evening. He, the one unequivocally royalist individual present, was the most sober by far. Although Danny had not been drinking anything like as heavily as the rest of the table. But Nick was no longer sure Danny was unequivocally royalist. Unlike Nick he was permitted his sword and Gyfford seemed to treat him more as a comrade in arms than an enemy prisoner of war.

"You should tell us a story, Danny," Gyfford said, putting his free arm, the one not holding his ale, around Danny's shoulders. "Tell these good gentlemen here about how you met that black-hearted bastard nephew of the king at Breda. Go on, you tell them."

Danny sat back.

"Well, if you want a city with full modern defences, Breda is the queen. Walls, revetments, bastions, hornworks, forts and more artillery than you'll have seen in one place. And the Spanish held it," he opened his hand palm-upwards, then closed it into a tight fist, "like a jewel in their grip."

He started drawing on the table using the spilt ale, "So the first thing, we invested the city and built defences around ourselves, a double circle of them, like this. Dammed a river or two, here and here, so the ground past them was flooded. Breda became an island, encircled by us and by water. That way we made it about as hard for any relieving force to get close to the city as we could." The enthusiasm in his voice was plain. "And then we—"

"Who cares about that?" Gyfford snarled and thumped his fist on the table. "Just tell the bit with the princes."

Danny shrugged. "Very well. It was when the Spanish were still trying to fight back. I was out in one of the counter ditches we'd been digging, there were hopes we could set a mine and I was helping with the exploratory work. That had to be done at night of course, or the defenders would have seen what we were about. I went alone as that was both fastest and quietest. There I was, trying to work my way in silence up to the walls when there is a splatter of mud and someone cursing in a low whisper. Then another joined them. They must have been not much further from me than Sir Nicholas here. That close. They didn't see me. It was dark with only the stars and a thin moon to help. I had no idea who it might be, and my sword was drawn when I heard what they were saying and realised it was two boys."

"Boys?" One of the men at the table jeered. "That must have been scary."

Danny ignored him.

"I stepped out of the shelter of shadow and asked them in good English, who they were and what they were doing in my trench. 'Your trench, sir?' says one boy, also in English, 'This trench is the property of His Highness Frederick-Henry, Prince of Orange and Stadholder of the United Provinces.' 'Then', said I, 'perhaps you can show me which part of it the Prince of Orange dug himself and I will avoid going there.'"

There was laughter around the table and Danny grinned until it subsided. "At which point I introduced myself as being in the service of the man they said owned the trench and explained I was there with his express permission, whilst casting some doubt over whether their own claim to be in his trench had as good a pedigree. To which, the prince—who was all of seventeen at that time—replied with his own and his brother's identity and that the owner of the trench was their great-uncle and then declared: 'My claim is with my sword if you wish to dispute the matter.'" That raised the loudest laugh yet and Danny had time to sip at his cup before picking up the account again. "Of course, I said I was willing to do so, but suggested that first, we complete the work we had all come there to do, which—in my case at least—was to get in close to the walls. This their highnesses agreed to as it seems they had arranged some dare with each other to the effect of touching the very walls of the city."

"And did you?" someone asked.

Danny shook his head. "The princes failed in their self-appointed mission, and I failed in the one with which I had been charged."

"You failed?" The same man who had mocked before was derisive. "Where's the tale in that?"

"We failed," Danny went on, "because I knew the princes were not going to depart without completing their intentions and they might easily either draw attention to themselves—or worse to me—if they continued alone. So I abandoned my survey and took them close to the walls by what I conceived of as the safest way. And then, in the dark and under the very noses—and musket barrels—of the Spanish, we overheard a discussion from the walls regarding a planned sortie to the east of where we were. It was to be the following morning at dawn, which would have taken us by surprise and netted them some valuable supplies. Instead, the news was taken right away to the high command by the princes and a warm welcome was prepared for the Spanish, many of whom found a cold grave as a result."

There were cheers at the thought of dead Spaniards and Nick realised that were the same story told in a tavern in York or Newcastle there would have been exactly the same response. It made him wonder just how deep the divisions between those fighting in this war really ran.

THE PHYSICIAN'S FATE

"A shame you never got around to following up on that duel the devil's whelp asked for," one of Gyfford's cronies said. "You could have stuck that blade of yours through his brisket and saved many good men a lot of trouble."

There were more noises of agreement.

"Oh, but I did follow up," Danny said, surprising them. "Or rather the prince did. The very next day, I was—"

There was a commotion by the door and a group of armed men pushed their way in. Danny stopped talking and closed his mouth. Nick could see his skin had paled beneath the freckles. Following his gaze, as did everyone else at the big table, he saw Mags, like a warship in full rig, stride into the space his men had just cleared. He stopped with enough distance from the table to make those seated at it into his audience rather than himself a petitioner to any there. Then he hooked his thumbs into his sword belt and rocked back on his heels, glaring at Gyfford.

Nick looked back at Danny and realised the paling had nothing to do with fear. His eyes had the feral darkness Nick had seen before and fury tinged with something more grim shimmered in the air around him.

"Major Gyfford," Mags said, his tone brooking no dispute, "I have come to relieve you of a burden and take your prisoners here into my custody." He had started speaking, needing to raise his voice over the speculative babble in the inn, but when he stopped there was almost complete silence.

Gyfford sat up in his chair and frowned

"Who the devil do you think you are to order me *Captain* Child?"

Mags grinned.

"You have the wrong name, Gyfford. I am *Colonel* Sir Francis *Coupland* of Howe."

Nick felt the air sucked out of his lungs as an invisible force squeezed his ribs. He was not even aware of the movement, but he was on his feet.

"You are a lying bastard," he snarled. "Your parents were never married, you are no Coupland, far less a legitimate one. You have no right to Howe, it is mine."

ELEANOR SWIFT-HOOK

It was only when his words were met by hostile looks, he realised the enormity of his mistake. In this company, no matter how any might feel about Mags, they would back his claim—which was doubtless being upheld by Parliament—over that of any Royalist. The strength went from his legs as Mags gave a snort of contempt and spat on the floor. Nick found he lacked both the will and the ability to resist Danny's hand pulling him back to his seat.

"You have nothing and are nothing, boy," Mags said, scornfully. "As soon as this fighting is done with and the king brought to his senses, I will claim Howe. I hope you keep it well for me in the meantime—or rather I hope your brother does. You are to be hanged. I have the order here." He tapped his chest and smirked. "You and that rat beside you."

Nick's stomach twisted tightly beneath his ribs. Danny made no reaction. He still had one hand firmly gripping Nick's arm. On Danny's other side Gyfford shook his head. He was drunk, but this seemed to have sobered him considerably.

"If you have orders, I want to see them, colonel," he growled. "These two are my prisoners, taken by my men and if there were to be any executions, I'd be the man to do them."

Mags' smile became a little stiff as if his honour were being affronted by the request.

"*Major* Gyfford, as a more senior officer it should be enough that I require you to hand over the prisoners."

"You're not my colonel, sir," Gyfford retorted "and even if you were I'd dispute that you outrank me. General Fairfax today told me I'm made Sergeant-Major-General, which is what myself and my friends here have been celebrating. Now show me these orders or leave us be."

It was then Nick understood why Danny was sitting so still in all this. He must have known of the promotion.

"Very well." Mags reached into his coat and pulled out a fat-bellied leather purse, weighing it in his hand. "These are my orders, I think you'll find them in good standing," and he threw the purse onto the table.

Gyfford was on his feet, hand on his sword, face nearly puce.

THE PHYSICIAN'S FATE

"How dare you, sir."

Mags just shrugged and put the purse away again.

"I'll take the men," he said, "whether you'll have the money or no. If you wish to press the matter, you'll find whatever your rank might be, I sit higher in the favour of those who matter now. You would spare yourself much grief if you just let me take them."

"Never, and for what you just did I will have an accounting."

Mags had been looking almost indifferent, but now a flicker of interest lit his face.

"An accounting? You want to try me with that pigsticker you wear? I am your man if so." He stepped back and drew his sword, the blade of it catching in the candlelight."

For a moment Nick saw the doubt on Gyfford's face, but the bravado of alcohol was clearly stronger, because he slammed a fist to the table. "I'll make you—"

Danny stood then, placing a hand on Gyfford's shoulder.

"This man wants me, John, I think that gives me the right to defend my own honour here."

"But the knave tried to buy me," Gyfford protested.

"He was trying to buy *me*," Danny said quietly. "To buy me from you as if I were a dog." He was not looking at Gyfford as he spoke, his gaze was locked with Mags. Nick saw something stir in Mags' expression, perhaps of satisfaction or anticipation, it was hard to be sure.

Even through whatever haze his inebriation must have placed about Gyfford's thoughts, something of the intensity of that hostility must have penetrated because he finally nodded. "He did too, tried to buy you from me. We have witnesses to that."

There was a rumble of assent around the table, with a slowly growing sense of excitement as the men sitting there realised what was going to happen. One of the wiser heads, perhaps more sober than the rest counselled restraint.

"The general's not going to like hearing there's been duelling."

"Then he better not hear," Gyfford snarled, his belligerence growing even more now it was clear Danny would be the one fighting.

After that it happened very quickly. Tables were pulled back, making a crude arena of the large room, edged on one end by the big hearth and on the other by a wall. Danny stood arms folded as it was all set up. Nick wanted to ask him if he was sure he would win, but his expression was closed as if he was seeing what was before his eyes but not really aware of it.

Mags stayed with his men and Nick noticed he had posted a couple outside as well as those in the room and it was Mags who strode first into the cleared space. He had shed the heavy deer hide buff coat and was now wearing his shirt with a sleeveless jerkin over it. He stood under the still swinging chandeliers which had been pulled up on their chains to keep from catching a sword in the fight.

"You going to hide in the corner now, Danny?" He called and there were derisive cheers from the men behind him. Nick had counted a good fifteen or twenty, which was probably as many as were with Gyfford. Danny did not respond, he still seemed immured in his own thoughts, as if the outside world did not exist.

"See? He *is* a coward. He won't come and fight for all his bluster. He says I called him a dog, but now he gives the truth to that, the cowardly cur."

The jeers and calls got louder, and Nick gripped Danny's arm, then nearly went flying backwards. Danny slammed an elbow hard into him as he strode into the crude fighting-pit that had been created in the middle of the room. As he went, he pulled off his coat and dropped it on a chair, followed by the baldric and the pistol he kept in it, then he undid the buttons on his doublet, and pulled at the lacings on his shirt so it fell open at the neck. He had been left the end of the room with the hearth behind him and as he reached it, he drew his sword. Its blade caught the firelight looking more of a gold than silver.

Nick wondered if there would be any formalities or statements of honour, then realised that he was being naive to even think there might be any such thing as honour between these two men. It was, for them both, just a thin facade. As the painted backcloth in a play gave the appearance to make the scenes on stage believable, so they used the trappings of an honourable duel to give a similitude of decency to what was a simple fight for power.

Or so he thought.

Standing in the firelight, framed by flames like a denizen of hell, Danny Bristow lifted his sword in what could have been taken as a salute to his opponent.

"This is for you Matt," he said, his voice so low only those closest to him as Nick was could possibly have heard. But he had little time to wonder who Matt might be because Danny brought the sword down and lifted his voice. "We'll see who the true coward is here."

Even before he had finished speaking he had closed the gap between them and forced Mags to give a pace backwards under the onslaught of his attack.

The blade he fought with, Nick could see, was double-edged and had a vicious point. It was as sharp to thrust as it was to cut, and Danny could use its back edge with sudden reversals as readily as its fore, which he did with a speed that left the eye dazzled by the light reflecting from the blade. The basket hilt with oddly set curving quillons, was as much a part of the way he used the weapon as the blade, deftly catching a cut and by a turn of the wrist sending it away.

If Nick had been the one fighting Danny it would have been a brutally short encounter, but Mags was another matter. He wasn't disturbed by the speed of the attack and his own economy of movement showed he knew how to manage men who were faster than himself. He fought defensively, parrying three times for one attack.

It was clear from the first that the energy of Danny's assault could not be sustained and the ferociousness of it had to burn out. Even though he drove Mags back he was not breaking his guard. Calls came from those who supported Danny telling him to press harder and some from Mags' men scoffing at Danny's failure.

Nick began to wonder if what Danny had claimed about his swordsmanship had been an empty boast. He was good, yes. Much better than most men Nick had seen wield a sword. But why would a man with the mastery he claimed fail to penetrate Mags' defence?

Both men had sweat on their faces. Neither was finding this an easy match. Around the edge of the room, money changed hands as people placed bets. Nick found he had no stomach for that. It was becoming clear as the fight went on that if he was defeated Danny would be killed, Mags wasn't going to allow any other outcome. If Danny was killed, then Gyfford would have lost his pledge and that would make Nick himself Mags' prisoner.

You are to be hung.

He found that his own face and shoulders were prickling with a sweat that had little to do with the warmth of the room.

The intensity of Danny's attacks was flagging. The strain of maintaining them showed on his face. His hair, plastered against his scalp, was darkened by sweat, his breathing ragged. Mags was able to make more ripostes and even slide in some close attacks himself. One such cut the fabric of Danny's open doublet and caught the shirt beneath, a small blossom of red stained the fabric.

Mags grinned, his teeth bared like a wolf and a whoop went up from the men at his end of the room whilst Danny's supporters gave a collective gasp. Nick said nothing, but his heart that had been hammering skipped a beat before it resumed. He could see Danny had paid the cut no heed, not even stepping back or in any way attempting to disengage. If anything for a short time his ferocity seemed to increase, forcing Mags to turn to avoid it being forced to the wall, so his back was now to the hearth.

There seemed to be very little technique left to Danny's swordwork. It had become a pedestrian rhythm of moves, which he varied only a little. Mags was smiling, toying with him, letting him exhaust himself more and more.

"Not so much the swordsman now are you, Danny?" he taunted, stepping back having delivered another successful cut. This time it was to Danny's shoulder after he failed to fully stop and turn the blade allowing it to gouge into him sufficiently to draw blood. "I'd heard you were good. You're not even a challenge."

Mags had to stop talking then as the response he got was a series of hard attacks which forced him back a couple of paces before he was able to contain them again. Danny's expression was rigid, a face chiselled from stone, his freckles the only remaining touch of colour against the pallor of his skin. His lips pulled back from his teeth with the effort of each blow and his feet no longer moved with speed and grace, but with a heavy tread.

By contrast, Mags careful conservation of energy throughout the fight was paying off. It was clear he would have reserves call on when Danny was spent. Nick began to understand the respect and fear which Mags was held in by his men. He was not just an excellent soldier and commander of soldiers, he was also an excellent fighter. He knew when to act and when to withhold, how to draw out his opponent into ever more wasteful moves, weakening and wearying. There was a morose silence now at Danny's end of the room. They had even given up calling encouragement and the disappointment was turning to disgust. A gleeful buzz surrounded those who were supporting Mags. They cheered his ripostes and urged him on.

Nick had the impression that neither man was aware of their audience now. From his own place, close to the hearth, he saw Danny making a final supreme effort to use his speed and skill against the implacable and steady resistance Mags held up with apparently very little effort.

But it had forced Mags to give a little more ground and that meant Nick was right beside the duellers when something changed. Nick saw the sudden shift in Danny's posture a moment before Mags' sword flew up in a parabola to land with a clatter on the floor under the chandelier.

That was when Nick understood that what had gone before, what had appeared a desperate fight, had in fact been deliberate scene-setting by the man who still held a sword. For a moment he was in another inn and Danny was speaking. *I didn't want to just defeat Mags, that would have been easy. I wanted to humiliate him too.*

The turmoil in the room was instant, shouts and groans, but neither of the principles paid it any heed. Mags looked shocked and stared at his hand as if unable to believe the sword was gone. Danny lifted his blade and spoke so softly that Nick could barely hear him. "I hold you to account for the killing of Matthew Rider.

Though you richly deserve this for so many other lives taken and ruined, just know as you die, I'm doing this for Matt."

Mags met Danny's gaze then and his eyes widened, seeing his death. But even as Danny spoke Mags' doom, the door burst open, and Sir Thomas Fairfax strode through it. With him were four men bearing primed muskets that they brought to bear on Danny.

"Hold. Drop your sword."

For a moment Nick thought Danny was going to deliver the killing blow anyway, no matter the consequence to himself. His face had become a mask, eyes dark with hatred and Nick was far from sure he was even aware of the danger.

"Danny," he said urgently.

Perhaps that made the difference. Danny's shoulders slumped and the sword he held fell to the floor beside him. Then he turned to face Fairfax and somehow his feet became entangled with Mags as he stepped back too quickly when turning.

There was a moment in which both men seemed to struggle to stay upright, then Danny was falling forward to catch himself on his hands and Mags fell backwards into the open maw of the hearth, his head cracking hard on the stone before he landed in the fire.

THE PHYSICIAN'S FATE

Chapter Eight

Sir Philip Lord's reaction to learning Gideon had handed over a goodly amount of his disposable wealth to a lieutenant at the Châtelet in return for nothing more than promises was more restrained than Gideon had expected. They were sitting in Lord's room with its view over the evening street and Gideon was thinking how dark it was compared to such a street in London where householders would habitually put a light outside their door in the winter evenings. Here it seemed every man had to carry his own if he wished to see.

"*For we brought nothing into this world, and it is certain we can carry nothing out. And having food and raiment let us be therewith content.*" Lord shook his head as if despairing. "I am sure you did what you felt was needed, but perhaps next time you could consider distributing largesse on a smaller scale?"

"You think Anders is not worth that much of your money?"

Lord shook his head. "You mistake my point. It is not so much what you gave away as the fact that you have now created an expectation which will become increasingly expensive to fulfil."

"You cannot afford any more?" Gideon felt a tightness in his chest. Having seen the wealth in land that Lord held it hadn't occurred to him for a moment.

"I can afford it, of course," Lord assured him. "However, if you lavish every man we need to bribe with my gold to that degree, then there may come a point when I am less able to replace what you spend." He sighed. "It is more that you wouldn't give an angel to the boy who takes your horse."

Gideon felt his face flush. For a moment he was again a child being given a lecture by his father on the value of money.

"I know that," he snapped. "But had you been there and seen Anders—"

"I'm sure I would have made an appropriate decision." He spread his hands, palms facing out, wiping the topic away. "What matters more is how we use what you have learned."

"I need to visit this Théophraste Renaudot," Gideon said.

"We will go tomorrow."

"We? I thought—"

"If Richard Browne objects," Lord said, "I'll tell him I can't afford to let you out alone or you'll beggar me."

In the event, the following morning, which was a Thursday, Browne greeted Gideon with an apology and explained he had some pressing business to deal with in regard to provisions for the chapel which had been either deliberately or accidentally misdirected. Browne no doubt intended to deal with that problem and then return to accompany his supposed friend from England to the Bureau D'Adresses.

Instead, leaving word where he might be found with Elizabeth Browne, Gideon took to the streets of Paris with a well-turned-out servant, who tragically suffered from a pocked face, at his heels.

"In Paris thefts are often committed by servants and lackeys," Lord observed as they stepped into a doorway to avoid a rare passing carriage. "But you are safe enough. Most wait until after dark when it is easy for them to perform their theft and then act as if they were in fact attempting to aid their master against the thief."

"I can't imagine that is a problem that has ever affected you much," Gideon said, which at least raised a brief laugh.

"Not as yet," Lord admitted

The island in the river Seine was the heart of Paris and the keeper of its soul. Gideon heard the bells even from the bank before they crossed the bridge and could see a multitude of thrusting spires and towers. There had to be a score or more of churches and chapels, with Notre Dame as their supreme queen.

"You should feel right at home here," Lord murmured, keeping to English. "It is the legal district, home to the Paris *parlement*, the highest court in France. Here we have nobility conferred for venal office holding rather than by the usual idea of land and military service—the 'nobles of the robe' as opposed to 'nobles of the sword'. If you lack a title, once you have bought your office you purchase one. A man with two hundred thousand livres to his name and some education can easily acquire both the office of a judge and a fiefdom for his sons to inherit."

THE PHYSICIAN'S FATE

Gideon would have guessed the nature of the place anyway from the number of robed judges and regular lawyers that they passed or stepped aside for. Many wore the arrogant confidence of men who knew themselves better than their neighbours.

"Richard Browne told me anything could be bought in Paris," Gideon said.

Lord laughed. "That is little exaggeration."

But the Île de la Cité was also a centre of compassion.

The buildings of the hospital known as Hôtel-Dieu sprawled along the river south-west of the cathedral. Then there was the Bureau D'Adresses, their destination, established at the Sign of the Cock on the corner of the Rue Calandre and Rue du Marché-Neuf.

The place heaved at the seams, appearing more like a bazaar than a place of charitable works. As well as the medical consultations and preparation of remedies about which Anders had spoken, Théophraste Renaudot, in his role as Commissioner General of the Poor, Browne had explained, also ran a shop where poor people could pawn or sell items and buy others second-hand. Many people other than the poorest were keen to both contribute and purchase, making the Bureau into a marketplace. In addition, the Bureau served to bring together those seeking employment and those in need of servants or labourers. It helped the poor to find work.

Once inside Gideon asked direction to Renaudot and after much prevarication, they were sent to a print shop in the basement of the building. Renaudot was there, engaged in a heated argument with the printer about the quality of a batch of pages. At least it was heated on the printer's side. By contrast, Renaudot, a plainly dressed man in his mid-fifties with thinning wisps of hair on his head and a neatly kept beard, was calmly explaining his issue with the work. He listened politely to the printer's snarling rebuttals, before gently rephrasing his case.

It was a technique Gideon admired. Renaudot eroded the printer's belligerence, then brought him around to see the point, and finally secured a promise to sort the thing at no extra charge.

Gideon and Lord had been standing in the shadows by the door of the print room, and as soon as he had made his farewell to the printer, Renaudot turned to Gideon with a smile.

"Are you looking for me, or is it monsieur here, that you wished to see?" He gestured to the printer. There was a warmth to the man. Gideon noticed that when he gave his attention it seemed as if no one and nothing mattered to him except the one he addressed.

"I was hoping to speak with you, Monsieur Renaudot," Gideon said. "I am Gideon Fox, a friend of Anders Jensen and—"

Renaudot interrupted him, smiling. "Please, you must come with me to my cabinet, we can have greater privacy there."

It seemed impossible in the bustle of people that anywhere in the building could afford anyone privacy. Renaudot was greeted on every side. He had to stop on three occasions to deal with some urgent matters before he led them upstairs and into a comfortable room which resembled a parlour more than a cabinet. The sole concession to formality was a neatly kept lockable desk with a chair beside it, which stood in one corner, upon which neat stacks of papers and documents could be seen.

"You are English? Then this place must be something very new to you," Renaudot said, as he held open the door. "Your man is welcome to stay with us or he may prefer to look around."

Gideon glanced at Lord who gave the slightest nod. "I think he had better stay," Gideon said.

Renaudot took a seat and gestured that Gideon should do likewise "Can I offer you some refreshment...?"

Gideon sat on a fauteuil. "I thank you, but no. However, I am keen to discover what you might know about the accusations made against Anders Jensen."

"Not as much as I might wish," Renaudot said. "The evidence seemed damning, but I will admit to being more than a little surprised at the accusation. It is not something I would ever have believed of Anders. But what is your own interest in this?"

There seemed little point in any untruth. Renaudot's familiar use of Ander's name suggested a warm relationship. Besides, he had a feeling Renaudot would be quick to spot falsehood.

"He is a good friend of mine. I went to see him in the Châtelet yesterday and he was being kept under terrible conditions. I hope I have provided him with some relief from that, but what he needs is proof of his innocence."

"And you think I might be able to help you with that?"

"I am hoping so."

Renaudot got up and crossed to the hearth, warming his hands for a few moments. "You seem convinced of Anders' innocence," he said. Then turned to face Gideon, his back to the fire. "I would ask why that is?"

"Having spoken with him, I have no doubt," Gideon admitted. "He didn't even know what he was accused of until I told him."

"I see." Renaudot looked down at his hands. "It is a very difficult matter. It touches on so much more than this one terrible act. There are those who would seek to use it to destroy all that we are doing here and with the Cardinal gone…" He broke off as if realising he might have said too much. Then he looked up with a wan smile. "I am relieved to hear you have been to see him and been able to offer some succour."

"Surely if it could be shown that Anders was not responsible for this, then it would relieve your Bureau of any possible culpability?"

Renaudot went back to his chair and sat down again and sighed.

"There is no doubt the laudanum came from here," he said. "It was in a bottle such as our apothecaries use to dispense medicines. There are few, if any, other places in Paris that will make it. Most apothecaries would not dare to flout the Faculty by doing so."

Gideon thought about that but before he could reply Lord spoke.

"But even if it was someone here who made it, it would not need to be Jensen who took it, would it?" Lord paused, then added, "Sir Philip Lord. My apologies for the deception but I cannot be officially here."

Gideon glanced round at him, not entirely surprised he had chosen to reveal himself but wondering why he chose to speak up now. Renaudot's lips lifted into a smile.

"I had wondered why you were happy to stay rather than, as any other servant, eager to see what is to be seen here." Then he looked thoughtful. "Anders mentioned having worked for a Philip Lord for a time whilst he was in England. You are the one they call the Schiavono?"

Lord inclined his head.

"And this is...?" Renaudot gestured to Gideon.

"As he introduced himself. Gideon Fox is my friend and a lawyer."

That left an odd sensation in Gideon's chest. Normally it was 'my lawyer'—which was true enough as Lord was paying his keep—but today he had said 'my friend'.

"I see." Renaudot tapped the ends of his fingers together. "I also see that Anders has good friends who wish to help him. It may be you can. I would if I could, but once the evidence was found..." He trailed off with a sigh.

"It is difficult for you to intervene directly without creating more problems for the Bureau and undermining your credibility," Lord said and Renaudot gave him a look of gratitude.

"Exactly so," he agreed. "That being the case, how might I help you without placing the Bureau in greater hazard?"

Lord rested a hand on Gideon's shoulder. "This is the right man to tell us that," he said, then stepped away to take a chair by the window, making it clear he wanted Gideon to hold the floor.

Renaudot looked towards Gideon. "Indeed, a lawyer should be able to know what is needed to show a man's guilt or innocence, if anyone does."

Still reeling a little from his abrupt, public, change of status, Gideon gathered his scattered wits to focus on what he needed to know.

"Anders told me that he wasn't the only man from here with access to the Palais de Cardinal. Can you tell me who those others were?"

"Myself, of course, Claude Charron, Gaspard Proulx and Josselin Voclain."

Gideon felt a lift of relief that there were only three new names. He had feared there might be many others he would need to consider.

"Were any of those in the Palais that evening?"

THE PHYSICIAN'S FATE

Renaudot looked thoughtful.

"I was not there myself as that was a Tuesday. Tuesday evenings I work on the next edition of *La Gazette*. Of the rest, Anders was there and so was Josselin. I do not know if Gaspard was, although I am sure that can be ascertained, but Claude was away from Paris. He had a funeral to attend."

Gideon felt his spirits lift a little further. It must have been one of those two, Voclain or Proulx. This was far easier than he had thought it would be.

"Has anyone looked into where Dr Voclain and Dr Proulx were that evening?"

"Why would they?" Renaudot sounded genuinely puzzled.

"Because if Anders didn't—"

"What Mr Fox is trying to say," Lord broke in quickly, "is that it is possible one of the two gentlemen might have observed something that could point us towards the real culprit."

Renaudot's face cleared, and Gideon realised the nature of the faux pas he had been close to making. It must be bad enough for this man to have one of his physicians in prison for murder, even if innocent. But to face the possibility that one of the others might truly be a murderer would perhaps lock his tongue. Gideon nodded quickly.

"Exactly so," he agreed. "Would it be possible to speak with them, please? I would also like to talk to any of your apothecaries who might have made the laudanum. Perhaps one might have had a bottle stolen or missing."

For a moment he thought he might have gone too far too quickly. The frown was back on Renaudot's face. Then he was nodding.

"I can see how that would be valuable," he said. "I should have thought to ask myself. Although I had assumed it was taken from the dispensary where we keep small supplies of many remedies. To the best of my knowledge only one of our apothecaries has been making any laudanum, and she isn't here today. I will find out for you if others have made some."

"She?" Gideon failed to keep the surprise from his voice.

Renaudot smiled.

"Truly. Yolande Savatier. She is one of my very best apothecaries. But she doesn't work every day and will not be back here until Monday."

Gideon spoke without thought. "But that might be too late. Will you give me her address? I will visit her at home."

He realised his mistake at once as Renaudot's expression closed.

"That would hardly be appropriate," he said "You are welcome to talk with her here on Monday. For now I will go and see if Josselin is available to speak with you."

"And Gaspard Proulx?" Gideon asked.

Renaudot looked troubled and got to his feet.

"I wish you could. Poor Gaspard was killed in the street on his way home after dark a few days ago. Someone stole his medical bag. Perhaps they misunderstood what it was because it was found thrown in the river the next day and nothing gone from it. He shouldn't have been out alone, but he was young and carried a sword. He probably thought he could defend himself at need. Sadly, there is no defence when three men come upon you from the shadows."

"Three men?" Gideon asked. "You sound very sure."

"There was a witness. Yolande Savatier was also going home. She saw the three men run off and tried to tend poor Gaspard, but it was too late. It is a tragedy, but these things happen in Paris."

"No one has been apprehended for the crime?"

Renaudot shook his head and crossed to the door. "That is also often the way it is in Paris," he said sadly. Then, "I will not be long," and he left the room.

Gideon decided he needed to find a way to speak to Yolande Savatier as soon as possible.

"*For now we see through a glass, darkly; but then face to face: now I know in part; but then shall I know even as also I am known.* Or so we can hope," Lord finished prosaically. "You seem to have uncovered something which makes our Monsieur Renaudot a little uncomfortable. I would suggest you tread henceforth in stockings not buskins."

Gideon had to laugh at that.

"I think even stockings might not be fine enough for Renaudot. I can see by his work here that he is a good man, well intentioned, and yet he did nothing to help Anders."

"He is hamstrung," Lord said. "He has enemies enough and has lost his greatest protector with the death of Richelieu. As you say, he is clearly both a good and well-intentioned man, but there are limits. If he reaches out a hand to Jensen and Jensen is found guilty, that would give much ammunition to his enemies. We need to avoid asking him to walk upon such thin ice and then I think he will do all he can to help our cause."

Gideon was thinking how to respond to that when the door opened and Renaudot returned with Voclain. He was a man of around Gideon's age, well dressed, black hair unfashionably short, curling about his ears and wearing an expression of puzzlement and concern. Renaudot looked questioningly at Lord who shook his head and was thus left out of the introductions.

"If you will excuse me, messieurs, I will leave you to talk as I have much work that needs doing." Renaudot said once the social essentials were done. "I will send some refreshments for you and if I may borrow your man, Monsieur Fox? Thank you."

Whatever reason Renaudot might have for taking Sir Philip Lord with him, Gideon was very sure it would not be so he could bring a tray. He hoped that it might be to share some more information.

Josselin Voclain took the seat Renaudot had left and treated Gideon to a frown.

"Théophraste said you were here because you think Anders is innocent. Is that true?" He leaned forward, his eyes holding a troubled look that Gideon would never have expected. "Have you seen him? How does he fare?"

This was the man who Gideon hoped was the real killer, but from the way Voclain spoke his concern for Anders was obvious. Of course, that could be an act.

"He hasn't been tortured—or at least hadn't been when I saw him yesterday—but he was being kept in little more than an oubliette. I left money for his keep and from the venal glee of his gaoler, I think he will be in a decent room now."

Voclain crossed himself in the Popish fashion and murmured a prayer.

"Thank you for that. I couldn't go myself. I begged Théophraste, but he said that if any of us went it would seem that the Bureau was involved somehow and I could see the sense in that."

Gideon nodded and gave a professional smile of understanding. In truth, even assuming Voclain was genuine, he found it hard not to think that a true friend might have found some way to get help and support to a man in the Châtelet even if at second or third hand in a way that need not reflect upon his employer.

"If I am to redeem Anders I will need your help," he said and Voclain nodded, his serious looking face intent.

"If I can help in any way, any way at all...?"

"You can tell me if you were at the Palais de Cardinal at all on the twenty-ninth of November?"

Voclain nodded again.

"I was, I went there with Anders. He had spoken to Demoiselle Tasse the evening before on behalf of Théophraste and he asked me to be with him when they spoke again to receive a reply. He thought if there were any objections to the proposals the two of us might be better able to come up with solutions. That was why I was at the Palais as I had no real reason to be otherwise."

"Why was that?"

"I went in the beginning because I truly believed that there was some possibility we might have our views considered in the physician's consultations for the care of the Cardinal. I would have done anything to save him. He was a truly great man. But the physicians from the Faculty wouldn't even allow us into their meetings and I wasn't permitted to see the Cardinal either." He shook his head, and his tone became bitter. "None of us were until it was too late. Only when the Faculty men had all but killed him with their methods were we allowed in. He had one day of lucid brilliance thanks to our care, but that was all we could do. He died the day after, and they would have set that at our door too if they could."

THE PHYSICIAN'S FATE

"Who was there then, with the cardinal?" Gideon was not at all sure it had anything to do with what he needed to know but at this point just getting Voclain to talk was a good start.

"Myself, Claude and poor Gaspard—he was killed by thieves, you may have heard. Théophraste couldn't be there, much as he wanted to. Anders would have been, but he had just been arrested, but it was one of his remedies we used in the end—one that gives strength even to the ailing, although the price for that is high."

Gideon thought back to a desperate sword fight when he had been injured and Anders pressing a small bottle on him with the warning that whilst it would give him strength it might also kill him. It very nearly had as well.

"I believe I know the remedy you mean," he said. "But, thinking back to the night when Demoiselle Tasse was killed, were you with Anders all the time?"

Voclain shook his head.

"We all arrived together, myself, Gaspard and Anders. There was something Anders said he needed to do. He had found a copy of Paracelsus' *Opus Paramirum* with a formula for Theriac handwritten in it. He was convinced it might be genuine and from the hand of Paracelsus himself, though I have my doubts, but he went to copy it on the understanding that if Demoiselle Tasse should send for him in the meantime we would find him. But he returned, and soon after word came of the murder."

Gideon could see how it would be easy to make a case against Anders, with the laudanum bottle merely confirming what could be seen as obvious.

"And you were with Gaspard Proulx all that time too?" he asked, feeling a little sick now.

"No. Gaspard had a friend who was one of the Faculty physicians and went to find him to discover what the latest news of the cardinal's health might be. I was alone too." Voclain's face paled. "Whoever decided to put the laudanum bottle in Anders' bag could have as easily chosen mine and then I would be in the Châtelet instead."

"You seem very sure it wasn't Anders and that someone is trying to make it seem as though it was him," Gideon said. "He is my friend, but even I had a moment of doubt when I heard about what had been found."

"And you claim to be Anders' good friend," Voclain said, an odd tone in his voice. "I'm not sure how that can be if you could harbour any such suspicion." He shook his head, frowning, then looked at Gideon with a sudden challenge. "How well do you know Anders Jensen?"

That was a difficult question.

"I think well enough to be sure of his innocence. We've shared a room and even a bed at one point."

Voclain's expression had cleared as if something he had not understood before was now plain to him.

"You do not know, do you? If you knew, you would also know there is no possible circumstance under which Anders might be thought guilty of giving a woman laudanum and then raping her."

It was Gideon's turn to be puzzled.

"Then tell me," he said.

Voclain sighed. "I can see no reason not to now. It would benefit him more than harm him. Besides, if you can't save him, what difference does it make if you know or not?"

"Know what?" Gideon's mind was shaping fantasies of Anders as a vowed celibate papist monk, or perhaps like Shiraz, a eunuch. What he didn't expect was what Voclain told him next.

"Anders Jensen has no interest in women in that way. He never has. His only lovers have been men."

THE PHYSICIAN'S FATE

Chapter Nine

"How could you not have told me?"

Gideon almost exploded with fury. He had given Lord an account of what Voclain had told him, finishing with the shocking news about Anders, only to be met with cool indifference. Lord had known already—and thought it nothing of any moment.

"I failed to see what business it might possibly be of yours," Lord said. "It was—and remains—a matter that is private to Jensen. It has nothing to do with you. The very fact that you react in such a way as this tells me it was the right decision to keep it from you."

They were in Lord's room in the Brownes' house. Lord, upon glimpsing the expression on Gideon's face after his interview with Voclain, had insisted that they wait to return to the relative privacy of his room before discussing what they had learned. Now Lord leaned his length against the wall by the window and Gideon paced and gesticulated.

"But to be...to do...that is...that..." Words failed Gideon and those of his father railing from the pulpit came to him. "It's an abomination before God."

"You are saying the man who has saved your life, saved the lives of your friends is an abomination?"

"I shared a room with him—I even shared a *bed* with him," Gideon protested.

Lord shook his head in incomprehension. "And that is why I can see no reason for you to be like this. You shared a room and a bed with him and remained as chaste as a virgin. You named him your friend, and *a friend loveth at all times*. What is your problem? Are you planning now to leave him in prison to suffer for a crime he did not commit and perhaps let Kate die because of this?" Lord asked.

Put that coldly, Gideon felt a sudden shame.

"I wouldn't—" he faltered, out of his depth and torn between what he knew to be true and what he had been taught to believe. It was a sensation he had come to know well in the months since he had joined Sir Philip Lord.

Of all the men he had ever met Anders was perhaps the most decent, principled and compassionate—and undeniably so. He was a man who willingly placed his own life in hazard for his friends and his commitment to healing meant that even when he had shared accommodation with Gideon, he was often absent from it tending those in need at all hours of the day and night.

"I think you should be very careful what you condemn," Lord told him, his acerbic tone sharpening like a knife drawn over a whetstone. "Your moral outrage is misplaced here. You should keep it for what happened to Geneviève Tasse."

And that gave Gideon's emotions further pause, allowing him to begin to think.

"There is no comparison," he said weakly. "Whoever abused Demoiselle Tasse is a monster."

Lord said nothing for a moment then he bowed his head as if with a weight that was hard to bear, but when he spoke it was with no discernible emotion.

"When I was little more than a child, those who held me in ward knew that the old king—King James—was much more taken by young men than young women and having scant other use for me that they could see at that time, thought to promote me and their ends by putting me in his path. I was all he might have been expected to fall for, young, impressionable, comely, athletic, but also intelligent and highly educated—he was a man who had a great intellect and appreciated that in others above almost all else."

Lord pushed himself away from the wall and crossed to a small table which was occupied in part by a book he must be reading, and in part by a tray with a glass decanter and three cups. Lord moved the book and Gideon caught the beginning of the title *Meditationes de Prima Philosophia...* Filling two of the cups, Lord offered one to Gideon, who accepted it as a token rather than as a drink and held the cup untasted in his hands as Lord went on.

"At the time I met him, the king was in a melancholy state quite often. His son, then still Prince Charles of course, had gone with the man the king loved most in the world—George Villiers, Duke

THE PHYSICIAN'S FATE

of Buckingham—to try and woo the Spanish Infanta in person. He missed them both sorely and it was hoped I might fill the breach and perhaps displace the duke, who was widely despised, to become a new favourite, thus putting power into the hands of the men who had raised me." Lord paused to drink off half his wine then he stared into the cup as if seeing some vision there of the past he was recalling. "He was an amazing man, King James. You'll hear much of his faults spoken now, but he saw what was being done with me when I was too innocent and arrogant, too full of confidence—too *young* to see it myself. And he could have abused that and made of me the distraction he so badly wanted just for those few months. Of course, there were those who indeed believed he had done so. We were often and close in each other's company all that summer. But he was the greater man and much in love with his Steenie, as he called Buckingham. Instead, he gave me his friendship and taught me things about the world none other could have, including that how and who we choose to love makes no difference to the kind of person that we are."

Then Lord fell silent and for a time the sounds of the city outside and the soft popping of wood on the fire were the only things to break the quiet in the room.

"Friendship," Lord said at last, "is a difficult thing sometimes. Our friends are not as ourselves. We love them for who they are even as we may occasionally struggle with what they are. But true friendship bridges all differences. *Love alters not with his brief hours and weeks, but bears it out, even to the edge of doom.*"

"What happened," Gideon found himself asking, "with King James?"

Lord looked up as if he had forgotten Gideon's presence then finished the wine with a final swig.

"What anyone could see would happen. Buckingham returned from Spain to find me in a place he thought threatened him. He pretended liking and friendship—but instead set things up so I appeared the villain and was discredited. Then to ensure I was no further threat, he helped me flee abroad so as to avoid arrest and all risk of the truth coming out. Thus I was attainted for treason. I was fifteen years old, afraid and didn't realise that had I stayed the king would have protected me. By fleeing I as good as declared my guilt and so made him unable to do so." Lord broke off and Gideon could see his throat constrict briefly as some emotion lodged there for a moment, stopping his speech. "He sent me a letter, the king did, saying he believed me innocent of all of it and that he was sorry Steenie had taken so much against me when he had hoped we might be good friends. But by then it was too late. *Iacta alea est.*"

Feeling suddenly humbled, Gideon knew that he had been given something Lord would not share with any but those he held in closest trust, and he also understood why he was sharing it now, which made of it an even greater gift.

"Anders Jensen is still Anders Jensen," Lord said, finally lifting his gaze to meet Gideon's. "He is your friend now as he always was. He protected you, as a friend, when he could. Surely you will not turn your back on him at this point, when he needs you most, just because of this one thing you have found out that has no bearing on anything except his own life?"

Gideon had no reply to offer. Part of him knew it didn't matter and that it never should. No more than it mattered that Zahara followed another faith or that Lord lived in a very different world to the one Gideon inhabited. But part of him still heard the thundering voice of his father condemning the evils of Sodom and Gomorrah. Then he thought of the evils being done to Anders, and that thundering voice was strangely silenced to be replaced by his mother's, her voice quiet as it had been so often when she countered the harshness of the religion his father expounded, with the tolerance and gentleness of her own. "Yes, but does it not also say in scripture *He that is without sin among you, let him first cast a stone?*"

His troubled thoughts and emotions were not soothed or settled, but they were subdued by the needs of the moment. Lord was right, Anders was still Anders. A good man and a good friend. This new knowledge Gideon had of him served one valuable purpose—it meant that there could indeed be no doubt of his innocence.

"No, of course I won't abandon him," Gideon said.

THE PHYSICIAN'S FATE

Lord studied his face a moment more and nodded, as if satisfied by what he saw there.

"We have work to do then," he said and set down his cup long enough to refill it. "Whilst you were talking with Voclain, I learned the address of Yolande Savatier, although Renaudot does not know I have it and would, I am sure, not approve of our making use of that knowledge."

"But you think we should?"

Lord nodded and drank from the cup before replacing it almost reluctantly on the tray again. "I think we should, and I think we should do so before our host, Mr Browne, returns to demand anything of us or before Renaudot himself thinks to send word to Demoiselle Savatier to warn her of our interest."

So, a very short time later and for the second time that day, Gideon took to the streets of Paris with Lord at his heels clad as a servant. As on their previous outing, Lord didn't have his cat's head sword on his thigh, replaced instead with a neat, long-bladed knife of the kind a man of the station he was imitating might carry.

Yolande Savatier lived not too far from her place of work, on the Rue de Saint Landry. If Lord had not obtained careful directions to her residence, it would have been easy to miss as it lay off a side alley that backed onto the chapel itself and the entranceway was so narrow Gideon had to turn slightly sideways to be able to get to the door.

The girl that answered was much too young to be an apothecary, perhaps twelve or thirteen, with hair as dark as a raven's wing and skin the colour of fine ale, so he smiled politely and asked if Demoiselle Savatier was at home.

"But I am Demoiselle Savatier," the girl told him. "I am Susanne Savatier."

"Then it is your sister I need to speak to. She works as an apothecary in the Bureau D'Adresses on the Rue Calandre."

"*I* know that," Susanne agreed, "but what is *your* business here?"

Behind him, he heard Lord cough to disguise his mirth and Gideon had an idea.

"It is my servant, mademoiselle, he has a strange cough, and I was told that Demoiselle Savatier is a fine apothecary and could have a remedy to help him."

"Your servant?" The girl made a noise that indicated doubt. "When a gentleman comes to knock on our door it is always for himself and always because he needs a treatment for—"

"Susanne. That is enough." The woman who appeared behind the girl was around Gideon's own age and as dark in hair and complexion as the child. But where in Susanne there was a promise of beauty to come, in Yolande it was there in full blossom. She was lovely. Even the slight scarring on her face which showed she must once have had smallpox did nothing to detract from that.

Gideon realised he must be staring and quickly sketched a polite bow.

"Demoiselle Savatier? You are highly recommended to me."

She surveyed him from astute brown eyes.

"You are English, I think."

"Gideon Fox," he told her, "I am indeed English and a lawyer, and I am hoping to consult you." He produced a coin whose value he had established might make it close to a crown. "May I come in?"

She eyed the coin then held out a hand so he could place it in the palm. "That will pay for your consultation, but any remedies will be more." The coin disappeared into an apron she wore over her gown, and she stood aside, shooing the girl out of the way, to allow Gideon and Lord to enter.

Gideon had expected that the dwelling would be small but this one was much smaller than he had even imagined. It had no kitchen, which he discovered was something of a luxury for houses in Paris and that many of even the better-off households in the city would cook in their hearths or bring in food. They were shown into a reception room which had a table folded back so was clearly also used as a dining room and Gideon glimpsed a tiny family parlour beside it.

"Who is it?" An older man's voice came from the parlour.

THE PHYSICIAN'S FATE

"It is a gentleman seeking a remedy, papa," Yolande called out, "I am taking him and his servant upstairs and when they are gone, I will make some food for you."

She gestured to the stairs and Gideon went up them. Upstairs were two rooms, one that was clearly a bedroom and the other, a small chamber which had a view onto the street, which was home to books and jars and bottles, with two chairs and scarcely room for three people. There was a rickety ladder of a staircase going up again, perhaps to where the sisters slept.

If Yolande was at all intimidated she didn't show it, gesturing Gideon to one chair and taking the other herself, ignoring Lord who managed to squeeze in beside the door just enough that it could be closed.

"What can I help you with, monsieur?" There was something in the way she asked that told Gideon she already doubted he was in need of her professional advice, and he decided that there was little point maintaining any pretence anyway.

"I must apologise for not being entirely honest," he said and went on quickly, holding up a hand as her expression changed. "I am a friend of Anders Jensen, and I am trying to discover anything that you might know which would help me to show he didn't commit the crime for which he stands accused."

For a moment he thought he had made a mistake because her face seemed to freeze. But then she glanced briefly at Lord and then back to him.

"Dr Jensen was kind to me," she said. "I would be pleased to learn it wasn't he who did that terrible thing, but I have no idea how anything I could say might help show that."

Gideon decided the less direct approach might work better in building Yolande Savatier's confidence.

"May I ask in what way he showed you kindness?"

She hesitated as if there might be some trap in the question, then nodded.

"Many of the doctors at the Bureau won't come to me for their remedies and most of the tablets and potions I make are put in the dispensary for those who come in most desperate need. But Dr Jensen would always ask me to make his remedies; he said he had more faith in me than in some of the other apothecaries who work there."

"I am sure he was right to do so," Gideon said. He could see from her look that she assumed it was flattery. "I never knew Anders to praise falsely."

She gave a small lift of her shoulders. "The difference is I *have* to work there as I wouldn't be permitted to work anywhere else. Monsieur Renaudot allows me to. The men who work there are often those too lazy or too uncaring to have their own establishments."

"Isn't it unusual for a woman to work as an apothecary?" Gideon realised there would have been a time not so long ago when he would have thought in much the same way as those physicians who refused to offer her work. "In England it would be."

"It is so here as well," she agreed. 'But I have little choice. When my family were struck with smallpox, my mother and two brothers died, and my father was left blind. I began to work then under his instruction, mixing the remedies for him. I learned as well as any apprentice. Then it came out that I was the one preparing the remedies and even prescribing them, and my father lost his licence. If Monsieur Renaudot had not taken me on we would be paupers." Then she leaned forward a little in her chair, brushing her hands over her apron. "But you haven't come here to hear my woes. You want me to do something to help Dr Jensen."

She treated him to a gaze as direct as her speech.

"That is true," he agreed. "I was hoping you might be able to answer a few questions."

"I'm sure that would not be beyond my ability," she said, and Gideon felt the colour rise in his face.

"Monsieur Renaudot told me that you're the only one of his apothecaries who makes laudanum, is that so?"

"I am the only one, yes. The men are afraid the Faculty might hear of it and punish them—as if working for the Bureau was not enough to earn them the dislike of the Faculty already. But I had no reason not to make it and any other remedy that the physicians asked me to make. And yes, before you ask, it was a bottle of my laudanum that was used to kill poor Demoiselle Tasse."

"No one asked you about that?"

She shook her head. "Why would they? It is not as if it was anything illegal. It was enough for the prévôt to have found the bottle in Dr Jensen's bag."

"So did you make the laudanum for him?"

"No. But it was to a new formula he had uncovered, he said, in England. He gave it to me because he thought it might be more effective than other versions he had used in the past. I made some up to see, enough for five bottles. It was one of those bottles that the murderer used. And before you ask, I had put a mark on them to show they were a new formula and should be administered with care as a result."

Gideon heard Lord straighten up a little behind him and understood why.

"How many of those five bottles can you account for?"

Yolande shook her head. "None of them. I made them then put them in the dispensary. It is where we keep supplies of common remedies or put any less common if we have more than is needed."

"Who has access to the dispensary?" Gideon asked but feared he already knew the answer.

"All the physicians and apothecaries and some others too."

"Is no inventory kept?"

That made her smile. "Of course, but it's never accurate and up to date. Someone will grab a remedy and intend to return to write up that they did so, but then forget."

Gideon made a mental note to ask to see the inventory on his next visit to the Bureau.

"There is a different matter which I wanted to ask you about," he said. "I heard you were a witness to the murder of Gaspard Proulx."

Yolande's eyes narrowed in sudden suspicion.

"What has that to do with Dr Jensen?"

"I don't know," Gideon admitted. "It might be nothing at all. But it strikes me as strange that Proulx was killed and his bag stolen then thrown in the river with nothing taken."

She lifted her shoulders again.

"That is no mystery. The men were sent to kill him, and they robbed him only to make it look more as an unintentional thing."

Lord drew in a sharp breath that echoed Gideon's and for a moment he thought the other man might be going to say something, but instead he rubbed at his chin.

"He was deliberately murdered?" Gideon struggled to keep the surprise from his voice. "Have you reported that to anyone?"

"Who to? Gaspard Proulx was an inveterate gambler. He could have been a truly great physician, all the others who work at the Bureau used to go to him for advice, but he was a lost cause. The reason he worked for Renaudot was that no one else in Paris would employ him as he was known to be a man who would steal from his clients, or even threaten to expose their secrets so he could make money from them to pay his eternal gambling debts." She shook her head and sat back in her chair. "The wonder is that no one murdered him before, not that he was killed when he was."

Gideon digested that for a moment trying to see how, if at all, it could in any way be related to Anders' plight, but from what Yolande had said that wasn't very likely.

"Did you see the men who killed him?"

She didn't answer and stood up, crossing to the small window and standing there looking out as if the memory was too difficult. Then she turned back to them.

"You must forgive me, Monsieur Fox, I need to prepare food for my sister and my father. Gaspard Proulx was killed for his gambling ways. I don't see how it can have been anything to do with Dr Jensen or the murder of poor Demoiselle Tasse."

Gideon rose too and thanked her for her time, placing a second coin of the same value as the first he had given her, in her hand as he did so. "I am staying with Monsieur Browne, the man who is agent in Paris for the King of England. If you think of anything more that might help Dr Jensen, please send word to me there."

She showed them out of the small dwelling and into the narrow alley off the Rue de Saint Landry.

Much as he wanted to talk about what they had learned, Gideon knew it would have to wait until they were back at the Brownes' house. The streets were busy and there was no real chance to discuss anything. He was getting more used to Paris now and the ways in which it was like London as well as those in which it seemed very different. The calls of the street sellers had the same rhythms and cadences but different words and lilts. There were more bells, seemingly all the time one would be being rung. The houses were taller and more pressed in and the dwellings within them smaller.

In London the Thames was a thoroughfare, boats taking people and goods about the city, in Paris Gideon found the Seine was as much a place of industry as a means of transport. The mill boats with their big paddles were moored along the banks or even to bridges, moving to catch the best flow of water. Then there were the laundry boats, partly covered flat barges where women would bring laundry to scrub. Some boasted small cabins, where the linens could be soaked in bucking-tubs, in a lye of ash or urine, before being scrubbed and then rinsed in the river.

"Do not react or look around," Lord said quietly as their road took them over the river. "We are being followed by some men who do not look as if their intentions are very gentle."

It took all Gideon's willpower not to look around. He took a steadying breath and kept walking as if unaware of anything untoward. Instead of keeping on their road, Lord turned at the end of the bridge taking one that ran along the riverbank. It was a well-used way to access moorings.

"How many men?" Gideon asked, his heart thumping, his hand wanting to reach for his sword and his legs telling him that now would be a good time to start running. The only people he could see on this street were women going to and from the boats with their laundry, the water sellers refilling their buckets and others who worked or had business along the river itself. Not the sort of people to intervene if weapons were drawn.

"I counted half a dozen," Lord said, sounding cheerful. "There may be more who have anticipated our route and gone ahead."

"You think they would attack us in broad daylight in the heart of Paris?"

"I have no idea," Lord said. "However, I think it would be safest to assume they plan to do so."

"Who are they?"

"Street ruffians. Two a penny to hire and only really effective after dark or in great numbers. And that does make me wonder who is hiring and why." Lord's tone was speculative. "I wonder if we can ask one of them?"

Which was when Gideon knew that his day was about to get extremely hazardous.

They walked briskly along the bank of the river and Gideon found his hand resting on his sword. He wanted to glance back, to see the men who followed them, whose presence he felt like a breath on the back of his neck even though he knew they must still be at some distance.

"Can you swim?" Lord asked.

Gideon's heart leapt up his throat and back again.

"No. No one in their right mind would swim in the Thames—or the Seine. Just look at it." Nearby a dead dog swirled past in a mess of other rubbish.

"It is considered clean enough to wash clothes." Lord observed, then he gestured back to a passing water seller. "Everyone drinks from it."

"I still can't swim," Gideon said firmly.

"Then let us hope there is no need. Oh look, our friends have friends. They must have sent a runner when we changed course."

Ahead of them, coming from the city streets, was a group of five men who were trying to look as though they were sauntering along the river. None of them carried a sword but Gideon was sure they would have weapons of some kind hidden in their coats. He was thinking that perhaps a concerted rush might take them through and past, when he saw two more emerge onto the river path.

"I have a feeling they're not here to fetch their laundry," Lord said. "Indeed, if I didn't know better, I might assume you had cuckolded some Parisian notary and he is out for revenge." Lord shot him a glance, tone suddenly serious, "You haven't done so, I assume?"

"What?" Gideon looked at him in horrified disbelief.

THE PHYSICIAN'S FATE

"Much better," Lord said. "Now you look as if you have just realised you are going to be murdered. In a few moments we will run. Keep looking exactly like that."

"Right now, I can't see any reason to think we won't be murdered," Gideon admitted, and Lord gave a low chuckle. It struck Gideon then that Sir Philip Lord was enjoying himself. The smile he wore was of feral delight.

"Have faith. We have them outmatched. They are only a dozen and mere rogues. Whereas you are a man of great wit and resource and I have some passing grasp of stratagems as a highly experienced military commander. What chance do they stand?" As he spoke, they had drawn level with the first of the laundry boats in a small armada of such, two or three deep out from the bank in places. "Tell me, when you were a child did you play that game where unless a certain name or phrase was used before a command was given you had to ignore it?"

Bemused, Gideon nodded. "Yes, Simon Says…"

"Were you any good at it?"

"I—I can't recall. But what—?"

Lord clapped him hard on the back as if with urgent warning. "You only do what I say in English. Ignore anything I ask in French. And now, we run."

Chapter Ten

Gideon ran.

To one side of the way was the river and the laundry boats shackled to the shore with planks to enable the women washing to come and go. On the other side was a bank with a seemingly solid row of houses above it, as impenetrable as a castle wall. In front, were seven men who were quickly spreading out to make the way ahead impassable. Behind, another six bravos were starting to run too, making any chance of retreat impossible.

Not that Sir Philip Lord seemed to have any thought of retreat. The last glimpse Gideon had of his face before he took the lead running, was of a scarcely subdued hilarity and delight. That was scant comfort to Gideon though, who could only see that they were trapped between the river and their attackers.

At first, he thought Lord planned simply to rush the men in front and they thought so too as they shifted their positions to make a line that could hold and close about their victims, no longer moving forward themselves. Weapons had appeared in their hands now, ugly knives, cudgels and saps.

"With me," Lord said.

It was the only warning Gideon got, but it was enough that when Lord jumped over the gap from shore to a laundry boat, one of the larger ones with a little roofed cabin, he was ready and able to follow. Lord had seized the plank which connected the boat to the shore and ducked into the door of the cabin. Almost at once, Gideon heard the laundresses yelling at him. When Gideon reached the door himself and went in, he saw why. Lord had started pulling out the dirty linens that were soaking in the bucking-tubs—shirts, shifts, even a sheet.

"You could," he said, as Gideon ducked his head to get through the low door, "give me a hand here."

Confused and very aware that their pursuers were not far behind, Gideon helped move the bucking-tubs to the shore side door. Their dolly-sticks Lord draped with the soaking linens, stinking of lye.

THE PHYSICIAN'S FATE

The first men who reached the door would be confronted by the need to jump from the bank through a barricade of sopping linens, and then confront the small problem of the tubs where they would need to land, making their entry an inevitably messy and awkward one.

But Lord was already leaving the cabin by the other door, to the narrow deck where women would rinse the cloth in the river once it had been well soaked, scraped and scrubbed on boards. Lord paused to bestow a brief bow and a gold coin on the most vociferous laundress as he passed, ducking under the blow she aimed at his head, which Gideon received in the chest instead.

Catching his breath and murmuring apologies in French, Gideon caught sight of two drenched and linen bedraggled men, at the other end of the cabin, clearly torn between turning to help their fellows by moving the tubs or pursuing Lord and Gideon.

Gideon decided not to wait to see their final decision. He went through the other door and found the narrow deck was replete with washboards and buckets. If there had been any women working there, they must have run inside already because there was no one in sight.

"No, *monsieur*, run to the next laundry boat," Lord called urgently. "*Il y a une cabine…* it has a cabin you can hide in. I will distract them." And for a moment Gideon was about to do so when he realised that Lord had been speaking French. Instead of turning towards the next boat, he went the other way.

At first, he couldn't see Lord. Then a hand came down from above and grasping it, Gideon swung up, and flattened himself on the roof of the cabin beside a grinning Sir Philip Lord, who's other hand held his long-bladed knife.

The first of their pursuers who had made it through the linen and tubs, boiled out of the door and hared away towards the next boat. It would be a jump to make it, but not a very difficult one with a bit of speed. From his perch at the other end of the boat and on the roof, Gideon could not see what happened, but he heard the yells and splashes.

"Soap," Lord told him, by way of explanation. "There was a small bucket by the door. I carelessly spilled it over the end of the deck."

Footsteps came running their way. Lord pulled himself up to crouch briefly on the edge of the roof and dropped down. The first man died without even knowing what had happened, a second had his mouth open drawing breath to yell when Lord's blade took him through the throat. A moment later the two bodies were being carried away in the other flotsam of the river. The third man had been furthest past them, and he turned to see Lord's knife point, the blood of his friends on its blade. He stood frozen, not needing to be told that any sound would be his last.

"You can come down now," Lord called softly, in English. "Be quick, we need to leave before this man's other friends catch on."

Gideon lowered himself from the roof and stepped over a deck now slick with blood to where Lord had found a small boat tied to the back of the laundry boat. It came complete with a set of oars. As their prisoner turned towards it, Lord's hand moved, striking with the pommel of his knife. The man slumped down unconscious. Catching him, Lord rolled him as much as lifted him into the boat.

"This," Sir Philip Lord explained as Gideon clambered in behind, "is a water seller's boat. They must go out into the middle of the river to collect their water and it is cheaper to pay the launderer for a mooring than the city rate."

The river was flowing fast, away from the men who had been chasing them and back towards the bridge. Within a short time, Lord was using the oars more to steer than to propel. Once they were close to the bridge an invisible force sucked them ever faster towards it. Gideon had too many memories of shooting through the arches of London Bridge to feel at all reassured. At least they were being carried well away from their pursuers and at speed. This bridge had narrower arches than London Bridge and he could see the concentration on Lord's face as he fought to manoeuvre the small craft to take a safe path and not be smashed against the pilings and supports.

THE PHYSICIAN'S FATE

Just as the bridge loomed over them, the tall houses that lined it rearing cliff-like above them, unconscious man moaned and pushed himself up, then collapsed back onto the side of the boat. One moment they were gliding under the arch, well clear of the sides and the next Gideon was tumbled into the freezing water.

It was so fast he had no time to think. He took an instinctive gasp of breath as he hit the water, but a moment later had lost all sense of up or down or knowledge of anything but the omnipresent ice-cold water that seemed to boil about him, pulling him down and hurling him along.

Struggling close to blind panic, he felt his cloak weighing him like an anchor and managed to pull the clasp free. For a single blissful moment, he was released and there was fresh air on his face, but scarcely more than long enough to catch another breath before the river reclaimed its grip and pulled him back down.

He tried to push himself up to where there was air, beating his arms against the water. Beating, but getting nowhere. The cold sapped all strength from his limbs and the weight of his boots pulled him down until the air in his lungs had become fire and the urge to simply let the breath go was intense. He knew he was drowning and that there was nothing he could do.

For a few moments fear crashed through him like a tidal bore, and in the panic, he almost gave way and tried to draw breath where there was no air. But then it was gone. In its wake came a strange acceptance. It was real. It was happening to him. Now. And fighting it would only prolong his own agony. What reason was there to hold out against the inevitable for, just another moment or another two?

His mind spun away, and he was with Zahara. She was wearing his ring and looking through the window over the college green, waiting for him to come back. Waiting, and he would never come.

Something in that vision seemed to give him a renewed strength and he kicked hard pulling himself with his arms and the last reserves of his breath, in the direction he believed lay air. Praying now in the hollow cathedral of his mind, he begged for God to give him the strength he needed. Instead, he felt only a numbing weakness and the edge of his consciousness seemed to be creeping inwards with darkness. Then his prayers changed, he no longer prayed for himself but only for Zahara and in so doing he felt a little of the peace she always brought him which held a sense of comfort as the ache in his lungs became unbearable and darkness closed in.

There was pain and chaos and someone calling his name. But by then a big part of him didn't want to let go of the darkness and peace. The demanding voice called again, and Gideon drew a breath to reply, which ended instead in a choking agony. Coughing up water from lungs that burned as if they had been scoured. For a long time he lay on his side coughing up and then vomiting the Seine, oblivious to his surroundings. He knew only that he lived and that it hurt to do so, and that he could do nothing except physically reject the river water.

"By God, Gideon, you need to learn to swim." Lord's voice, speaking English, though Gideon could not see him and felt too weak to move. Then Lord spoke in his rapid-fire French, "Thank you again. I hope this will go some way towards recompensing your speedy action and kindness and if I could please impose upon you to take this message to the house of the English agent, Monsieur Browne? He will send assistance. Monsieur Fox is his guest."

Gideon heard footsteps recede and a door close, then he must have passed out because when he came around it was to realise he was lying shivering on a floor covered with flour, which made so little sense he wondered if he was delirious. He had been stripped of his outer clothes and wrapped around in a dry sack.

Lord crouched beside him wearing clearly borrowed clothes, worn and drab beyond even the servant's attire he had originally adopted for the outing. All trace of his disguise had been taken by the Seine.

"Ah, you are awake and if you can bear to move a little..." As he spoke Lord hooked an arm under Gideon's shoulder.

With the assistance that gave, Gideon was able to pull himself up and shuffle back to sit against a wall. There he was able to take in his surroundings which seemed to be a storage cupboard for sacks of flour. It was then he noticed the familiar swish and clack of a waterwheel.

"Where are we?" he asked, between chattering teeth.

"Oh good, you are back with us. You had me worried for a while," Lord said. "We are on one of the floating mills that we were lucky was moving its mooring. They saw us in the water and when I hailed them, came to our aid."

It all made sense then. Gideon thought of the strange boats he had seen with their water wheels to one side, some even with one placed between two hulls, grinding flour for the city. Then the import of Lord's words caught up in his numbed brain.

"I was drowning," he said.

"Very nearly. It took me a while to find you even I saw you break the surface briefly. It's not a good river to fall in, you can't see much at all underwater." Then he shrugged off the coat he had and put it around Gideon. "Here, I have no wish for my good work pulling you from the arms of the Seine to be wasted. I was wondering how I was going to explain things to Zahara if you had drowned and have yet to come up with something I think she would accept as a reasonable excuse for losing you."

That cut too close to the bone for Gideon.

"What about the man who was with us?"

Lord shook his head. "Unfortunately, he couldn't swim either. I had to choose between him or you. A shame as I would have liked to have known who sent those men after you."

"After *me*?" Gideon took a moment to absorb that and then realised there was no other explanation. Lord had been out with him as a servant, and no one had followed them until after they left Yolande Savatier's house. "Someone objected to my visiting the apothecary?"

Lord nodded. "Objected very violently too. It is hard to see why else they would have risked trying to murder you in broad daylight. I am willing to bet that whoever paid those men offered them well over the going rate for the additional risk."

"Whoever it was must have ready access to such street roughs," Gideon observed. "Assuming the very fact I was visiting Yolande

Savatier was the problem, we were there for a very short time. Not long to gather such men."

"Unless…" Lord trailed off and bounced to his feet. "Unless I have been an utter fool and missed the obvious."

"If so, you're not the only one," Gideon said. "I cannot see this 'obvious' even now."

"What if someone was watching the Savatiers' house for specific visitors—visitors enquiring about the death of Geneviève Tasse?"

Gideon thought for a moment. "Or the death of Gerard Proulx?" he suggested.

Lord looked down at him sharply. "Or indeed the death of Gerard Proulx, which would make sense as we know that Yolande Savatier was a witness to that."

"Maybe whoever this man is, he knew I had already visited Bureau D'Adresses and if Renaudot or Voclain said anything about my enquiries there..."

"Perhaps," Lord said, but it was very clear to Gideon he was not in full agreement on that point. "I must admit I have been wondering if the deaths of Demoiselle Tasse and Dr Proulx were connected, but I am struggling to find any possible link. I had toyed with the idea that perhaps Proulx was the one who had killed Geneviève Tasse, and someone knew they could not prove it so had him murdered—a lover perhaps, maybe even her mistress. Richelieu himself was not above such methods at need."

Gideon bridled at the thought. "And leave Anders to die for it, knowing him innocent?"

Lord sighed. "What is he to them? Would you be so quick to Jensen's defence if you knew him innocent, but he was not your friend?"

"I'd like to think so," Gideon said, stoutly. The law was as much his passion as his profession, and any miscarriage of justice he would oppose.

"And if you knew he was one who loved men and not women?"

Gideon felt the colour rise in his face.

"I'd like to think so," he repeated. "I take your point there might be those who would know Anders' innocence and yet still find reasons—excuses and justifications—not to lift a finger to help him. But if the murderer was Proulx and he is dead, what hope do we have for proving Anders falsely accused?"

"And that," Lord said soberly, "is the problem. But the fact remains whoever sent those men after you were intent on your death and having failed once they may try again."

That was a thought to chill Gideon's blood even more than the waters of the Seine. He knew he needed to bring his clearest thinking to the matter but, shivering and exhausted, it was difficult to keep his thinking any less murky than the waters he had just escaped.

"That is why," Lord went on, "I asked Browne to come for you with a sizable and obvious escort. He has named himself, publicly, as your friend so he can do that. For your safety I am tempted to send you back to Saint-Léon-du-Moulin. At least until I have completed my work for the king."

"No," Gideon pushed himself to sit upright. "No. You mustn't do that. I'm the only hope Anders has. I gave him my word that I'd do everything I could, and I'll not abandon him just because someone tried to kill me because of it."

Lord's expression was unreadable.

"If it is indeed because of that," he said. "It might not be. From what you have said Proulx had a ready ability to make his own enemies. We might be wrong to link his death to that of Demoiselle Tasse." Then Lord sighed. "But you are, of course, right. You are not a child I can overrule and insist that I protect. You are also correct that any hope of proving Jensen innocent rests in your hands right now, not mine." He crouched back down bringing his gaze to the same level as Gideon's. "But I'm very aware of your vulnerability and today has shown us both we need to be more careful. There are clearly more threads to this weave than we yet see."

That was where they had to leave the discussion because Richard Browne arrived with an armed guard, a sedan chair and porters. Gideon was provided with dry clothes and a warm cloak, which Lord himself helped him dress in. But something was not as it should be. Browne seemed to struggle to be solicitous as if some other problem was totally dominating his thoughts.

"We must hurry and get you back safely," was all he said to Gideon, then turned his attention to Lord who was refusing to be rushed.

"There is very little time. If you miss this opportunity—"

"You said at seven? Then we have over an hour. That is enough time." Then to Gideon. "Let me help you with that," as Gideon's fingers fumbled with buttons.

In a very short time, but one that was clearly not short enough for Browne, they were going through the dark Parisian streets. Gideon was carried in the enclosed chair by the two porters, like an invalid—which he supposed he was. He was escorted by Lord and Browne, some half dozen well-armed men and two runner-boys bearing lanterns.

Paris being a small city, they were back at Browne's residence within a quarter of an hour. Gideon was installed in his room under the solicitous care of the lady of the house, who was keen to send for a physician, but Gideon managed to dissuade her. Instead, he accepted a posset and let the warmth of that restore him as best it might.

Lord came to see him, dressed in an extreme of fashionable finery and looking immaculate. White hair brushed out and gleaming against the peacock blue of his clothes and sword restored to his thigh. He wore a hat boasting a white plume and the same kerchief Gideon had seen on their arrival in Paris.

Aside from a small bruise on his face, and a slight shadow around his eyes, there was no mark of Lord's exertions of the day visible on his face. No sign that not much more than two hours before he had risked his life diving again and again under the filthy water of the Seine trying to find Gideon before he drowned.

It struck Gideon that this was a man for whom such adventures were commonplace. No less urgent and vital than they might be for anyone else, but a usual part of life that required no more than the time and effort of the moment before moving to the next thing that demanded his attention. And yet, unlike so many who took their own experience of life as something all should manage and achieve as they did themselves, Sir Philip Lord understood that for those around him such a thing was not their regular experience. That was a rare grace Gideon had seldom encountered in others and wasn't sure he bestowed himself.

"How are you feeling now?" Lord asked.

"Like a man who nearly drowned in the river."

Which made Lord laugh at least. "I apologise that I cannot sit with you, but I am summoned to see King Louis. That is why poor Richard Browne has been so anxious."

"You are going to have an audience with the King of France right now?" Gideon struggled with the notion.

"No. This is no formal reception. My understanding is I am just to be a guest at the same event as his most Christian Majesty. A well-arranged chance encounter where I will be presented and recognised. The king is still hoping to avoid offending the envoy from Parliament, so we must play a game," Lord explained. "It is not the best timing, but at least once this is done, we will be able to pursue the work to redeem Jensen more openly."

That was something to be glad about. But Gideon could see problems ongoing.

"So you will not be able to discharge your commission from King Charles?"

"Not tonight," Lord admitted. "But I am hopeful the diplomatic dancing will mean that I am able to do so soon. Meanwhile, it allows me access to court circles should we need that."

There came a tap on the door and Richard Browne's harassed face appeared around it.

"Sir Philip, we need to go now."

Lord acknowledged him with a nod then turned back to Gideon briefly.

"Hopefully tomorrow you will be much restored, and we will see what we need to do next. Rest now."

Not that Gideon had much choice in the matter. His body felt bruised and battered inside and out. Once Lord had left him, he fell quickly asleep.

Chapter Eleven

When Gideon woke it was full light. The sounds coming through the window were of a busy city caught up in the daily demands and activities of a Friday morning. There had been snow overnight and the frozen slush was being churned on the street below. In England it was still early December, but here in Paris it was already the nineteenth. In a few days' time, it would be Christmas and the city would give itself over to festivities—the wealthy for the full twelve days. But for now, it was still a working day.

Having dressed himself, Gideon went downstairs. He was greeted by Elizabeth Browne who informed him that Lord had returned late the previous night and already left again, first thing that morning, in company with her husband.

"I am sorry, but they did not leave word of where they were going," she told him, "I think it was something to do with Sir Philip's mission for the king. But he left you a note and there is another one that arrived for you a short time ago too."

Accepting the very welcome offer of something to eat, Gideon apologised for rising late and having put his hostess to extra work. But she told him they always kept food ready for chance arrivals. Gideon supposed that it must be part of the duty of any ambassador or agent in a foreign country—providing shelter and succour to fellow countrymen in need, often at short notice.

As he sat alone, waiting for the food to arrive, he opened the note written in Lord's elegant, fluid hand.

I trust you will be feeling recovered and well rested, so you can give some thought to what we need to do today. I have to play a game of tennis or two but hope to return by dinnertime with some news that may be helpful. Keep within doors until then.
P.

The other note was addressed to 'Monsieur Gideon Fox' in an impeccably neat, small script. Even before he opened it Gideon was sure he knew who it was from. Gideon felt his heart rate pick up speed as he read.

Monsieur,
I am very scared and I believe that I am in great danger. There are things I did not tell you yesterday that I wish I had done. I dare not leave the house or I would come to you. Please come at once, every minute I wait I think it might be too late.
Yolande Savatier

Then in a much less neat hand beneath that, she had added.

It is not just myself I am afraid for, it is my father and my sister. Please come, monsieur, and quickly.

Gideon read over the note a couple more times as if the words might somehow tell him more. It was possible she was not on the side of the angels, but then she would know of the attack and that he wouldn't be likely to respond as she was asking. Only a fool would go back having barely survived an attempted murder. But if he waited for Lord to return and what Yolande had written was true, it might be too late.

He got up and went in search of Elizabeth Browne, encountering her at the bottom of the stairs, talking to one of the servants who was holding a bucking basket full of dirty linen.

"Could you tell me who delivered this note?" he asked.

"It was just a regular running boy as far as I know." She gestured back to the dining hall with a smile where a servant had just gone through. "Your food is being served, if you would like to go and eat, I will find out how the note arrived."

Gideon did as she asked and had finished eating when she came in looking flustered.

"I do apologise, Mr Fox, I was delayed because there was an Englishman calling at the house, demanding to speak with a Mr Lennox who he said he was sure was staying here. It was one of the gentlemen with the delegation from the Parliamentary rebels.

My husband has made it very clear that we will have nothing to do with their sort."

Gideon hoped his face did not betray the horror he felt. It was not entirely unlikely that one of his acquaintances, or even one of the handful of men he had considered as friends in London, might have been amongst those sent by Parliament to speak to the French king.

"Did this man give his name?" he asked, then realised he must have asked the wrong question as Elizabeth Browne gave him a quick look of surprise.

"He did not offer a name, but I am sure my husband would know who it was. He was here with one of the others when their delegation first arrived, seeking to persuade Richard to join their rebellion."

Gideon nodded as if it was of no real account—and indeed compared to the other matters he had to manage at that moment it wasn't. "And did you find out who had brought that message?"

"It was brought by a water seller."

"Did your servants know the man?"

"He was not our usual one, but perhaps, if it is important, I can ask the regular man if he knows who it was. He should be here any time."

"I would speak to him," Gideon said quickly, an idea taking shape in his thoughts.

Only a fool would go alone, but perhaps there was a way...

A short time later, Gideon left the house ignoring Elizabeth Browne's tightly clasped hands and the anxious look of disapproval on her face.

He had written a note to Lord and folded the message from Yolande Savatier into it explaining his absence. If any further information was needed, he was very sure the means of his departure would be described in some detail by Mrs Browne. And Lord could always speak to the water vendor who was happily sitting in the kitchen in one of Richard Brown's old shirts and a pair of breeches that were close to being turned into cleaning rags. Which finery, together with the jingle of silver in his purse, Gideon had thought was more than enough recompense for losing an hour or so of work.

Meanwhile, Gideon himself was clad in the water vendor's clothes. The holed shoes, straggled stockings and ripped breeches, were partnered with a tatty but colourful slashed doublet that had apparently been given to the man in lieu of payment by a customer. The whole was topped off by a jaunty hat with two pheasant feathers, which Gideon pulled down over his face hoping against all hope that it was not crawling with lice. He had darkened his beard and moustache with soot and the same for his hair and had to trust that the ominous clouds overhead would not give way to icy rain or snow.

Carrying the water was not as easy as it looked. A broad leather strap went over one shoulder and attached to the two buckets, either one of which had it been full Gideon would have struggled to carry very far, but these were left half full. They could have been empty, but he had no wish to make the perilous journey to the river to fill them and arriving at the Savatier's house as a water vendor with no water would have certainly drawn attention.

The most difficult part was managing the hoop which was wedged between the bucket handles as he held them and stopped the buckets from being slopped against him. It made for an awkward way of carrying, with arms uncomfortably wide whilst helping bear the weight that the strap was putting on his shoulder. The fact that there were still places where the slush was icy underfoot did not help matter at all.

By the time he made it across the bridge to the Île de la Cité, he had needed to stop and change shoulders and although he knew that was something all the water vendors did now and then he worried that his unfamiliarity with the manoeuvre meant he was not cutting a very convincing figure.

Mercifully the only people who gave him any attention were a couple of other water vendors who clearly knew the man who normally wore the clothes Gideon had adopted. One laughed aloud and went on his way, the other began to approach him calling out as he did so.

"Antoine? Is that you?"

Gideon nodded and smiled and stopped as if for a chat, pressing a coin into the other water vendor's hand, which sent him on his way looking puzzled but pleased.

Feeling he might have overestimated his ability to carry off the role, Gideon hurried on, head down and when another voice hailed 'Antione' he kept walking as quickly as he could under the awkward encumbrance of the buckets and hoop. He was left in no doubt that by the next day there would be tales of a gentleman dressing up as a water seller which would only grow ever more unlikely in the retelling.

He almost decided not to carry on but having made it to the Chapel of St Landry and not noticing anyone paying him more attention now than any other water vendor, decided that it would be more foolish to withdraw than to go on. He walked up the road past the Savatiers' house and noticed two men who looked out of place in the streets so close to Notre Dame. Men reminding him of those who he and Lord had evaded the day before.

They paid him little heed and he realised that from where they stood, they would have a good view of the side of the Savatier's house. The window of Yolande's room looked out over the road there. Continuing past them, he made his way along the road and then turned into a street that would take him to the other end of the narrow passage that led to the Savatiers' house.

It was even more tricky to get to the door than it had been before. Turning sideways to get along the narrow alley, meant pushing the hoop up his back and letting it go lower at the front and that made carrying the buckets twice as hard as they came in against his body. He knew then that he would never look at a water seller in the same way ever again.

When he finally reached the Savatiers' door he rapped on it and sang out, "*L'eau...au!*" as he had heard the water sellers do. When there was no response, he tried again.

"*L'eau...au!*"

He had his fist lifted for a third try when the door opened a crack.

"Demoiselle Savatier," Gideon said quickly in a low voice, "I got your message."

THE PHYSICIAN'S FATE

The door closed and for a moment Gideon thought he would be left to stand there. Then it opened again and wider than before. Yolande was there, her expression questioning, clearly recognising him despite the soot. She held out an empty bucket. Gideon took it and under the cover of filling it and the splash of water he spoke quietly.

"You said you needed to tell me something."

"You should not have come." Yolande was wide-eyed with terror. "I was about to leave. I am not staying in Paris. They will—"

"Kill me?" Gideon managed his best insouciant smile. "They already tried on my way home yesterday."

"You must understand, I could not say anything before. Susanne is only a child. They would have—" She broke off and Gideon felt his anger growing.

"Are they with you now?"

"No. But they will be watching the house."

"You sound very sure of that."

The bucket was filled, and Gideon handed it to her, she put it down just inside the door.

"Yesterday they came and said there was an Englishman asking questions at the Bureau and if he visited me, I was to stand in the window upstairs. Then they came back this morning, soon after I sent you the note and told me if you visited me again any time, I was to give the same signal as before."

Gideon was absorbing that when she spoke again.

"I did not want to do it," she said fiercely. "I wanted to help Dr Jensen. But I had no choice. After you left, I made arrangements to send my father and Susanne away from Paris. They have gone already, and I have only stayed to make sure all our affairs are settled. If you had come in another half an hour I would have been gone too—and perhaps that would have been safer for both of us."

Gideon could sense the courage that had prompted her to write the note to him evaporating.

"You just need to tell me the name of the man who threatens you." He had thought about that on the walk there. One name was all they should need.

Yolande bent to pick up a second bucket and held it out to be filled, shaking her head. Gideon was starting to get worried now. As soon as the second bucket was full, he would have no more reason to stand there and would risk drawing attention. If Yolande did not speak…

"Pierre Firmin," she said, her voice low and shaking. "He works for the money lenders. If you do not pay, he will visit. Before I had a job at the Bureau I had to borrow, and he came to collect sometimes he offered to take my payments another way and was angry when I refused and gave him the money. I saw him leading the men who attacked Dr Proulx. He came around the next day and said I must never tell anyone, or he would take my sister." She looked grey with fear and her eyes darted along the alley as if expecting the man she had named to appear.

"Where can I find him?"

"Le Cheval Rouge."

Gideon handed her the second bucket.

"Thank you for what you have said. If you want to come with me, I can—"

"No. I am leaving Paris."

He thought then how she was the breadwinner for her family and how she would struggle to find work as an apothecary anywhere else.

"Where will you go?"

She stared at him then and he realised that she had taken his question in completely the wrong way. But before he could correct that, she had shut the door in his face.

Aware that unless he was to expose himself as the fraud he truly was, he could not bang on the door again, Gideon turned and went back along the narrow alley, choosing a way that did not go past the watching men. Then he retraced his steps across Paris in his increasingly uneasy disguise, reaching the Browne's residence with relief.

The real water seller was almost as pleased to have his yoke of buckets returned as Gideon was to restore them to him. Elizabeth Browne seemed the happiest of all that he was back. She returned the note he had left with her. Clearly, she had not relished explaining Gideon's absence to her husband and Lord. Though, other than ordering the servants to physically restrain him, Gideon was not sure what she could have done to prevent him from going.

Lord and Browne returned soon after. Browne looking thoughtful and a little perturbed, Lord his usual untroubled self and with the glow of someone who had been engaged in energetic pursuits. Gideon noticed the kerchief Lord had been wearing the night before was no longer in his hat band. When Gideon suggested quietly that they needed to discuss matters, Lord glanced at the case clock in the entrance hall and nodded.

"We have time as I change. Our hosts have arranged a dinner, it would be rude to not attend."

Gideon followed Lord to his room, waited as he dismissed the servant who had been sent to help Sir Philip dress, and decided that as time was apparently short full explanations could wait.

"I know who killed Gaspard Proulx," he said as the servant's footsteps receded down the stairs. "It was a man who works for money lenders who feel they need force to collect on their debts. Which would make sense as we know Proulx was a gambler."

"It would," Lord agreed, quickly pulling a fresh silk shirt from a chest. "Although if he was killed for his inability to repay a debt then his death is no more than a coincidence and we have no interest in it."

"Except Yolande Savatier was told that she should be on the lookout for an Englishman who had been asking questions at the Bureau, and I asked no questions regarding the death of Proulx that I recall."

Lord paused, half-stripped, old scars and fresh abrasions and bruising visible on his torso.

"Now that is a very good point," he said, pulling on the new silk shirt. "I take it from this you did not heed my advice to stay here this morning but went to visit Demoiselle Savatier?"

Gideon had expected censure and maybe even anger that he had disobeyed Lord's injunction. But there was nothing more than mild curiosity in the question.

"She sent a note asking me to do so, saying it was urgent and had I waited for you she would have been gone from Paris, so it was as well I did. I went in disguise as a water vendor."

"You went as...?"

"A water vendor. I borrowed the clothes and buckets from the one who serves the Brownes."

Lord looked at him, mouth open in exaggerated disbelief and then he burst out laughing.

"I can see," he said when he recovered, "you have spent altogether too much time in my company. Clearly you made it there, buckets, hoop, water and all—and back again too." He had laid out on his bed a doublet and breeches in a pale blue satin, with white and silver braid and a matching cape and now started putting them on. "What else did you learn from Demoiselle Savatier?"

"That was all. The man is called Pierre Firmin and we may find him at Le Cheval Rouge. There was not a lot of time for conversation, The Savatiers' house was watched, and Yolande was about to leave. She had sent her sister and father out of Paris already as Firmin had threatened Susanne."

"I look forward to making his acquaintance then." Lord was working the gemmed points, quickly doing up the lacings on his clothing as he spoke. "We need the name of his employer I think, and I have a feeling it will not be one of those disreputable money lenders on this occasion. We will pay a visit to Le Cheval Rouge this evening, I doubt it will be one of the finer taverns in Paris."

"And what have you found out?" Gideon asked.

"Last night I discovered that the Most Christian King Louis will do everything he can to assist his good-brother Charles in his war against his rebellious subjects, apart from providing money or troops to aid his cause any more than he has already done so. As a Catholic king, he can hardly succour a monarch who declares himself to be head of a church, although he can—of course—give money and military support to his Protestant allies who fight the Hapsburgs. Strange how religion matters so much right up to the moment raw power politics comes into play." Lord finished the lacings and picked up his cape. "And I learned that the king is thinking more about the upcoming festivities and his hunting dogs than the unfortunate death of Demoiselle Tasse."

"I don't see how that helps us with Anders at all," Gideon said.

"It means the king has very little interest in the matter, which is both good in that he will not press for a rapid execution of 'justice' and bad in that he will not stir to seek if they have the right man. However, this morning's visit was more profitable. After the tennis, I managed to secure a brief audience with the Duchesse d'Aiguillon, niece to the late and much-lamented Cardinal Richelieu. I had performed a small service for her in the past for which she had rewarded me with a small token against future need, it gave me immediate admittance to her presence."

"The kerchief?" Gideon guessed.

"The kerchief." Lord snatched up his hat and brushed some invisible dust from it. "The Duchesse, it transpires, was very fond of Geneviève Tasse, seeing her more as a companion and friend than as a maidservant and she was most interested to learn that the man in the Châtelet might not be the one who killed her friend. I cannot say she was as moved by the thought of Jensen suffering a terrible fate so much as that the man truly responsible might go free, though to do her justice I could be wrong."

Lord strode to the door, looking his usual immaculate self.

"So how does that help?" Gideon asked.

"Aside from securing her goodwill should we need it at some point, I'm not sure it does. However, she told me that Geneviève Tasse was supposed to have summoned another of her ladies to be present at the meeting, but she did not. She was to have met in a public room but was found in her bedchamber. It suggests she was acquainted with her murderer at least enough to trust herself with him alone." He lifted his hand and frowned at Gideon. "You still have a trace of soot in your hair, but there is no time to remedy that. We must go and be good guests. Eat well and then later we shall pay a visit to Monsieur Firmin."

The guests were all exiles or visitors from England, and they sat for a pleasant enough dinner at which a broad range of subjects were raised and discussed from politics to philosophy.

One of the guests was Mr Thomas Hobbes who Gideon knew had deemed it wise to leave London after his last treatise had been found displeasing to just about everyone of any political persuasion, but particularly Parliament. In the relative safety of Paris, Hobbes seemed keen to engage those present with his theories on the nature of society. Despite Elizabeth Browne's best efforts to change the subject to everything from her daughter's latest accomplishment to the vagaries in the price of fish in recent weeks—it being a Friday—Hobbes kept returning the discussion to the political sphere. At one point Gideon came dangerously close to expressing his own thoughts on the topic when Lord intervened, lifting his voice to carry over the increasingly agitated conversation.

"I recall your thoughts upon colour quite impressed me, Mr Hobbes."

The learned gentleman broke off mid-sentence and scowled.

"Colour, sir?"

"Yes," Lord ran a finger around the rim of his glass, and it sang a note. "Colour, you say, is not inherent in an object, but is an effect upon us, as sound is an effect upon the air and so our ears." He stopped the ringing. "I wonder then at dyes. If the colour is not inherent in the dye, how can it be transferred to the cloth?"

Hobbes laughed.

"My dear sir, you misunderstand my meaning. The colour is caused by the imperfect reflection of light from other objects."

"Yes, but were I to take dyes of red and blue and yellow and drop them into water then they would be red and blue and yellow water. So what rough, uneven or coarse property in water is giving the different colours?"

Which neatly curtailed the conversation from politics to optics, even as it left Gideon more bemused than enlightened, but he knew from the glint in Lord's eyes that he was playing with the philosopher and at the same time saving his hostess from the embarrassment of political argument at her table.

Once the guests had left, Lord brought the Brownes close to hilarity doing an impersonation of the pompous and doughty Hobbes defending his theories on the nature of the physical against

THE PHYSICIAN'S FATE

Lord's ingenuous and mischievous disputation. It was only once the laughter was done that Lord told them he and Gideon would be going out that evening in common dress.

"But surely, Sir Philip," Richard Browne protested, "now you have completed your embassy for the king, you don't need to go so discreetly in Paris. You can be more open. You are recognised as being present and acknowledged as who you are now."

Lord looked regretful.

"If you would rather I did not remain under your roof whilst I engage in these activities, I quite appreciate your right to ask me to leave. I can take myself and Mr Fox back to Saint-Léon-du-Moulin. I am sure His Majesty will understand your reservations."

There was a slight, appalled silence.

"There is no need for that, of course, Sir Philip," Browne said hurriedly. "You and Mr Fox must stay here as long as you have business for the king in Paris. It is just that I was not aware that this matter with Mr Jensen *was* the business of the king."

"It is not," Lord said. "It is, however, a matter that closely touches me and the king's nephews, the Princes Rupert and Maurice."

Browne's expression cleared at that.

"Then I repeat, you must stay until this problem has been resolved."

Lord must have seen the look on Elizabeth Browne's face. "We'll not need to spend the Christmas season here," he reassured her. "Matters will be set to rights by then, of that I am most confident."

Gideon, however, was not. In five days, the Christmas festivities would begin, normal life be set aside, and their task become much harder.

They went out after dark.

Lord had abandoned any disguise except he was clad much as Gideon himself, in the style of a well to do but not wealthy individual. They were accompanied by four very determined-looking men, armed with street weapons. No doubt men from Lord's estate. It was another bitterly cold night and Gideon was glad to have a warm cloak about his shoulders.

"Why do we have company this evening?" he asked.

Lord laughed softly, his teeth white in the light of the lantern he carried.

"Well, whereas you are indeed a man of great wit and resource—as you demonstrated this morning—and I have some passing grasp of stratagems as a highly experienced military commander, the place we go tonight might outmatch even us."

"And four men will make a difference?"

Lord looked thoughtful. "I am hoping they will have a peaceful time and we will enjoy a drink undisturbed. But yes, if they are needed then they will undoubtedly make a difference."

The streets had become even less well-lit, and the houses seemed to close in about them. Lord stopped and spoke softly to the four men.

"From here, keep a distance. Wait outside the tavern unless I call you in."

After that, Lord and Gideon went on apparently alone.

When they reached Le Cheval Rouge, there was nothing to betray either the name of the tavern or even that it was one. It could have been just another house on one of the many struggling-to-be-prosperous streets in this less than salubrious part of the city.

Surprisingly, once inside, the tavern was not as its environs suggested. Whilst hardly spotless or richly appointed, the tables and seats, made of plain undecorated wood, were all reasonably clean. Though dark, each table had a candle, and some had two, putting pools of light about the room. The fire blazed in its hearth and added a little illumination of its own along with its heat.

It was busy but not full, with the odd empty table here and there. Towards the rear of the room two tables had been pushed together where an excited group were playing a dice game. But the true nature of the establishment was shown by the number of women, most of whom were sitting with the men, or holding onto the arms of the dice players and their audience, but a couple sat together, watching the room from a table by the hearth.

Another woman appeared as they walked in, hair grey, eyes astute. Gideon could see her doing a rapid mental calculation as to their worth as customers.

THE PHYSICIAN'S FATE

"Messieurs, it is always an honour to welcome new gentlemen to Le Cheval Rouge. Please be seated, I will send a couple of the girls over to find out how we may serve you tonight."

"Now I know why Richard Browne gave me such an odd look when I told him our intended destination." Lord said as he sat. "I think we made it above the penny-ha'penny whores in Madame's estimation, but I do wonder how far above? That will be interesting to see." Then he caught the expression on Gideon's face. "Don't tell me you have never been in a bordello before?"

Of course he had. It would be all but impossible to be a regular student in Oxford or at the Inns in London and not be dragged into one now and then by enthusiastic friends.

"It's not that," he protested.

Lord laughed. "Fear not, Sir Galahad, you will not be required to test your chastity tonight."

The two women who joined them were certainly well above the penny-ha'penny level. Both were young, with clear complexions, slender waists, generous smiles and bosoms. One had golden hair and the other was dark, it was she who spoke as they sat at the table.

"I am Manon, and this is Angélique. What can we do to entertain you gentlemen this evening?" As she spoke her gaze moved between the two of them then settled on Lord, the lashes lowered over her eyes and her lips slightly open in a pout. Gideon glanced away and found himself looking into the summer-sky eyes of Angélique who smiled at him almost shyly.

"Manon," Lord said, taking her hand in his and bestowing upon it a kiss. "I am delighted to make your acquaintance and I am very hopeful that you will be able to meet the needs of myself and my friend here."

Manon fluttered her lashes and breathed deeply so her breasts surged. "We can be *very* obliging, monsieur. Whatever your needs may be."

Gideon was painfully aware that Angélique had moved closer to him.

"Would you like me to serve you some wine, monsieur?" she asked breathily. "Or shall we go upstairs?"

"Wine," Gideon said quickly. "Yes, some wine. Thank you."

Angélique rose and Gideon saw her roll her eyes at Manon as she went off to get the promised drink. Lord, meanwhile, had pulled Manon onto his lap where she sat, giggling.

Gideon felt a little sick. Surely he did not mean to…?

"I am hoping you have what I need, *ma petite*," Lord was saying, and Manon smiled and ran a finger down his cheek, tracing the line of his jaw.

"For a man as handsome as you, always."

"Anything?" Lord asked

"*Mais oui,* anything at all," she agreed.

Lord leaned in and whispered something in her ear. Manon froze and her expression changed suddenly from playful to shocked. She turned in Lord's arms and tried to push him away, but he held her and finished what he was saying.

"*Non*," she said, struggling now. "Let me go."

Lord held her easily with one arm and with the other produced a gold coin, which he pushed into her cleavage.

"Does that make any difference?"

"No. I won't, and you can't make me." Her voice was rising now, and heads turned in their direction.

"For the love of God, what are you doing?" Gideon demanded, torn between shock and disgust. This was a side of Lord he would never have suspected. "Let the girl go. She has said 'no' clearly enough."

Angélique had come back with a jug and cups on a tray. She stood wide-eyed, uncertain whether she should rejoin the table. Gideon saw her shoot an anxious glance at Madame, who was frowning at Lord. Seeing she was reluctant to intervene made Gideon more determined to do so himself.

"Put her down," he demanded.

Lord laughed and released his unwilling companion abruptly.

"Thank you, Manon," he said as she slipped free of him. "You told me all I needed to know."

That made her face go white, stark against her dark hair.

"I said nothing," she hissed. "Nothing."

THE PHYSICIAN'S FATE

Then she ran for the door but before she could reach it Madame caught her and pulled her to one side. Lord watched them, looking amused. Then he beckoned to Angélique, still standing in nervous uncertainty nearby.

"Bring the wine then," he said.

"If you—" Gideon started, but Lord spoke across him.

"I only want the wine, but oh look, it seems we are to be honoured by the company of Madame as well."

Sure enough, like a galleon in full sail, Madame bore down on them her face thunderous.

"You must leave at once. You have no business here," she said sharply. Gideon had to admire her courage speaking like that to two armed men. Then her voice dropped. "Pierre Firmin is dead. You will not find him here."

Lord's lips tightened and he got to his feet. Gideon could see some of the men at the dice game had stepped aside from it and were walking over.

"You are right," Lord said. "If Firmin is dead we have no business here. All you need to do is tell me how he died, and we will be on our way."

Chapter Twelve

"Who is Matthew Rider?"

It was something Nick had wondered ever since Danny had hurled the name at Mags and this was the first opportunity there had been since to ask.

"He *was* a friend," Danny said, lying on the bed, his hands behind his head, staring up at the ceiling as if he might read portents from the patterns on the plaster.

They had been moved from both the immediate custody of John Gyfford and from the tavern he occupied and were now held in a comfortable enough townhouse in the middle of the well garrisoned town of Selby.

Nick had been taken there right after the duel and left alone overnight, locked in what must have been the guest room of a prosperous Selby resident. The smell of burning hair and flesh as they had pulled the unconscious Mags from the mouth of the hearth stuck to his nostrils. Danny had been taken by Fairfax. With whatever ordinances there must be against duelling, formal or informal ones, Nick had feared he might be made to pay the ultimate price.

It had been a relief when Danny was pushed into the room late the following day, clad only in shirt and breeches and no longer wearing his sword. In answer to all questions about what had happened he said nothing. After a while Nick stopped asking and slept.

In the morning they were brought a simple meal. Having eaten, Danny seemed only a little more communicative.

"Rider was a friend Mags killed?"

"That's right."

It was like persuading a stone to bleed.

"And you knew Mags had killed your friend before you went to work for him?"

"Yes."

THE PHYSICIAN'S FATE

"So you never were Mags' man at all. You just lied to win his confidence so you could betray him?"

It was something Nick had thought a lot about and that seemed to be the only way to make sense of the hatred he had seen in Danny's expression. He had thought the decision to kill Mags had only occurred after Danny changed his allegiance to Nick himself, but that no longer made sense.

Danny sat up and swung his legs over the side of the bed. Nick was occupying the only chair in the room, by the hearth, but he had turned it so he could see Danny.

"I joined Mags. Served as his man. Pretended loyalty and won his trust all with the sole intention of destroying him. Yes." From beneath his untidy hair Danny seemed to be studying Nick intensely, looking for something in his face.

"This man Rider must have been a good friend," Nick said. He was trying to think if there was anything or anyone, he would do the same for.

Danny stared at Nick for a few moments more, then shook his head as if in disbelief at something and lay back on the bed. "Yes," he said. "A very good friend."

By which point Nick was irritated with his attitude. Since Danny had made it clear any questions about what had happened to him since the duel and his appearance in the room were not going to be answered, he tried another tack.

"Is Mags still alive?"

There was a long silence before Danny replied.

"Mags lives. He may well recover, but he'll not ride or fight for some time."

"Which also means he may not recover?"

Danny rolled over onto his side and propped his head up on one hand.

"Which means he might die," he agreed. "But the word I have is that is not a likely outcome. Unfortunately."

It was strange. As if the man who had come back was not the same as the man he had sat beside in the tavern two days before. Nick was at a loss.

"What happens to us now?" he asked, not expecting any reply.

"To you, you mean?" Danny gave a sharp sigh. "I expect you'll get to enjoy an honourable imprisonment and be exchanged at some point unless you make the offer to change your allegiance. But as long as Mags lives, he will do his best to prevent that as he wants your title and your estate."

Nick felt the same sickness that had assailed him when he first heard Mags make the vile claim on Howe. He knew then that if there were any way to prevent that he would take it, no matter what it might mean. Even if that meant renouncing the king.

"And you?" he asked.

"And me...what?" Danny sounded genuinely confused by the question.

"What happens to you? I have some claim to being a man of rank, you haven't. Perhaps if I make it clear you are my man, I might be able to give you some protection and..." He trailed off suddenly aware that Danny was looking at him as if half-expecting him to start barking like a dog or clucking like a hen.

"This is no danger you can shield me from," he said. "I'm hoping John Gyfford will persuade Fairfax my service is worth overlooking what happened. If so, I'll be given a simple enough choice."

Nick suddenly grasped what was behind the change in Danny.

"You mean they would execute you if you don't change sides? Surely by the laws of war—?"

"I tried to kill one of their colonels in a duel," Danny said soberly. "They could easily have my life for that, with no need to look to the laws of war."

Nick stared, a terrible sense of helplessness welling from somewhere deep within him.

"There must be something we can do. The Covenant men, perhaps they—"

Danny rolled onto his back again. "May rally to you, but not to me. They are men who reward success but deplore failure. I failed."

And that was unarguable. It meant for Nick that he had to make a hard decision.

"I understand," he said at last.

THE PHYSICIAN'S FATE

"Understand what?" Danny moved his head to look at Nick, frowning as he did so.

"I understand you will need to turn your coat to save your life." Nick broke off and had to swallow before he could go on. "And that is what you *must* do."

For a moment there was silence then Danny looked away and there was a laugh from the bed.

"What's funny about that?" Nick demanded. It had cost him much of his pride to say the words, to give Danny permission to turn traitor so he might live.

"It's nothing funny," Danny said. "I'd have never thought to hear you..." His tone changed and he inclined his head. "But thank you, Sir Nicholas, if I am given the choice, I will choose life as you said I should."

He wasn't given the choice.

Neither of them were.

When the door next opened an hour later, they were ordered out of the room and the house to where a troop of horse waited. In their midst, Nick saw the young Lieutenant Fane who had also been taken prisoner at Tadcaster, looking pale, his hands lashed to the pommel of the saddle of the horse upon which he was mounted. Beside him were two more horses, held ready.

Gyfford was there but not mounted, his face looking grim. He held out an old coat for Danny, who was still in his shirtsleeves in the biting cold and spoke to him as he slipped it on.

"They are my men, so you'll be well looked after on the first part of the journey at least," then he added some more in a low voice. Danny shot him a sharp look, listened a little more and gave a nod, but Nick could see whatever had been said Danny thought little of it. Then Gyfford clapped him on the shoulder. "I'll be keeping your sword safe for you, Danny, so you'd better come back for it, you hear?"

As he spoke, Nick was being pushed onto one of the two waiting horses and a few moments later Danny was mounted on the other. Then, their reins being held by two of the troopers, pressed in the middle of the horsemen, but at least with hands unbound, they were taken through the streets of Selby at a brisk pace, which increased to a ground covering one, as soon as they were away from the town, heading east. There was no opportunity to talk as their escort seemed focused on speed and when Nick tried to ask the man leading his horse where they were going, he received no reply.

The answer only came late in the day after a fast and hard ride with only the briefest of breaks for food at dinnertime, when Danny was taken to join the commander of the troop and Nick was left with the surly trooper assigned to him. The land they traversed was mostly flat and they made good time over it following the course of an ever-widening river. Nick was not too surprised to find they were approaching the port town of Hull. There were strong defences around the town, even enough water to make it seem an island between the Humber and the River Hull itself. The impressive defensive works reminded Nick that all Royalist attempts so far to take the port had failed, including one by the King himself.

It was approaching twilight before they finally rode through the Beverly Gate and into the town. Nick, who had been to Hull only once before in his life, had little notion of where in the town they were taken.

So far Nick and Danny had been kept and treated differently from the young Lieutenant Fane who had defied Gyfford, but now the three of them were hustled into a house and thrust together into a single chamber at the end of a ground floor passageway. It had a weary-looking bedstead that tilted to one side, a small hearth which someone had supplied with sea-coal and a table with two chairs where a loaf of stale bread sat, together with a plate that held a few slices of cold meat, a jug of small beer and two cups with a candle stub for lighting.

"It looks," Nick observed when the door had been locked behind them, "as if they had prepared for two not three men."

Danny was already by the window. "Barred," he said, then glanced at the table. "I think they were not expecting me. Now Gyfford's men are no longer our captors, we should expect little comfort."

"You know why we are here." Nick didn't make it a question.

THE PHYSICIAN'S FATE

But before Danny could speak their third companion, who had been standing just inside the door rubbing at his newly unbound wrists, cut in.

"Who are you, sirs?" There was a chill of both hostility and fear in his voice. Nick decided he was probably no more than seventeen or eighteen. "I know you were taken at Tadcaster but thought you had accommodated with the rebels since you weren't held with me."

"Captain Sir Nicholas Tempest of Howe," Nick said, avoiding his accusation. "And you are?"

"Richard Fane, sir, cousin to the Earl of Westmorland."

"That," Danny said quietly, "makes sense."

Nick stared at Danny with a frown aware Fane was shooting a look at him too.

"What does? What do you know of why we are here?"

"I know why you two are being sent to London. They need Royalist officers of sufficient status."

"Sufficient status for what?" Fane asked, adding, "And who are you, sir?"

Danny made an exemplary, neat military bow.

"Currently I am a lieutenant as you are, Daniel Bristow, and I meant that you and Sir Nicholas have sufficient status to ensure parliament will be able to negotiate for some of its own notable prisoners who stand in danger of trial for treason. If that happens and they are condemned, then you would serve as counter hostages to be equally tried and condemned."

Fane's mouth was open in horror and Nick felt his flesh tighten as the hairs on his arms and shoulders lifted,

"We are to be *executed*?" Fane's voice was close to a squeak.

"Only if the king decides to find guilty of treason those Parliamentarian officers currently held in Oxford."

"But I have a cousin who is a colonel for Parliament, he will never allow—"

Danny started laughing then and shook his head. "You have it all planned, don't you? Whichever side wins this war the House of Fane shall stand."

Richard Fane looked furious at that but before he could snarl any riposte, Danny went on talking.

"Don't worry. I think the idea is that with you sitting in the Tower, reason will prevail. Instead of mutual executions there will be a mutual exchange of prisoners."

"Is there no way we could escape?" Nick realised that he had been counting on Danny to find a way out of this situation as he had out of all the others they had been caught in.

"Anything is possible," Danny said, but he sounded doubtful. He filled the cups and offered one to Nick, who took it and one to Richard Fane who refused. Then Danny broke the bread in three and started to eat one portion. When they did not join him, he gestured to the food. "Whatever comes, I promise you from long experience that facing it on a full stomach is easier than on an empty one."

Nick quelled his growing nausea and forced himself to eat, then a thought occurred, and he found his already small appetite shrinking away. If Danny was not being given the chance to turn his coat, where did that leave him?

"What of you?" he asked. "You have no influence or title."

Danny eyed the untouched cup he had offered to Fane then picked it up and drained it, wiping his mouth on his sleeve when he was done.

"That is so true," he said. "I am, however, something of a problem for Black Tom Fairfax and his father. According to Gyfford they were set to have me up before a military court. But then changed their minds or had their minds changed for them. Gyfford seemed to think the latter. Either way they decided to send me to London."

"For trial?" Nick wondered if the Covenant was behind the change of mind.

Danny wrinkled his nose as if at a bad smell.

"I will have to hope it doesn't come to that," he said. "Perhaps my charming smile and beaux yeux will help."

"If we're going to London," Fane asked suddenly, "why are we come here to Hull?"

Nick wondered then if they had been saddled with a half-wit.

THE PHYSICIAN'S FATE

"Because to travel by road to London from Yorkshire would take over a week with prisoners to escort, and the risk even so of our escape or rescue." Danny answered as if it were a perfectly normal question. His tone was one Nick was familiar with from many replies he had received to his own questions. He found that realisation acutely embarrassing and he looked away as Danny went on talking in the same patient manner. "However, by sea we might be safe in Tilbury within two or three days if the weather obliges. As the navy is held solidly by Parliament there is next to no chance at all that any might seek to rescue us. But all that is for tomorrow. Now, you should eat."

In the end, the young lieutenant was persuaded by Danny to at least drink a cup of the small beer. A bit to Nick's surprise Fane was asleep on the uneven bed soon after.

"He's just a boy," Danny said. "I expect his colonel cousin will make sure they don't hang him whatever happens. That is as well because I'd feel bad leaving him behind otherwise."

Nick felt a sudden jolt as his heart picked up its pace.

"Leave him behind?"

"Yes. I won't have the time to train him," The stub of the candle they had been left was close to extinguishing but there was enough light to see the expression on Danny's face.

"You have a plan to get us out of here?"

"I do. We need to start a fire."

"But we have a fire." Nick pointed to the hearth.

"We have that one," Danny agreed. "But that isn't going to make them open the door to get us out."

Nick looked from the hearth to the door and back, then he realised and looked at Danny.

"We could die," he said.

Danny shrugged.

"We could if they get us to London."

Nick decided the idea was either the product of a brilliant mind or a fevered one, but as they worked, he realised the mind was brilliant. Danny wasn't just setting fire to a random pile of combustible objects, he had sorted and placed them with great care against the bottom of the door, considering where each should go.

"It's a question of how fast things will burn and how much smoke they'll give off," Danny explained when Nick asked why. "We can use the slower burning things here and here to keep this from spreading too fast, but too much smoke and we'll choke ourselves."

"How do you even know such things?" Nick looked at the pile of wood and fabric and shook his head in bemusement. It seemed a strange area of expertise to have and one for which he could see little use.

"It's my job," Danny said. He got up from his crouch by the pile they had set against the door, picked up the dish their food had been left on and went over to the hearth. "I also find it interesting to experiment."

He scooped some embers onto the plate then went back to the miniature pyre he had constructed and carefully deposited them. Then he put the plate aside and brushed his hands on his breeches, grinning. For all the world reminding Nick of a schoolboy set on some trick against his master.

"What do we do when they open the door?" Nick asked, as the smoke began to curl. "And what if no one comes to help us?"

"Go piss in the bucket," Danny told him.

Nick blinked.

"What?"

"I said piss in the bucket. No. Wait. Let me go first." Having done so, Danny gestured to it. "Now you."

Realising that whatever else, Danny was deadly serious, Nick obliged. By which time Danny was hammering on the door. Nick realised the way the fire was set most of the smoke and flames were being pulled out under the door. It wouldn't be for long, but for the moment it must seem much worse from the outside than it was within.

"Fire!" The shriek came from the direction of the bed where Fane was now wide awake. The smoke had begun to fill upwards and backwards as well as be drawn under the door. It was getting harder to see and Nick began coughing as it caught his throat.

THE PHYSICIAN'S FATE

"Here." Nick felt a wet cloth thrust in his hands and for a moment thought of the piss bucket, but then smelt beer. "Put this over your face."

It helped, but not much. Fane was panicked and shouting, choking between the screams. Nick was close to the edge of his own courage. Only his faith in Danny kept him steady.

His back to the wall by the door, ready for any chance to escape, Nick could do nothing as the coiling smoke thickened into a lung-clogging cloud filling the room. He stood it as long as he could then, half-blind and choking, he threw himself across the room towards the chance of life-giving air from the window. That was when the door burst open and as it did the flames suddenly lifted and blazed, throwing up a fiery barrier in the doorway and blocking their possible escape.

There were men shouting outside. Fane screamed and Nick heard a sudden hiss, as of water poured on the flames, after which there was more smoke and less fire.

Afterwards, he wondered if Danny had meant to leave him along with Fane or perhaps he had simply trusted that Nick would be right behind him and not need shepherding. But at the time all he knew was that Danny had thrown the piss bucket at the fire in the door, partially dousing the flames, making more smoke and sending the men who received it in the face recoiling as he dived past. It was only thanks to the thickness of the smoke Nick was able to follow him before the men at the door recovered.

He rushed up the passageway and stumbled over a body on the floor. Danny's work he was sure, and the man's sword was gone. There was still a pistol which looked to be loaded and primed. Nick grabbed that and hurried on.

Behind, he could hear the chaos caused by the panicking Fane and the men trying to put out the fire. Ahead there were four men blocking the way, but the width of the door meant Danny was only having to face two of them. With his skill and ferocity, that should have been plenty, but these men also had pistols.

How he thought of it, Nick never after was sure, but it began as just an instinctive shout.

"Hold," he yelled. "I have him."

It was enough to confuse the attacking men. Danny, no doubt recognising both Nick's voice and the intent, disengaged and stepped slightly back. The man who had been lifting his pistol lowered it and, in that moment, Nick fired the pistol he had captured into the group of men and charged forward, only to find himself a pace behind Danny. The man with the pistol went down to Danny's blade, his pistol discharging into the air, then there was a door open to the night air and no one before or outside it.

They were free.

"You're making a habit of this," Danny said, breathless beside him. "Let's head down to the docks. The best place to hide out will be there and our best chance of a way out of Hull."

Then he was off and running and vanished down an alleyway, Nick a few paces behind. Thinking back to his one previous visit Nick recalled that the only way to the waterfront was to go down one of the sets of stairs. He hoped Danny knew that too because as they threaded through the dark streets there was evidence of a hue and cry being raised behind them. And that was when Nick realised that if they were caught they were dead men. They had killed in making their escape and if recaptured tonight he doubted they would even be accorded the pretence of a trial.

By the time they had reached a set of stairs they were no longer running. Danny had slowed to walk so they could mingle with those who lingered late in the waterside taverns. These served those who worked the docks, and the sailors presently in port, with cheap food, bad beer and poxed whores. A short time later, Nick was following Danny into the cramped and foetid common room of one of those taverns. Nick decided it was the most disreputable establishment he'd ever had the misfortune to enter. It was dark, stinking and packed. Despite being only a pace behind him, Nick lost sight of Danny at once. He had to push through the squalor in the direction he hoped Danny had taken. Even so, it was a couple of minutes before he managed to discover him.

There was a table at the back of the room with five men already playing cards and more looking on. Unbelievably Danny had had a span of cards in one fist. Though where he had found any coin to buy himself into the game, Nick had no idea. Standing in a place where his head could just avoid the low rafters and with his back against the wall, Nick wondered why, in this time of such extreme peril, Danny thought it wise or needful to indulge in a game of cards. He didn't recognise the game but was not surprised that Danny was winning well after the first couple of hands.

Then as if suddenly aware of his presence, Danny scooped in the winnings from the hand and grinned over at him.

"Hey, Nick, get us some drinks organised and for these good people too."

Nick felt the flesh on his face stiffen into a mask at such insolence. He was about to snarl a rebuke in the kind of terms such demanded when the glint of cold in Danny's eyes, captured by the guttering candle flame from the table, gave him pause.

Danny was right, here they had to pretend to be as equals or be betrayed.

This tavern was the only one where they could seem not to be out of place despite their filthy condition. In the dark, it was to be hoped the finer quality of the cloth they wore might pass unnoticed. They could even hope that such a vile place might be passed over in any search for them.

Forcing a rictus grin on to his face, he took the handful of small coins and tavern tokens Danny was holding out. It didn't take long to find one of the slatterns who was supposed to be serving. She was wedged against the wall, skirts hitched up to her naked buttocks. One sagging breast hung loose over the lacings of her bodice with its painted nipple bobbing up and down as a customer, cock out of his breeches, took his pleasure in full view of the room.

Seeing Nick and his handful of coins the woman looked over and gave him a near toothless leer.

"You'll have to wait your turn, my pet," she said.

Nick turned quickly away.

Instead, he found a boy collecting pots and pressed a coin on him so someone would come to the card table to serve them. Then he went back to see Danny was now letting the other men at the table win some of the hands, as his own pile of coin was diminished. Either that or Danny had hit a run of extremely bad luck, but from his cheerfully intent expression, Nick decided it was a deliberate ruse.

By the time the drinks had arrived and been shared around, Danny was clearly bosom friends with his fellow gamblers, and the conversation changed. It seemed one of the men worked on a small goods barge which plied the river Ouse and could, for a fee, get them out of Hull with no one the wiser.

The fee was reduced over the next few hands of cards. By the time Danny and Nick were following the man through a stinking passageway at the back of the tavern, past someone relieving himself, it seemed they were doing him a favour letting him smuggle them from the town.

The barge was at an untidy mooring, and, by lantern's light, Nick could see there was little enough aboard to be taken upriver—some crates and a handful of barrels. But their new friend, Jarrett, said by the time they set out there would be fresh fish too.

"You can take us to York?" Nick asked.

Jarrett spat.

"Not what we agreed. The barge is for Selby, and you can take yourselves on from there."

Nick felt sick.

"Selby? But—"

"I know you're keen to get back to your girl in York," Danny said, gripping Nick's arm hard. "You'll just have to be patient another day or two."

Once Jarrett had left them, Nick wasn't so willing to be silenced.

"What are you thinking sailing us back to Selby?" he hissed.

They were sitting with their backs to the well roped barrels, looking out over the dark water of the Humber. The walls of Hull strode along the far bank of the river to protect the port.

"We don't have a lot of choice in the matter," Danny said softly. "The only way we'll be able to leave is on a boat and we don't have the luxury of choice. The one I found us is, by chance, heading up to Selby, so that is where we must go. Besides," he added, "my sword is in Selby."

Nick failed to see that as any reason to place their lives at risk.

THE PHYSICIAN'S FATE

"A sword is not hard to replace," he said scathingly. "It is folly to return to Selby, we would be like—like," he struggled to think of a way of saying how dangerous it would be, "like Daniel walking into the den of lions."

Danny laughed.

"I don't see my namesake did badly out of that in the end. And that sword would be impossible to replace. But think about it, where in all England would no one look to find us or expect us to go?"

"There's a good reason for that."

"Think. They'll be searching every vessel to Newcastle or abroad or points along the coast, looking them over tip to stern," Danny said. "If they bother doing a check on those heading upstream, it'll be no more than a glance because—as you keep saying—only a fool would head back."

It was the kind of logic that Nick had learned he would never understand nor master, but that Danny seemed to bring through all the time. Like setting a fire when trapped in a room. He sighed and let it go. It was just good to know he had a man like Danny at his side.

The night was cold and even with some of the heavy tarred canvas to put about them as a shelter, Nick was sure he would struggle to sleep. But he woke to the sound of movement and shouting, as the promised fish was being loaded in the thin light before dawn. There was no sign of Danny, but he decided it was safer to remain under the tarpaulin than venture out and risk being seen.

Then they were underway and looking out from under his concealing canvas, Nick saw the walls of Hull pass by and then they were in the estuary and rocking with the waves, the water, lifting and swirling about the barge, pushing them inland as it flowed up the river Humber with the force of the tide.

Danny appeared, wearing an old smock over his shirt instead of a coat, hair crushed under a knitted bonnet and looking his usual cheerful self.

"I've been helping them load. No one seemed much interested in this barge at all, though they have turned the whole town inside out looking for us and they are not letting anyone in or out of the gates this morning." He dropped down to sit beside Nick and reached under the smock to pull out a slightly stale loaf which he tore in two and held half out. "You stayed solid under fire back there," he said.

"Under fire? You mean in the fire," Nick said with a brief laugh, taking the bread and devouring it with real appetite. It was interesting how little thought he gave nowadays to the quality of the food he ate.

"No, I mean it," Danny said. "You could have panicked like Fane, left me to get killed."

Nick wondered what he should say to that. Then he had a thought.

"It is alright. I understand why you had to use my name as you did in that alehouse—and why you might need to again before we are safely back. I know you meant no impertinence by it."

Danny said nothing. He didn't even turn his head. His gaze stayed fixed on the swollen river which carried them upstream on the back of the tide, as the keening gulls overhead circled and called. Then he shook his head as if something had disappointed him.

"If you don't want to come into Selby," he said, "I'll find you a boat for York when we get there."

Nick sighed. He knew that this was a test of his ability. His father's words in York were no less vivid for all that had happened since.

"If your sword is that important, I'll come with you to Selby. Besides, there may be a chance to finish what you started with Mags, and we need to do that."

Then Danny looked at him, his expression one of bemusement. He shook his head again and laughed. "You defeat me, Sir Nicholas, completely defeat me. I only hope you are as much an enigma to the Covenant men." Then his face became serious. "And yes, it was always part of my plan to make sure of Mags. Both our lives depend on that, whatever else may happen."

THE PHYSICIAN'S FATE

Chapter Thirteen

When they returned from Le Cheval Rouge, Gideon was still smarting from the way Lord had behaved and his own complete misinterpretation of it. He wasn't sure whether he should be embarrassed that he had made the wrong assumption or outraged that Lord had acted in the way he had.

Lord met Gideon's accusation, hand on the latch of the door to his room, without rancour.

"*Thou hast chastised me, and I was chastised, as a bullock unaccustomed to the yoke.* I am sure you feel you have good cause. But I do put it to you that causing Manon a few moments of distress by threatening her if she did not reveal what she knew of Firmin, was a better way to gain the information we needed than making the floor slippery with blood. Besides," he went on, "she was recompensed more for those few minutes she spent with me than she will receive from all her other clients together for the rest of the night. As for what we have learned, let us talk of it in the morning." And with that he had gone into his room and closed the door.

With so much on his mind, Gideon assumed sleep would evade him, but almost as soon as he closed his eyes, he was opening them again on a new day. As soon as he was dressed, he descended the stairs to knock on Lord's door.

The bed looked so neat it might have been unslept in, and Lord himself was sitting in the window, knees supporting the book he was reading. He closed the book as Gideon entered the room and set it aside on the table beside him, without getting up.

"Pierre Firmin was poisoned with laudanum," Lord said. "Which leaves us where we started. Someone is determined to ensure that their tracks are covered."

Firmin, the Madame had told them, had been found dead in his rooms at Le Cheval Rouge earlier in the evening and he had an empty bottle of laudanum with him. The Madame said she had no idea if he had received any visitors that day. He had a separate entrance to his rooms and no, no one had seen or heard anything and whilst she had thanked Lord for his coin, it made no difference to her memory or that of anyone else. After dark anyone could come and go and not be marked.

Gideon had concluded that the woman wasn't lying. Aside the fact that the amount of money Lord was willing to offer her would have been enough to persuade even the most reluctant, she was also in obvious terror of being reported to the authorities. It was only the assurance that wouldn't happen which had opened her mouth and secured her honesty.

"Except," Gideon said, "why leave the empty bottle?"

Lord took it out of his pocket and studied it.

"I don't know. Perhaps to make it look as if the man took his own life? Although that doesn't seem to have occurred to our Madame. If she were to have allowed the authorities to know of his death, this bottle would strongly suggest that. Though in the case of such a man I doubt anyone would have cared about the cause of his death or troubled to look into it."

"But whoever did it was risking a link being made between the deaths of Demoiselle Tasse and Pierre Firmin." Gideon pointed out.

"If there were anyone to make that link."

"We have."

Lord nodded. "Yes. We have. By chance. A chance the murderer could not foresee. But what does it give us to help Jensen?"

"I am not sure, except it shows someone is killing with laudanum who could not possibly have been Anders." Gideon thought as he spoke. "It tells us one thing though, whoever killed Geneviève Tasse it was not Gaspard Proulx."

Lord put the laudanum bottle on the table with his book and sat up, swinging his legs down from the window embrasure. "You seem very certain of that."

Gideon considered for a moment shuffling his thoughts as he might when trying to set out the facts of a legal issue.

"Alright. We had a theory that someone killed Proulx because he had killed Geneviève Tasse and had managed to cover his tracks and successfully blame Anders. That theory would have had

THE PHYSICIAN'S FATE

Yolande Savatier threatened so as to keep the name of Pierre Firmin from us—from me as your name was not and is not linked with this yet."

"Except by the duchesse, she knows of my interest and the Brownes..." He trailed off then shook his head. "But, no. I don't think that is important. Go on, I interrupted you."

"Well, the point is that Proulx was only a suspect because of the laudanum and being someone with access to that and to Demoiselle Tasse. By using laudanum to kill Firmin, it tells us that his killer—the man who surely hired Firmin to kill Proulx—must also be someone with access to supplies from the Bureau. So, that would make it much more likely that the killer of the two is the same man than that there are two rogue physicians murdering people with laudanum."

Lord frowned and then pushed himself to his feet.

"You believe that Firmin was killed by laudanum because the murderer lacked any other means of doing so—and unaware that Madame would never inform the authorities—left the bottle to make it seem a suicide?"

Gideon nodded.

"But then why use laudanum? If our killer has access to the dispensary of the Bureau, why not choose another poison? It would risk a link being made between the two killings"

That was not so easy to answer.

"Because it was what he happened to have with him when the opportunity was there? Or perhaps because he knew how to put the laudanum into Pierre Firmin's drink without him noticing? After all, we know our murderer had already achieved that with Geneviève Tasse. Why take any risk of a violent man like Firmin noticing an attempt to poison him?"

For a moment Lord stood like a statue.

"You think our rapist and murderer set Pierre Firmin to kill you because he knew you were asking about the killing of Gaspard Proulx? After Firmin failed to kill you, he had to kill Firmin because Firmin could identify him, and he couldn't risk that you might track Firmin down."

"That's the only conclusion that makes sense of it all to me," Gideon admitted.

"Then why kill Gaspard Proulx? Because that is what led to all this. Had Proulx not been killed all we would have learned from Yolande Savatier was that she had made the laudanum."

Gideon shrugged. "I truly do not know. Perhaps, like Yolande Savatier, he saw something he shouldn't have. But I do believe if we can find out who hired Firmin to kill Proulx, then we will have the man who killed Geneviève Tasse."

"Except our killer seems very good at covering his tracks with ever more murders."

"I think he is a superb liar too," Gideon said, "a clever man who thought he could throw me off the scent by pretending sympathy and then shocking me so I was disoriented and could not think clearly. A very clever man."

That made Lord stare at him.

"Josselin Voclain?"

"Who else could it be?" Gideon observed. "Renaudot gave us the list of those allowed entry to the Palais de Cardinal. Himself, Anders, Gaspard Proulx, Josselin Voclain and someone called Claude Charron. Renaudot says he was working on *La Gazette* at that time, I am sure we can ascertain if that is true. Claude Charron was not in Paris at all that day, Renaudot said he was attending a funeral. Only Anders, Proulx and Voclain went to the Palais. If it wasn't Anders or Proulx…"

"I think," Lord said softly, his tone dangerous and intent, "we need to have a quiet conversation with Monsieur Voclain, a very private, quiet conversation. We need to find where he lives. In fact, I think—"

He broke off and glanced at the door and a moment later Gideon heard the sound of footsteps. Then came a soft knock on the door.

"Sir Philip? Might I have a word?"

Richard Browne.

Lord crossed to the door in three easy strides and opened it, standing back as soon as he had done so and holding an arm out to his side in a gesture to show Browne he was welcome to enter.

"Of course. Is it a confidential matter?"

THE PHYSICIAN'S FATE

Taking the hint Gideon stepped towards the door, but Browne lifted a hand and shook his head, carefully closing the door behind himself.

"Actually, it is a matter which concerns you both. Do either of you know a man called Ellis Ruskin?"

There could have been worse moments for his London life to catch up with him, Gideon was sure, but at the time he found it hard to think of many.

"Who is he?" Lord asked.

"He has called twice at the house now saying that a friend of his is staying here, a Mr Lennox who he says is a Chancery lawyer from London. He harangued my wife yesterday, becoming most insistent. He even implied I might be detaining the gentleman against his will as he could think of no reason for a man of Mr Lennox's sympathies to be staying under my roof."

At which point Gideon knew he had to speak up. He had no doubt at all that Lord would produce a bland denial. But Gideon knew Ellis well enough to be very certain he wouldn't desist if he thought Gideon might be in any danger. That could cause not just a socially awkward situation, but one with international ramifications. After all, Ellis was attached to the Parliamentarian delegation in some capacity and Gideon was staying in the house of the king's agent and in company with his special envoy.

"It is me he is seeking to speak to," Gideon said, and two sets of eyes looked at him, Browne's wary and Lord's curious, as if he wondered why Gideon had chosen this path and how he would walk it. "I have been mistaken for this man Lennox before. We share the same given name and I have been told we look very much alike. If you can tell me where Mr Ruskin is staying, I will visit him and ensure he understands his mistake. I wouldn't have him troubling you and your family, especially at such a sensitive time."

He hoped the doubt he read in Browne's face was around the wisdom of allowing Gideon to deal with the matter himself rather than his claim of it being mistaken identity. But whichever it was, Lord resolved the issue.

"I will go with you," he said. "I can vouch for who you are if need be and besides, I have some interest in speaking with someone from his mission and this would give me the excuse to do so."

"If you are sure, Sir Philip. I would not wish to in any way compromise your embassy from the king," Browne said, frowning.

"Neither do I," Lord assured him. "And far from doing that, this might even assist in the matter. At the moment the entire French court is set on keeping our two embassies apart, as if to allow us to meet would be to place match to frizzen. That has caused me no end of problems. This meeting will settle things between us socially. After which we can cordially loathe each other in the same company if need be."

Browne looked troubled still but nodded. "Very well. I will leave it in your hands. I am sure you will let me know if there is an outcome from this that I need to bear in mind ongoing."

He left with a brief bow to Lord and a nod to Gideon.

"We need to find out where they are staying," Gideon said. Then he sighed. "It is another complication in affairs."

"I already know where they are," Lord assured him. "I have men watching their every move and reporting on each conversation the Parliamentarian mission has engaged in. I have had since I learned they were here. It seemed safer."

Gideon stared at him.

"Then you already knew that Ruskin had been here—yesterday and today?"

"Of course. I had planned to raise the matter with you and discuss what we should do about it, but this with Firmin seemed a little more pressing." He paused and looked thoughtful. "I think we will pay a visit unannounced to our rebellious compatriots. Meanwhile I shall put matters in hand and discover where friend Voclain can be found. But first who is Ellis Ruskin and what is he? More specifically, what is he to you?"

"Ellis Ruskin is, like me, a lawyer. We studied together. Unlike me though, he has always been a bit of a firebrand politically. He has close friends who are much caught up in justifying the cause of Parliament against the king and he is an admirer of men like Pym and Lilburn."

Lord looked thoughtful. "He is a friend of yours?"

Gideon hesitated to answer. Had someone asked him a year ago, when matters were tense but had not yet reached the point of war, he would have undoubtedly said that he counted Ellis amongst his circle of friends and as a man he admired. But even then, he had instinctively stepped aside from the fiery words and heated debates, absented himself when he knew such were likely to happen. Not that he wasn't interested in them and he often found himself in agreement with much of what they said, it was simply he had no wish to make himself a target for hostility—or to lose any clients.

Then a few months ago, with armies being mustered even if no war had officially been declared, it had become ever more difficult to walk the neutral line and most of the men he knew had given up trying to do so. It had been those like Ellis Ruskin that had made him decide to remove himself from London when the chance came with an offer of work from the Hostmen of Newcastle. He had fondly imagined that away from the political bonfire London had become he might be able to keep himself free of the problematic demands to nail his loyalty to one extreme cause or creed or another, only to find the entire nation had caught fire as he did so.

"Ellis was a friend when I was last in London," Gideon admitted. "I am not sure he would be now. I worked for his father quite a few times, Sir Isaac Ruskin, who is a Serjeant-at-Law."

Lord nodded but didn't say anything right away. It dawned on Gideon that Lord might already know that anyway. How many enquiries had Lord made about him since they first met? He was very sure Lord had the reach and the network to do so, but that he might have done, sat ill.

"You could be advised," Lord said, breaking across his thoughts, "to allow Mr Ruskin to think he still holds your friendship. Let him believe that your presence in Paris under an assumed name is not so far removed in purpose from his own."

That took Gideon aback.

"You mean I should imply that I am a spy for Parliament in the Brownes' house?"

Lord smiled approvingly. "That is exactly what I am suggesting."

"But he'd know," Gideon objected.

"Would he? My understanding is that with the profusion of committees that have sprung up to oversee the various aspects of government in London and the pushing for power and influence between them, it is often a case of the left hand being completely bemused by what the right is doing." Lord made a dismissive gesture. "If he asks your authority, you just hint that it is a secret committee, so secret even the secret committee he answers to has not heard of it."

"But when he returns to London—"

"He will either say nothing, because he will feel he knows a secret that his secret committee do not know. Or, if he does speak out, all that will happen is that the various committees will be chasing each other down rabbit holes trying to find out which one you work for. They will all deny it, but then none of the others will believe them as if it was their committee you were working for so secretly, they would deny it too."

Gideon realised he was gaping and closed his mouth. "And on what pretext are you visiting the Parliamentarian embassy?"

"I am going to summon them to their true loyalty. I shall ask them to abandon their rebellious ways and submit—through me—to the king, who will then in his mercy grant them pardon."

"You have the authority to do that?" Gideon was shocked.

Lord considered. "I was not told I didn't have that authority. But seeing as they will refuse and harangue me anyway, it will not matter."

"What if they refuse to receive you?"

"That is why I travel with you," Lord said, and he gave Gideon a brief grin. "You are my entrée into these elevated circles. You are my John the Baptist—*the voice of him that crieth in the wilderness, Prepare ye the way of the Lord*. So I am very sure they will receive me."

An hour later they set out. The four men who had been with them the previous evening were now joined by two more. All were well mounted, dressed and equipped as an appropriate escort to a man of Lord's rank and status. It wasn't quite the show that would have greeted Paris had Lord been able to ride in on that first day, but it looked impressive enough.

"Did the king get his horse?" Gideon asked as they navigated through the narrow streets as well as they could manage. Paris really was easier to cross on foot.

"He did," Lord said. "Yesterday. He was very pleased with it too. Not that it changes anything diplomatically for us, of course. I am hoping this visit will help us more with that."

The Parliamentarian delegation had been accommodated in the home of a wealthy merchant—a wine merchant. A detail which made Lord laugh as he pointed it out.

"In Paris," he explained, "they have six merchant guilds—the drapers, fine grocers, furriers, hatters, goldsmiths and the most powerful of all, the mercers. They live like a merchant aristocracy lording it over all others who they see as mere tradesmen no matter their level of wealth. The vintners have been trying since the dawn of time to gain entry to that cabal. But no matter how much they might fight amongst themselves, the Big Six will unite in a solid front against them. They have declared that," Lord put on a pompous, self-righteous tone, "*avarice, fraud and deceit are the inseparable characteristics of wine merchants.*" He shook his head in disbelief. "Which means it is truly ironic that these men are staying in the home of a mere vintner."

"More to the point," Gideon said, thinking of the kind of men he had encountered who were most strong against the king, "most of them probably abstain from alcohol anyway."

"You think so?" Lord shook his head. "This is hardly a goodly and godly delegation unless your friend Ellis is of that persuasion. They sent a viscount as titular head of the embassy, and he is anything but abstemious by reputation from any vice you care to name. He would not be my choice of ambassador, but then they could hardly send merchants and lawyers to treat with the King of France."

At which point their conversation had to stop as they were entering the narrow gate to a stable yard. In Paris that meant little more than a carriage house with a couple of stalls. They alighted and Lord leaned in to whisper one last warning.

"Do not mind me. Remember, we're not supposed to be friends."

Then they were shown into a house which was the wealthiest Gideon had yet seen in Paris itself. Like most Parisian dwellings it wasn't spacious, but it was richly accoutred with precious art, gold plate and costly hangings. The vintners might not be permitted the status of a guild, but this one at least was not allowing that to set any limits upon his material aspirations. Gideon later discovered that the wealth he saw owed less to wine and more to the fact that this particular wine merchant was also one of the men who acted as financiers and bought and sold everything from government bonds to government offices.

But whatever its source, the wealth was self-evident and on display. Monsieur André Villeneuve, their owner, however, was not. Instead, they were greeted by a group of three men, one of whom was Ellis Ruskin. He frowned hard at Gideon. Of the other two one was a man in his fifties soberly dressed and with a wary expression, but the man who stepped forward to greet them looked almost as suave and fashionable as Lord himself. He was in his late thirties or early forties, with very blue eyes and a charming smile.

"Philip Lord? Your reputation precedes you. I wish we had been given more notice of your visit then we could have entertained you in a more fitting style. But please, come through, I am most interested to hear what you might wish to say."

Lord made a deep bow, with a flourish.

"My lord viscount, it is Sir Philip. I was made knight banneret on Kineton field after defeating those in arms against the king. But I forgive you. I am sure such news is slow to travel to London." He gave a brief and most supercilious grin.

"Sir Philip," the viscount corrected himself and the charming smile was renewed, "I am pleased to make your acquaintance."

"And I am most interested to make the acquaintance of a man who, having been raised from the commonality by one monarch to a position of rank and status, lavished with gifts and honours, proceeds to repay that largesse and generosity by taking arms against his benefactor's son."

There was a frosty silence and the viscount's smile became fixed.

"Fine words from a traitor," one of the men behind him murmured in an overloud undertone. It was hard to be certain which of the two, but Gideon thought it sounded like Ellis.

"The viscount and I do have some things in common," Lord said amicably, "but not that. We were both acquainted with King James in our younger years. Perhaps we can compare notes?"

That made the viscount draw in a sharp breath.

"We have much to discuss," he said, his tone now much less friendly and welcoming than before. "You'd better come through."

Lord inclined his head and followed the viscount into the chamber indicated and the older, unknown, man went with him. Gideon assumed that would be the real leader of the embassy of which the viscount was the figurehead. He made a move to follow but a hand touched his arm.

"Gideon? It *is* you. What on earth are you doing in Paris—and in company with such a man as that malignant monster whilst staying under the roof of Richard Browne of all men?"

Gideon glanced at the backs of the departing group and then back to Ellis.

"I am afraid you have mistaken me for someone else," he said in an almost theatrically loud voice whilst dropping a wink at the startled Ellis. "I am Gideon Fox and am staying with the Brownes as we have mutual friends."

"Oh."

Ellis seemed lost in uncertainty and Gideon realised that his recent enforced training in dissimilation had far exceeded anything most of his contemporaries had yet been pushed to learn. In fact, seeing Ellis, a man he had admired less than a year before, Gideon felt an odd mix of new emotions. It was as if he was looking into a mirror that reflected his past and the stark contrast between the man he had been and the man he was now momentarily shocked him.

"I—er," Ellis cleared his throat. "Perhaps you would take some refreshment then, sir, as we wait for the others to conclude their discussions."

It was a clumsy save and had there been any other than servants to witness it Gideon would have thought them both condemned as liars. But he smiled and made a polite bow before following Ellis to another room that had a window onto the small courtyard behind the house.

There were expensively upholstered fauteuils and beautiful little inlaid tables as well as a hearth with decorative firedogs upon which sat a glowing log fire, warming the room against the cold winter's day outside. It was a delightfully cosy and welcoming room, but Gideon remained standing, and Ellis seemed no more inclined to sit once he closed the door firmly behind them.

"Gideon? What is going on?"

When Lord had outlined the plan of deception Gideon had wondered if he would be able to carry it off. But seeing Ellis now, he knew it would be no issue at all. The man he remembered as being perceptive and astute, he saw was, in reality, naive and idealistic. As naive, he realised, as he himself had been four scant months ago before he had met Sir Philip Lord. Four months? It seemed half a lifetime.

"I'm here for much the same reasons you are," Gideon explained. "My loyalties haven't changed, I assure you."

"But..." Ellis shook his head in obvious confusion. "Where have you been? The last I had heard you took some work somewhere in the north—Carlisle, was it?—last summer. Then nothing until I see you in company with that delinquent, Lord, going into the house of the king's man here in Paris. I couldn't for the life of me understand how that might happen. You were always a sound man, Gideon. Your father was—"

Gideon broke in quickly. He was not in the frame of mind to hear any kind of panegyric about his father, the man who Gideon had seen make his mother's life a misery and his own feel oppressed and empty.

"I can't tell you the details," Gideon said. "Last summer I was approached by someone, and they asked me to undertake work on

THE PHYSICIAN'S FATE

behalf of those who are of our mind. It is work that means I need to appear to hold views other than those I truly do, so I may gather intelligence for our cause." Ellis was staring at him now with wide eyes. "These are very dangerous and very dark times, and I am doing my small part in it."

The words echoed hollowly in his own ears. In truth he was in closer agreement with the political views Ellis held, more than those of any he had met who supported the king. His only tie to the royalist side was Lord's own affiliation and that itself had nothing to do with politics or religion. He pushed the thought away. This was not a time or place he could afford to think such things.

"I understand," Ellis said. "It was much the same way for me when I was approached about this mission and told I must speak of it to no one."

"Then will you keep my real identity—and that you have even seen me here—a secret?" Gideon asked. Suddenly ashamed of himself, and ashamed that he was glad Ellis was so willing to accept his lies. "Even when you get back to London? Because if those who I am working for thought I had betrayed myself in even the smallest degree…"

He realised then he had overplayed a little because Ellis was frowning.

"I could not conceive that such good and godly men would—"

"I meant they would remove me from this work," Gideon said quickly. "I am well established now so that would set back our cause maybe months."

Ellis' face cleared.

"Yes. Yes, I can see that." Then he gripped both Gideon's shoulders. "You need have no fears on my account. My lips are sealed. I will tell the rest of the embassy that I was mistaken. That you are not who I thought you were, but that you were most gracious about the matter."

Gideon managed a smile.

"Thank you. That means a great deal."

"What you are doing is hazardous and brave," Ellis went on. "I always admired the way you stood firm for justice and the rule of law, but this is something I would never have believed you might do. You were the one of us most wanting a quiet life when you could have it, the one urging us to caution and decrying the pamphlet writers as dangerous fanatics. Of all the people, I would never have suspected you of such a thing."

"That is perhaps why I was approached," Gideon suggested, thinking how the man he had been last summer had regarded travelling to Newcastle as the very height of adventure. "Why were you asked to come to France?"

Ellis laughed. "Much as I would like to say it was my wit or my standing, I believe it was probably my linguistic ability. My mother is French, a Huguenot, and she taught me from the cradle. The others here all have some grasp of the language, but I am the only one fully fluent. I have been much involved with the negotiations."

"They are going well?" Gideon now had no idea whether he wished that they prospered or did not. He was struggling with a sense of disorientation as if he no longer had solid ground beneath his feet.

"Not as well as we might wish. At first, King Louis was refusing to meet with that base mercenary who came rattling a begging bowl for Charles Stuart. At that point we had some hopes we could persuade him to declare his neutrality in the affairs of England at least. But then, two nights ago, Browne managed to arrange for Lord to be admitted to a court event. As soon as King Louis saw him, he was fawning over the man. Saying he was the saviour of Paris or some such rubbish. It was unedifying to witness, as if...." Ellis broke off and shook his head, his lips pursed in distaste.

"You mean it was improper?"

"Let us just say their behaviour was not as is befitting men of any status. But then this French court is the most dissolute place. Exactly as one might expect from Popish heathens." He shook his head. "Anyway, after that King Louis was so taken by the mercenary that we are now all but ignored. Unless the others can make some headway with him, I fear our agenda has been swept away. Or unless..." He looked at Gideon speculatively. "Unless there is any way you could find to thwart Lord's petition or ensure he is kept from court these next few days until they begin their pagan celebrations of Christmas? You would be doing our cause a great service if you were able to arrange that."

Gideon felt sick. If it weren't so horrible that he was being asked to somehow incapacitate Lord, the impossibility of it would be laughable. But from somewhere he dredged a thoughtful look, as if the idea was not as abhorrent as it was foolish.

"If there is a way, I will look to find it," he lied.

It was as well that they were disturbed then, summoned back to the room they had left. Matters between Lord and rest of the Parliamentarian mission had clearly deteriorated. Lord seemed at ease, his expression as amiable as it had been when he arrived. But the faces of all the other men were tight with controlled anger.

"Oh, look who it is," Lord greeted them. "Now, did we decide if this is the Gideon from Ephesus or Syracuse? Or indeed if this is not a Gideon at all but perhaps an Esau or a Jacob? Though with that hair surely Esau?"

Gideon recognised the tone and forbore to reply, merely taking his leave politely and then following in Lord's wake, teeth gritted. He was subjected to a running commentary on the vintner's possessions, which Lord picked up and discarded as they passed them.

"Garish and crass. This man thinks to impress by encrusting all he owns with cheap, poorly cut gemstones. And look, the foot of some poor Greek god. I wonder what he did with the rest. Probably dismembered it and sold off each portion separately to ensure the highest profit. I can only guess which part of anatomy earned him the most. Oh, and what is this?" Lord stopped and picked up a beautiful, chased silver goblet clearly of some antiquity. "It looks to me as if André Villeneuve has been raiding the sacristy of his church—or perhaps he made a trade against supplies of communion wine. I suppose we will never know."

Lord carried the chalice with him to the door in a careless grip, twirling the precious thing by its stem in his fingers, then dropped it into the surprised hands of a servant as they left the house.

With his intestines shrivelling from embarrassment, Gideon was grateful to be back on the horse that had brought him across Paris and returning to the Brownes' residence. Having been forced to drink to the dregs the grim reality of his situation in conversation with Ellis, the grotesque masquerade of Sir Philip Lord at his most despicable was not a good second draught.

"Whatever it is that is giving you the look of someone fed for a week on a diet of lemons," Lord said as they dismounted, "it will have to wait until after we have been to see Josselin Voclain."

And that was something Gideon couldn't argue. Whatever else he might regret he could not regret or abandon his efforts to see Anders cleared of the charge against him. Placed against the cold knowledge that he and Lord were all that stood between an innocent man and a guilty verdict, everything else was unimportant.

"You know where we can find Voclain?"

"Right now, I might hazard a guess he will be at the Bureau, but I hope to have his address shortly," Lord looked at Gideon with a critical and appraising gaze. "We will need to avoid attracting attention and whereas I would pay good money to see you in your water-vendor attire, I think something a little less remarkable in appearance is probably more in order."

THE PHYSICIAN'S FATE

Chapter Fourteen

In the end Gideon's outfit was much less remarkable in appearance than that of a water-vendor. Both clad much as any servant might who worked for one of the many reasonably affluent households, he and Lord walked anonymously through the cold streets of Paris. Hunching shoulders beneath his thin coat, Gideon shivered as the snow swirled about them. It was getting on for twilight and the dark skies and narrow streets did little to help with what illumination there was. At least now, Gideon thought, they could see where to walk to avoid the worst of the muck and slush puddles. He hoped Lord had given some consideration to providing them with light for the way back.

Josselin Voclain rented rooms that were situated above a glover's shop. The shop was clearly prosperous. If not catering for the very wealthiest Parisians, it served the better off of the middling sort. It had spread its front over two buildings and the owner lived in one and rented out the rooms above the other. The servant who let them in didn't trouble to show them up, merely gesturing to the stairs. A baby was crying somewhere.

The lower floors would be the more expensive, but Voclain had his rooms two floors up, on the level below those who were right under the roof. It was clear he was not a wealthy man despite his profession, which would usually be the gateway to a very comfortable income.

That was the first odd thing Gideon noticed. The second was that as they approached his door it became obvious that the baby they had heard crying since they entered the building was on the other side of it.

Exchanging a glance of confusion with Lord, who shrugged in return, Gideon rapped on the door. It was opened by a young woman who was well dressed, holding the baby and seeking to soothe it. Gideon wondered why he had not heard that Voclain had a wife and child. But that didn't mean, of course, that he was any less likely to be a rapist and murderer.

The woman frowned.

"What do you want?" she demanded, her brown eyes anxious. "I paid the rent on time. The baby is teething so she will cry sometimes. I have given her something to make her stop."

Gideon realised that to her they might well appear to be the kind of men an irritated landlord might employ to pressurise a tenant.

"We are not here about the rent or the baby," he said, offering what he hoped was a reassuring smile. "We're here to talk with Monsieur Voclain."

Her expression changed to relief, chased away by a polite smile.

"My apologies, the landlord here is very strict, and he has threatened more than once that if the baby cries we will have to find somewhere else to live. That is not easy in Paris as I am sure you will know. You had better come in." Then she turned and called. "Josselin!"

She took them through the small dwelling to what was clearly a mixture of parlour and dining room. Voclain must have been sitting by the window trying to catch the last of the light on the pages of his book, because he got up quickly, clutching the book to his chest in momentary alarm as Gideon and Lord turned came into the room.

"Josselin, these men have come to consult you," the woman said. "I will be in the bedroom with the baby."

Then she was gone, and the sound of the baby crying was softened again by there being a door between them and the cries.

"Do I know you?" Voclain asked, squinting his eyes to see them better.

"We met at the Bureau," Gideon explained, and at once Voclain's face cleared.

"Of course, Monsieur Fox. I didn't recognise you. You look..." He trailed off awkwardly.

"Indeed, I do," Gideon said, agreeing with the unspoken assessment. "I apologise for my clothing, but I had to come here without half of Paris knowing. I needed to speak with you privately."

"Is this about Anders?" He put the book down and gestured to a chair set by the hearth. Gideon made no move towards it. He was wondering how he and Lord were going to manage to question Voclain with the woman and baby in the next room.

"It would be best if we could speak privately," Gideon repeated.

Voclain spread his hands in a helpless gesture. "I can hardly throw my sister out onto the street at this time of night. You need have no concerns. Hélène is used to keeping my confidence." Despite that claim he lowered his voice as he went on. "She knows about me and Anders."

Gideon took a breath. He was rapidly reassessing the woman from wife to sister.

"You and Anders?" he asked.

Voclain nodded.

"It was when he was here in Paris for a time last year. I should have said this before, but talking about it at the Bureau... I would lose my place there if Renaudot found out. He is an understanding man, but few men are *that* understanding."

"You and Anders?" Gideon repeated, wondering what he was missing.

Lord spoke over him. "You were lovers?"

Voclain glanced sharply at Lord then nodded. "For a short time. But that is all it could ever be. Too long and people might suspect. We have been good friends since and if there is anything I can do to help him, anything at all, you need only ask."

"What makes you think we will not take this confession to Renaudot?" Lord asked, his tone cold.

For a moment the blood fled Voclain's face then he swallowed.

"I would deny it, of course. Théophraste knows me and trusts me, so without proof—and there is none—it would be your word against mine."

Lord inclined his head in acknowledgement.

"Monsieur Fox here and I are both good friends of Dr Jensen. You have nothing to fear from us on that score, but your admission has made what was simple, not at all so."

Voclain was frowning and Gideon stared at Lord. He was no longer sure what their purpose here was now. It seemed to him that Voclain's reaction to the threat had been too natural. He was not lying about his relationship with Anders.

"You are not, I think, a servant to Monsieur Fox?" Voclain said, his confidence rebounding a little.

"No," Lord agreed. "I had the privilege to employ Anders Jensen for a short while in England before he came to Paris, and I am hoping to be able to do so again."

That made Voclain's eyes widen. His voice dropped to little more than a whisper. "Then you are the Schiavono?"

Lord nodded. "I have nothing but good will towards Dr Jensen and your secret is as safe with me as his has been."

It was only then Gideon realised that Voclain had been removed from any suspicion in Lord's mind too.

"What can I do to help? I told Monsieur Fox all I know about what happened already."

"You can perhaps help us to discover who really murdered Demoiselle Tasse," Gideon said.

Voclain looked between them, comprehension visibly dawning on him.

"You thought that I—?" He shook his head in disbelief then gave a brief laugh. "But why? Why would you think it might be me even for a moment?"

"Because it was not Anders or Gaspard Proulx," Gideon said. "That was the only reason. I am hoping you might be able to think of someone else it might have been, or we are left with no way forward to see Anders freed."

Saying the words out loud made them suddenly more real. It was the simple but devastating truth. With Voclain removed from the list of possible murderers, there was no other candidate. No one else who had ready access to both the laudanum from the Bureau and to the Palais de Cardinal that evening. And with no other possible murderer, Anders remained condemned.

"Are you sure it was someone from the Bureau?" Voclain asked. "There were many men in the Palais that evening, it could have been any one of them. They might have bought some laudanum from elsewhere—from outside Paris. They might have—"

"The laudanum that was used was in a bottle from the Bureau," Gideon said heavily, "Yolande Savatier was very certain of that."

"It was also used to kill the man who murdered Gaspard Proulx," Lord said, and produced the bottle they had been given by the Madame of Le Cheval Rouge.

"To kill the man who..." Voclain's eyes had gone wide.

"The killer, we think," Gideon went on, picking up the tale, "is not a man of violence but of medicine—or of medical knowledge at least. We believe he killed the man he had hired to murder Proulx so that he could not be paid—or made—to betray who his paymaster was."

They were all still standing but at that Voclain's legs seemed to give out and he sat back on the chair he had been occupying when they came in. It was getting too dark to see clearly and Lord crossed to the fire, lit a spill and used it to light the candles.

"I understand now why you thought it must be me," Voclain said, a hoarse rasp to his voice. Then he looked up at Gideon. "I promise you I would never harm Anders, but if it had to be someone from the Bureau and you are sure it was not Gaspard, then that only leaves Théophraste and Claude. No one else from the Bureau had permission to be there. But Claude was not in Paris that evening, he had a funeral to attend in Gisors; he had travelled there the night before and he was staying overnight after it. I had to see some of his regular patients that afternoon."

"And Renaudot said he was working on *La Gazette*," Gideon said, remembering.

"At least he was in Paris," Lord said thoughtfully. "We do not know if he was working alone or there were others who can say he was there with them."

Voclain was looking at them open mouthed.

"*Non. Non. Non.* I will not believe it could have been Théophraste. He would never do such a thing. He's not such a man."

Lord's lips tightened.

"I wish I could say I am as sure," he said. "I have known too many men who in their public lives are unimpeachable in their conduct but who in their private lives are much less restrained." He paused and in the quiet that followed, Gideon realised that the baby had finally stopped crying. Lord's expression changed as if he had just opened a door and seen something within. "But I will agree I think it is unlikely in the extreme. It is also something we should be able to ascertain without too much difficulty."

"You have an idea?" Gideon asked.

"I have several ideas," Lord agreed. He turned to Voclain. "I don't believe that Théophraste Renaudot is the man we seek, but we need to confirm that. Would you know who else should be there on a Tuesday evening when Monsieur works on *La Gazette*? If we can talk with those he was with, he need never know there was any suggestion of his involvement."

Voclain thought for a moment, still clearly outraged that the man he worked for could be considered for a moment to be connected with the murders. Then he shrugged helplessly.

"I have never been involved with that project of his, but I am pretty sure the printer from the Bureau is one of those who would be there."

Lord inclined his head. "Thank you for both your insight and your forbearance. If we succeed in freeing Anders, then I am confident it will be because of this meeting. In the meantime, if you think of anything at all that you believe might help us in any way, please send a message to me or Monsieur Fox." He turned to the door then hesitated and turned back. "Your sister, she is alone with her child?"

Voclain's face tightened.

"She is my sister, and her child is my niece. She is not alone."

"They live here with you?"

Gideon wondered what Lord was up to. He had already clearly decided Voclain was nothing to do with the murder, so why not leave the man alone?

"Yes." Then Voclain lifted his hands as if in defeat. "My sister was seduced by a man who promised her marriage and she loved him very much. It was only when she was with child, she discovered he was already married and had abandoned her."

Lord nodded.

"It must be difficult for her here with the infant. If she is interested, please tell her I can offer her a position where she would be able to keep and care for her child, not far from Paris—

a place called Saint-Léon-du-Moulin. You would be able to visit her easily there and she would be with people who would be less judgemental. It would be a happier place for your niece to grow up."

Voclain's mouth opened and closed a few times and Gideon found himself reminded forcibly again that here Lord was not as he was even in England. Here he was a man who could make such offers and they would be upheld.

"Anders told me you were a good man," Voclain said. "He didn't tell me how good, only that he believed you were being turned by circumstances from being so. I think he is wrong in that."

"I hope he is," Lord said, then smiled and the smile held sadness and reflection. "I am also sure it is what Dr Jensen himself would have done for you both, were it within his power. Ask your sister. It is for her to decide her own future and that of her child."

They left then and Gideon discovered that Lord had indeed anticipated the need for lighting the journey back. They stepped a few paces into the road when they were joined, as if by chance, by two of Lord's men one of whom carried a lantern. Friends meeting up by happy coincidence and walking home together. In retrospect Gideon supposed he should not have been surprised. Lord was a man who neglected very few details.

Which was also why he was not too surprised when Lord announced quietly to their two companions that they were taking a detour on the way back and would be going to the Bureau D'Adresses at the sign of the cock on the Rue Calandre.

By the time they got there Gideon's feet were frozen. Although it was after dark it was still only late afternoon, and the Bureau was open. People were coming and going through the doors, stepping reluctantly from the warmth within to the bitter cold of the dark streets without. Inside there was a festive atmosphere as everyone seemed to be anticipating the coming holiday. Leaving his two men to enjoy what there was to see, Lord led Gideon through to the bowels of the building and the printer's workshop.

They found the man locking his door. He looked over them suspiciously. "If you want any work done for your master you'll have to come back after Christmas,"

"Are you closing until then?" Lord asked, the quality of his French matching the quality of his appearance. "Even for *La Gazette*?"

"What's that to you?"

"I've some news that could go in it. For a price."

The printer sniffed. "News about what?"

"About the murder of Geneviève Tasse."

"That is old news," the printer scoffed.

"Not if they have the wrong man."

Now Lord had the printer's attention.

"That would be news," he agreed. "So, who was it?"

"You tell me," Lord said with a conspiratorial wink. "Who wasn't at the Gazette meeting the evening it happened? Would have been Tuesday three weeks ago."

The printer frowned.

"What are you on about? We all were there. There was an argument about what we should be saying about how ill the Cardinal was—he was dead the next week."

"No one left early?"

"No. It finished late. I got a right earful from the wife for being home past time."

"Oh," Lord managed to sound as if he was deflated. "Word was one of the men who was gathering news was missing from the meeting."

"Word is very wrong then," the printer said. "You need to be careful what you go around saying. Could earn yourself a beating. Now get out of here and be glad it's the season of goodwill so I won't tell Monsieur Renaudot about you."

They left quickly, trudging out into the cold darkness. Lord's men must have been watching the door because they had taken only a few paces before the two followed them out.

"So where does it leave us now?" Gideon asked quietly and in English as they neared Browne's residence.

Lord did not reply then, only a while later when they sat together in the sanctuary of his room, a cup of mulled wine in hand and a good fire in the hearth. Lord was restored to his usual dress and Gideon still in servants' attire. Stretching his feet towards the fire, warming them after the cold sludge of Parisian roads in winter, Gideon remembered he had intended to take Lord to task for his behaviour at the vintners. But it no longer seemed to have the same imperative it had at the time. In fact, he decided, it really didn't matter at all anymore.

"Tomorrow is Sunday," Lord said heavily, "which makes things much more difficult. After that there are only two more days before Christmas begins on the twenty-fourth. Then it will be impossible to get much done for some time."

Gideon heard the note of resignation in Lord's voice and his own heart sank.

"When we were at Voclain's you said you had several ideas. One, I assume, was asking the printer about Renaudot, but there were others?"

Lord nodded. Perhaps it was the flickering light from candles and hearth casting shadows, but he looked very tired. His eyes were hollow, and the flesh stretched too finely over the bones of his face.

"There are others, but not ones I wish to employ. *The art of our necessities is strange, that can make vile things precious.* I had hoped that you might..." He stopped himself from going on and it was obvious it cost him an effort to do so.

Gideon felt the bite then. Lord had been about to say he had hoped Gideon would manage to prove Anders innocent so Lord himself wouldn't need to resort to whatever desperate means he had in mind. It stung sharply. He cast around for something, anything, he could say to show he had not yet finished the task.

"There is still one more name on the list," he said. "I've yet to confirm that Claude Charron was indeed at a funeral in Gisors that day."

It hadn't even occurred to him to do so until that moment, but once the words were said, he realised it was needed. If they had gone to the extreme of making sure a man as far above suspicion as Renaudot surely was, had been where he claimed that evening, then they needed to do the same for Claude Charron, who was a completely unknown quantity.

Lord nodded, but it didn't lift his mood.

"Tomorrow I will send a message to the duchesse with the names of all on our list and ask which of them were admitted to the Palais that day. It is a long shot, but it is possible we might find that despite his denials Renaudot was there." Then he sighed. "That is, of course, *if* she is willing to undertake the task, *if* she can find the men on duty and *if* they recall. It was, after all, nearly a month ago now. And that is a large number of 'ifs'. We should also go and see Jensen. Visiting those in prison seems an appropriate act of charity for the sabbath. It is possible he may have some information to offer that we have missed."

"And then Claude Charron?" Gideon asked.

"Yes, and then Charron. I will find out where he lives if I can," Lord agreed. "After that, if we can make no progress, on Tuesday I will have to do something which I have no wish to do."

Gideon could hear the weight in Lord's words, as if whatever he was contemplating would place an intolerable burden upon him.

"Judges can be bribed?" he hazarded. "My understanding is that everything here in Paris is for sale for a price, even justice."

"Judges can be bribed," Lord agreed. "But I doubt they would be willing to let anyone free with such evidence as they have against Anders. Not without another to stand condemned in his place. I might, by such means, at least save his life and have his sentence commuted to the galleys. But no," he shook his head. "That is not my plan. I can arrange that Anders receives a pardon and I will if I must, both for his sake and for Kate. King Louis has already made it clear that he would like to employ me. I have pleaded that I am presently engaged in serving the cause of his sister and her family, but if needs must…"

Gideon stared at him, but Lord sat looking into the fire as if scrying visions of a future he did not wish to see.

"You mean you would be willing to sell your army to the French for their wars against the Emperor and Spain?"

Lord looked at him then.

"What choice do I have? And they would not be sold but gifted—at least in large part—and it would be myself as well as my men. But the very last thing I want at the moment is to become caught up again in these hopeless, pointless and endless wars for years to come. I want—I *need* to resolve the matter of my own history and heritage, to free myself from the chains others have cast about me, to know the truth for once and for all about who I am. And in the process, I hope, prove myself innocent of treason. So no," he finished his tone bitter, "I would not be *willing* at all, but if that is what is necessary, then that is what I will have to do."

There was no reply Gideon could think to make to that.

Lord stood up and refilled his cup, swallowing the warmed wine in a few gulps and then filled it again.

"I'm probably not the best company," he said, staring down at the wine which he held in both hands. His face was in profile to Gideon, features hidden by the silver curtain of his hair as he bent over the cup. "You should go. Sleep well. We have much to do tomorrow and not so much time in which to do it."

For a moment Gideon hesitated, wondering if he should stay regardless. Then Lord looked up and met his gaze.

"I promise you I am neither mad nor maudlin, merely weary. I will sup the last of the wine and seek my sleep." He smiled and lifted the cup he held in a silent toast. "Go to, my friend, whatever tomorrow holds it is better to face it rested."

For once it was Gideon who reached out to place a hand briefly on Lord's shoulder and then left him standing by the fire.

Chapter Fifteen

It had occurred to Nick to wonder why they hadn't been sent to Hull by water and he had his answer soon enough. Although there were places a boat could be towed, most trade had to run with the tides.

For much of the day, progress could be made downstream with the river flowing towards the sea and carrying any vessels with it. But twice a day and for some hours each time, the tidal surge pushed the ships heading inland upstream. Whichever way a vessel travelled, most would simply moor and anchor when the tide turned against their passage and wait for the next favourable flow in the direction they wished to go.

The result was that far from it taking under a day as the journey had been on horseback, it took the best part of two for them to regain Selby, meaning they arrived around mid-morning on the eleventh of December. Nick had traded his coat for a smock and been given an ancient bonnet. The bored gaze of the watching soldiers saw nothing untoward in either himself or Danny as they assisted the regular barge crew with unloading.

It turned out that Jarrett had a house in Selby and since Jarrett and Danny were now seemingly close as brothers, the bargeman offered to take them there to sleep the night if they needed.

"So long as you'd not mind the wife and bairns."

Danny accepted gladly and Nick could see the advantage even if it meant spending the night in a filthy lice and flea infested hovel.

Although Selby was heavily populated by soldiers, no one challenged them as they went up from the docks to Ousegate and turned along the road towards Micklegate. But then, Nick reflected, they must cut very different figures to the captured cavalier officers that they had been on their previous visit.

There was one shout of recognition from a soldier that sent his hand reaching for a sword that was no longer there. But it was Jarrett who was being hailed. It seemed he had promised these soldiers he would bring them something from Hull and they were stopped and surrounded in the street whilst Jarrett explained why he had been unable to procure what they wanted on this latest trip, but that he hoped to oblige them on the next.

Nick's heart was beating a sharp tattoo against his ribs, so hard that he feared it must surely be noticed by the soldiers about them. He kept his gaze lowered and tried to remind himself that to these men he was just a labourer of no account or interest. Someone to whom they would scarcely give a moment of attention. It didn't help that Danny stood with an idiot's grin on his face, every inch the labourer, from his tousled hair under a scrappy bonnet to the well-scuffed shoes. He scratched at his beard, as if oblivious to any danger.

But by some miracle, the soldiers accepted Jarrett's excuses and promises and, having failed to recognise either of the two men who were with him, stood back to let them pass.

Jarrett's house turned out to be a modest but pleasant and clean dwelling. For all his rough appearance and ways, it seemed that Jarrett was part owner of the barge they had travelled on, not just a casual worker on it as Nick had thought. He had a neat and pretty young wife, and two children with a baby on the way. His house was small and the accommodation they were offered was clearly the room the children slept in.

"I hope we'll not need to take up the offer," Danny told Jarrett, whose wife quickly hid her look of relief. "I have some business I need to see to in Selby and if it can be done quickly, Nick will want to be away to his lass in York. But just in case..." Danny slipped a coin from the pocket of his breeches and held it out smiling to Jarrett's wife as if he had performed a magic trick. She probably thought he had as the coin was a shilling. Where Danny had stolen that from Nick couldn't guess.

After that, of course, Jarrett's wife couldn't do enough for them and sent the oldest child, all of about four, to fetch an extra loaf. Then sat all three men at her kitchen table and served them dinner of pottage of some kind. Nick was sure it had been left in the pot for a day or two too long already, but he was too hungry to really care.

After they had eaten Danny excused himself and Nick only just managed to catch him before he left the house.

"Where are you going?" he demanded in a taut undertone.

"I told you already." Danny's voice held its usual patience, which Nick, having heard that same tone used on Fane, felt increasingly uncomfortable with. "I need to redeem my sword. Then I will find out where Mags is and will deal with him. The best thing you can do is stay here and keep out of sight until I get back. Then we can head to York, hopefully before nightfall."

"I'll come with you," Nick insisted. "You need someone to watch your back and if Mags is to die, I need to tell the Covenant men I know it was done."

For a moment Danny studied him.

"Alright," he said. "But you keep your mouth shut and your eyes on the ground if anyone stops us."

It was only after they set off together it struck Nick that he had been taking orders from Danny for some time now. The thought was intensely uncomfortable. It was an inversion of the natural order of things. Admittedly they were in circumstances where Danny's expertise made it essential that he take the lead, but Nick promised himself that as soon as they left Selby, he would find a way to reassert his authority.

He was surprised how little attention they drew. Then he considered how things had been in Newcastle, York and the other garrisoned towns he had been in recently. Two unarmed men who walked with purpose going about their business would not catch the eye of any soldier. He followed Danny, trying not to let his nervousness show. By the time they had reached the market square, he was sure he knew where they were going, but was far less certain how they might proceed.

The inn was the one that Major-General John Gyfford had taken over with his staff and prisoners. Leading the way to the stables behind the inn, Danny paused briefly to ask, "Are you any good with horses?"

What kind of question was that?

"I've been riding since before I could walk," he said, stiffly.

"That's not quite what I meant. It will have to do though."

THE PHYSICIAN'S FATE

The man in charge of the stables looked harassed. He was shouting at a boy who cowered from him as if expecting the shouts to turn to blows.

"...an' tha'll get a good braying from me if tha.."

"Mr Cobbett, sir," Danny's voice had acquired a sudden local lilt and the man turned scowling.

"Ye want sumat?"

Danny gripped his bonnet in his hands, screwing it around in his fingers as he spoke and explained—convincingly in Nick's opinion—that he and his friend had come to Selby from Hull and been told Mr Cobbett was looking for two men good with horses to replace the two who had left to be soldiers a couple of days past.

Mr Cobbett, Nick decided, was a desperate man. After only a brief interrogation as to where they had worked before, which Danny's invention supplied to Cobbett's satisfaction, and a few questions to make sure they knew the basics of horse care, he took them on a trial basis. They could sleep in the loft over the stables stores and have a meal a day from the kitchens, for which he would deduct tuppence from their meagre pay.

Nick was soon thoroughly fed up with having to make brief grunts like a half-wit whenever he was addressed. Worse was having to do such menial and disgusting work of a kind that he hadn't done since childhood, when helping out in the stables had seemed an adventure. By contrast, Danny set to with as much enthusiasm as if it were his lifetime's ambition to be a stablehand.

Cobbett eventually left them in the middle of the afternoon. Before he went, he told them that the officers would be back with their horses later. If he were not returned from his supper by then, he instructed that they were to treat those mounts more lovingly than the last woman they had slept with.

After he had gone Danny leaned on a rake and laughed then walked into the storeroom, threw the rake down and climbed the ladder-like steps to the loft above. A few moments later his head reappeared, and he was holding a lit lantern. He looked down at Nick with a grin.

"You'd best come up here."

Nick joined him to find two well used straw pallets, a table and some dirty cups. The boy he had seen earlier had already curled up in the corner and was sleeping the sleep of exhaustion.

"What are we doing here?" Nick demanded, being careful to keep his voice low.

"I told you I want my sword back," Danny said as if explaining the obvious, turning and testing one of the pallets with his foot. "John Gyfford is staying in the inn and his horse will be stabled here. I shall take the opportunity to talk with him. He should also know where we can find Mags."

"And why do you think he will do that and not simply betray us?"

Danny sat on the pallet and then lay back with his hands behind his head.

"I don't intend to give him a choice," he said.

Nick heard from the tone that he was not going to get any more answers about that. Instead, he sat on the other of the pallets and looked down on the stalls below. It reeked in the loft of both horse dung and human.

"Jarrett told you Cobbett was looking for men?"

"No. I knew he would be as I recruited the two he had working for him into John Gyfford's cavalry. Gyfford was down a few men but had horses spare and bet me I couldn't find him decent recruits in all Selby—men who at least knew how to sit on a horse. I won the bet."

"But Cobbett—"

"Is a lazy man. He wasn't here when I did the recruiting and I think he'll not be back today now we've shown him we know a horse's head from its arse. Get some rest. When Major-General Gyfford gets back we'll be a bit busy."

Nick hadn't expected to fall asleep, but he was shaken awake by Danny to the sound of hooves on cobbles and followed him and the stableboy, blearily, down the ladder. He'd seen the job done enough times to have some idea of what he was supposed to do, assisting any of the men who asked in dismounting. Mercifully only one did, a grey-haired man who was surely too old to be on horseback anyway.

THE PHYSICIAN'S FATE

He wound up nodding and saying 'sir' a great deal as he was given explicit and precise instructions on what each rider wanted for his mount, be that specific proportions of feed, a particular blanket or some treat.

"No water until after she eats, or she'll not stop drinking."

"Make sure you pay close attention to that back hoof, I think the shoe might need tightening, if it does you can have the farrier round first thing."

"Make sure you get all the mud out. He was in a state today."

Someone even flipped a coin at him—a groat. Nick recalled his supposed position enough to bend and pick it up from the dirt of the cobbles and mutter thanks. He was struggling to see how this was going to help them as Danny seemed to do nothing except keep his face in shadows and take the horses into the stables.

After the men had gone into the inn, Danny insisted that the three of them worked to settle the horses in their stalls, ignoring all the extra commandments that might have been given for any specific mount. That done, Danny chose two of the handful of horses in the stables that had not been ridden that day and started saddling them, then gave a coin to the boy and sent him into the inn with a message.

"Tell Major-General Gyfford his gelding looks to have a swollen hock and can he come and see right away. Then use that to buy yourself something to eat from the inn, then you can go to your bed for the night."

The boy scampered off. Danny finished saddling the horses and pointed Nick to the stall beside the one that held Gyfford's mount.

"You wait in there. If anything untoward happens, I'll call you. Otherwise, just keep out of sight. If Gyfford thinks I'm on my own, he is more likely to agree to letting me go and we can avoid any need for violence."

"So why did we just do all that work?" Nick asked, gesturing to the settled horses.

"Because when he comes in here, he would notice right away if the horses were not well-tended and that would make him suspicious," Danny explained, patient as ever. "Besides, someone had to look after the horses."

"But—"

Danny pushed him into the stall as the boy's voice could be heard from the yard then the sound of boots and slightly less than sober grumbling came closer. Keeping in the dark beside the horse and hoping the beast was not the kind to object to having someone so close, Nick saw Gyfford, bearing a lantern, walk past the stall where he was hidden to where another light glowed in the next stall.

He couldn't see what happened, but he heard Gyfford make an exclamation of surprise. There was a sudden flurry of movement, a snort of protest from the horse, some gasps and a heavy thud. Then Gyfford's voice.

"God's wounds, Danny, you could have said 'hello' like any decent man would. No need to greet me with a knife to the throat. I thought you were away to London, man. How did you get back here?"

"I came for my sword," Danny said. "I see you've been keeping it safe by your thigh. Thank you for that. I'll take it now."

"It is a fine blade, and I couldn't see you needing it again," Gyfford protested. "Not after the way things fell out. I was sure you would rather it was being used than left lying around."

"That was very thoughtful of you," Danny said, his voice cold with menace. "Almost as thoughtful as how hard I heard from your men that you argued on my behalf with Fairfax."

There was a sudden and chilling silence.

"You have the wrong notion there, I did my best, I promise you. But they weren't listening." Nick could hear an edge of desperation in Gyfford's tone. "Didn't I see you safe as far as I could?"

Another silence followed and Nick could picture in his mind the dark-eyed hate he had seen on Danny's face a handful of times and the hairs over his arms stood on end as his skin prickled.

"You are a lucky man this evening, John." Danny's voice was almost gentle. "I don't want half of Fairfax's army chasing me to Pontefract tonight, so let's say I believe you. If you're wise, you'll be keeping this to yourself as well. It wouldn't be a good look for you, newly promoted as you are."

THE PHYSICIAN'S FATE

The breath of relief Gyfford let out was audible.

"What more is there? You have your sword."

"I want Mags. Where is he?"

Unbelievably that made Gyfford laugh.

"You are clean out of luck there Danny. He was sent where you were headed. Seems there are those in some faction of the Parliament party who are keen on him. He could hardly ride, so he was floated downriver the day before yesterday, a physician with him, tender as you please. He's for London on a ship by now."

Nick's guts tightened at the news. It was a bitter twist of irony that they must have passed whatever vessel carried Mags at some point on their journey from Hull.

"And his men? Where are they?"

"Were sent south with some other troops two days ago. For London too for all I know."

"He had a woman. Did she go with him?"

"Someone you were sweet on, Danny?"

"Did she go with him?"

Gyfford gave a grunt of pain.

"Hey, no need for that. There was no woman with him when he left and I've not heard of any mentioned. If he had one she'd have stayed with the army."

"Then I have all I came for," Danny said. "I'll need your help to leave though."

"I can't do that, if I do, I'll be—"

He stopped talking abruptly.

"You don't need to worry. I'm not planning on taking you with me. I just need the word of the day and something that will convince them to let me through. A message to deliver, perhaps?"

"Looking like that? You would never be believed."

"That is my problem not yours."

"Very well, the word is 'Lady Anne's Birthday' and if you try in the bags I left with the saddle from my horse there will be something in there you can use, for sure."

"Careless of you," Danny observed.

"Nothing of any importance, but the seals will get you by if you have the word and the right look, though why I'm obliging you when you..." Gyfford's voice was suddenly muffled.

"If you take care, John," Danny said, "you'll be able to reach the knife and cut yourself free, unless you want the boy to find you when he comes back. If you're wise, you'll free yourself and go back to the inn moaning about how useless the stable staff are here and be as shocked as the rest in the morning. But the choice is yours."

A few moments later Danny appeared at the entrance to the stall Nick was occupying and held a finger to his lips then beckoned. Nick followed across the stable yard and around the back of the inn. It took him a moment to recognise the place where Danny stopped and held up a hand. Ill-lit and smelly, this was the place where those drinking in the inn would come to relieve themselves.

"We need soldier's coats," Danny whispered in his ear by way of explanation.

They didn't have long to wait. Two men, clearly the worse for drink, staggered out of the inn. They took a few paces into the gloom before undoing their breeches, talking together the whole time and oblivious until Danny and Nick grabbed them from behind. There was a brief tussle before they had the needed coats. One man was unconscious, the other dead.

"There was no need to use a knife," Danny hissed furiously. "Now when they find these two there'll be a hunt for us as murderers. John Gyfford may feel he has to speak up, even. Christ, that is the most—" He broke off abruptly. His voice had changed when he spoke again. "We have the coats so let's go."

A few minutes later they were mounted and riding at a brisk trot down Finkle Street and along Mill Lane towards the Mill Gate and the road for Cawood. Even in the dark and dressed in soldiers' coats, Nick was far from convinced that they would get through. Had they tried the same trick by daylight he was certain they would not.

The road was not very wide. A small knot of men was on guard duty, their mere presence blocking the way. As they approached, Danny called out.

THE PHYSICIAN'S FATE

"Lady Anne's Birthday—do not delay us, we have vital messages from the Major-General to Captain Hotham."

In Nick's experience, sheer boredom would encourage men on guard duty to be officious. But these were clearly either convinced by Danny's imperative urgency or were preoccupied with some discussion they had amongst themselves. A minute later, Nick almost giddy with relief, the two of them were riding fast and hard away from Selby.

Danny reined a good two miles north of the town.

"We need to go with care from here," he said "There will be patrols out from Cawood and thanks to your action we may get pursuit from Selby at any time too. We'll have to get around Cawood and towards Tadcaster to be back with Newcastle's army."

"What then?" Nick asked, caring little for whatever slight difficulties might now stand between them and safety.

"Then we'll be back with Newcastle's army," Danny told him, an edge to his usual patient tolerance. "Isn't that what you want?"

Nick had no idea how to reply to that. What he wanted was to ensure that he and not Mags was confirmed as the master of Howe and now he could see only one way to be sure of that. He had to do what the Covenant men required of him. But right now, he wasn't sure how to achieve it. He recognised that he was too tired and worn by recent events to be thinking clearly and regardless of all else, Danny was correct, his first duty was to get back to York. But then he would need to consider his next step with care.

There was also the matter of re-establishing the correct relationship between himself and Danny Bristow.

"Very well, lieutenant," he said. "Now we are away from the most pressing and immediate danger. I see no reason to continue as we have been with you assuming command."

It was much too dark to see Danny's face but there was a silence after Nick's words and when a reply came, it sounded as if the speaker was on the verge of laughter.

"Of course, Sir Nicholas, I understand the importance of getting our respective rank and status clarified. Would you like to choose the path we take from here, sir? Or would you prefer it if I did?"

"Until we reach Tadcaster, I am content you should do so."

Nick realised he must sound much as his uncle had always sounded—cold, detached and distant. It was, Nick knew, the only way to command. He had allowed Danny much leeway since they were captured. That had to end. Better sooner than later.

But as they rode on through the night, taking a broad arc around Cawood, a part of him felt as if he was losing something precious. For the life of him though, Nick couldn't say what that was.

Chapter Sixteen

Sunday started, naturally enough for Gideon, with a church service.

Held in the Anglican chapel that Browne maintained in his residence, there were a surprising number of attendees and the notable absence of Sir Philip Lord. But for Gideon the comfort it brought was much needed. The familiarity of the words and ritual of the service soothed him whilst the hope of grace uplifted his spirits. As always, he prayed for Zahara and as always, he wondered if his prayers for a woman who followed another faith were somehow sinful.

Standing there, Gideon was reminded how much religion had been a journey for him. From the terrifying blood and thunder of his father to the gentle moderation of his mother, who had always maintained that faith was in the heart and deeds of the believer more than in the church he or she attended. He was grateful for her influence as he knew it had left his heart open to allowing Zahara her own faith.

He found himself wondering what faith Sir Philip Lord followed. When they met, Gideon had accused him of being an atheist. Now he was not so sure. But whatever faith Lord had been raised in, it was not any usual form of Christianity. Gideon recalled him talking of how those who had controlled his life when he was a child had foreseen an era with a new religion, which had led to the Rosicrucian tracts being published. That was something about which Gideon knew very little, but he had to wonder if that was why Lord seemed reluctant to make an appearance at any religious service.

On the tail of that thought and as if to give it the lie, the door of the chapel opened quietly and a few moments later Sir Philip Lord was beside him, head bowed reverently. He was exquisitely dressed in deep blue silk, decorated with silver braid sewn with pearls, and a matching cape. The priest was saying the closing prayers and Gideon heard Lord's murmured 'amens'. A short time later they went from the chapel with the blessing of the celebrant warm in their ears.

"You were busy?" Gideon hazarded as Lord expertly navigated past those who might seek to detain him, a word here, a brief bow there.

"I was, as you rightly deduce, busy," Lord agreed, increasing his pace as he reached the entrance hall. "If you are ready and both physically and spiritually refreshed, we will visit Anders Jensen. On the way I will tell you what my busy-ness achieved."

They went to the Châtelet on horseback and in some state. Sir Philip Lord's banner was missing, which maybe added a small element of anonymity but, apart from that, the four men who rode with them were clearly the escort of a man of importance.

"My busy-ness," Lord said as they rode to the seemingly incessant sound of bells, "has resulted in my discovering both the home address of one Claude Charron and the despatching of a man of some discretion and intelligence to Gisors to ascertain if he did indeed attend a funeral there on the day he claimed not to be in Paris. I have also sent a polite request to the Duchesse d'Aiguillon asking if she would be willing to set in train enquiries with the Palais guard as to who on our list asked for admittance that day. You never know, being Richelieu's men, they might even have needed to keep a written record of who they admitted. We can hope."

"So that is what kept you from worship?" Gideon asked, his thoughts from before not yet dislodged.

"No. That is what I was attending to. It did not keep me from anything."

"People will notice."

"People always seem to notice me," Lord agreed. "Kate thinks it is my hair, Matt always blamed my gait, Danny swears it is the intensity of my gaze and Zahara claims it is my taste in clothes."

Another time Gideon might have pressed the point, but the shadow of the Châtelet was looming and it seemed less important the closer they got. There would be other opportunities for such a discussion.

THE PHYSICIAN'S FATE

"You are not exactly discouraging attention today," he said, gesturing to their immaculately turned-out escort. "I am surprised you didn't employ hautboys and clarions. I take it you no longer have any concern about showing your interest in Anders?"

"Having fulfilled all that our king required of me with His Most Christian Majesty, King Louis, I am here and acknowledged. I no longer need to creep in the shadows. Besides, it would not go amiss to let it be seen that I have an interest in Dr Jensen's fate, especially if I need to resort to the action I spoke of yesterday evening."

Gideon found himself wondering, suddenly, what he would do if Lord stayed in France. So far their fates had been tied together, first by chance then by circumstance and now—now, perhaps by friendship. But he wasn't sure that should circumstances change to that degree he would be happy to follow Lord. Having encountered Ellis Ruskin, he was also not at all sure he had any desire to return to his old life in London. He was no longer even sure that life was there to return to. What had been cracks in society, were now rifts and he knew he wouldn't find London as he had left it.

But could he commit to life as a mercenary? Then it hit him with force that he already had. If he chose to stay with Lord in France, it would be no more than a continuation of what he had been doing already—fighting for a cause he didn't believe in. In fact, he realised, it might even be preferable, if he had to do so, that it happened in a nation other than his own. And, of course, there would be Zahara.

His thoughts were cut short as they reached their destination and the same man who had been guide to Gideon and Richard Browne on his previous visit, bowed and scraped and fawned on Lord as Gideon remembered in time he wasn't supposed to speak any French. Of course, the monsieur was more than welcome to visit the prisoner, who monsieur's companion had generously provided for on his last visit. Oh, merci monsieur! How generous. More than generous. Most assuredly for that price a good meal could be served in the prisoner's room. Yes, and with wine if the monsieur wished that.

Lord clapped Gideon on the shoulder.

"Go on ahead. I will be there in a short time."

A little confused but gathering from the look that accompanied the words that he was wiser not to question, Gideon was shown up some stairs within the Châtelet. The stench of human filth was still present, but not as marked as it had been in the lower levels where he had been escorted before.

Anders had been moved to a room that was, if not light and airy, at least enjoyed a small measure of daylight through a narrow, grated, window. He had been provided with some essentials, a simple bed, a small table with a chair by the window, and a bucket he could cover. He was properly dressed now, even if in such coarse clothes that Gideon felt guilty, he hadn't thought to bring anything better with him. There was no hearth and the room was very cold.

In the light it was possible to see the change in him. The Anders sitting on the one chair in the room looked akin to a skeletal parody of the sturdy man he had been before. His fair skin was almost grey and his hair and beard a tangled mess. But the intelligent hazel eyes were the same as ever and they lit up from within as Gideon was allowed into the room

"You did this." He gestured to the bare room around him as if to a luxurious chamber and his smile was of genuine gratitude. "Thank you, my friend."

It was then Gideon knew for sure that what he had discovered about Anders didn't matter. He made himself a promise that wouldn't ever reveal that he knew by word or deed. He had a strong feeling it would be something the Dane would struggle to come to terms with and Gideon didn't want to put any more burdens onto the shoulders of a man who already had too much to carry.

"It was Sir Philip Lord's money," Gideon admitted. "He has resources here in France I was not aware of before."

"*Sir* Philip Lord?"

Gideon remembered then that their last conversation had been exclusively about Anders and his plight. Somehow, here in the light and air, it seemed easier to talk of other things. So he took the time to tell the tale of how Lord came to be knighted.

"You were clearly courageous yourself. I have never been in a battle although I have seen the aftermath enough to know I would not wish to be so," Anders said when Gideon finished. "And from this I must also assume Sir Philip is no longer held to be a traitor?"

"He was granted a pardon thanks to the intervention of Prince Rupert with the king, but he wasn't happy to accept it as it meant he was still held to have committed the crime."

"I can imagine he would not like that," Anders said. "Sir Philip is nothing if not a proud man."

The last words were spoken as the door opened and Lord stepped into the room.

"I can confirm that is true," he said amicably. "Although I am fortunate to have friends who are kind enough to make a regular effort to keep me humble."

Anders laughed and got to his feet, but the laughter finished with a grimace. Lord crossed to him in two swift strides and to Gideon's surprise, embraced him quickly. That forestalled any attempt on Anders' part to try and form a bow, which had clearly been his intention.

"It is good to see you," Lord said, stepping back, his hands still on Anders' arms. "Please sit. I have asked for a meal for us all to share which should be here soon and I have sent for some better clothes for you and a barber to visit." He shook his head as Anders sat again. "It is to my shame I have not thought to do such for you before. I have been overly occupied in seeking ways and means to ensure your liberty. And you must have no doubt that you will walk from this place a free man before Christmas. You have my word on that."

Anders' expression was difficult to read behind the sprawling beard that occupied most of the lower part of his face, but his eyes were overbright.

"You do not need to promise me, Sir Philip. I know it is not a certainty. Unless you have found the man who committed the terrible crime of which I am accused?"

"No. Not yet," Lord admitted. "But what you need to understand is that you will be freed whether we can prove your innocence or not. I know what it is like to live under the shadow of a false conviction, but I also know that it is better to live."

Anders' eyes narrowed a little as he stared at Lord, as if he were trying to understand a riddle or solve a puzzle.

"If you cannot show I am innocent, then I fail to see how…?"

Lord dropped into a crouch, placing himself at eye level with the Dane.

"You do not need to know the how or why of it. Only understand that if we are unable to prove your innocence, you will have a pardon. I tell you this, so you need not hold any fear in your heart. No one will torture you and you will not be executed or sent to the galleys." His voice carried absolute conviction.

Anders closed his eyes and bowed his head with a relief that was almost unbearable to witness. Mercifully, the promised meal arrived covering the moment two stark tears escaped his eyes. With it came two more chairs and a pile of cloth which proved to comprise two outfits, both clean and of decent quality, with new shirts and stockings. There was even a pair of shoes. Then the promised barber arrived, who quickly trimmed Anders' beard and hair.

As they sat to eat, they were interrupted a final time by the arrival of a man with a feather bed and another bearing bed linens and new warm blankets, whilst a third set a small brazier filled with coals and lit it. When they were left alone, Anders was smiling.

"Even a small star shines in the darkness," he said, his voice hoarse with emotion. "Yet you have given me an entire constellation. Thank you both. You have brought me hope between you, my friends."

The meal itself was not particularly good and, by then, warm rather than hot, but Anders clearly relished every mouthful. It was painfully apparent that whatever food he had been given so far, even in this new accommodation, was neither plentiful nor nutritious.

THE PHYSICIAN'S FATE

The conversation was light. Gideon and Lord sharing such news as they might of those Anders knew. When they spoke of Zahara Gideon recalled the book she had mentioned by Ambroise Paré. Anders smiled sadly at him.

"I understand why she asked you to speak to me of that book, although I am sure she knows I left with her as a gift. It is her gentle way of telling me I am needed." He bowed his head for a moment then raised it and looked at Lord. "You said when I left your service that I would always be welcome to rejoin it. If I do leave this place alive, I would like to return to England with you, Sir Philip. If you will have me. I do not think the climate of Paris agrees with me."

"Consider yourself reemployed from this moment, Dr Jensen," Lord said. "You will leave this place tomorrow or the day after and be in England before they celebrate Christmas there."

After that the atmosphere of the meal was lifted and by the end they were even laughing a little, a sound that Gideon felt sure was rare within those dread walls. It was only after they had finished eating and Anders was allowing himself the luxury of a small cup of wine, that Lord gave Gideon a slight nod ae he poured himself a full cup.

"We have run up against something of a stone wall in seeking the true killer," Gideon admitted and then went on to outline concisely and briefly all they had so far ascertained. That the murderer was not Voclain or Proulx and seemed most unlikely to be Renaudot or Charron as both had witnesses to their not being at the Palais de Cardinal that night.

"It is not Théophraste," Anders insisted. "He simply is not such a man. Claude was definitely not there that day. Josselin and I had to share out his most urgent work at the Bureau between us." He shrugged a little helplessly. "I am afraid I can see nothing I know which would assist you. Though I would say that if I was not completely certain he was absent that day, Claude Charron would be a man I might think capable of such a deed."

Gideon felt a sudden tingle over the flesh of his forearms.

"You did not say that before," he said. "What makes you say so now?"

"Nothing, except you mentioned Charron as now being a man to consider. Although I am still not sure why he should be as he was not in Paris at the time."

Lord leaned forward in his chair a little.

"Tell us about Claude Charron," he said.

Anders looked thoughtful and took a sip of his wine then drew a breath and let it out again.

"You need to understand that Théophraste is not a judgemental man. He will take help from all who offer it. His view of the world is that even the worst of us can be turned to good works. That is why he employs men like Proulx and Charron, it is why he was able to work with the Cardinal and to produce *La Gazette* which sings the king's praises whilst also telling people the truth of what is happening in the world. It is why he kept all the published notes on his weekly conferences anonymous. In brief, Théophraste is not a man to let ideals mar pragmatism. He would say that evil can be the horse upon which good may ride. If a man is able and willing to serve his cause and heal the poor, Théophraste will not question his morals, only his capacity. It is hard to blame him for such an approach. It is difficult enough to find qualified and competent physicians willing to work for free or just a pittance amongst the poor, risking the wrath of the Faculty, let alone insist that those are also saints." Anders gave a nod towards Lord. "That is something I think you might understand, sir, although Gideon I fear might struggle with it more."

Gideon opened his mouth to object then closed it again and felt his face colour.

"This man Charron has a less than savoury personality?" Lord asked.

Anders nodded. "He is not a man I would wish to have as a friend, and he is not one I have been happy to have as an associate. But that was not anything I could choose. None of us liked him. Except Proulx, and that is saying little as he seemed to be most undiscerning in his choice of friends."

"What do you find so distasteful about him?" Gideon asked.

"He is the kind of man who believes that what he wants he should have. An arrogant man of the worst kind, a man who revels

THE PHYSICIAN'S FATE

in what power he has over others. He told me once that it was one of the greatest delights of his work that he had the ability to dispense life or death." Anders shook his head. "Such a man should not become a physician."

"It seems unlikely that an arrogant man would choose to work at the Bureau," Gideon said. "Is there some reason he works there so much rather than in his own private practice?"

Anders shrugged.

"You would need to ask Théophraste. You must remember most who work there have their own practices and give a little time each week to the charitable consultations. There are not many of us who put all of our time into the work of the Bureau. I did hear there were rumours that Charron had to leave Gisors where he had built up his practice because of some scandal involving the wife of one of his clients, last year sometime. But to be honest, I disliked the man, so I paid little heed to him or anything about him unless I had to do so." Then he stopped talking for a moment and frowned. "There was one odd thing though, on that dreadful day I had to see one of his clients, a young woman. She sent a friend saying she needed treatment, so I included her in those women I visited that day. Women are not allowed in the consulting room at the Bureau, you see. But when I got to her, she seemed healthy enough. When I explained Charron was away, she asked if he had left anything for her. She said something about pictures and that he had promised her some money; she sounded quite desperate. But when I asked what she meant, she suddenly denied that was what she had said. That she had made a mistake and I should go. I had others to see so I went."

"Did you tell Charron about it?"

Anders shook his head. "We have a lot of strange and troubled souls who come to the Bureau and with the death of Demoiselle Tasse and all that followed, I did not think of it again until now. I am not even sure it is important. She was probably just another disturbed young woman."

"Do you recall where she lived?"

Anders shook his head. "But there should be a note of it in my papers for the day. I always try to keep a few details about everyone I treat. Théophraste could tell you where to find them, if it were important."

"Where were you staying in Paris?" Lord asked suddenly and it struck Gideon that he really should have thought to ask that question himself—and on his first visit.

"I was a guest of Théophraste," Anders said. "He had told me I could stay with him until I was able to find myself some decent rooms, which is harder than it might seem in Paris."

"So your things are at the Bureau?"

Anders nodded, looking uncertain now. "In a manner of speaking. Théophraste has some rooms of his own as part of the building, I was staying there." He looked downcast. "One of my worst regrets in all this is that by being the one accused I have brought such trouble to Théophraste."

"You can hardly hold yourself responsible for that," Gideon said, reasonably, but he knew from experience as a lawyer that people would often feel guilty for legal issues beyond their control when someone they cared about was affected. "But you can help him and yourself best by thinking if there is anything else about Charron that might mark him out as a man who could have committed such a crime."

"Truly, no. I gave him as little of my time and attention as I could and I still do not see how he can be the murderer, even if of all men he is one I could picture in the role." Anders was looking distressed and weary now. The events of the day whilst joyful for him had clearly taken a toll.

For Gideon it was painful to see the man he had known as always calm, reassuring and self-assured reduced so much by circumstances both undeserved and unjust. It struck him then that a lesser man than Anders would have been broken by the experience. But the Dane, whilst clearly buckled to his knees, was still the same man. It gave Gideon great hope that unlike many he had seen emerge from imprisonment as shadows of who they were before, the Anders he knew might yet be restored in full.

"Is there anything you need that we have forgotten to provide for you?" Lord asked.

Anders smiled tiredly and gestured to the things Lord had already given him.

"How can I ask for more? But if there was any way I could have a book to read, then I would think myself as blessed as I could be without my liberty."

"A book, of course," Lord slapped his brow with his palm. "How could I not have thought of that? And I will ensure you have light as well so if you wish to read after dark you can do so." He got to his feet. "But now we must go. If anything occurs to you that might help us, anything at all, tell the turnkey and I will make sure he understands it is worth his while to get word to me immediately." He put a hand on Anders' shoulder. "No. Do not get up. Rest. Regain your strength and be ready to leave here with me when I come again, which will be no later than the day after tomorrow."

"You spoke of a pardon," Anders said quickly. "That would surely come with a price. I am not willing that another should pay such for me."

Lord smiled then and released him. "That might be so, but it is not your choice to make. It is mine."

Anders looked as if he might be going to object again, then thought the better of doing so and nodded instead. "As the saying goes since we cannot get what we like, let us like what we can get. I am in your hands, sir and I am most grateful to you."

Gideon made his own farewell then, with Anders gripping both his hands.

"Thank you, my friend, I knew when we first met you were a man to trust."

"I will try to live up to your faith in me," Gideon promised.

As the heavy door was slammed shut and locked behind them, Gideon realised that in all this he had forgotten something just as important as securing Anders' freedom. For Sir Philip Lord it might be enough to procure a pardon, if need be, and so ensure Anders was free both for his own sake and to aid Kate. But Gideon was thinking of a young woman he had never known. A woman who had friends and family that must surely be grieving, her life having been ripped away from her and themselves so callously.

He was thinking how it was easy to lose sight of that and how he neither wanted to do so nor was willing to allow that to happen.

Of course, he wanted to find the murderer to free Anders, but beyond that, he wanted to find the murderer so Geneviève Tasse could have justice. And so that no more young women might be at risk from the man who had killed her in the cause of slaking his own lust.

THE PHYSICIAN'S FATE

Chapter Seventeen

After what they had learned about Claude Charron it was no great surprise to Gideon to find that the physician had taken rooms in a smart new house in the Marais area of Paris. The Marais was presently the place where all the more wealthy who couldn't afford a traditional Parisian grand house had been building. What was less clear was how a man working as a physician for the Bureau D'Adresses could possibly afford to live in such a place.

"Perhaps not so difficult to understand when you consider that if he is our man he counts—well counted—such people as Pierre Firmin amongst his acquaintances." Lord observed when Gideon raised it. "That would suggest he has some contacts amongst the criminal fraternity which could mean he is serving that community in some way."

They were walking towards the Marais in the thin winter sunlight of a December afternoon, clad again as servant and master, Gideon the master. Lord had suggested that if Charron were the guilty party, he would expect to be questioned by the man he had already met. Of course, if Charron was indeed the guilty man he might very well try to murder Gideon too.

"I can't see physician skills earning him much from such criminals." Gideon said. "Surely most are, by definition, not very rich at all?"

Lord gave a brief laugh.

"There are many wealthy men who are criminals by trade. Pirate commanders for example, I can promise you that makes good money." He grinned briefly. "Then there are smugglers, many of whom are both engaged in legitimate trade and criminal activities at the same time. There are those who make and sell reproductions of antiquities or of well-known and respected craftsmen's work, like the men in Geneva who make replicas of English clocks and watches and forge signatures upon them. Then there are—"

Gideon lifted a hand. "Yes, but what would such people want with a physician?"

"A procurer or procuress of a more upmarket kind than the Madam of Le Cheval Rouge might need to employ a physician if one of his or her more expensive young ladies was to wind up pregnant, for example." He must have seen Gideon's reaction of disgust because he went on quickly. "There are ways all men can turn their skills to crime. Surely you must see it with your colleagues in the law? Losing vital contracts or forging documents. One need not be out on the street at night with a knife to make money as a criminal. In fact, that kind of criminal is the one who makes the least money."

They had reached the house. It looked as fresh as a newly minted coin with the dirt of the city yet to make too much of a mark on its smooth and fashionable facade. A smartly dressed servant greeted them at the door.

"You are here about renting the rooms, monsieur?"

Gideon didn't even blink.

"Yes," he agreed swiftly. "I'm from England, a lawyer, and need to stay in Paris for a few months. This would be ideal for me."

The servant explained the lower floors of the house belonged to a gentleman of finance. Clearly still a mere apprentice at his chosen calling, Gideon decided, as he needed to rent out the upper floors to those who wished the cachet of living in such a coming area of the city.

"The rooms are only available to professional gentlemen," the servant informed them. "Monsieur is very particular about the quality of those he has living here."

The rooms they were shown were spacious but with a view that gave onto little more than the narrow way between this house and its close neighbour. The servant was keen to explain that they were situated not far from various facilities and that such things as food and water could be delivered, laundry and nightsoil collected. If the monsieur was a man alone, female company of a most obliging and prestigious sort could be arranged for him also.

"And who are the people in the other rooms?" Gideon asked.

"They are all most respectable gentlemen. Just across the landing is a notary, another man of law like your good self,

THE PHYSICIAN'S FATE

monsieur. The other rooms on this floor are taken by a physician, which might be very useful if the monsieur is ever taken ill."

Lord caught Gideon's eye behind the man's back and gave the slightest nod.

"I'll take it," Gideon said. "It is exactly what I have been looking for."

"But I have yet to show you the courtyard garden to which you will have access in the summer and—"

"It is perfect." Gideon smiled at the man. "I have looked at a number of other places and none I like so much. I can leave you the first month's rent right away and I will move in before Christmas. How much do you need?"

The amount the man named would have made Gideon's jaw drop under normal circumstances, instead he nodded.

"You will write me a receipt?"

"I—er—I will need to fetch pen and paper, if you will just wait here for a few minutes please monsieur."

Once they heard the sound of footsteps retreating down the stairs, Lord led the way to where they had been told the physician lived. It would surely be too much of a coincidence for there to be another physician staying upstairs as well. Gideon knocked on the door and waited. A minute later the door opened, and they were confronted by a portly man in his middle years, with receding brown hair which was still long enough to curl fashionably to his shoulders. He was dressed in the way any of his profession might choose to dress and had a pair of spectacles perched awkwardly on his nose. Behind the lenses his eyes widened as he saw Gideon.

"I apologise, but I do not work on a Sunday," he said stiffly and was about to close the door, but Gideon stepped forward quickly with a smile.

"I'm not seeking your professional services," he said. "Merely to ask your advice as a potential resident of this house. I'm about to take out rent on the rooms over there and I was hoping you might be able to give me some insight as to whether they are indeed worth the cost and if the local facilities that I have been regaled with at length are as I have been told." He saw refusal waver in the other man's face and pressed on quickly. "May I come in? I wouldn't take much of your time. As we are likely to be neighbours it would seem appropriate to get to know each other. I'm Gideon Fox, a lawyer from England staying here for a few months."

For a moment Gideon was sure he would be refused, but at his last words something changed.

"Well, yes. In that case I suppose we should," the man said. "I am Claude Charron, physician. Please do come in, but your man had better wait out here, I have enough of muddy boots and careless elbows from my own servant. Thank goodness he is out."

"Of course," Gideon said and turned to Lord. "Wait for me in my new rooms. I'll not be long."

Lord made a brief bow and stepped aside. His gaze held a silent warning which Gideon didn't need. He had no intention of trusting Charron an inch.

The pleasant but formal room to which Charron took him was clearly one set aside for private consultations. There was an unused look to much of the furniture, only the old oak table set as a writing desk seemed to be well used. It was covered in papers and some sheets Gideon could see had columns of figures that seemed to be accounts. The walls were decorated with well executed framed sketches of Paris and her people. Gideon noticed one included a water-vendor and grimaced internally.

"Do take a seat, Mr. Fox." Charron gestured to the two other chairs apart from the one set beside the table.

"It is kind of you to take the time to talk to me," Gideon said, as he did so. "I know very few people in Paris as I have only been here a few days."

"You have employment in Paris?"

"I have indeed," Gideon agreed, searching his mind for a possibility. "I have recently been offered some work by one Sir Philip Lord. It is well paid and should keep me occupied for a few months. Hence why I am taking these rooms."

"Lord. Hmm." Charron spoke the name as if it had a faintly familiar flavour. "I may have heard of this man. He is an Englishman and a commander of armies, is he not?"

"He is a very successful military entrepreneur," Gideon agreed.

THE PHYSICIAN'S FATE

Charron smiled. "Then in this day and age you can be sure of your pay as his services must be much in demand."

"I believe so, but I am not involved in that. I am concerned with other affairs of his here in France to do with his lands near Paris."

"Surely I recall you from somewhere recently?" Charron's face furrowed into lines of concentration for a moment then cleared. "Ah, of course. Has your business taken you to the Bureau D'Adresses at the sign of the cock on the Rue Calandre at all?"

Gideon decided honesty was a good way to go. If nothing else it meant he could discuss matters openly and see what, if any, reaction he had from Charron,

"Yes. You might have seen me there. I was there making enquiries about a friend of mine, Anders Jensen. He was working there the last I had heard. I discovered he now stands accused of murder."

"You are a friend of Anders?" Charron's face slipped into a look of condolence. "It is so sad when one has to face the hard fact that a friend is not the man you believed him to be."

"You are mistaken, monsieur," Gideon said. "I know for certain that Anders is falsely condemned, and I have been working to prove his innocence and find the man who should truly be accused."

Charron's spectacles slipped on the bridge of his nose. Their silver frame caught a stray ray of sunshine and sent a mote of light dancing over the wall beside Gideon. Clutching at them, Charron took them off and put them flat on the table.

"I see," he said gravely. "It is understandable that if he is your friend you would believe that. Do you have any alternative candidates for the role of murderer?"

"Rapist and murderer," Gideon corrected. "I believe that the man had no intention of killing Demoiselle Tasse, merely of availing himself of her body whilst she was insensible under the influence of laudanum." He watched Charron carefully as he spoke, but the other man merely nodded and frowned a little.

"Truly terrible—but that would make sense, would it not? A man driven by lust." He leaned forward as if imparting a confidence. "It is in his heritage. Dr Jensen is Danish. His ancestors used to rape and pillage along the coasts of civilised nations, did they not?"

"Er…" Gideon struggled to find an answer to that, but Charron seemed not to notice and warmed further to his theme.

"Look at how the Swedes have been across Germany. But I digress, you were going to tell me of those who you think might have been the perpetrator."

"Not 'those'," Gideon said carefully. "Just one man."

Did he imagine that Charron's face froze for a moment before the polite, interrogative smile appeared? Gideon was unsure.

"Which man? Surely not Monsieur Renaudot?" Charron laughed at the ridiculousness of such a notion and Gideon joined in.

"Of course not," he said, "Monsieur Renaudot is above reproach. I meant Gaspard Proulx."

"But Proulx is—"

Gideon might not be a master of recognising guilt or even concern, but he had not spent several years in chancery without knowing very well the signs of relief.

"Yes. And that makes it harder."

"You are sure of this?" Charron was solicitous now. "I mean, you have some proof?"

Gideon nodded.

"I think so, but I am reluctant to talk of it before I am certain."

Charron nodded.

"Of course. I am sure the prévôt and the courts will uncover the truth. The trial is tomorrow so we will soon know."

Gideon felt his blood run cold.

"Tomorrow?"

"So I believe," Charron said. "Then the execution can be dealt with on Tuesday before the Christmas season is on us."

"Then I will need to talk to the prévôt," Gideon said. It must be a mistake. It had to be.

"Indeed you will." Charron pushed himself to his feet. "We must drink to your success. I have some rather fine wine you might like to try. It has an odd and rather sweet aftertaste. You will like it I think."

THE PHYSICIAN'S FATE

The muscles across Gideons stomach tightened and he got to his feet as well, pushing a smile onto his face.

"That is most kind and as soon as I have moved in I would be delighted to join you to try it. But my servant is waiting, and I need to go and arrange the details to rent the rooms here, finding a suitable place has been a nightmare." Still smiling, Gideon stepped past Charron who made a half-hearted attempt to detain him with one hand. From the safety of his place by the door to the landing, Gideon made a slight bow. "It has been a pleasure to meet you, monsieur."

As the door closed, Gideon was relieved to be on the far side of it from Charron and on the same side as Lord, who was leaning a shoulder against the wall beside it. He made himself draw a breath. The offer of wine was surely not any attempt by Charron to murder him. After all, he had just said that he believed Proulx was the guilty party and besides Charron would have struggled to explain away someone poisoned by laudanum in his own rooms. And with Lord standing outside the door, even in servant guise, he could hardly hope to commit murder and dispose of the body unnoticed.

"Monsieur, I paid the first month of rent as you asked me to," Lord said in a French accent that belonged to the streets of Paris. "If you wish we may leave immediately."

Gideon did wish, very much so.

"You look a little pale." Lord spoke in English as they made their way back to Browne's residence.

"Charron said that Anders is due for trial tomorrow. Do you know if that is true?"

Lord shook his head. "I should surely have been told this morning if so." Then he frowned. "Although I didn't ask directly, so it might have been assumed I knew, and my largesse was by way of final comforts for a condemned man."

Gideon felt his heart contract.

"We must—"

"What we must do," Lord said, his tone sharp, "is find out first if it is true. Charron could be mistaken or seeking to mislead you. Fear not, I will make the necessary enquiries. But you haven't told me if you think he is our murderer?"

It was not easy to push aside this fresh anxiety, but Gideon tried. He forced his mind back over the conversation.

"In all truth I could not say so for sure. He seemed to me to be relieved when I said I thought Proulx was the real murderer, but does that show him as guilty? Not in any way that one could persuade a court of law."

"We have no need to persuade a court of law," Lord said grimly, "I am sure he could be persuaded to confess his guilt if he is indeed guilty."

Gideon bridled at that, remembering too vividly what he had seen being done to a man in the dungeons of the Châtelet.

"Yes, I am sure he could. He could also be persuaded to confess to guilt even if he is innocent, by the use of torture."

"Then you are unsure indeed," Lord said. "I have found you somewhat less careful about such things when you think you have right and justice on your side."

Gideon opened his mouth to protest then closed it again. It was hard to argue. He had stood by and let Lord torture a man he was convinced was responsible for the capture of Kate and raised no protest. It was not a very edifying thought.

"I'm not convinced of Charron's guilt," he said shortly. "But I'm also not sure he is innocent."

"Then we keep friend Charron under close observation."

"You sound as if you think he is involved in ongoing crime," Gideon said.

"We already discussed this," Lord reminded him. "I think he has to be. If he were not, he wouldn't be able to afford living in that house. I will arrange for my men to keep an eye on him. Perhaps we can catch him doing something illegal."

It started snowing again and by the time they got indoors Gideon's feet felt like blocks of ice tied loose onto his stockings. He sat in Lord's room, holding a cup of warmed wine, naked feet near the fire and stockings hanging to dry from the hearth like those in the tale of St. Nicholas. He had a moment's sympathy for the men Lord had just sent out to keep a watch on Claude Charron.

THE PHYSICIAN'S FATE

"What do we do now?" he asked as Lord changed from servant to master with his usual unnerving alacrity. "Charron believes I think the guilty man is Proulx."

Lord paused in the middle of doing up his points.

"That is true. And if he is the guilty party since he killed Firmin, and Yolande Savatier has fled Paris, he probably feels safe enough with that."

Gideon sipped the warming wine and felt it settle in his stomach with a glow.

"I think you believe Claude Charron is the man who killed Geneviève Tasse."

"I think I do too," Lord agreed easily. "Of course, I could still be wrong, but it seems to me we are extremely limited in possible killers. We know it was not Jensen or Voclain; neither would have any desire to rape Geneviève Tasse. It seems it was not Gaspard Proulx as his killer was then murdered in the same manner as Demoiselle Tasse had been and that strongly suggests it was the same man who did the deed. We have established that Théophraste Renaudot was at the Sign of the Cock at the time of the murder, which only leaves Claude Charron as the man with both the ability to obtain the laudanum and with access to the Palais de Cardinal."

Put like that, Gideon had to agree it seemed very probable that Charron was the murderer. He opened his mouth to agree when there came a tap on the door. Lord strode over and opened it then closed it again.

"I will return in a moment. The man I sent to Gisors is downstairs, I would spare the servants the mud traipsed through the house and him the walk upstairs as he must have ridden hard and changed horses at every post to be there and back so fast and undertaking enquiries about Charron whilst he was there."

Gideon looked at his bare feet and nodded. Much as he would like to hear the news first hand he could hardly walk downstairs into public view with half-bare legs and no stockings or shoes on his feet. He stayed where he was, enjoying the warmth and a second cup of the wine, rising only to light the candles with a taper as he realised it had been growing dark.

Lord was gone longer than Gideon had expected and when he came back he looked less than cheerful.

"There is bad news?" Gideon asked, his mood of a moment before evaporating.

"It is not exactly good news," Lord said. "It seems that Claude Charron did indeed attend a funeral in Gisors that day. Charron had travelled to Gisors the day before, which was a Monday, and he usually does not work—at the Bureau at least—on a Monday. He went to see the priest that afternoon to talk about the funeral—which incidentally was for a sister.

"My man found two people prepared to swear they had seen him there, one of which was the priest officiating at the funeral, the other being another sister who added that she wished he hadn't come and couldn't believe he would dare show his face there again, but wasn't willing to explain why."

"I take it your man asked others about that?"

Lord nodded. "It was the priest again. He was very forthcoming for a man of the cloth who you might think would be most averse to scandal, rumour and gossip."

Gideon had to laugh at that.

"You clearly never met my father. He adored a good scandal. It meant he could find fuel for his more vituperative sermons. In the absence of anything provable he would settle for gossip or rumour as an example."

"I have a feeling he and I might not have got along," Lord said, which gave Gideon a brief moment of amused horror at the thought of such a meeting.

"It is as well it's no longer possible," he agreed. "What did this priest say?"

"He said that Charron had a reputation as a womaniser and more than one young woman had fallen for his false promises. Then a couple of years ago there had been some talk of Charron trying to seduce the wife of a local merchant at which point he left for Paris."

"Which is all very interesting, but if Charron was at the funeral then he was not in Paris."

"Yes," Lord agreed. "But also no. The funeral finished mid-afternoon. He could have been in Paris in time to commit the murder."

"What do you mean? It has to be fifty miles from Gisors to Paris, it took us most of a day when we rode from there to Saint-Léon-du-Moulin."

Lord nodded. "We were riding the same horses all the way. You forget, this is France and there is an established network of posting stages where anyone who have the status and the means can hire a horse to ride between posts. It is how my man got there and back in one day."

"So why did we not do that?"

"Because there were four of us and... Nevermind. The point being post houses will keep records of who has taken a horse and when."

"So we can find out if Charron used them that day?"

Lord nodded. "If it was indeed him, I somehow doubt he planned to murder Demoiselle Tasse therefore I also doubt he took many pains to hide his progress back to Paris." He lifted a hand as Gideon opened his mouth to ask the obvious next question. "Yes. I have already dispatched someone to take Charron's description to every staging post between Paris and Gisors if need be. It was a while ago, but it is possible someone will remember him if he used that route."

"So where does that leave us now?"

Lord sank down into a chair beside Gideon and picked up his wine from a small table set beside it.

"You must have patience, Rome was not built in one day: and he that hopes, must give his hopes their Currents. For the present time we must be like the broody hen upon her eggs who waits for what she has worked upon to hatch." He sighed and tipped the last of the wine from cup to mouth, then set the empty cup down again. "Tomorrow we will have much to do but for now we must steel our souls against adversity and restocking our feet. We are summoned to supper with our hosts and their guests who, I fear, will again include the redoubtable and most irritating Mr Hobbes."

Gideon knew Lord was trying to lighten their burden, but somehow the attempt missed its mark. As he pulled on his still damp stockings, his thoughts were not of supper or Thomas Hobbes but of the morrow and what it might bring.

Chapter Eighteen

Nick had hoped that once back in York he might secure permission to return home to Howe for a time. After all, it was winter and conventional wisdom said that in winter one didn't fight wars, one withdrew to winter quarters and awaited the spring campaigning season. But this war between the king and his parliament seemed set to defy that convention. He wanted to go home to spend some time there and see if things had changed with Christobel. Surely by now she would be more accepting of her new position as Lady Tempest, mistress of Howe and willing to consider the notion of beginning their marriage afresh? He desperately needed to secure his position with the Covenant and if Mags was no longer in reach, it seemed that having a relationship with his wife was the sole key left to that.

But things in York were not what he expected. He expected to be welcomed back much as the Prodigal Son, celebrated for having escaped imprisonment by great daring and through much danger. Danny had warned him they wouldn't be praised, but that made little sense to Nick. When waking him to say the summons to the earl had arrived a scant handful of hours after they got back to York, Danny pushed a roll of paper into Nick's hand saying that it should help matters.

The earl was in his new war room in Clifford Tower at the heart of fortified York. He was alone apart from a couple of men of civilian appearance who Nick didn't know, and acknowledged Nick's bow with a cold nod, face set in an unpromising frown.

"I am surprised to see you, Sir Nicholas. Rumour is torn between your desertion and your death. Personally, I had considered the second more probable. The reports from the men who escaped from the house you had been defending gave the impression that was the most likely outcome."

"Desertion?" Nick was aghast. "Why would anyone think for a moment that—?"

"The Earl of Newport informed me that he sent you to me the night before we attacked Tadcaster to ask my will, having received a message he assumed was of malicious intent purporting to be from me to delay him. He said that he had great suspicion regarding the note, but you assured him it was genuine. He then sent you to ride to me to discover if indeed it was."

Nick was still exhausted. He had endured four days of intense danger with too little sleep only to return to accusations of perfidy. His first response was fury. He opened his mouth to deny the charge and say that the Earl of Newport was a coxcomb, a coward and a traitor. Then some small corner of his mind, with a voice very like Danny Bristow's, counselled caution. He closed his mouth again quickly and drew a brief steadying breath.

"I think my lord, the Earl of Newport is perhaps mistaken in what he recalls," he said instead. But that proved very little less incendiary.

"Are you saying the earl *lied* to me?" Newcastle asked, his brows knitting.

Nick shifted uncomfortably.

"Of course not, sir. I think he just might have been a little confused or—"

"Speak plainly. Did you tell the earl the note was genuine?"

Nick tried to remember what his exact words had been. So much had happened since that it was not easy. He just remembered the supercilious expression on the face of Mountjoy Blount and being so angry that Danny had needed to take him outside.

"I didn't think it genuine, sir. But I do not recall what I said to the earl."

It was very obvious to Nick that since he had been captured Blount had thought him the perfect scapegoat for what had happened around his own failure to support the attack on Tadcaster. Especially since until Nick rode into York he had been assumed killed in the fighting.

"And did you ride to Tadcaster on his orders to ask me about the note?"

Nick wondered how he should answer.

THE PHYSICIAN'S FATE

"I rode right away with Lieutenant Bristow to inform you that the earl wasn't coming and why."

Newcastle shook his head.

"You did *not* do that," he repeated. "If you had, perhaps we would have lost fewer men."

Nick swallowed hard, remembering his own frustration at the time in not being able to do precisely that.

"I was prevented from doing so, sir. When we reached the edge of the fighting, just by the mill, we encountered Lieutenant Colonel Atkins, and he commanded me and Lieutenant Bristow to join his attack force."

The earl looked at him then, frowning.

"That can hardly be confirmed or otherwise as Atkins is dead."

Nick thought desperately. "The men we were given to command, they can confirm it, sir."

Now the earl looked both troubled and perplexed, his expression dark

"You are asking me to believe your account over that of the Earl of Newport. That and this unlikely tale of escape from Hull and Selby. It seems to me you were treated rather well for a prisoner."

And that was when Nick realised that this was more than just a conversation about what he had done. This was an interview at the end of which the earl was going to decide whether or not to try him in a court-martial. Blount had covered his own inaction and incompetence by making it seem that Nick and Danny had misled him, and he would be likely to continue to press some such lie against them

The realisation of what that could mean made Nick feel abruptly weak-kneed. Then he remembered and reached into his doublet where he had thrust the papers Danny had given him and clutched them like a talisman.

"I did my best, my lord. I was taken prisoner and fought free. I also recorded anything of note that we could remember—myself and my lieutenant who was kept captive with me." He held out the papers and the earl took them carefully with just a finger and thumb as if expecting they might bite him. He turned away as he opened them and held them up to the light from a nearby window.

Nick could see the pages were dense with lists, labelled sketches and annotated plans and he realised Danny must have been working on them all the time he himself had been sleeping.

As he read the earl muttered "Good God," under his breath a couple of times. Then he passed the pages to one of the men, telling him to get copies made immediately. When he returned his attention to Nick, the earl's expression was very different, more speculative and appraising.

"If that information should prove to be accurate…"

"It is, sir," Nick said confidently. He was very sure anything Danny had drawn up would be precise and detailed.

The earl seemed thoughtful then and lifted a hand in dismissal.

"I will need to speak with you again shortly. For now, keep within the city. Ensure your movements are known and refrain from the taverns and bawdyhouses. I need to consider matters and once I have settled this with Newport, I will have work for you."

Nick made a neat military bow and left quickly, wondering if he had said what he should or spoken too fully—or worse, if he had left out something of import. That he hadn't been detained boded well, but the earl had told him to remain available and keep in York, so things were not yet settled.

He found Danny asleep and shook him awake.

"Mountjoy Blount tried to have us declared deserters," he explained when Danny sat up, bleary-eyed and shaking his head as if to clear it.

"Did he succeed?" Danny asked. "Are we to be hanged?" He sounded as if he was too tired to care.

"No. I think I persuaded the earl that it was calumny against us. That was not easy to do whilst not accusing Blount."

Danny nodded and rubbed at his face. "You did well, sir."

Then he lay back down again and closed his eyes. Nick shook his shoulder and Danny opened his eyes again but did not sit up.

"We are to keep ourselves ready. The earl said he will have work for me."

"Then," Danny said, "I might suggest, sir, we both get some sleep so that we can be properly awake when any orders come from the earl."

THE PHYSICIAN'S FATE

"But—"

Danny groaned and rolled so his back was to Nick. "We both need sleep."

Nick wasn't so sure that he did. Having had a brief sleep and been grilled by the earl he was in no mood to return to bed. He was about to insist that Danny got up when it occurred to him that there was something he needed to do without any other company.

Leaving Danny sleeping he headed across York to the merchant's house where his father had taken up residence.

When Nick arrived, he was informed that Colonel Sir Richard Tempest was having dinner and was shown through to the same parlour as before to await him.

His father entered the room, and Nick thought how grey he looked—grey all over, grey hair, grey eyes and a grey tinge to his skin. He pulled in his lips when he saw it was Nick standing by the fire.

"They said you were dead," he said coldly, his tone almost implying that it would have been better if that had been so.

Stung, but used to his father's ways Nick managed a riposte of sorts.

"Well, now you see I am alive. You can kill the fatted calf."

"That would be a waste. Only two of us to eat it. Did you succeed in what you set out to do?"

"Which part?"

Nick's father got up and poked at the fire in the hearth viciously, sending a small cascade of sparks and embers flying up the chimney.

"You are still acting as if this is some kind of game that you can win, Nicholas. You always were boneheaded and easily led astray. I told you last time we spoke that we were in a bad position. You were the one who suggested a possible solution."

The failure stuck in his throat and Nick shook his head.

"If I recall *you* did that," he said.

"I suggested a delaying tactic only. You were the one who offered a remedy." Putting the poker back in its rack, his father straightened up. "Clearly you failed, or you wouldn't be so reluctant to speak up. You were exactly the same as a child.

Anything to avoid admitting you did wrong. Who are you going to blame for it this time, hmm?"

Before God he had tried, Danny had tried, to kill Mags. After all he had been through and the accusations of desertion and betrayal, he had faced down from Mountjoy Blount, it was more than Nick could bear. His fist had lashed out and his father staggered backwards and fell. By good fortune he was beside the chair he had been sitting on and he collapsed back into that.

Appalled at what he had done, Nick stepped forward hand lifted now in supplication.

"I'm sorry, I have no idea what—"

"Oh, stop whining," his father wiped at the small trickle of blood that was running from his mouth. "That's the first time I've seen you stand up for yourself properly, though of course, you choose the wrong time to do so." He pushed himself upright in the chair and for a moment Nick saw in his face a little of the ferocity that had made him fear his father so much as a child. "I sent you to Coupland all those years ago because your mother had made a milksop of you, and you needed toughening up. You are still a milksop, but whether I like it or not you're one who has to carry my name."

"I have always done my best," Nick protested. "All you ever asked of me."

"I don't blame *you*," his father let out a sigh. "You cannot help who you are. What you are. I blame the Covenant for that. And Coupland. I'd seen what he had done with Philip Lord, and I believed he could do the same with you. But instead, he left you in the hands of his servants, men like Hoyle. Good men, solid men, but servants with nothing beyond the basics to offer. No. I don't blame you at all. It was my fault for thinking Coupland would give you the same fire he gave to Lord."

That stung as salt rubbed into the open wounds in Nick's soul.

"I am a better man than Philip Lord," he snarled. "I'm not a traitor or a murdering rapist."

"Better man?" His father laughed. "I doubt any of us are *better* men than Lord on just about any count you might care to name. He was bred and raised to be the best of men."

THE PHYSICIAN'S FATE

Nick gaped at his father.

"Oh, for goodness' sake, boy. Do you think that means anything in this world? Sir Philip Lord is a dangerous man only because he is as he is. Were he feeble, or flawed, or incompetent he would have been swept away long ago and not be any problem to us today. It is because of his greatness that he must be destroyed."

"Then I don't see the point—"

"The point is I wanted that for you also. I wanted that kind of greatness for the Tempest name. But Coupland didn't oblige even though you were his heir as well and I was too slow to realise it. By the time I'd understood the depth of his failure to do so it was too late. But what is done is done. And it is not as if Henry has shone much more brightly despite my very best efforts with him, so perhaps breeding makes less difference than I once thought it did."

Nick bridled at that, his anger kindling.

"I did my best to learn all I was taught. You can hardly blame me if the lessons were lacking."

"I just told you I don't," his father said. "Besides, the clay was weak. Your mother was a dull-witted woman, caring only for fashion, gossip and entertainment." He sighed and Nick realised his father had no awareness of the pain his words were causing, like a dagger in Nick's chest, being turned in his heart. "Anyway, you will hear it from the earl soon enough I'm sure, but I am being given leave to go home. I can scarce ride now as it is. The physician tells me if I rest through the winter, I might be a man reborn in the spring."

"I am sure he is right," Nick said quickly, though in all truth he was far from certain. His father didn't look at all well.

"You do?" his father sounded surprised and dismissive. "Personally, I think the man is a mountebank, but I will take his judgement as far as it goes. However, the clear point is that if I'm not here the regiment we raised lacks a commander. I was going to give it to Henry, but as you have come back it will fall to you."

Nick tried to make sense of that statement.

"Fall to me?" he echoed.

"Oh, for goodness' sake are you addle-pated? You will have to take command of our men."

Nick realised then and was horrified.

"You mean I am to be made commander in your place?"

His father nodded, still looking exasperated.

"Yes. You will be Colonel Sir Nicholas Tempest and most men would think that a high honour, so why is your face set to curdle milk?"

But Nick knew he couldn't answer that in any terms his father would accept so he just shook his head.

"It's an honour I hadn't considered," he said honestly. "The earl said he wanted me to keep myself available. I thought perhaps he might appoint me his scoutmaster. I'd not—I'd never expected promotion to colonel."

"Well, it's your right," his father said. "The men were raised from Coupland and Tempest lands in the main and it was our money that equipped them."

"It would mean I'd not be able to go back to Howe to keep Christmas."

His father blinked.

"Are you a child that you need to keep Christmas with more than a visit to church? There is a war, and we are fighting it. These puritans have no notion of festivities or Christmas, they won't stop the war for it, you can be sure."

Nick bit down on the words that ran to his tongue, that if his father went home, it would be to a household that was indeed keeping Christmas this year, even if perhaps less flamboyantly than in other years. What he couldn't say, of course, was that he needed to get home so he could attempt to resolve matters with his wife. That he had seen the Christmas season as an opportunity to try and ensure that instead of having to lie to the Covenant men about her being with child it could be an undisputed matter of fact.

"I have arranged for you to have this house when I leave," his father continued. "The owners are keen to depart. I think they've decided the political weather here is not in their favour. They were quick to ride out to greet our army but seem less persuaded now

THE PHYSICIAN'S FATE

we are here. When I'm gone you can have it and can arrange your household as you see fit."

It was a princely gift in the city which was so tight on accommodation and if he was indeed promoted it would allow him to live in a manner appropriate to his status. On the heels of that thought came the first stirrings of another idea, an idea which could perhaps solve many of his problems. Thanking his father, he returned to the issue in hand. "And what about the Covenant now?"

His father looked at him and for a moment Nick thought he was going to say something dismissive. Instead, he nodded.

"If all else fails, we have one last card to play, but better you have no knowledge of that yet."

Nick was beside his father's chair in one swift stride. "Tell me," he demanded.

His father lifted a weary hand. "You are too hasty, Nicholas, you always were. There's no point burning down the house just to get a few rats out of the cellar. Besides, maybe it is better destroyed or left alone. Something to be unearthed in a future times when our descendants a hundred years hence will laugh at the folly of their forebears." He fell silent for a few moments. "Regardless, now is not the right time and I've said enough."

Nick felt as he had done as a child. It was as if he were being shut from the room when the men were talking secrets within secrets and making decisions that shaped his life. But he knew his father well enough to be sure he would get no more on the topic no matter how hard he pressed.

"I shall await your convenience, sir," he said, not even attempting to hide the sarcasm.

His father frowned. "Of course, you will, you have no other option." He pushed himself to his feet, making it clear the discussion was done. "Just remember whatever happens you bear the name Tempest."

What was it the Covenant man had said? *Would you not wish a new royal dynasty to have the Tempest name?* It was a sobering thought and troubled Nick as his father walked with him to the door.

"I'll be leaving York in two days then this house will be yours. The owners plan to be gone by the end of the week."

"But you will move back here and to the army when your strength returns," Nick said, which made his father laugh.

"If God is willing," he conceded. "Until such a time you are in my place, and I expect you to uphold the Tempest name with as much honour as I would."

His father stopped on the threshold and put a hand on Nick's shoulder.

"Despite everything, I am glad you came back." He touched the place on his jaw where a bruise was beginning to purple. "You have more steel in you than I thought at least."

Like all his more meaningful exchanges with his father, Nick was left feeling confused, although this time less angry than usual for some reason he couldn't fathom. But he had long since stopped trying to work out how to please his father. Instead, as he made his way back to his quarters, he was thinking through the idea that had come to him when he learned his father had leased the house.

This time when he found Danny asleep, he insisted.

"You must wake up. I have work for you."

Danny pushed himself up at that, skin looking pale behind his freckles and stifling a yawn. "Work that can't wait even a couple of hours, sir?"

"You have had a couple of hours," Nick pointed out reasonably. "Now I need you to leave for Howe immediately. I am not permitted to go, but you were not mentioned by name so there is no reason I shouldn't send you."

Danny rubbed his eyes.

"Howe Hall?"

"Yes," Nick snapped, suddenly impatient. "I have a house in York now and I want you to go to Howe with your best men and fetch my wife here."

THE PHYSICIAN'S FATE

Chapter Nineteen

Gideon woke early, the sounds of Paris, now familiar, as the city stirred itself for the day. He had been in France just over a week and in Paris for five days, but it seemed much longer. Thoughts drifting to Oxford, he prayed as he did every morning—for Zahara and Kate, for Anders, Shiraz and then for Lord whose soul he was sure was in sore need of redemption.

He was in a reflective mood as he went downstairs. A voice from behind stopped him as he reached the second flight.

"Look how yon one-ey'd waggoner of heaven
Hath, by his horses' fiery-winged hoofs,
Burst ope the melancholy jail of night;"

Gideon turned to see Sir Philip Lord, as immaculately clad as ever in his guise as knight banneret and envoy of King Charles, an appearance Gideon knew now was no more or less adopted than his servant guise. He wondered who Lord would be if he were not forever having to act a role as the world required.

"And with his gilt beams' cunning alchymy
Turn'd all these clouds to gold, who, with the winds
Upon their misty shoulders, bring in day.

Then sully not this morning with foul looks… or perhaps not foul so much as distracted," Lord decided, catching up with Gideon and studying his expression with mock intensity. "I hope not distracted by too much as we have work waiting. Even before the one-ey'd waggoner took to the road, my man was checking the post stations in Paris as they stirred for the day—those where a man returning on the road from Gisors might have finished his journey."

"And?" Gideon was suddenly anything but distracted.

"Our friend Dr Charron did indeed hire a horse from Paris on the twenty-eighth of November last but there is no record of him returning."

"He didn't come back by the following evening?" Gideon knew a stab of disappointment. He had been increasingly sure Charron was the guilty man.

"You miss my point," Lord said. "There is no record of his return at all. On the twenty-ninth or any other day."

Gideon tried to think what that could mean.

"He stole a horse?"

Lord laughed and clapped Gideon on the shoulder then headed downstairs, glancing back up at him.

"No. And since he is clearly back in Paris now, it means either he used another name, or he left his last horse outside the city. If the latter, we should know soon enough. Now come eat and fortify yourself for the day."

They ate a brief meal in which Lord laid out what he had clearly already considered regarding the day's agenda.

"I also had a man go to the Châtelet and he returned with word that Charron was correct. Somehow Jensen's name has been moved forward on the list and we need to make sure he is not brought to trial this afternoon." Lord must have seen his horror because he placed a hand on Gideon's arm. "That is not cause for alarm, it simply means I must pander myself to those with the power and ability to prevent it. But your first step is, I think, a visit to the sign of the cock. Charron will not be in the consulting room today as we know Monday is a day he is not working there, but you could ask Renaudot and others about him. We may learn something of interest. You will have two of my men with you in case our friend decides to make another attempt to relieve you of the burden of your life. Meanwhile we may yet get confirmation of Charron's return by post horse."

"And there is the woman," Gideon said.

Lord frowned.

"The woman?"

"The one Anders mentioned who he went to see on Charron's behalf that day. She said something strange about pictures. If I am at the Bureau I will see if I can find Anders' notes with her address and look over the room where he was staying."

Lord nodded.

"Very well. Then we can hopefully both return here for dinner bearing the laurels of success. If I am detained, which might be needful, I will send word."

Lord set out this time in a hired carriage with outriders, looking as flamboyant and imposing as any noble in France. With him, at his request, went Richard Browne. Between them Lord seemed confident that they could petition, intimidate or bribe whoever was needed to ensure Anders' trial was deferred.

Gideon took to the streets in much less dramatic fashion, on foot. As well as the French servant he had been lent by Browne he was also being shadowed by two of Lord's men, something that made him feel a little safer.

He left the servant to inspect what was for sale in the Bureau's shop and crossed to the consultation room where men were holding their numbered tickets and waiting to be seen. He was about to ask where he might find Dr Renaudot, when he appeared from one of the side rooms in deep conversation with another man whom Gideon did not recognise. Glancing up, Renaudot caught Gideon's eye, then touched the man he was talking with lightly on the shoulder and excused himself, before crossing over.

"You have news of—" Renaudot caught himself and went on almost at once, "of our mutual friend? Josselin said you had been to see him."

Gideon opened his mouth to explain he was still trying to find out what was needed, but Renaudot lifted a finger.

"One moment, I must quickly see to a couple of urgent matters then we can talk in my cabinet." He vanished again into the throng and Gideon was left, like flotsam stranded at high tide, watching the flow of people into and out of the building.

"Monsieur Fox."

He turned to see Josselin Voclain.

"I am glad I saw you here or I would have had to send a message. You said I should do so if I recalled anything that might help."

"And you have?"

Voclain nodded. "Or I think so. You see I was talking things over with Théophraste and he was saying how sad he was about Anders as of all the physicians we have had here he was the one who was the most humble, the happiest to help and the least likely to argue with others."

"That does sound like Anders," Gideon agreed.

"Yes, but it reminded me of the fact that I saw Claude and Gaspard arguing quite heatedly a couple of times in the days before Gaspard's death and yet before that they had seemed to be very good friends and much in each other's company. At the time I thought it was just a falling out of the kind that can happen between friends and as I liked neither of them, I thought no more of it. But after what you said, it made me wonder if it might be of some significance after all."

Gideon felt his pulse lift its speed.

"Did you hear what they were arguing about at all?"

Voclain shook his head. "I had no wish to know so I kept well away. But Claude seemed very angry, and Gaspard was being insistent, that is all I can say for sure."

"It might well be significant," Gideon told him, his thoughts racing. What if they had missed something important? What if Proulx and Charron had somehow both been involved in the murder? Proulx was a man always desperate for money, with a known record of using extortion to try and fund his gambling habits, and Charron seemed to have a source of finance from somewhere.

Then Gideon realised Voclain was still talking.

"...and she would very much like to accept the Schiavono's offer of a place at Saint-Léon-du-Moulin. I wonder if you might be kind enough to enquire of him when it would be convenient to call on him to make the arrangements?"

"Of course," he said, "I will speak to Sir Philip for you."

Voclain was effusive in his thanks then took his leave just as Renaudot reappeared, apologising for the time he had taken and ushering Gideon up the stairs to his cabinet.

"It is very sad for me," he said as they went into the room. "Before the death of the cardinal I would have been preparing to hold another conference at this time on a Monday. They were such fascinating events, we had topics from across the whole realm of human experience, from science and metaphysics, to practical issues and the organisation of society."

Gideon thought for a moment, as he took the seat he was offered and Renaudot settled himself beside the escritoire.

THE PHYSICIAN'S FATE

"I may even have read something about one," he said, remembering. "It was a pamphlet I picked up discussing the idea of whether there was anything new or if all knowledge was merely being rediscovered. I recall it pointing out that even things we think of as having only been around for a couple of centuries, such as printing and gunpowder were known to the Chinese for over a thousand years."

That made Renaudot nod enthusiastically. "Yes, I remember that one well. You would have enjoyed attending them I am sure, monsieur. Anyone with an open and enquiring mind did. But now…" He sighed and spread his hands. "Without the assured protection of the cardinal we would be open to all kinds of accusations, so I deemed it safer to stop."

"What about the other projects you run from here?" Gideon asked. It had not occurred to him how much Cardinal Richelieu had facilitated the charitable and educational causes Renaudot espoused.

Renaudot lifted his shoulders and spread his hands. "In all truth, I do not know. I cannot see what harm anyone can find in what we do here. It is all for the good of the poor people of Paris. The employment exchange, the place to sell and redeem possessions, the consultations—all we do is for the poor."

"Even *La Gazette*?"

That made Renaudot laugh. "Most importantly *La Gazette*. It keeps all our citizens informed of what is going on and sells widely, carrying advertisements of importance to what we do here at the Bureau."

"You are a very busy man," Gideon said, feeling he had given enough time to acknowledging Renaudot and his work. "I will not keep you from all you need to do for long, but I understand that I might be able to gain access here, with your permission, to some documents which could be of assistance to the task of showing Anders' innocence."

"Of course. Naturally. What would you like to see?"

"The dispensary listings for the week before and after the day of the murder would be very useful. Also, Anders told me I could access his personal notes. They would be in his possessions in the room he had here."

"And that is all you need of me?"

Gideon hesitated. He would have very much liked to ask what Renaudot thought of Proulx and Charron and what he knew of any links between them, but from the previous visit he had learned caution. As Lord had warned, if Renaudot thought another of his physicians might be accused he could become defensive and even uncooperative.

So instead of asking anything more he just nodded. "That would be most helpful, if you can arrange it for me."

Renaudot got to his feet. "As it happens, I have the last month's dispensary lists with me here to be gone over and costed, I will give them to you and show you up to the room Anders was staying in. His things should all be there. Then I will have to get back to my work." He shook his head as he pulled a pile of the papers towards him, strung together and then held them out to Gideon. "It will be harder now we have lost Demoiselle Savatier. She was such a good and efficient apothecary, but she had to leave to help nurse an aunt in Rouen or Rheims, I forget now which she said. Perhaps she will come back when that is done."

Gideon bit on his tongue as he stood and took the string of papers, pushing them into his doublet to keep them safe. It was, he agreed, always sad to lose a good and skilled worker. Renaudot took him up a flight of stairs and then along a passageway and up another flight before stopping by a door and producing a key to unlock it, revealing a further passage beyond with a door on each side and one at the end. The building was clearly much bigger than its frontage suggested or perhaps had sprawled over more than its own street level facade below.

"Here," Renaudot said, holding out a key. "I will leave you with this so you can lock up when you are done. If you need me for anything else, I shall be in the consulting room for a time. These are all rooms where those who work here and need a place to live are allowed to stay until they can find suitable accommodation. The one on the left is Anders'. Claude was staying here for a short time recently too, when he lost his previous dwelling, but since he moved out, I have no one staying." He sighed. "Perhaps after Christmas. I am so short on physicians now."

After he was alone Gideon went to the room he had been told was Anders' and felt a wash of emotion as he opened the door. The room was sparsely furnished but he recognised the familiar leather bag which Anders had always carried, containing his medical materials. It had been left open on the small table in the window and its contents pulled apart. Someone had made a small attempt to restore it to order but had clearly given up, perhaps uncertain where things should go. Knowing the care with which Anders had always kept it before, it was painful for Gideon to see.

The notebook was there but written in Danish so he could make very little of it. He looked at the last few pages and could see 'november' which seemed to be the same in Danish as in English. Then he found the twenty-ninth. The address was there, and Gideon stared when he saw that Madeleine Froissart lived in rooms beside Le Cheval Rouge. That would not necessarily mean she was of the same occupation as the women he had met in that place, but the coincidence was an odd one.

Keeping the notebook in his hand, Gideon left then. He felt glad to end his intrusion into Anders' possessions. He had just relocked the main door to the passageway and was about to make his way back downstairs when he had a thought. Unlocking the passageway door again, he took the time to investigate the other rooms along the short corridor.

It was not hard to work out which room Claude Charron must have been using. It was the only one of the other two that showed signs of relatively recent occupation and less undisturbed dust. It was as sparsely furnished as Anders' room had been, with just a bedstead, a table, a chair and a washstand. Gideon realised he had no real idea of what he might hope to find there and turned to go, pushing the notebook into his doublet for safekeeping. That was when he realised, he still had not studied the dispensary listings, so he sat at the table by the window to get the best of the light and started to go through them.

He was not really surprised to find that there was no mention of laudanum on the lists at all for the entire two weeks. It was possible, he supposed, that he could go back even further and check, but he had no idea how far back he would need to go. He wished he had the foresight to ask Yolande Savatier when she had put the laudanum in the dispensary. Irritated at himself he stood up and snatched the lists, but one of the pages had torn from the string and fluttered to the floor. Of course, it landed in an inaccessible place behind the table, and he had to put the table away from the wall to reach it.

As he did so another sheet of paper dropped down from where it had been trapped behind the table against the wall. Curious, Gideon picked up both pages and examined the one that had dropped down. It was big enough to cover his hand and rectangular in shape. The paper was a thick variety and it had on it an inked over sketch of a street scene in Paris which reminded him of some he had seen recently, but at that moment he could not recall where.

Pushing the table back, he picked up the papers and carefully undid the string, making a new hole to reattach the loose sheet as he had done many times for his own papers. Then picked up the sketch and studied it. Wondering if it might say who had drawn it on the back, he turned it over and then, catching a glimpse of what was there, dropped it again as if it had burned his fingers.

There was another inked sketch on the back, and this was not of a Paris street scene. He had no doubt that the subject was most likely a Parisienne, but she was completely naked, in a pose which was meant to display and left nothing at all to the imagination. It was a view of the feminine form Gideon had been vouchsafed perhaps twice before in his life and whilst it was undoubtedly alluring on one level, something about it sent a chill down his spine that had nothing to do with arousal.

He turned it over again to hide the picture and it was then he realised where he had seen that same sketched Paris street scene, or one very similar—on the wall of Claude Charron's consulting room.

The next few minutes passed in something of a blur as he slid the sketch into the protection of Anders' notebook, left the room and headed back downstairs, locking the door to the passageway behind him. Renaudot was in the consulting room, mercifully

THE PHYSICIAN'S FATE

between appointments, so Gideon was able to return the key and dispensary lists. He was sure Renaudot must have said something and Gideon himself no doubt replied politely, but his next clear awareness was of being back on the streets of Paris. He had walked almost to the bridge before he remembered he had come out with a servant and had to return to fetch him. That responsibility helped to sober him again and he made the walk back to Richard Browne's residence as quickly as he could.

Gideon had hoped to find Lord returned so they could go straight away to visit Madeleine Froissart, but neither he nor Richard Browne had yet got back. Common sense dictated that it would be very unwise for Gideon to try and go anywhere near Le Cheval Rouge on his own, or even with the invisible presence of two of Lord's men who would no doubt follow him wherever he chose to go in Paris that morning.

Besides, although the pictures might be salacious and in very bad taste for a physician to produce, it was neither illegal nor yet any kind of proof that he had been involved with the murder of Geneviève Tasse. All that Madeleine Froissart could do was confirm what Gideon was now very sure about, that Claude Charron was making a lucrative living producing lewd sketches and hiding them behind innocent images that their owners could keep on open display.

It did speak to the nature of Claude Charron though and Gideon had no problem imagining that a man who was happy to earn a living in such a way might be capable of dosing a woman with laudanum to take full advantage of her. If the nature of the sketch he had was typical of Charron's work, it spoke to a disrespect for women that bordered on the obscene.

It occurred to him that whilst it might not be safe to venture into the tangle of streets around Le Cheval Rouge, the Marais was a very different prospect with its wide new streets and houses. Besides he had just rented some rooms there, so he had every reason to go without in any way causing consternation to Claude Charron.

He set off with a confident stride but had barely left the house when he found his path barred by two men he recognised as being

Lord's. The same two who had accompanied them when they returned from visiting Josselin Voclain and, no doubt, the two who had been following him when he went to the Bureau D'Adresses.

He waited for them to step aside, but instead one of them spoke in a rasping English.

"I'm sorry, sir, but the Schiavono said we were to be sure you remained in the house once you were safely back from the Rue Calandre."

Gideon bridled at that.

"Sir Philip has no business telling me where I may and may not go."

The man who had spoken shrugged.

"You work for him, same as we do, sir," he said, his tone phlegmatic. "He tells us where we may and may not go. Today he told us we may not go away from the house once you were back here, and we were to keep with you at all times until he got back. He's not back yet so that means as we can't leave here, you can't either, sir."

Gideon had a strong feeling that, ridiculously easy as it would be to pick apart that logic, it would not alter the substance of the issue. For a moment he wondered what they would do if he simply pushed past them and carried on his way. But somehow he doubted they would even allow him to do that much. Knowing defeat as much as frustration, he turned away to go back into the house. This was clearly a matter he would have to take up with the high-handed Sir Philip, not his men.

"And sir, the Schiavono said we should keep a close eye on any water-vendors or other people who might be leaving the house as well."

Gideon felt his ears redden but didn't turn around. He could hear the grin he would see if he did. His anger at Lord growing, he was hard pressed to rein it in and produce a polite smile when Elizabeth Browne intercepted him.

"Oh, thank goodness you are back so soon, Mr Fox," she said, sounding flustered. "A messenger from the Duchesse d'Aiguillon has just called asking for Sir Philip. When I explained he was absent, your name was offered instead. The duchess is asking you to attend upon her at the Palais de Cardinal. She is sending a carriage which will be here shortly. The messenger was sent ahead so Sir Philip would have time to prepare but as you are here, and he is not..."

Gideon barely hesitated. If the Duchesse d'Aiguillon wished to speak with himself or Lord, it could only be about one matter.

"Please tell the messenger I will be ready momentarily," he said. "I just need to get changed."

"But Sir Philip—"

"Is not here," Gideon said, his tone very reasonable. "Thank you for letting me know."

A sliver of glee glowed in his soul that whatever orders Lord might have left, neither Elizabeth Browne nor Lord's men could prevent his leaving.

He had little that was suitable wear for meeting with a duchess, except the extravagant outfit that Lord had gifted to him for their original entry into Paris. A short time later, clad in blue and silver, he was shown into the carriage by a liveried servant. Its path, assured by outriders, took him as fast as a wheeled conveyance could travel in Paris, through the streets to the grand building that had been designed and built according to the wishes of Richelieu himself to be his Parisian home.

The Palais de Cardinal was truly magnificent.

As they approached along the Rue Saint Honoré, Gideon could see the beautiful modern facade with large windows on two floors and smaller ones under the gables. It was set opposite to the royal palace of the Louvre and looked very little less grand. The carriage swept past the guards, through the gates and into the cloistered building, where it came to a halt. A servant opened the door and once he had alighted Gideon was escorted swiftly through room after room, each more eye wateringly lovely than the one before.

Finally, he was shown into an apartment of rooms where some of the furniture and decorations were being packed and carried out. The last room overlooked the formal gardens, and he was ushered towards a group of three women who stood by the window looking out at them. They were all dressed in black, two slender and younger, one rather well rounded and close to her fortieth year on one side of it or the other.

It was the older woman who wore the most expensive gown, in embroidered silk taffeta gemmed with clusters of jet. Her light brown hair was arranged in a fashionable confection of ringlets framing her face and the rest pulled back with black lace and ribbons and even black feathers. She had a small mouth and full cheeks and wore a necklace close about her neck of fat pearls and had matching earrings. The front of her gown was decorated with a black bow pinned by a broach which had a similar pearl suspended from it. In her sleeve, Gideon could see the same kerchief that Sir Philip Lord had been wearing before.

He needed no introduction to know this was the Duchesse d'Aiguillon, the favourite relative of Cardinal Richelieu, widowed at the age of eighteen and never remarried, but made by her uncle's influence, a duchess in her own right. Gideon gave a deep bow and felt painfully aware that his clothes, far from looking fashionable here, when set against the trappings of mourning, were completely out of place. But the duchesse seemed not to notice, or not to mind if she did.

"You must be Monsieur Fox," she said, her voice a pleasantly low and gentle one. "Philippe spoke highly of you. I will assume he is engaged with urgent business, or I am sure he would be here."

Gideon stumbled over his words for a moment then cleared his throat.

"He is engaged in the most urgent business of preventing a great miscarriage of justice, madame."

She gave a nod that seemed to barely move her head at all as she glided a couple of steps towards him and away from her ladies.

"I had thought he might be, and that is why I summoned you in his stead. Philippe said you were as his amanuensis in this matter, and I could trust you as I would himself." She stopped talking and for a moment studied Gideon's face as if seeking something there. "I firmly believe that God sometimes tests us by placing the path of truth and lies side by side and it is up to us to look closely and discern the difference."

THE PHYSICIAN'S FATE

Gideon was unsure what to say to that. It was the kind of sentiment he often heard from his more puritan acquaintances, but this woman was surely a Catholic.

"I believe seeking truth and justice is indeed work God sets us too," he said, and his sincerity was unfeigned as that was surely the keystone of his professional life.

She gave him a smile, her small mouth opening to reveal teeth that looked strong.

"I can see why Philippe likes you," she said. "But to business. He asked that I discover who of a short list of men was granted access to the Palais the night my poor, dear, Geneviève was killed. She was such a wonderful friend. That is her in the portrait of me with my uncle." The duchesse gestured to a picture that was being removed from the wall on one side even as they were talking. "And please excuse the activity, I am moving my things as this Palais now belongs to the king as my uncle wished."

Gideon heard her words but didn't really absorb them. He was staring at the face of Geneviève Tasse and trying to keep the cold horror from showing in his expression. The face of the woman in the portrait was the same face as he had seen before for the first time just that morning. The face of the woman in the much too revealing sketch. Pushing that information away as he couldn't think what it might mean and had no time to consider it more deeply, he forced his attention back to the duchesse.

"I made enquiries. Though to do such things has been more difficult since the passing of my uncle," she was saying. "I managed to engage the sympathy of one of the captains who asked amongst his men, and they said that all those mentioned on the list were admitted to the Palais that day. Dr Renaudot was here in the morning and the rest were all here at some point in the late afternoon and evening. The guard recalls three of them arriving together and then one coming a while after."

"Dr Claude Charron?" Gideon asked.

The smile reappeared and the duchesse gave another of her tiny nods.

"That is right. It is strange as Geneviève mentioned his name to me before. It would have been in October soon after my uncle returned here—he was bedridden even then, poor man. Geneviève had been consulting with Dr Charron over a health issue with her feet and had found his treatment effective. I might have said something to Philippe about it, but I forgot until Mariette here reminded me," She gestured towards the women waiting together by the window although Gideon was uncertain which of the two was the one being indicated. "Does this information help you at all?"

"It is of very great value indeed, madame," Gideon assured her. And it was. It explained why Charron might have been allowed private access to Geneviève Tasse's rooms alone. She already knew him and had no grounds to suspect he was anything other than a devoted physician. Gideon wondered how many other women had been gulled in a like manner. "Truly I believe your actions in this matter will help both save an innocent man and ensure the guilty party is brought to justice." He made a gallant bow, sensing that the audience was nearing its end.

"It has been a pleasure to meet you, Monsieur Fox. Please tell Philippe I hope he will visit me in *Le Petit Luxembourg* before he leaves Paris."

A short time later, Gideon was being escorted back through the Palais. He was a little surprised to find that the same carriage that had been made available to him before was waiting to take him "wherever in Paris monsieur might wish to go."

Monsieur, Gideon decided, wished to go to the Marais.

He alighted from the carriage a little way from the house where he now rented rooms. To arrive in such a conveyance would be marked and noted, and Gideon didn't want to draw too much attention to himself when he reached the house where Charron had rented rooms.

The same servant as before opened the door and welcomed him, enquiring effusively after his plans for taking up residence. Gideon escaped upstairs saying he wished to consider the decoration and such furnishings as he would need to bring. Once in the rooms, he waited until he heard the footsteps of the solicitous servant retreat then quickly crossed to the door of Charron's rooms and knocked. There was no reply and he knocked again. After a while he realised

THE PHYSICIAN'S FATE

that Charron was out, and his visit had been in vain. He would have to return later in the day with Lord.

"If you are after the physician, I rather think you are out of luck."

The speaker had just emerged from the other door on the landing and was betrayed by his garb as being the notary who lived there.

"I'll have to come back another time," Gideon agreed politely. His accent betrayed him.

"Ah, you must be the English lawyer who is to be my new neighbour," the notary sounded enthusiastic. "I am sure we must have much in common. Is Dr Charron your physician? If so, I think you may need to find a new one. When he left today he was carrying much luggage and was in a hurry. He didn't say so, but it seemed to me he was leaving Paris for good."

Chapter Twenty

Gideon was not molested on his walk back to the Brownes' residence, despite being alone and with only the sword by his thigh as a defence. It was just one more confirmation, if any were needed, that the man who had killed Geneviève Tasse, paid for the murder of Gaspard Proulx and the attempted murder of Gideon Lennox was indeed Claude Charron.

The two men Lord had left to be his guardians made no attempt to conceal themselves. They scowled at him as he returned. It occurred, belatedly, that having failed in their orders Lord wasn't going to be pleased with them. He was a man who wasn't hesitant in showing his displeasure in active ways. Gideon hoped his own news would be distraction enough to keep the worst of any wrath from their shoulders.

He wasn't too concerned that Charron had fled. Lord had said he would set men to watch the physician. Wherever he might go, Gideon was confident they would follow. The question that troubled him more was whether Lord had succeeded in delaying the trial and if all they had gathered to try to show Anders' innocence and Charron's guilt would be enough.

It was certain that even some of what they had found out could never be presented in any court case. He couldn't see himself showing the Duchesse d'Aiguillon the sketch he had with the face and features of Demoiselle Tasse put onto the sprawled, displaying, body of another woman entirely—perhaps that of Madeleine Froissart.

Gideon was also sure that any attempt to bring that picture into court would be prevented by any judge as being a gross obscenity And without it proving that Charron was obsessed by Geneviève Tasse and thus was a man one could expect to be guilty of seeking to drug her so that he might have his way with her, would be very difficult.

THE PHYSICIAN'S FATE

"You will be pleased to know I was successful in delaying the progress of justice," Lord's voice stopped Gideon with one foot on the stairs. "How fares *la duchesse*?"

Gideon turned back. It was always impossible to tell what Lord's true feelings were when he chose to hide them and at that moment the face he showed was bland and sculpted only into mild curiosity.

"She fares well—and despite it being most evident that she would have preferred your presence and not mine, was still most helpful. The duchesse did, however, demand your presence at *Le Petit Luxembourg*, whatever that may be, before you leave Paris. She still carried the token you had returned." It felt like a rather petty form of revenge for the indignity of being prevented from leaving the house.

But far from seeming perturbed Lord produced a smile that was close to a smirk. "*Le Petit Luxembourg* is a charming house seat beside the beautiful Luxembourg Gardens, and I will, of course, obey the summons in due course." Then his expression grew serious. "But such pleasures will have to wait until we have resolved the present issue. If you will come to my room, I have asked for food to be sent up so we can eat, share what we know and plan as we need."

"I will join you," Gideon agreed. "May I get changed first? You have a dozen such costumes. This is my only one." He turned away and then remembered and turned back. "But before I do so, I assume your men will have told you Charron has fled Paris."

Lord's head lifted and he looked at Gideon sharply.

"No. But then they may not have had any opportunity to do so if they have had to follow him with no notice. As soon as they are able, I am sure they will send word. However, that might not be until he stops for the night. I gave no orders that they should prevent him going anywhere, merely that they should follow him and tell me where he goes." Lord thought for a few moments then nodded. "There is nothing we can do about it until we hear where he has gone. Go and get changed and we can eat and discuss what we know."

Gideon went.

By the time he had dressed in a more appropriate style and gone back down to Lord's room, the meal had been served. The food was good, if not as hot as Gideon would have liked, but with their being late and it being carried through the house that was hardly surprising. As they ate, Lord explained he had spent the morning distributing his wealth and favours between the prévôt and a trio of senior judges at the end of which he had succeeded in persuading them that Anders' trial could wait until after Christmas.

"I am hoping that you have something that will make that use of mine and Richard Browne's time worthwhile." Lord had finished eating and moved to the window where he sat holding a cup of wine. "If after all that I still have to seek a pardon, on top of the amounts I have just distributed it will add not just insult to injury, but injury to injury."

Gideon was still eating but wiped his fingers and, reaching into the modest doublet he had put on, pulled out Anders' notebook, which he had placed there to bring downstairs. He slid the sketch out with the side that showed the Parisian street scene uppermost.

Lord took it and frowned.

"A good artist. He has an eye for perspective and is able to give life to his figures in quite a realistic way. Charron?" He looked at Gideon, who had his mouth full by then so nodded and made a gesture with one hand, miming turning the picture over.

"A very good artist," Lord said, eyes narrowing slightly as he studied what he found there. "Excellent portraiture and a superb understanding of the anatomy of the female body, although I have the strangest feeling the two are not from the same source and this is a form of human chimaera." He put the sketch down with the obscene side facing upwards. "It seems Claude Charron had an obsession with Demoiselle Tasse."

Lord must have been shown the same painting Gideon had seen.

"According to the duchesse, he was treating her for some problem with her feet a couple of months ago, so he must have had a degree of close access to her at that time. The duchesse also managed to discover that all the men on the list were at the Palais at some point during that day. Renaudot in the morning, Anders,

Voclain and Proulx together in the early evening and Charron a little later."

"So Charron was there, had an excuse to be alone with Demoiselle Tasse and could have performed the deed. Perhaps Proulx saw him and tried some blackmail. Or perhaps..." Lord paused, and his gaze became speculative. "Perhaps Proulx was involved in the drugging in some way."

Gideon nodded and, swallowing down the last of his meal, tapped the notebook.

"We have the address of the woman Anders mentioned, she is called Madeleine Froissart and she lives hard by Le Cheval Rouge."

"And makes her living, or at least part of it, by posing as an artist's model is my guess," Lord said. He picked up the sketch and studied it again. "I might like to meet Demoiselle Froissart."

"I think Kate might object," Gideon said acidly.

"I think Kate would like to meet Demoiselle Froissart too, truth be told," Lord said. "She has always found much to recommend bold women."

"Hardly bold if only her body is being used." Then Gideon stopped as a sudden thought occurred. "Perhaps that is why Charron is making such good money. What if instead of just pictures of a whore posturing, Charron will add the face of the purchaser's choice to whatever exposing or humiliating pose takes his patron's fancy?"

Lord looked back at the sketch and nodded.

"That would make sense. He would combine his evident skill at portraiture with his ability to copy from life the precise human form and that would indeed be something many men would be willing to pay for. It would explain both his wealth and his criminal connections."

"Then perhaps we should visit Madeleine Froissart," Gideon suggested.

Lord shook his head. "I want to be here when word comes of where Charron is to be found. All that we have here is not enough to free Anders. We need Charron himself and his confession."

"Where would he go?" Gideon wondered aloud, not really expecting a reply.

Lord shrugged. "Any big city in Europe. He could set up the same scheme all over again. My guess is that he was doing it on a smaller scale in Gisors before he came to Paris. But now he has mastered the technique, he would find a ready market for his wares just about anywhere."

There came a knock on the door and Lord was up from his seat and opening it almost at once. He was there listening to the man outside for less time than Gideon needed to count to ten, then he turned back, an almost viscous look of delight on his face.

"We have him."

Perhaps because of his familiarity now with the speed and efficacy with which Lord moved from his relaxed and at ease persona to the brutally efficient military one, Gideon was not too surprised that within less than a quarter of an hour they were mounted with a well-armed escort of four and demanding a path through the streets of Paris which was ceded as if by right. Then, free of the city at last, the horses were put to a ground-covering pace.

The ground they covered was hard with frost and in places a brittle layer of snow. Around them was a countryside that reminded Gideon of parts of England, a mix of woodland, forest, and farmland, mostly flat but with some low hills lifting the terrain. With few major obstacles to constrain it, the road ran straight, and they made good progress. It was afternoon and the winter sun was low in the clouded sky. These were the very shortest days of the year and the sun seemed to struggle to lift itself far over the horizon or shed more than the slightest modicum of warmth upon the earth.

It was only when Gideon saw they had ridden past the turn-off on the road that would go to Saint-Léon-du-Moulin that he remembered to ask where Claude Charron was expected to be found.

"At this moment he will be on the road," Lord said, having to lift his voice over the pounding of their horses' hooves. "He is a passenger in a coach to Gisors. He had a good amount of luggage with him."

"A public coach?"

Lord grinned, his teeth as white as his hair.

"That would have made things very awkward, but no—it is a privately hired one with a well-armed escort. However, it will no doubt be changing horses along the route."

"And we are not?"

"We are not," Lord agreed. "But then we are travelling three times faster at least and having to stop to change the horses will slow him even more. We must hope we catch him before we lose that advantage as our horses fatigue."

Despite that, it was getting dark, and their mounts were beginning to tire when they caught up. Indeed, Gideon had not even realised that had done so, his focus being on the road ahead and not on the coaching inn they had passed on the edge of a small town, the name of which he had not learned.

The first Gideon knew was when Lord turned them from the road and reined beside a small wood, the horses blowing clouds about them. It was twilight and hard to see features at any distance in that strange quality of light where day and night met.

"Why have we stopped?" Gideon asked.

His question was answered almost immediately by the arrival of another man.

"He is in the inn, Schiavono. Eating a meal. I overheard him telling the four men with him that they will stay the night and set off at first light."

"That is convenient," Lord said, the tone in his voice one Gideon recognised. It was the same tone he had used just before they jumped on the laundry boat. The tone that said for Lord this was a dangerous puzzle which he would take pure delight in solving with whatever of violence might be required. It was a tone that chilled Gideon. He knew Lord was no longer thinking of saving Anders or of what had happened to Geneviève Tasse. His thoughts were only on the immediate task, and he brought to it every aspect of his being.

"Do we take them when they leave?" one of the men asked.

"And spend the night shivering in the fields when there is an inn with warm beds and good food?" Lord laughed. "That would be folly. No, gentlemen, we will enjoy the hospitality of the coaching inn."

"Except," Gideon said, "Charron knows me and might find it a little suspicious that I am here."

Lord's eyes widened as if in discovery.

"But of course—you will be the bait."

Gideon felt his heart sink.

"Last time we did this I nearly drowned."

Lord gestured around them.

"I see no water here. Besides which you have myself, five of my men and your own sword. *Danger hath honour, great designs their fame; glory doth follow, courage goes before.* I have never known you lack courage."

A response Gideon didn't find particularly reassuring. But he knew that there would be little point raising an objection. Lord in such a mood would counter each with ease, wit and conviviality.

"Did Charron say he was here to meet someone?" Gideon asked instead. It seemed odd to him that having been so keen to escape Paris at speed and with a private coach, Charron had chosen to stop here for the night instead of pressing on further.

Lord looked towards the man who had just joined them who shook his head.

"Not in my hearing."

"It makes little difference," Lord said. "We need to secure him alive and ensure he gives us a full confession. Which with the resources we have at our disposal should not be hard to achieve."

"The plan being?"

"You will ride into the inn and take a room for the night. If Charron is visible, you greet him and explain you are heading north on some legal matter—or whatever seems appropriate to you at the time. Strive to join him and when you may, encourage him outside on some pretext. Then it is simple. We can have him away and thence to my house at Saint-Léon-du-Moulin within a couple of hours. There he will confess in writing to his crimes and tomorrow we deliver him, alive, together with the confession, to the prévôt at the Châtelet. Jensen will be exonerated, and we will leave Paris post-haste to be back in England in time to celebrate the Christmas season with our friends and loved ones in Oxford."

"And if he won't accept my company? Or decides I'm a danger to him and orders his men to attack me?"

"In the first case, you will tell me, and we will reconsider. In the second, he cannot do so in full sight of all in the inn so would need to order the men to follow you outside, where I will, of course, be at hand to rescue you." Lord shook his head. "But I truly do not consider that a likely outcome. I think he will see you, want to know your business and then once he is reassured, lower his guard."

"I suppose we'll find out," Gideon said. It was true he could see no better way to achieve the effective kidnapping of Claude Charron even if he disliked the proposal. "And what if he is meeting someone here?"

Lord laughed.

"In the worst case we may need to bring them along to Saint-Léon-du-Moulin as well, but I doubt it would come to that." He turned to beckon one of his men. "Dennel here will go with you as your servant." It was the same man who had refused to let Gideon leave the Brownes' residence. "If you go now, I will follow."

There was, Gideon could see, no reason to delay and every reason to move with speed to make an encounter with Charron more natural. After all, it was possible he might plan to retire early and eat in his own room.

Leaving Lord by the small wood he returned to the road with the reassuring presence of Dennel close behind.

The inn was busy but by no means full. Stepping into the cheerful warmth, as Dennel arranged stabling for their horses, Gideon was met by a plump man with passionately expressive hands who gestured with every word. Of course, the monsieur was most welcome. There was indeed a room available which he could share with his servant. Yes, monsieur could of course dine and—

"Mr Fox?"

Gideon turned to see Claude Charron descending the stairs, clad in clothes suited to travel and with a red manteau around his shoulders. Shaping a polite smile, Gideon tried to appear delighted to see a familiar if unexpected face.

"Monsieur Charron is it not? What on earth are you doing here?" If nothing else Gideon had learned from his legal practice that attacking first was always the best defence. He modified his smile then as if embarrassed. "I apologise, that must have sounded rude. I was just surprised to meet my new neighbour in a coaching inn."

"I have relatives in Gisors," Charron said, his own expression relaxing. "I had hoped to make the journey in one day, but…"

"I am for Rouen," Gideon said. "A small matter of a contract gone awry."

"This close to Christmas?" It might have been surprise or doubt that made Charron's eyebrows knit.

Gideon's pulse jumped. He had forgotten how close it was to Christmas here in France. He nodded and managed a long-suffering sigh. "Yes. This close to Christmas. I have to get there tomorrow afternoon. I have an early start and a hard day of travel ahead of me."

Charron's expression shifted almost instantly to solicitous sympathy.

"It will be a hard day indeed. But come, you must surely eat before you sleep. Join me and we can talk a little, get to know each other for the neighbours we are to be."

Gideon wondered then if the notary in the house in the Marais had been completely mistaken and Charron had been leaving Paris simply to spend Christmas in Gisors after all.

"I would be delighted," he said and asking the host to provide food for his servant, followed Charron to a private dining room which he had reserved at the back of the inn.

There were two men already in the room. One sat at the table with a glass of wine. The other was standing by the window and looking out over the poorly lit stable yard.

The man who was sitting Gideon recognised with shock. He had met him briefly at the house of the vintner André Villeneuve and in company with Ellis Ruskin. This was the viscount Lord had been abominably rude to when they were there. Because of that rudeness, he hadn't been presented by name. The same bright blue

THE PHYSICIAN'S FATE

eyes and attractive features but dressed much less finely than he had been on that occasion. The clothes were not just for travel, it was almost as if he had no wish to be marked for his rank.

The man at the window turned and frowned. Gideon had no idea who he might be, but he had spent enough time around such men over the last three months to know what he was. He was tall and broad set, wearing a very serviceable back sword on one thigh and a pistol by his hip.

"Who is this?" the viscount demanded as Charron closed the door behind them.

"Monsieur le vicomte," Charron said, his tone that of a polite introduction. "This is Monsieur Gideon Fox. He is a lawyer from England. He is travelling to Rouen."

"Fox?" the viscount echoed. Then looked more closely at Gideon, the first stirrings of recognition in his expression. "Isn't that the—"

"Yes," Charron said a little too quickly. "It is."

It was as if the temperature had dropped in the room. The well-armed man seemed to straighten a little, his gaze fixed on Gideon as a cat might look at a mouse.

"He is here alone?" the viscount asked.

"With a servant," Charron told him.

Gideon took a small step back. Charron was no fighter and Gideon had an idea to seize him and use him as a shield. Then the viscount nodded, and he gave Gideon the most charming smile.

"A pleasure to meet you again Mr Fox. I apologise for my rudeness. I was simply surprised. Dr Charron mentioned he had a new neighbour and I had not recognised the name. And please forgive my lack of formality, I have urgent need to return to England and must travel somewhat incognito. Let us be seated and eat."

Uncertain now if he was starting at shadows, Gideon made a brief bow and took a seat at the table. He had barely done so when the meal arrived and for a time there was no talking as everyone, except the armed man who stayed watchful standing beside the window, concentrated on the food.

Conversation when it developed remained very general, the state of the roads, the coldness of the season, the quality of the meal. Gideon found he had very little appetite. It was becoming increasingly hard to see how he could persuade Charron outside and the undercurrent of hostility directed at himself made him uncertain he would be allowed to leave the room alone.

"The vicomte is also travelling north," Charron said, helpfully as they finished the meal. "In fact, he is leaving tonight as he is in a hurry. Perhaps since Monsieur Fox is needing to get to Rouen tomorrow…"

"No."

"Thank you but no," Gideon's voice clashed with the viscount's.

Charron shrugged and smiled. "I just thought it might be easier."

The viscount pushed his plate away and got up, glaring at Charron. The charming facade had vanished.

"You presume too much, sir. Our business is done. Descoteaux and his men will take care of you. I need to go. My horses will be ready now." He gave Gideon a brief nod of farewell then turned to the armed man who had straightened up at the mention of the name. "You will look after *both* these gentlemen when I have gone, Descoteaux. As I have told you." Then without waiting for any acknowledgement the viscount turned on his heel and left the room.

If Gideon had been in any doubt as to the meaning of the viscount's parting words, the gleam in Descoteaux's eyes would have removed it. A coldness slid through his veins and shivered the flesh across his back. He was sure that Charron, sitting there looking myopically at the remains of the meal and clearly contemplating another serving, had no idea of the danger he was in. Heart hammering, with one hand Gideon picked up a cup of wine as the other rested on his sword hilt, out of sight under the table. The problem was not just that he had to get himself out of the room alive, but that he had to get Charron out alive too. Without Charron's confession, there would be no way to exonerate Anders.

He couldn't shout for help as that would simply speed the attack and there was no guarantee he could keep himself and Charron alive long enough for any rescue. He was very sure that Descoteaux would not want to use his pistol as that would make too much noise. He was also sure the man would not think either himself or Charron any real challenge. The only issue Gideon could see was whether he intended to kill them here and leave, not caring about the consequences, or try to get them both away from the inn.

He had to hope it was the latter.

Other than that Gideon had few options. Dennel would be watching the room from the outside, not thinking Gideon might be in danger within. And even if Lord recognised the viscount, there was no reason he might think to stop him from leaving.

"The viscount is kind, but I think we can manage very well without you, Monsieur Descoteaux," Gideon said, trying to keep his voice light and untroubled. "Please do not remain on our account, you will have your own affairs to arrange, I'm sure."

"Oh no," Charron said quickly. "The captain is here to look after me. It is not safe to travel without protection in these times."

"Surely not at table?" Gideon protested. "It can't be good for the digestion."

He had forgotten he was talking to a physician because Charron promptly launched into an entire lecture on what was and was not good for the digestion. Descoteaux rose and moved around the room as if heading towards the door. It would mean he would be behind Gideon and that was not something Gideon was willing to permit. Fortunately, Descoteaux's path to the door took him past Charron, not Gideon himself. The short-sighted, middle-aged and overweight Charron was no threat at all to a man like Descoteaux. The younger, stronger, sword-wearing Gideon, even if clearly a mere pen-pusher in the captain's eyes, would be the man he would want to deal with first.

"Of course, Galen has it that digestion begins with the reduction of food by chewing, which he compares to a workman preparing wheat before it is ground for flour." Charron gestured with his spoon to emphasise what he was saying.

Gideon caught the movement only in the corner of his eye, his focus being on Descoteaux whose hand had rested on his sword as he crossed the room. Leaving it until the very last moment as the captain passed by, Gideon pushed his chair back and spun from the seat, the wine in his hand still as against all expectation Descoteaux drew his pistol. Had Gideon not already been committed to his action he knew he would never have had the courage to risk a pistol ball in the head.

But his hand was moving at the same time as the captain pulled the pistol free. Before Descoteaux could pull the cock and level the weapon, Gideon had thrown the wine in his face and followed it with the pewter cup, his hand already pulling his sword free.

The pistol clattered to the floor as Descoteaux reacted with unthinking instinct to protect his face. Had he realised he was facing more than just a lawyer, he might not have been taken off guard so easily, but thus far Gideon's sword had been mostly concealed by his cloak so Descoteaux could not even have known from the nature of the blade he carried that Gideon was more than a typical clerk.

Now, however, he knew and by the time Gideon had his sword drawn, Descoteaux had recovered and drawn his own. Unfortunately, at the same moment, Charron leapt to his feet and Gideon had to jump to catch the blade that was casually aimed to cut Charron.

"Get down," he snapped, aware he had overextended his reach. It was his sword that saved him, the quillons of the basket hilt catching his foe's blade as he lifted his hand to guard himself. He tried to turn his hand in a disarming movement he had seen used by others, but Descoteaux avoided it, stepped back and cut again, this time at Gideon.

There was no telling where the men the captain had with him might be, which made Gideon reluctant to call out as whilst that might summon Dennel and Lord it might, for all he knew, as easily summon Descoteaux's men instead. So, he kept silent and was glad that Charron, seemingly petrified by fear, had backed away behind him at least.

He concentrated on the deadly dance of blades, knowing that what for him was an exercise in intense focus, for the man he fought was a natural rhythm, wearing down Gideon's guard and looking for any way through it. But the blow, when it came, Gideon nearly missed, because it came from behind not from the front. Charron had grabbed the near-empty jug of wine and swung it at Gideon's head.

It was such a clumsy swing, he saw it in plenty of time to duck away, but that meant Descoteaux was able to scrape a blade along his ribs as Gideon struggled to turn it. Fighting on two fronts now and striving to defend one of his attackers, he kicked out at Charron, hard on the side of his knee which pushed him back staggering. At the same time Gideon had to bring his sword up to stop the descending blow that would have sliced into his throat, catching it only with his hand pressed against his shoulder, the basket hilt acting as a gorget, armouring him briefly.

But Descoteaux had snatched up a knife from the table and thrust it hard towards Gideon's body, as they were locked closely by their swords. Gideon saw the blade and could do nothing to stop it, his muscles tensing uselessly against the impact of killing steel. Someone gasped and screamed, but Gideon felt nothing. It took him a second to realise it was Charron. He had lunged forward to tackle Gideon and the knife had cut deeply into in his shoulder.

Pushing Charron hard into Descoteaux, Gideon broke the lock the captain had on his sword so he could wrench it free. Descoteaux was briefly half-entangled in the panicking Charron's weighty embrace giving Gideon the moment he needed to bring his blade up and drive it into the captain's stomach.

Which was when the door opened and Gideon, unable to pull his own blade free of the dying man, snatched up Descoteaux's sword to face whoever came in.

"I think you have done enough," Lord said, his tone conversational as he easily countered the blade that Gideon had lifted to his face, striking it down and turning it. The relief was so intense Gideon's legs weakened with it and he had to drop the sword to brace himself on the table breathing hard.

"I apologise for our delay in coming to you," Lord went on, stepping into the room to allow Dennel in behind him before closing the door. "Charron's guard took a little dealing with. They are presently riding hard to the west in the belief he was in a coach that left ten minutes ago." He looked down at Charron himself, who was now curled into a ball, one hand clutching the ripped cloth and flesh where Descoteaux had stabbed him. "Is that his only injury?"

Gideon nodded, then found his voice. "I believe so. He took a blade meant for me."

That made Lord raise his eyebrows.

"Not intentionally," Gideon said quickly. "At the time he was trying to attack me from behind. He did not—probably still doesn't—realise that Descoteaux there was supposed to kill the both of us."

"But who—?" Lord's expression changed. "Of course, the viscount. I had wondered why he was here but assumed he was heading home incognito to England as the embassy he was on had failed quite spectacularly. I wonder what Charron did to cross him."

"Where is he now?" Gideon asked, uncomfortable to think that a man who had been willing to see him so casually murdered was at large.

"He left travelling north and a good riddance, I think." Lord prodded Charron with his toe. "Is there a man in there, or just a worm?" But Charron remained as he was. Lord stepped over him and examined the window freeing the casement. "Alright, Dennel, please get the horse we have for Charron in the stable yard. I think Dr Charron is fat, but not so fat we can't ease him through this window and avoid bringing half the inn about our heads with the resulting inevitable further spilt blood and the trouble that would bring."

As Dennel left, Gideon did what he could to help Lord gag Charron then tend his wound enough to be sure the flow of blood had stopped. They had just done so when the window was pulled open from the outside. They had a struggle to get man through it until Lord leaned in and whispered something in Charron's ear which seemed to both deflate him and make him cooperative to the extent that he was manhandled and bound on a horse without further protest. The body of Descoteaux followed.

THE PHYSICIAN'S FATE

Closing the window behind them, after Gideon was through it, Lord handed him the reins of the horse he had been riding from Paris. Then, mounted, they set off with one dead man and another alive but unwilling in their midst and turned south for Saint-Léon-du-Moulin.

Gideon missed most of what followed once they got there, for which he was grateful. He knew whatever Lord had planned for Charron was not something he had the stomach to witness so didn't protest when Lord told him to go to bed. Following Gervais Poirier upstairs, he was taken to the blue room where he had slept before. Despite the sickness in his heart, sleep claimed him quickly.

When he woke it was to the stillness and scant birdsong of a winter's day in the French countryside. The twenty-third of December, the day before the Christmas celebrations would begin on Christmas Eve.

Lord was eating a small bowl of frumenty in the dining room where a fire had been set so the chill was not too great. Gideon accepted a portion of the grainy porridge for himself and added a spoonful of honey from a pot of it on the table as the servant retreated from the room.

"Charron wrote his confession?" Gideon asked, when the warmth from the fire without and the frumenty within began to penetrate through his body.

"In the end, no," Lord said between spoonfuls. "I had to write it for him, his arm is not very good, and his hands seem rather damaged. He lost a couple of nails. But he signed it and is now speaking his truth to anyone who will sit still for five minutes to listen to him."

"And is his truth *the* truth?"

"I doubt it," Lord said. "But it is as close to the truth as we are likely to come now." He pushed the empty bowl away and sat back. "Claude Charron was indeed already making a living creating pictures of women in the most salacious of poses, but then it occurred to him he could make even more were he to have the face of whoever his patron might desire placed upon the body. Naturally enough those were not things he could sell openly and his friendship with Proulx, who already had contacts in the more socially prestigious criminal world, gave him access to a ready market. Men like the viscount, for example, who apparently had the desire to have the face of King Louis' consort, Queen Anne on his pictures. That Charron had a sketch of one still on his person is going to seal his fate whatever else might happen."

"So how does this fit with the death of Geneviève Tasse?" Gideon asked. "Pictures are one thing, but that..."

"The first thing you need to understand is that she was not the first to suffer from his laudanum in the wine trick. He had used it before both for himself and for other gentlemen and seemed to think nothing of it as if 'done well' as he put it, the lady herself had no memory of the event—which, disturbingly, he seemed to think made it perfectly alright. Anyway, he had been much entranced by Demoiselle Tasse, obsessed indeed, although he did not use the word. He decided to have her, despite the obvious risk.

He knew there wasn't much more time before his opportunity would be gone as the cardinal was not far from death and after that his chance to access her so easily would be lost. She had shown no sign of wanting to re-engage his services as a physician after their first consultation. Charron planned a rapid return from the funeral and asked Proulx to bring the laudanum as he knew he wouldn't have the time to arrange that himself."

"So Proulx knew of the plan?"

"Charron was paying Proulx very handsomely to both provide the laudanum and to keep any away from the room until he was done."

"So not guilty, but hardly innocent," Gideon observed.

Lord poured himself a cup of small beer. "Exactly so. Charron knew from Proulx Demoiselle Tasse was to meet with Jensen, so he knew where to find her. He told her he had a new remedy to help with the pain she had in her feet which he was happy to provide to her to try without any charge. She agreed to allow him to examine her feet and to take the laudanum."

"But how did they expect to get around the fact that Anders was supposed to see Demoiselle Tasse that evening?"

"That was a complication Charron hadn't expected. They decided Proulx was to tell Anders not to worry, that he would speak to her for him. But Anders went off to copy his latest Paracelsus discovery before Proulx could do so. Charron decided he could tell Anders afterwards. Unfortunately, 'afterwards' was not as Charron had planned."

"He gave her too much?"

Lord sighed. "Charron blamed that on Anders Jensen. This was, if you recall, a new formulation of laudanum. One that Jensen had found, and Yolande Savatier made up to his new receipt. It had much greater efficacy and potency than the remedy Charron was used to. In his mind, even though he admitted the bottle had been clearly marked as a new formulation, it was Jensen's fault not his own that Geneviève Tasse died. He thought—still thinks it right that Jensen should die for that."

Gideon shook his head in disbelief.

"And Proulx?"

"Proulx was a threat because he was always desperate for money. Even though he had already been well paid for his assistance, he tried blackmailing Charron. He maintained as he had known nothing of what Charron had intended to do he could not be held to be an accomplice. I very much doubt Proulx would have dared to carry it out, but Charron was rattled enough not to want to take the risk."

"Rather than pay him Charron had him killed?"

Lord nodded. "Ironically by some of the same people to whom Proulx had introduced him. Then you started taking too much of an interest and Yolande Savatier recognised Pierre Firmin and Charron's world began to fall to pieces even more. He killed Firmin as the only person who could name him and made plans to leave Paris, funded and assisted by his latest client."

"The viscount?"

"The viscount. Charron took a leaf out of Proulx's book and used blackmail, not realising that there are some people whom it is simply foolish to attempt that with. The viscount was to provide him protection and safe passage from France to England but told Charron they must not travel together, which Charron foolishly accepted. He is not a very intelligent man in such matters. Having met the viscount at the coaching inn, he handed over the last of the pictures and trusted himself to the protection of Descoteaux."

It was unedifying to hear the whole laid out so bleakly. Gideon left the frumenty unfinished, his appetite vanished. He reminded himself of the positive outcome to it all.

"At least now," he said, "we can deliver Charron to the Châtelet, free Anders and head back to England, Oxford—and Zahara and Kate."

There was a tap on the door and Gervais Poirier came in.

"There is a letter come for you sent under royal seal from England, Schiavono."

Lord thanked him and took the letter, examining the seal with a frown as Poirier withdrew again.

"Yes, we are now able to redeem Jensen," he said as he broke the seal and unfolded the sheet. "But I would have him stay for a few days over Christmas here before we travel. He needs to rest and recuperate his strength a little." Then Lord started reading, his frown deepening.

Gideon thought of Anders as he had last seen him.

"That would be wise," he agreed. "Better a few days delay now than Anders falling ill on the way. I am sure Kate will be patient for your return."

Lord looked up from the letter, his expression grim.

"Unfortunately, it appears Kate will have to be very patient. Dr Jensen will recuperate here at Saint-Léon-du-Moulin and then you and he will need to travel back to Oxford without me."

Gideon stared at him, bewildered.

"But why?"

Sir Philip Lord lifted the paper he held by way of explanation.

"I am commanded immediately on the conclusion of my embassy here, to join Her Majesty Queen Henrietta Maria in The Hague in order to assist her in completing her task of finding, selecting and purchasing arms for the king's cause and then to remain with her, in command of her escort to ensure her safe return in due course to England."

THE PHYSICIAN'S FATE

Howe Hall, 16th December 1642 (Julian Calendar)

The way to Howe had been hard.

Danny had pressed on even though it was bitterly cold. Showers of heavy snow made progress slow and horses founder to their hocks at times as they rode through Weardale.

Having reached the house that was more fortress than manor, the engineer in him had admired its strength and noted its weaknesses, but he had wondered at its lack of grace when there was a lady to govern it as her home.

That mystery was quickly solved.

Tempest had said his wife was unhappy and hoped she might find the house in York more to her liking. But in that, as in so much else, the arrogant little shit had lied. The truth was so much more brutal.

Danny had been given the key to her rooms as they said she was disturbed, given to outbursts and could be violent to herself or others if the door to her chamber was left open, so they had to keep it locked. Danny unlocked it and walked in. The bars on the windows sent shadows like scars across the sunlight entering the room.

What kind of man kept his wife locked in a room with a barred window?

The room contained little: a tester bedstead with a featherbed, two chests, a table with a single chair. There were two strongly set women seated on a settle by the window, their hands folded, watching the third woman who sat at the table, back straight as a scouring stick, reading over something she had clearly just been writing. The two women appeared wary, as if at any moment they expected her to seize the pen and attack them with it.

Who wouldn't do that if kept locked up endless day after endless day against their will?

From behind he saw only that she was slender, her hair was covered in a matronly coif and a small, jewelled cap, the gown she wore was wool, not silk, and in a tired shade of blue that boarded onto grey. It was laced at the back so she would need her women to escape it. She must have heard him enter but made no move to turn to see who had arrived.

How many bitter disappointments must it have taken to kill all natural curiosity?

Danny stood there watching her write for a few moments, then took a step forward and in doing so caught her face in profile. He could not prevent the sharply drawn breath the sight elicited and that made her turn, eyes wide but incurious. Philip's eyes in a face that was a younger, feminine reflection of his and yet—and yet held its own mystique which owed nothing to him, which was uniquely and compellingly hers and hers alone.

Who...?

He opened his mouth to speak then closed it again as something in her face changed. It was as if she had expected to see a wolf when she turned to look, but instead saw it was a familiar hound. Danny's breath faltered. He had vowed a thousand times—a million times—that he would never, ever...

It was a moment Danny knew must have been fated from the beginning of time or at least from the beginning of his time on earth.

Nothing else could explain it.

"Who are you?" she asked and the women by the window startled and looked at each other in surprise. They had told him she never spoke.

Who would speak when no one listens to what you say?

He swallowed the emotion in his throat and made a bow.

"Daniel Bristow, my lady, and I am come to take you from here."

She rose, brushing her skirts down.

"Is... is the man I am supposedly married to here with you?"

Supposedly?

Danny shook his head. "If you mean Sir Nicholas, then no, my lady, he is in York."

Her eyes were as clear as the Mediterranean and their gaze met his questing, as if seeking his very soul. For once he made no attempt to hide anything. So she must have seen the grief and the pain, the hate and the fury, smouldering within him and witnessed the awakening of wonder her own presence evoked. Something in her face changed as if with discovery, and she gave a small nod.

"I will go with *you*," she said.

And it was done.

ELEANOR SWIFT-HOOK

Author's Notes

This book is dedicated with all my love to my mother. Her unswerving encouragement of me as a writer began as soon as I picked up a pencil and started writing stories. As a lifelong Francophile and teacher of French, her inability to instil in me more than the basics of that wonderful language was entirely my fault, not hers. I hope this book might show her that some of it did rub off on me after all.

The battles of Piercebridge and Tadcaster are historical events and both took place pretty much as I described. Although I did take one liberty. There is, to the best of my knowledge, no indication John Hotham damaged the bridge in the first engagement in the manner I describe, something which will undoubtedly upset purists, but which I included to allow Danny to shine a little. However, Fairfax certainly holed the bridge at Tadcaster. The existence of the note supposedly forged by Hotham, purporting to be from the Earl of Newcastle telling Blount not to advance is recorded in Drake's 'History And Antiquities Of The City Of York', written a century later and is most likely untrue. But it is certainly true that Blount failed to march, something commented on at the time.

If you go to Paris, you will not find a Saint-Léon-du-Moulin on any map, and there never has been. I must also admit that (to the best of my knowledge) there was no delegation of condolence such as I describe sent to Paris at this time by either King Charles or Parliament.

There are, however, a number of historically based individuals who appear in The Physician's Fate. It is important to emphasise that their words and deeds as invented by me and expressed in this book, are a fictional representation and not an accurate historical one.

Whilst all those I mention as working for him are my own creations, Théophraste Renaudot was indeed Commissioner

THE PHYSICIAN'S FATE

General of the Poor in Paris. His headquarters was the Bureau D'Adresses, established at the Sign of the Cock on the corner of the Rue Calandre and Rue du Marché-Neuf on the Île de la Cité. He was a force of nature who as well as running the Bureau as a pawnshop, employment agency, clinic and dispensary for the poor, also held weekly debates on issues of scientific and philosophical interest and published their proceedings. These he stopped as soon as Richelieu died as he was already under pressure for them with murmurs of heresy. In addition, Renaudot might have a good claim to be the creator of the modern newspaper as his *La Gazette de France*, which he began in 1631, contained news, editorials and advertisement and was printed weekly.

Sadly, he met much opposition for his good works. In particular from the Faculty of Medicine in Paris which disapproved both of his methods of medical practice and of his freely dispensing of them to the poor. Within a year of the death of Cardinal Richelieu, the Faculty that Renaudot had fought so hard against, succeeded in banning him from medical practice. At their instigation the parlement of Paris forced him to close his Bureau and end all the services it had offered to the poor of Paris.

He remained the editor of *La Gazette*, however, and in 1646 Mazarin appointed him Historiographer Royal (the official court historian) to Louis XIV. *La Gazette* continued to be published even after his death in 1653, covering the French Revolution in the late Eighteenth Century and surviving in one form or another until 1917.

If you would like to know more about this remarkable man, I would point you to the book I learned so much from myself: *Making Science Social: The Conferences of Théophraste Renaudot, 1633–1642 by Kathleen Wellman*.

The ambassador for King Charles to the French court in Paris from 1641-1660 was indeed Richard Browne and he did maintain an Anglican chapel in his house. His daughter, Mary, was married to the diarist John Evelyn in 1647, when she was just twelve years old. Evelyn and Browne became friends after they met in 1643, an event recorded at the end of the entry in Evelyn's dairy for Monday 16 November 1643:

ELEANOR SWIFT-HOOK

We lay at Paris at the Ville de Venice; where, after I had something refreshed, I went to visit Sir Richard Browne, his Majesty's Resident with the French king.

Browne impoverished himself in the king's cause and was rewarded with a baronetcy by Charles II in 1649.

I also drew on Evelyn's diary for the account of torture at the Châtelet which you can find in his entry for 11 March 1651.

Marie Madeleine de Vignerot du Pont de Courlay, Duchesse d'Aiguillon was the daughter of Richelieu's sister. After a brief marriage in 1620 (her husband died in 1622) she became, through her uncle's influence, the lady in waiting to Marie de Medici until her fall from grace. Usually that was an honour reserved for the highest of nobility and it placed Marie Madeleine in control of the wardrobe and immediate household of the king's mother. In 1638 Richelieu had her created Duchesse d'Aiguillon in her own right. After her uncle's death she retired from court and concentrated on her charitable works. She never had a companion/maid Geneviève Tasse, who is purely my invention.

I could not finish these notes without making known my debt of gratitude to one book in particular: *City on the Seine: Paris in the Time of Richelieu and Louis XIV, 1614-1715 by Andrew Trout.* Whilst its main focus was on the reign of Louis XIV, it allowed me to get a good sense of the city and how it was in the first half of the Seventeenth Century. Amongst other delights, it contains the wonderful picture upon which I based Gideon's guise as a water vendor.

If you have enjoyed The Physician's Fate, I would love to hear what you thought about it so please do leave a review. You can also follow me on Twitter @emswifthook or get in touch with me through my website www.eleanorswifthook.com where you can find more about the background to the book including the origins of the various quotations in the text.

Meanwhile you will be pleased to know The Physician's Fate is the fourth of six books In the Lord's Legacy series, which follow Gideon Lennox through the opening months of the first English Civil War. As he unravels the mystery of Philip Lord's past, he finds himself getting caught up in battles and sieges, murder investigations and moral dilemmas as all the while he bears the heartache of his seemingly impossible romance with the beautiful Zahara.

Printed in Great Britain
by Amazon